PRAISE FOR THE NOV

"A fantastically _____ _____ _____ _____ y story
with emotional _____ _____ _____ fan and
she's at the top _____ uld be
reading her boo_____

—Lor_____ author

"Sarina Bowen is a master at drawing you in from page one
and leaving you aching for more."

—Elle Kennedy, _New York Times_ bestselling author

"I not only bought this book and devoured it, I bought—and
read—this entire NA series (The Ivy Years) in a WEEK. It
is OMG-awesome-NA-at-its-finest."

—Tammara Webber, _New York Times_ bestselling author

"Bowen writes great dialogue and wonderfully realistic
characters."

—_Kirkus Reviews_

"This page-turner will have readers eagerly awaiting Bow-
en's next book."

—_Publishers Weekly_

"[A] terrific read."

—Dear Author

"So well done that I just want to read it over and over."

—Smexy Books

Berkley Sensation titles by Sarina Bowen

ROOKIE MOVE
HARD HITTER

HARD HITTER

SARINA BOWEN

BERKLEY SENSATION
New York

BERKLEY SENSATION
Published by Berkley
An imprint of Penguin Random House LLC
375 Hudson Street, New York, New York 10014

ISBN: 9780399583452

First Edition: January 2017

Printed in the United States of America
1 3 5 7 9 10 8 6 4 2

Cover art by Claudio Marinesco
Cover design by Rita Frangie

For Kyla, whose presence in the yoga studio is always inspiring. Not only have you made my body more flexible, but also my heart.

ONE

Standings: 4th place in the Metropolitan Division
19 Regular Season Games Remaining

Patrick O'Doul knelt on his yoga mat, eyes closed.

"Let your breath find its natural rhythm," came a soothing voice at the front of the room. "Become aware of its temperature, and of the sensation of your breath as you exhale."

He exhaled slowly, obeying Ariana, the team's massage therapist and yoga instructor.

O'Doul didn't give a crap about yoga. He didn't know where his chakras were, and he didn't remember any of the names of the poses. But on game day he never objected to this mandatory hour of Simon Says with the beauty at the front of the room.

She had them holding child's pose for a couple of minutes. Since he stunk at yoga, he needed to listen closely to her instructions. The concentration yoga required was the best part—if the pretty lady in the pink sports bra was trying to twist your body into a New Age pretzel, there was no time to worry about the opponent you had to face down in five hours.

"As you hold the pose, reconnect your breathing with your body. Notice how the breath moves through the ribcage in this pose," she suggested. "Use each exhale to settle a little more firmly into the stretch. We're opening up the hips . . ."

Ariana circled among her students, making a posture correction here and there. She stopped at O'Doul's side, then got down on all fours. "Hi," she whispered.

When he turned his head, he met a pair of brown eyes, sparkling with mischief. "Hi?" She rarely began conversations during class.

"If this is too hard on your hip flexors, go back into tabletop."

"I'm good," he grunted. *Christ.* The whole world was focused on his weakness. Chronic muscle soreness shouldn't be such a big deal. Playing through pain was a rite of hockey.

"Do you have children?" she whispered.

"Fuck no," he whispered back. "And I never will."

Her smile didn't falter. "This pose is easier for them, because their limbs are shorter relative to their torso length. So take it easy. Let gravity do the work, okay? And do me a favor?"

"What?" He'd never had a conversation with anyone when they were both folded in two on the floor.

"Don't blow off your next massage appointment. You're making me look bad."

Aw, man. Ambushed in child's pose. "I'm sorry," he said immediately. The trainers wanted him to have some massage therapy for his hip. "Didn't mean to mess up your schedule."

She shook her head. "It's okay. You'll show up this time, right?"

"Sure," he promised, because it was hard to think up a decent excuse when you were sweating over your yoga mat.

Ari gave him one more killer smile and got up, moving on to correct another player's posture.

He watched her go, then felt guilty about missing his appointments and also for checking out her perfect ass.

Twenty minutes later, after yoga, he was ambushed a second time. But not by Ari.

"How's the hip?" Nate Kattenberger asked, his towel draped around his neck. The reason the Bruisers did yoga in the first place was because the team's young owner was a big fan of vinyasa. He sure didn't have any trouble holding Ari's poses, and always took a spot in the very front row.

"I'm good. Feeling stronger," O'Doul lied.

"Glad to hear it. I think we can beat Boston tonight," the billionaire said, wiping sweat off his forehead with a towel. He was wearing spandex shorts and a T-shirt reading, *Move Your Asana*. "Two game points tonight could really set us up for the weekend."

As if O'Doul didn't already know that. "We'll make it happen," he vowed.

"I think you will," Nate agreed.

O'Doul hoped so. They needed a third place finish in the Metropolitan division to be guaranteed a play-offs spot. If they ended up in fourth place, they might squeak into the last spot. It was possible. But, as O'Doul's team-issued phone told him every time he pulled it out of his pocket, their play-offs spot was not a lock. Kattenberger's sophisticated model projected their chances at 81 percent.

There was no room for error. And tonight's game meant a lot because Boston was one of the other Eastern teams in contention for those last couple of slots.

They were so close. So fucking close he could taste it.

"Get some rest before the game," Nate suggested, squeezing his forearm.

O'Doul fought the instinct to shake off the big boss's casual touch. "Will do," he agreed, knowing it was a lie. He'd go back to the hotel and lie down for a while. But sleep would elude him the same way it did on every game day. "See you tonight," he said.

Nate gave him one more nod and walked away.

* * *

Eight hours later, the fans roared as Boston made another attempt on goal.

O'Doul watched from the bench, feeling grim.

The most grueling part of his job wasn't the hockey game, or the constant travel. And it wasn't the fighting, or the stitches and bruises.

It was the *dread*.

Sitting on the bench between shifts, it sunk low in his belly. It was heavy, like lead. And each time he vaulted over the wall it rose up in his throat like bile.

If any team's enforcer ever told you he never felt dread, that man was lying. No human could put his body in the path of a six-three scrapper's fist three or four times a week without anticipating the pain.

Tonight's fight had been pre-arranged in the worst possible way, too. The other team's enforcer—a dick by the name of Trekowski—had called him out last night on social media. On fucking Twitter.

> Maybe O'Doul won't wimp out on fighting me tomorrow night. #AGuyCanHope #BabySayYes.

Of all the dick moves O'Doul had witnessed, this one took the trophy. He hadn't responded, because he didn't even have Twitter. He didn't tweet. Or twat. Whatever.

The team's publicist—Georgia—had responded on his behalf. He'd approved a pithy little quote for the Bruisers' Facebook page:

> Someone punched me on the interwebs?

he'd supposedly replied.

> Funny, I didn't feel a thing.

He had to admit it was a clever response. A hockey fight was supposed to have purpose. Usually, a fight was payback for a cheap shot that endangered one of his guys. Other times, the brawl was meant to fuel an ongoing rivalry, rallying the team and changing the energy of a game.

Fights weren't supposed to start because some bonehead wanted to flex his shiny personality on social media. And they sure as hell weren't supposed to be fueled by a *lie*. O'Doul had never ducked a fight in his life. But he'd missed the last game against Boston on account of a procedure on a tendon in his wrist.

Thankfully, and with the help of the best medical attention money could buy, his wrist had healed up fast. But lately he had a new problem—pain in his hip flexor muscles. It was a low-grade thing. Something to watch. But it made him feel a lot less invincible than he was used to. At thirty-two years old he was suddenly more conscious of the toll the game took on his body. And the fighting he did for his team made everything riskier.

So much could go wrong in those violent sixty or ninety seconds.

Still, the hours leading up to the fight hurt worse than a cross to the jaw. As tonight's game wore on, the dread got heavier. He'd already spent the first two periods trying to make plays while simultaneously taking it easy on his hip. While trying not to *appear* to take it easy on his hip. And keeping the warlike mask on his goddamn face.

Frankly, it was exhausting.

Earlier this season he'd had an unusually frank heart-to-heart with another team's enforcer—an old timer known as the Hammer. He was the nicest guy in the world— the kind who wanted to buy you a drink after you'd finished beating the crap out of each other.

Maybe it was the scotch, but that night he'd confessed how much mental energy the fights demanded of him.

"Doulie," The Hammer said, using his nickname. "Try

some chemical courage. I can share it with you now that we're not gonna match up again this season." He'd pulled out a pill bottle and shaken eight of the tablets into O'Doul's palm. "Take one of those before a game."

"What is it?"

"Uppers." Hammer closed O'Doul's hand over the pills. "You'll love 'em. Only one a game, though, okay? And you won't get hooked."

O'Doul wasn't proud of it, but he'd hidden those tablets in a bottle of plain aspirin. Parsing them out over the next three weeks, he'd taken one pill before each game. The results were even better than Hammer promised. The drug made him feel energetic and invincible.

But then they were gone. So he'd taken the risky step of buying a dozen more from a guy in a nightclub in lower Manhattan. For a few short weeks they provided exactly the lift he needed. When his stash was depleted again, he missed the fearlessness they'd granted him. But buying that shit was both embarrassing and tricky. So this month he'd gone without.

Consequently, tonight's game lasted eighty years. The score was still 1–1 in the third period. For what felt like the hundredth time that night, Patrick's coach tapped him on the back. Fifteen seconds later he leapt up for the line change. Again. And just as quickly, the other team's enforcer turned his back. His Twitter taunter wouldn't ask for the fight. The fans wanted it. The teams wanted it. But this dick was making everyone wait.

Fuck. Mind games were the worst. They distracted him from the business of blocking shots and scoring goals. And that, of course, was the point.

Now O'Doul accelerated backwards at top speed, face to face with Adam Hartley, Boston's youngest left wing, blocking the kid's path and being a general nuisance. The kid wasn't going to get a shot off if he had a say in it.

Meanwhile, his man Castro got the puck back on a breakaway and gave it a good try. But Boston's goalie got a lucky save and thwarted Brooklyn's attempt to break the 1–1 tie.

The shift ended without a score, and without incident, goddamn it. Trekowski stayed as far away as it was possible to do on a 200 foot sheet of ice. Bastard. Not all of the league enforcers were good guys like Hammer. This one was a real piece of work—the kind who'd insult his own mother on Twitter if it made him look tougher.

At thirty-two, Patrick felt too old for this shit. And he was keenly well aware of how obnoxious it sounded to claim to be too old for anything at thirty-two.

He sat back down on the bench, sweating, and reached for a water bottle only because it allowed him to surreptitiously stretch his hip for the hundredth time.

"You want me to draw him out?" Leo Trevi asked from beside him on the bench. "Don't know what Trekowski is doing over there. Posting your picture on Instagram, maybe."

When Patrick looked up, he caught an unmistakable look of concern behind the rookie's face shield. *Fucking great.* The whole stadium could probably tell he was on edge. Though Leo—or College Boy, as O'Doul liked to call him—was awfully smart. "Naw," he said, swilling water. "I'll get 'im soon enough."

The game dragged on, with Patrick's hip aching as the clock ticked down. When he was younger, pain was just pain. It was something to live through until you could have a nice whiskey and a couple of painkillers. Even now it wouldn't bother him so much if it weren't such a harbinger of doom. The Bruisers needed to make the play-offs. They had a new coach and some new blood and a decent record. The owner wanted it. Badly.

Competition—the good kind—had always fueled him. So he leaned into it now, taking the ice once again. They only needed one more goal tonight, and it would happen. He could feel it.

But first, a fight.

Trekowski gave him an opening, finally. It happened when the fool slid into Brooklyn's goalie a little too carelessly. It wasn't the worst offense Patrick had ever seen, but the crowd made a noise, and he went for it. Instead of campaigning the ref for a penalty, he got in Trekowski's face. "That's enough bullshit, big man. I'm done with you."

The enemy gave him a toothless grin. "You want to go right now?"

Do I have a choice? That was his last conscious thought. Fight mode was always a blur. His gloves fell on their own accord as he circled Trekowski, sizing him up, looking for the first attack. His opponent's arms were about as long as Sasquatch's. O'Doul was only six feet tall, two hundred pounds. He wasn't huge, and he wasn't heavy.

His only advantage was bone-deep grit.

To win against Trekowski, he'd have to yank him in hard and keep him close. So he faked a grab and the guy ducked. Patrick lunged forward on his good side and grabbed the guy's sweater with his right hand, throwing a punch with his left.

That was exactly the opposite of his usual move, and the surprise actually worked. Patrick landed two punches before he took one himself, right below the ear. It hurt like a bitch. But surprise was still working for him, so he presented that side of his head again, as if asking for another, then swapped his hands as fast as lightning. His next three punches landed in quick succession on the guy's ribcage. Not the most sensitive spot, but you had to go to war with the grip you had. And it kept his strained muscles away from this jerk's flailing limbs.

The crowd might have been chanting, *Fight! Fight!* Or maybe that was just the pounding of his own heart. Patrick's vision tunneled down to only the set of Trekowski's mouth—it was tight, meaning these punches were felt.

Patrick was taking blows to his shoulder, but they barely registered. It was his good side, for one. And the angle wasn't too intense. But time was slipping by. He needed to end this before the goon changed tactics. It was risky as hell, but Patrick tried a one-footed stance to knee the guy in the thigh and unbalance him. Then he gritted his teeth and landed one good punch a little higher up, right in his chest.

Trekowski went down, and Patrick narrowly avoided landing right on top of him. He tore himself out of the guy's grasp and righted himself just as the ref rushed in to pull him back. They always ended things when someone went down.

The crowd's roar—silenced before by adrenaline—now echoed in his ears. They screamed his name and waved foam fingers. Or jeered, depending on attitude, level of drunkenness, and team affiliation.

A few minutes from now a video of the fight would be up on a website where fans would vote on it. He'd earn an 85 percent or 90 percent win rating for this one. Crazy job he had. When the night went well, he felt relief first and then pain later. When a fight went badly, he got stitches and curses from fans.

He was a side show, like one of those circus freaks who used to bite the heads off chickens in front of a jeering crowd.

It worked, though. The energy in the arena shifted in Brooklyn's favor. Two minutes later his man Beringer scored a goal, bringing them into the lead.

Boston wasn't able to answer it in the remaining six minutes of play, and the Bruisers would go back to the hotel with two game points. So nobody could say his contribution didn't matter.

And nobody did.

In the visitors' locker room, he took the longest, hottest shower of his career. Adrenaline was an amazing chemical. It always kept the pain at bay until after the buzzer sounded. But the comedown was a bitch. He ached everywhere. The soreness radiated outward from his hip. It climbed down his quadriceps and into his groin. It wrapped around to his lower back, gripping him like a vice.

Every athlete played through pain. It's just that the trajectory worried him.

He was toweling off when Henry, the head trainer, stopped behind his bench. The man crossed his freckled arms and gave Patrick an appraising look.

"What? You checking me out? The female fans always say I have a nice ass."

Henry rolled his eyes. "It's top notch, which is why I want to see it out on the ice for the rest of the season. So I need you to cooperate with your training staff."

Patrick fished a pair of clean underwear out of his bag. "I always cooperate in the gym."

"I set up a massage appointment for you and you blew it off. Twice."

"Stretching works just as well," Patrick argued, pulling on his shirt. "Massage is too time-consuming."

"You know what's also time-consuming? An injury. By the third period you were skating like an old lady trying to protect her handbag. I'm setting up massage appointments for five out of the next seven days. And I'm checking up on your attendance." Without waiting for a response, Henry marched off.

Five appointments? *Hell.*

Patrick finished getting dressed. The screen of his Katt Phone lit up with a picture of a bus, meaning that one was now outside. And he was going to be on it. A good night's sleep would do wonders for his muscle strain.

But when the bus pulled up in front of their hotel, Leo Trevi didn't let him escape upstairs like he wanted to. "Come on," he said. "I want you to meet Adam Hartley. Can't believe I played an NHL game against my college buddy. Unreal."

Patrick knew he could beg off after one whiskey, so he let himself be led to a table in the corner of the bar where a couple of his teammates already sat. He eased himself into the chair like an old man, hoping the painkillers he'd taken would kick in soon. "Evening, Georgia," he said to the publicist, who was also Leo's fiancée. "Thanks for leaving me out of the press conference."

Georgia Worthington grinned at him. "Why, Doulie! If someone else said that, I'd think he was being facetious."

"Fuck, no." Everyone laughed. "Who skates off the ice, drenched, and says, *I'd love it if someone shoved a camera in my face right now?*"

"Nobody loves the camera itself," Castro argued. "You love being *worthy* of it."

"Dude, you'd *break* the camera," somebody said. Castro wadded up his cocktail napkin and threw it down the table.

Their drinks arrived, and Patrick had just taken his first sip when a voice rang out. "Somebody order some cookies?" A smiling guy approached the table with a giant bakery box in his hands. O'Doul recognized him as the rookie whose shots he'd blocked all night.

"Hartley!" Leo jumped up and hug-tackled the guy. "What's in the box?"

"Cookies. *Duh*. After I lose a hockey game to my buddy, I like to eat cookies." He slapped Trevi on the back. "Buy me a beer, punk."

Trevi introduced his college friend to everyone, starting with his fiancée.

"Damn," Hartley said. "Trevi's getting hitched? Who would have thunk it?" He gave Georgia a potent smile. "Can I just tell you how relieved we all are? He dated the most awful girls in college."

She laughed, and Trevi groaned. "This again?"

When it was Patrick's turn to shake hands, he reached across the table without standing up. If the guy thought he was rude, it wouldn't be the first time someone did. "Nice to meet you."

"Likewise."

Trevi sat back down, one arm around Georgia, the other around his college friend. Hartley opened the box and passed cookies around the table, and then the boys began to reminisce. They had several years of memories to chew through, apparently. Pranks and dormitory shenanigans. "And then you hid that thing under Orsen's bed! Gawd. The stench . . ."

Patrick listened with half an ear. He didn't have ye olde college tales, like these kids. And the idea of living in a dormitory gave him the willies. It sounded too much like the group homes where he'd grown up in Minnesota. Too many people. Too loud.

The minute he got his first paycheck from the minor leagues when he was nineteen, he'd started apartment hunting. He was still in the Midwest then, where housing was just cheap enough that he'd found something. It was a room over someone's garage, but it had a private entrance and it was all his. He liked his silence. On the team, he had a reputation for being fair, and a sturdy team captain. But he wasn't cuddly, that was for damn sure.

Across the table from him, Georgia sat up a little straighter and began to wave at someone across the room. A moment later, O'Doul caught a whiff of lavender. He didn't even need to turn to know who'd come to stand beside him. Ari Bettini, the team's massage therapist and yoga instructor, greeted Georgia. She did this by putting a hand on Patrick's shoulder and leaning over to kiss Georgia's cheek.

Against his better judgment, O'Doul took a deep breath of Ari's essence. There was something about her that really turned his crank. From her dark, unflappable eyes to the irreverent gemstone in her nose, he liked the whole package. The soft, coal-dark waves of her hair brushed his ear as she righted herself again.

Patrick took a sip of his drink, studying the ice cubes as if those suckers were interesting. Ari left her hand on the shoulder of his suit jacket, the warmth of her palm bleeding through a few layers of fabric to reach his skin. That was the only thing about her he didn't really appreciate. Ari was a toucher. A massage therapist would have to be, right? But he preferred it when his friends kept their hands to themselves. Even the gorgeous ones.

Turning her attention to him, she squeezed his shoulder muscle. "How are you doing?"

"I'm good, thanks. Can I order you a drink?"

She shook her head. "Thanks, but I'd better turn in."

"What?" Georgia yelped. "You're going to leave me here at this testosterone fest by myself? There's a pinot grigio by the glass. Just have one."

Ari gave Georgia an indulgent smile and then pulled out the only available chair—the one next to Patrick's. "I've been drinking a lot more often now that you've decided to become a party girl."

"Blame me. I don't care." Georgia waved to get the waitress's attention. "Besides, these guys are in on a plot to get you drunk so you go easier on us at yoga tomorrow morning."

"You guys do *yoga?*" Hartley asked, his face breaking into a grin. "That's something I'd like to see."

Ari put an elbow on the table and rested her elegant face in her hand. "Don't knock it 'til you try it. Maybe you'll win the next one."

"I really teed that one up for you, didn't I?" Trevi's friend asked, his smile widening.

"You did," Ari agreed. "And I do appreciate it."

"So what else is different about the Bruisers?" Hartley asked. "What's Nate Kattenberger like?"

It was a common enough question. The young billionaire was interesting to a lot of people.

"The dude really likes his hockey," Trevi said. "And we all have the same cool phone. They keep tabs on us with it, but it knows *everything.* And here's something funny." Trevi pulled his phone out of his pocket. "There's a gold star on the screen after we win a game. See? We got a gold star tonight. Haven't gotten those since second grade."

Hartley laughed. "What do they put up there when you lose? A middle finger?"

"Nope." Trevi shook his head. "It's just a void where the

star should be. And it's weird, but I kind of hate knowing it's missing."

"Then the mind games are working," Georgia said. "The man is a genius."

When Ari's glass of wine arrived, Patrick watched her lift the stem of the glass between elegant fingers. Everything on Ari was long and sleek. She turned her head suddenly to catch his ogling eyes. *Busted.* But her glance was more appraising then irritated. "Mr. O'Doul, how is your pain level this evening?"

Hell. "I'm fine. I've been stretching really well." In fact, the foam rollers he carried around in his suitcase had to be replaced every couple of months because he used them so often they tended to collapse from overuse.

She gave him a patient smile. As if she was just humoring him. "Henry spoke to me on his way out the door tonight. He told me to be sure to get you on the table five times in the next seven days. But I can't do that if you don't set up some appointments."

"Right," he said. "Send Rebecca some appointment times. She'll put 'em on my calendar and I'll be there." The last thing he needed was the training staff butting in, criticizing him for blowing off massage treatments. There were three weeks left before the play-offs started. He had to hang in there and play as hard as he could.

"Did you take anything for the pain tonight?" she asked, her cabernet lips pursed thoughtfully. Ari's expression had a wisdom to it that O'Doul was always trying to categorize. She was beautiful, but not in a careless way.

"I took some ibuprofen. I'll use some ice before I sleep." She was still studying him in that penetrating way she had, and he didn't like it. "How's your ankle healing?"

Her gaze slipped. "Oh, really well. Almost like new." She sipped her wine.

"How'd you break it, anyway? I never caught that."

She grimaced into her wine. "By being stupid. Tripped on a set of steps in my apartment."

"Ouch." There was something about her delivery that raised the hair on the back of his neck, though. He'd spent his whole life trying to read people, and he was pretty good at it. "Did you fall all the way down a flight of stairs?"

"Nope. And I installed a night-light in the hallway, so it won't happen again." She cleared her throat. "Georgia, how are the wedding plans coming along?"

"Okay, I guess? Ask Rebecca. She's the one who's keeping track. She wants me to pick out flowers this week, except she gets mad when I just point to the first thing we see."

"Flowers?" Leo asked, giving her a squeeze. "How could those be a big decision?"

"Right?" Georgia laughed. "Don't worry your pretty head over it. You just focus on hockey and stay in your happy place."

"Did I mention how much I love this woman?" Leo grinned like he'd won the lottery. "She doesn't care that I don't care about flowers! Am I winning at life, or what?" He high-fived Hartley.

"You are, honey," Georgia said. "Carry on with your important discussion about hiding each other's jock straps or whatever. Ari and I have got this."

Ari laughed, and O'Doul liked the sound so much that he didn't even mind that she'd changed the subject on him.

Across the table, Trevi asked his pal Hartley, "How's Callihan? When is she going to move to Boston and marry you?"

Hartley chuckled. "What are you, a marriage evangelist, now?"

"Born again," Trevi agreed.

"I've played on three teams in three years," Hartley said. "I can't wait to shack up with Callihan, but we're waiting until it looks like I might be able to stay put somewhere for more than a season. She's got a great job in Chicago, too. Another year there will only make it easier for her to find a job in Boston or wherever."

"Uh-huh. Sounds like stalling."

His friend pulled his phone out of his pocket. "Let's sober-dial her."

"What is that?" Georgia asked.

"We can't drunk-dial her because we're not drunk," Hartley explained. "Obvs."

"Obvs," Trevi repeated. Then, while his friend tried to raise his girlfriend on FaceTime, Trevi hugged the guy hard and gave him a noogie. "I miss the hell out of you!"

If anybody did that to O'Doul he'd probably chuck them across the room.

"Hello?" a voice came from the phone's little speakers. "Omigod! Look who it is! Trevi—I want to meet your girlfriend!"

The three of them put their smiling faces together in front of the phone, like a goddamn pack of puppies. He took a gulp of his Scotch, feeling like the Grinch. His hip gave a throb, and he set the mostly empty glass on the table. "I think it's time to turn in," he said to Ari.

"You take care of yourself," she said, her dark eyes sparkling. "Good work tonight."

The compliment made a warm spot right in his chest. Or maybe it was the whiskey. "Thank you," he whispered. "Sleep well."

She gave him a soft smile, and he carried the memory of it all the way upstairs.

TWO

Standings: 3rd place in the Metropolitan Division
17 Regular Season Games to Go

It was four more days until Ari got O'Doul onto her therapy schedule.

At first he'd agreed to see her at the rink in Toronto during the pregame warm-ups. But then "something came up," and he rescheduled. *Again*.

Now the team was back home in Brooklyn. Ari waited for him in her treatment room at the practice facility. She was perched on the countertop, wondering if he'd show. He was five minutes late already.

A girl could start to take this personally. She'd held this job for almost two years without ever seeing the captain on her massage table.

Before now she'd chalked up his absence to his exceptionally good health and flexibility. The wrist injury he'd had earlier in the season was not the kind of thing that sent a man off to the massage room, either. But now that he was in such obvious need of her help, it was odd that he wouldn't seek it. Many of the other players would book a massage *twice* a day if her schedule allowed it.

Not O'Doul.

She'd asked him once in casual conversation whether he saw a private massage therapist. Some players were so into massage that they paid up for a private masseuse to visit them at home every morning. As a veteran, O'Doul could afford to hire a staff of thousands if he wished.

But when she'd asked, he'd just shaken his head.

Ari had a theory about O'Doul, though. He didn't seem to like to be touched. At all. During yoga class, she never corrected him with her hands, because she'd noticed early on that his postures got worse instead of better when she adjusted him. At first she'd assumed he was embarrassed to be corrected by a woman.

But his reluctance to have a massage had shifted her thinking. Maybe O'Doul didn't like to be touched *at all*. She'd tested this theory the other night at the bar, laying a hand on his broad shoulder in passing. He actually flinched a little.

Weird.

The training team was worried about a strain to his right hip flexors, so they'd asked for her help. And now here she sat watching both the door and the clock. If O'Doul didn't show this time, she'd have to tell Henry—the head trainer—that she might not be right the right therapist for O'Doul's needs. If the man was sensitive to being touched, he might do better with a therapist he chose himself.

This possibility made her jumpy, though. It shouldn't be the end of the world if one player snubbed the staff therapist. But job security was always in the back of her mind, and she really wanted to do well for this team. She wanted to do well, period.

Every hockey team had a staff masseuse, but the role was usually held by a man. Ari was proud of her position on the Bruisers. And since the breakup with her boyfriend of eight years, her job was the one steady thing in her life.

Luckily, this train of thought was interrupted when the door to her therapy room flew open to admit O'Doul. Right away she was struck by how absurdly handsome he was. It ought to be against the law to have a jaw that rugged and eyes the color of a tropical sea. As a massage therapist, Ari believed that all bodies were beautiful and miraculous. However, some were more miraculous than others.

But when she checked his expression, her confidence faltered. O'Doul was the only player who walked into her treatment room wearing the same expression that another man might wear to have a tooth extracted.

"Good afternoon," she said, hopping down as he took off his coat.

He turned to face her the way a guy might face the firing squad. "Afternoon."

"I'll step out while you change," Ari said, placing a folded sheet on the table. "If you'd feel more comfortable you can leave your undergarments on. When you're ready, lie down on the table, using the extra sheet as a cover."

"Got it," he said, pulling his team sweatshirt over his head.

Ari stepped out of the room for a moment. She tied up her hair and fetched a bottle of massage oil off the warmer where she'd left it. Then she took a minute to close her eyes and visualize how she wanted the hour to go.

The team often snickered when she led them through visualization exercises, but Ari knew their power. It was hard to achieve something if you couldn't *imagine* it working. With her back to the door, she first formed his name in her mind. *Patrick.* When meditating on her clients' needs, she always used first names because they seemed more personal. When you put your hands on someone's body, it was personal whether you wanted it to be or not.

Today I'm healing Patrick.

In her mind's eye, he relaxed on the table. With firm but gentle hands, she'd probe his trouble spots. She pictured his hip flexor muscles, overlapping one another, the nerves stretching toward his groin in one direction and around to his lumbar spine in the other. She visualized her hands bringing him comfort, easing the strain, recruiting the deeper hip flexors. She'd try to ease any pressure he'd been shifting to his lower back. At the end of the hour, he'd be looser and more flexible. He'd feel more confident whenever he moved.

Ari opened her eyes. She could help Patrick if he'd let her. She knocked twice before reentering the room.

"C'mon in," came the gruff response.

She let herself in, then stopped for a moment at the stereo she kept on the countertop. She cued up a playlist and then washed her hands. "Daughter" began to emerge from the little set of speakers she kept on the counter.

"Pearl Jam?" he asked from the table.

"You don't like it?" she asked. She would have figured him for a grunge rock guy. He was thirty-two years old with a macho streak a mile wide.

"No, I love it," he chuckled. "Once I tried to get a massage at a hotel, and they were playing harp music. My ears were bleeding."

"Okay, no harps. Got it." Ari approached the table and looked her client over. Bodies were an everyday sight for a massage therapist. But this was a particularly stunning example. All athletes were muscular but O'Doul was *cut*. Even lying flat on a table he looked like a tightly coiled spring, ready for sudden physical exertion. The sheet had been casually draped across his waist, but everywhere else rippling muscle was visible, from his stacked shoulders to his thick calves.

He tucked his hands behind his head and stared up at the ceiling. "How long does this take?"

Ari laughed in spite of herself. "Sixty minutes, usually. And I haven't killed anyone yet. I swear."

"Okay. Sorry." His mouth formed a tight line.

Right. Ari rubbed her hands together to warm them. She was oddly self-conscious for someone who gave six or more massages a day. "I'm going to ease toward your hip flexor strain, okay? I'll want to relax the surrounding muscles, so they don't contribute to your pain. You'll let me know if anything hurts, and if you don't approve of the pressure." She folded the sheet back to reveal his thigh. She patted his knee to announce her presence, then used her left hand to palm his lower quad, and her right to slowly manipulate the muscle just above his kneecap.

Slowly she worked her way up the outside of his hip. So far, so good. "Just checking in, here. How's the pressure?"

"Okay," he said tightly.

Hmm. Not exactly a rave review. She worked on, and eventually he closed his eyes and sighed, which was always a good sign. If there were no risk of being caught acting silly, she would have given herself a victorious fist pump.

Taking her time, she loosened up all the ancillary muscles, the ones bordering his trouble spot. Her beat-up old iPod played a Red Hot Chili Peppers song and then transitioned back to Pearl Jam again.

All was right with the world until Ari moved her hands closer to Patrick's inner hip. One by one, all his muscles tightened up until his entire body had the consistency of a concrete block.

"Patrick," she said quietly, and his eyes flew open. "Are you in pain? Massage doesn't have to hurt to do you good."

"No pain," he said quickly.

Liar. "You're fighting me, though. Why is that?"

"Uh," he pressed himself up on an elbow, causing his chest muscles to ripple. "That's the . . . trouble spot, right? Why would I want someone touching it?" The expression on his face was cautious for once.

"Well . . ." Ari replayed the words he'd just spoken, trying to find a clue to his reluctance. "Because I can help you? I won't hurt you, I promise. Careful massage can reduce inflammation, and relax surrounding muscles, too. Is it possible that you had a bad experience with massage before?"

He gave his head a shake, as if her suggestion did not compute. "Nah. I just don't like having, uh, weak spots."

"Everyone does, though, right?"

"I suppose. But I don't grab yours."

She put a hand on his muscular wrist, the way she would anyone. But his eyes traveled down to that spot immediately, and she wondered if she'd just made another mistake. Had any other client ever been such a mystery?

"Hey," she tried. "You told me a few minutes ago that you'd tried to get a massage at a hotel once. What happened that time?"

"Didn't work out." He gave her a wry grin. "It's not you, I swear."

"*Why* didn't it work out? Besides the harps. Why did you book a massage?"

He gave what was supposed to be a casual shrug. "I'd slept funny on the jet, and my neck hurt. No big deal. So I booked a massage at the spa. Left after ten minutes. I guess I just don't like hands on me."

"You don't like to be touched."

He looked at his hands. "It isn't my favorite thing, no."

The hair stood up on the back of Ari's neck, and she had to restrain herself from asking why. Not liking to be touched wasn't a common attitude. "Everybody's different," she said softly. "But we still have to work on your hip flexors. I have one idea that might help you."

"Good." He made a sheepish face. "Because I'm fresh out."

She patted his wrist again—intentionally. If they were going to work together, he needed to become at least a *little* more accustomed to being touched. "Let's try a more active technique. It will feel more like a gym exercise and less like massage. Can you roll onto your good side and bend your knee for me?"

He complied, turning his broad back to her. She adjusted his bottom leg to be somewhat straight, and then wrapped her hand around his right ankle. "Bend this knee a little more for me." He did. "All right. I'm going to brace your outer hip. Like this." She gripped the muscle as far in as she'd gotten before he'd begun fighting her touch. "And you're going to put your *own* hand on the trouble spot. Show me."

He pushed his fingertips into his flesh between his hip and his groin.

"Now, don't use your back." She tapped the muscles of his lower back. "Don't activate these. Instead, use your hip and leg. Press down and straighten that leg. Go."

With a lazy-sounding rumble from his chest, he did as she'd instructed.

"Good! How'd that feel?" She dug her hands into the accessible muscle at his hip, warming it, working it as best she could.

"Not too bad."

"You wouldn't lie to me, captain, right?"

He chuckled for the first time. "No, ma'am."

"Ugh. You ma'amed me like an old woman. Just for that you're going to do it four more times." She grabbed his ankle again. "Bend."

"Yes, *ma'am*."

"For that? Six times."

"Yes, master." She watched the taut muscles of his back shake with laughter.

Ari placed her hands on his body again, her palm warmed by the taut skin of his lower back, the fingers of her other hand gripping his sturdy hip through the thin cotton of his navy blue briefs. "Ready, big guy?"

"Ready," he rumbled.

"Push and go." Together they worked around his trouble spot while he extended his leg. And the sigh he let out was a good sign. "Okay?"

"Yeah. It feels a little looser than it did a half hour ago."

Ari's small victory was like a warm tingle in her chest. Smiling, she made him repeat the exercise a few more times. "Now roll onto your stomach," she insisted. "For fifteen minutes I want you to pretend you enjoy massage. Just to stroke my ego, okay?"

Chuckling, he rolled over. She spread a bit of oil on her hands and went to work on his calves, slowly working her way up to his hamstrings. Bit by bit she felt his body relax beneath her touch. "How am I doing?" she asked. "Feel free to lie."

"Aw. This is the best massage I've had all year."

She let out an unladylike snort. "This is the *only* one, right?"

"Yeah, but still." He rolled his handsome face into the crook of his arm and sighed again.

Skipping his hips, she went to work on the muscles at the juncture of his lower back and his rather beautiful ass. "Do you have much pain here? The risk with a hip strain is that you'll overcompensate by using your lower back."

"By the end of a game, I'm feeling it there for sure."

The honest answer surprised her. She gave him a pat on the back. "Okay. At your next visit, we'll keep working on these trouble spots. Each time you put on a burst of speed on the ice, you demand a lot from these muscles. If we keep you loose, it's going to help. I'm going to work into your hip a little now—but only from the back. And I'm not going to hurt you. And you're lying on the trouble spot, right? No one can touch it." She hoped his defensive position on the table would prevent him from tensing up.

"Got it. Do your worst."

They were tough words from a tough guy, but now she knew better. Patrick O'Doul had some serious issues with having hands on his body. His reluctance probably stemmed from a refusal to make himself vulnerable.

She could work around that, though. She'd have to.

Eddie Vedder sang "Black" through her speakers and Ari hummed along, rolling the waistband of his briefs down just an inch, giving her better access to his skin. She oiled up her hands again and leaned into him, closing her eyes, applying all of her strength to the task at hand. Muscle and bone pressed against muscle and bone. Skin met skin. She let the oil do its work, reducing friction, bringing her hands into better contact with the body she was trying so hard to heal.

That's when she felt it—finally—that beautiful connection, the moment when the client opens himself up to the treatment. He seemed to go slack beneath her, his muscles relaxing beneath the rhythm of her hands. If it wouldn't have disturbed his newfound peace, she would have hooted in victory.

She finished up the massage at his big shoulders, now supple. His eyes were heavy. His breathing was steady. And if she checked his pulse, she knew she'd find it at a slow, relaxed rate.

It almost seemed mean when she had to pat the back of his neck gently and tell him that time was up.

His eyes widened. "Okay," he said a little sleepily. "Thanks."

"Here," she said, placing a towel on the edge of the table. "You don't want to get massage oil on your clothes."

She turned her back and washed her hands at the little sink in the corner, giving him a moment alone to peel himself up off the table and gather his things. "See you tomorrow in Detroit," she said over her shoulder. "I'll text you a location. I think we'll be at the hotel."

"Right. I'll be on time," he mumbled. "Thanks."

"Be well!" As he opened the door to leave, she stole a look at his face. The expression she found there tugged at her heart. It was a little dazed, as if he couldn't quite make sense of how he'd spent the last hour. She gave him a smile, and the corners of his rugged mouth turned up, too.

Then he was gone, probably to the showers. The hot water would do him some more good and keep him loose. But it would also give him a few minutes to pull himself together. Somehow it hadn't been easy for O'Doul to let someone touch his body. But he'd done it. He'd let down his guard. Now he'd have to pull it back up again for game night. In a few hours he was expected to mow down the visiting team from Washington D.C., and maybe take a few punches to amuse the fans.

Although Ari found some aspects of hockey barbaric, she had tremendous respect for the competitive demands these men placed on both their bodies and their psyches. While she was donning her coat and wondering what to eat for dinner before the game, two dozen men would think of nothing but victory for the next seven hours. Cameras would follow their every move on the ice, then reporters would argue afterwards about their odds of making the play-offs for the first time since Nate Kattenberger bought the team.

Ari walked home, heading north toward the tiny Brooklyn neighborhood of Vinegar Hill where the streets were brick and the buildings were barely three stories high. The houses here were smaller and older than in almost any other part of Brooklyn. The townhouse where Ari lived dated back to the Civil War. Someone had put a rather pedestrian brick facade on it during the sixties, which dimmed some of its charm. But as Ari approached from a block away, its blue-painted wooden door beckoned her home.

She was lucky as hell to live here. The building was worth a couple of million dollars at least, in spite of the Con Edison substation blocking the entire neighborhood from having a decent view of the river. The townhouse belonged to Ari's great-uncle. He and the rest of her Italian family had decamped for Florida a decade ago. She paid only a very modest monthly rent in exchange for looking after the building.

As she approached, though, she saw something that made her slow down. The back end of her ex's dark-red van was visible just around the corner. The sight of it made her stomach ache instinctively, but its presence wasn't necessarily bad news.

Three days ago she'd sent him an ultimatum—an e-mail notifying him that he had two days to finally clear the rest of his belongings out of her storage room. He hadn't replied at all. Just this morning she'd been wondering what to do about it.

If Vince was finally clearing out his junk from her basement, that was progress.

Ari dug out her keys—still shiny from their newness—and covered the rest of the block quickly. She jogged up the four steps to her front door and unlocked the brand new deadbolt. Then she closed and locked the door. And listened.

The only voices she could make out were muffled, and coming from the rear of the building. She set her bag down at the foot of her staircase and tip-toed through the dining room and on into the kitchen, stopping only to kick off her boots to silence the sound of footsteps on her hardwood floors. She hung back near the old refrigerator, taking a cautious, oblique glimpse out the back window.

Nothing.

Her heart was racing for no good reason. Vince was outside and she was inside, behind the safety of new locks. His presence unsettled her nonetheless. Vince Giardi was the embodiment of her worst, most embarrassing mistake. The grandmother who'd helped raise her—God rest her soul— had been right about Vince. *Thank you, Nonna. Sorry it took me eight years to notice.*

Ari leaned against the fridge, its hum at her back, and took a six-count breath, expanding her diaphragm. She wouldn't let Vince get her riled up today. There was no need, anyway.

She heard the distinctive slam of the exterior basement door, and stood on tiptoe to take another peek out the window. A beanie hat appeared. But when the man came into view, it most certainly wasn't Vince. That was obvious even with the guy's back to her. He was thin and wearing dirty jeans. Vince would never dress like that. And, damn it, the man wasn't carrying anything. If there were strangers coming in and out of her basement storage room, they'd better have moving boxes containing Vince's clothing and video games.

Damn. It. All. Now what?

More than a month had passed since the awful weekend their relationship had finally ended after an epic fight. Her flight was late in from Ottawa, and she'd gotten home to find Vince waiting up for her, drunk and angry. He wanted to know where she'd been. Why hadn't she called?

This was nothing new, sadly. As soon as she'd taken the job with the Brooklyn Bruisers, things had headed downhill. But that awful night he didn't bother to couch his jealous little jabs behind a tense chuckle. He flat out accused her of sleeping with hockey players.

Even as she'd taken out her phone with shaky hands to show him the official arrival time of their charter flight on her Katt Phone, she'd understood that he'd finally gone too far. That she couldn't live under a cloud of pointless suspicion anymore. It ended right then, even if Vince didn't know it yet. But instead of playing it cool like a smart girl, she'd raised her voice. Blame it on her Italian heritage, but her top blew right off. "I shouldn't have to *prove* it, Vince," she'd said angrily. "If you think I'm a cheat, then leave me already! Walk out the fucking door! Just *stop this!*"

He did stop it—by grabbing both her wrists and shoving her toward the stairs. In her wool socks, she'd slipped. Heart-stopping fear rose up in her throat as the staircase sliced into view. Her head bounced off the wall as she grabbed for the carved antique bannister.

Her foot stopped her fall, though—caught between two balusters. At first it was such a relief to stop falling that she didn't feel the pain shooting up her instep. And then, shaking with fury and freaked out, she'd tried to conceal it. But that's hard when you can't put weight on one leg.

At the sight of her injury, Vince had sobered up fast and used Uber to get them a ride to the ER. "I'm sorry, baby," he babbled. "Terrible accident. Never happen again."

She made sure it wouldn't. The next night, when he went to work at the club, she'd had an emergency locksmith come over to change the deadbolts. She'd asked her tenant, a flight attendant named Maddy, to help put Vince's clothing into trash bags. It was possibly the most embarrassing favor she'd ever asked of anyone.

It had been far easier to shake off the hospital staff's probing questions than Maddy's. "He did this, didn't he?" she demanded, pointing one long red fingernail at Ari's walking cast. "I never liked the look of him. Good for you showing him the door."

Ari had neither confirmed nor denied Vince's role in her tumble. He probably hadn't meant to break a bone, but it really didn't matter. A bone was broken, and he'd been the cause of both her trip to the ER and her sudden wake-up call. With Maddy's help she'd hobbled around, doing her best to be respectful of his things even as she scrambled to get them all out of the house and into the basement storage unit. Maddy made all the trips down those back stairs herself, which meant Ari owed her. Big.

"You'd do the same for me," Maddy protested. And surely it was true. When the job was done, Ari gave her a hug and a pre-apology for whatever grief Vince might give her if he happened to show up when Maddy was coming or going. "I can take care of myself, hon. You do the same."

The four A.M. pounding on the exterior door had been awful. When Ari didn't come to the door to explain herself, he'd begun yelling terrible things up at her bedroom window. "Fucking cunt! Get down here and let me in."

Maddy's chainsaw voice had rung out from her third floor window. "Go away or I'm calling the police. You have ten seconds. Tomorrow Ari will tell you how to get your stuff."

"Meddling bitch!" he'd returned. But when Maddy'd told him she was dialing 911, he'd actually left.

In the morning she'd e-mailed Vince to let him know he could retrieve his own things from the storage room with his old key. The fact that he didn't answer or turn up for a week only made her more anxious. It was unlike him to give up and walk away. Especially if his collection of expensive suits was on the line.

But then one day she'd spotted his van nearby. And she'd

heard the basement door open and close. It happened again a couple of days later. For the past few weeks he'd either been moving out one article of clothing at a time, or merely torturing her with his sporadic presence.

That's why her latest e-mail had threatened to change the locks on the basement door, too. She should have done that weeks ago. It's just that the basement was so inhospitable—its entrance barely a step up from the cellar door in *The Wizard of Oz*—she thought he'd get sick of the lurker charade and leave her alone for good.

Hopefully today was the day.

Hugging herself, Ari kept up her vigil by the fridge. Eventually the door slammed again and Vince strode into view, his back to the window, his swagger intact. He disappeared around the corner of the building. A moment later she heard what had to be the van's engine start up and then drive away.

Finally, she relaxed.

With her heart rate returning to normal, she checked her messages and reheated a square of lasagna she'd saved for dinner. She even poured herself a half glass of wine to go with it. Everything was fine, or soon would be. Tonight her team was going to beat the visitors from Washington D.C., and tomorrow she'd relieve their aching muscles.

After her early dinner she lay down on the couch with a book. The house was so very quiet. She still wasn't used to living alone. She'd met Vince when she was just twenty-one and bartending at one of his clubs. She'd never been an adult on her own.

It was obviously time to start. She read her book and tried to think soothing thoughts.

By six thirty it was time to get ready for the game. She went up the creaky narrow staircase to her bedroom and chose a knit dress with three-quarter sleeves and tights. The NHL liked its staff to look professional, even if she might be called upon for some last-minute attention to stiff muscles. It had taken her a few months on the job to figure out what to wear. Now her closet held four comfy game night dresses in shades of eggplant (the team color). She wore ballet flats to keep herself comfortable and mobile.

Ari grabbed her bag and headed out the door. Before heading to Water Street where cabs were more plentiful, she took a moment to circle the block for a moment, casing her own building like a thief. She peeked into the alley. The basement door of her little house was closed, as it should be. There was nobody in sight. Checking over both shoulders like a paranoid fool, she walked around back, slipping her keys out of her pocket.

But she stopped at the rear door, confused. There, gleaming against the beat-up metal door, was a new lock. Even though it didn't make sense, she tried her key anyway. This was her building, for God's sake.

The key wouldn't even fit in the lock.

Anger rushed through her veins like a drug. *Damn you, Vince!* He was like a cockroach that couldn't be killed off. He'd locked her out of her own basement.

What the hell?

The only windows back here were narrow and just above her eye level. Shaking with fury, she stood on tiptoe to peek inside. She cupped a hand over the glass to try to reduce the sunset's glare. It took her eyes a moment to identify the shapes in the basement's dim light.

The first thing she could make out was the strip of lights on a computer modem, doing their little dance to announce their connection. And their light helped illuminate a sort of folding table which held the rest of a computer setup—a screen and a keyboard and mouse, with a chair pulled up to them. But the item which really drove home the problem was the wastepaper basket on the floor. There was something so freaking civilized about it that it could almost make steam come out of her ears.

Vince had set up an *office* in her basement. He was conducting some kind of business on her property! With a wastepaper basket!

She was mad enough to spit. She stomped toward the corner, calm mood ruined, and stuck her arm in the air for a taxi.

Two hours later she was feeling a little calmer, even though the problem remained unsolved.

But the game was about to start, the stadium filling with ten thousand fans. It was hard to feel crabby with so much expectation bouncing around the arena.

Ari had already given a couple of last-minute chair massages to players with upper body pain. By this point their fate was out of her hands. She stood in the owners' box, a soda in her hand, a notebook at her side. She would watch the first period of the game from this premium location and make some notes about who suffered the hardest hits, so she could follow up with those players during the intermission or tomorrow.

Hockey was pretty freaking exciting, too. Just because she'd never been a fan before she took this job didn't mean she didn't enjoy it.

Beside her, the Brooklyn Bruisers' office manager stood sipping from a glass of wine. "How's O'Doul today?" Becca asked, watching the ice team sweep the surface one more time. "I heard rumors that they sent him to you for his hip."

"He seemed fair," Ari said, considering the question. "A little rest would probably help him. But I don't think it's any worse than a lot of the strains the guys play on."

In her heart of hearts, Ari would never understand the risks these players took with their bodies every day. That was their job, and they were highly compensated for it. She'd never be rich, but she'd never take a punch to the face, either.

Though you let yourself be pushed down the stairs, her subconscious prodded.

"Is Doulie a diva in the treatment room? He's so freaking bossy. The travel team actually calls all the hotels where he stays and gets duplicate receipts to submit for him, because they've learned it's a bigger pain to ask for his cooperation than to just take over."

"Really?" Ari laughed. "Sounds like he has them trained." Everyone was supposed to submit his or her own receipts, or pay an assistant to do it for them. Ari did her own, but it was a pain in the gluteus maximus.

"He has an ego the size of the stadium. If you have any trouble with him, I'm happy to play the part of bad cop."

"You do that part well." Ari squeezed her friend's shoulder.

"Fuck," Becca moaned. "Do that again. Please? I spent too many hours at my desk today."

Ari set down her drink and stood behind Becca. She put her hands on the younger woman's shoulders and began to rub. "You only like me for my hands," she complained.

"Not true! You make a mean margarita, and you always turn in your personnel forms on time."

"I feel so much better now." She put her thumbs at the base of Becca's skull and rubbed. This was a brand-new friendship. Ari had always liked Becca and her sidekick, Georgia, the publicist. But Ari's ex had resented all the traveling that Ari did for the team, and when she was home in Brooklyn he got pissy if she went out without him.

His attitude had kept her away from developing normal friendships with the girls at work, and she hadn't even realized it until after she'd broken things off with him.

During Ari's yoga training, a wise yogi had told her that pain always brought new awarenesses. He said pain brought gifts with it. Or, as her Italian grandmother would have put it—when God slams a door, he opens a window. Becoming friends with Becca and Georgia was that window.

"Marry me," Becca breathed as Ari rubbed her shoulders.

"I would, but I've sworn off relationships. Today was a good reminder of why."

Becca spun around, cutting off her massage. "Oh, no! What happened? Did he pound on your door again?"

"No, but his stuff is still in my basement storage room, and . . ."

This conversation was interrupted by the arrival of Nate Kattenberger, the team's owner. He walked in wearing his trademark hoodie and dark wash jeans. Ari had heard that the old guard of the hockey league hated the young billionaire's personal dress code, and its governors occasionally made snide comments about his "athletic shoes" in the press.

Becca had let it slip that Kattenberger's Tom Ford sneakers ran six hundred bucks, though. The man liked expensive clothes, but he did not like to conform to a bunch of league rules. And Ari loved him for it.

"Evening, ladies," Nate said with a wave. He walked right over to the front of the box and looked down, surveying his dominion.

A young woman breezed in after him. Lauren was Nate's Manhattan assistant, not to be confused with Becca, his Brooklyn assistant. The contrast between the two women was more than a little amusing. Lauren wore a designer suit in an expensive shade of pink, stockings and high heels. Her hair was swept into a glamorous up-do that must have taken forty-five minutes to accomplish. And at seven thirty P.M., it still looked perfect.

Becca wore Dr. Martens, purple tights, and a leather dress. Her hair was purple and her eyebrow and nose were proudly pierced.

The biggest difference, though, was in facial expression. Becca raised a hand to give the other woman a friendly wave. "Hi, Lauren! Want to have a glass of wine with us?"

The only acknowledgment that Becca had spoken was a sidelong glance flicked in their direction. As if she hadn't heard at all, Lauren went over to the drinks table herself and poured her boss a Diet Coke over three ice cubes. She perched a wedge of lime on the rim, snapped a cocktail napkin into her hand, and scurried over to him to present it as if to royalty.

"I'm always nice," Becca whispered under her breath, "but I'm really not sure why."

"Because it feels better to be nice," Ari whispered. "And you're a beautiful person."

Becca shot her a grateful glance. "She makes ugly look pretty good."

It was true. Queen Lauren (as they sometimes referred to her) was beautiful. But Ari wasn't even a little jealous of that silky pale hair or those blue eyes. Lauren exuded stress and unhappiness. A decade of yoga might not even make a dent in Queen Lauren's steel facade.

"Rebecca," Nate called. "Do you happen to have tonight's ticket sales?"

"But of course!" she chirped. "Do you really think I'd stand here and slurp wine if I hadn't brought them with me?" She balanced her glass in one hand and dug through her briefcase with the other. "It's here somewhere. Ah." When she finally tugged a file out of her bag, Nate took the folder with a smile. "Anything shocking in here? Should I hit the whiskey early?"

"It's always cocktail hour somewhere, boss. But the numbers looked good to me."

Nate flipped the cover open and scanned the summary page while Lauren glared over his shoulder at Becca. "These are good numbers. And I like the time series graph."

"Thanks! I got sick of flipping backward to see the prior weeks' numbers."

When he was through, Nate handed the folder to Lauren for safekeeping. Lauren stashed it in a leather satchel while simultaneously attempting to incinerate Becca with her eyes.

"Thank you," Nate said in Lauren's general direction. "That's all for today, I suppose."

Lauren said good night to her boss and buttoned up her impeccable jacket.

"Aren't you staying for the game?" Becca asked.

"I hate hockey," Lauren declared. Then she walked out, her heels clicking importantly across the walnut floorboards.

Ari exchanged a loaded glance with Becca. Her friend's

eyebrows lifted as if to ask, *can you believe Nate's assistant would say that right before a game?* Maybe the girl didn't understand how superstitious men could be about their sports.

The door opened again, admitting Georgia Worthington and the brand new publicist, Tom. This was his first week on the job.

"How'd the press take it?" Nathan asked by way of a greeting.

"*Lots* of questions," Georgia said. "There's going to be speculation."

"Take what?" Becca asked, voicing the same question that was on Ari's mind.

"O'Doul was scratched at the last minute," Tom said. "The trainers want him rested. That's our story and we're sticking to it."

Oh, boy, Ari thought, staring down at the ice. The players were lining up for the national anthem now. She couldn't even remember a night when O'Doul had been scratched before. The only time she'd known him to sit out games was that brief span when he was on the injured list while his wrist was healing.

She didn't know him all that well. But she knew enough to say he was *not* going to like it.

THREE

Standings: 4th place in the Metropolitan Division
16 Regular Season Games to Go

A day later, stepping off the bus in front of their Detroit hotel, O'Doul had to admit that his hip was better. But not his attitude.

They'd fucking *scratched* him last night at the last minute. "We need to rest you," Coach Worthington had said. "I need you to play a long postseason. Can't do that if you're injured."

Needless to say, he had not agreed with this decision. He hated the way it looked—like he needed rest, like an old fart. His team had struggled without him, too. They should have owned that game against D.C. But by the end of the third period, it was a 2–2 tie. And then a lucky shot in the overtime period by the opponent's rookie lost the Bruisers the game.

No gold star.

"We got an overtime point out of it," Coach had said last night, sounding uncharacteristically sanguine for someone who had slipped in the standings. Since Boston had won their game the same night, the Kattenberger model now had their play-offs chances slipping to 73 percent.

O'Doul knew the numbers would have gone the other way if he'd played.

He wore a grimace while he waited beside his teammates for their luggage to be offloaded from the bus's storage hold. His hip didn't hurt, but his ego sure did.

The new backup goalie, Zac Sullivan, was horsing around on the sidewalk, trying to steal Bayer's bottle of Gatorade out of the side of his duffel without getting caught. It was all fun and games until the guy almost crashed into a woman pushing a stroller.

"Whoa! Sorry ma'am," he said, backing off.

She gave him an evil look and pushed her baby quickly past the group of hockey players.

"Twenty bucks, man," O'Doul said. "Pay up."

"What? Why?" the goalie argued.

"For almost mowing down that kid. Jimbo?" O'Doul said, pointing at the young man on the travel ops team. "Sully owes you twenty."

"Got it," Jimbo said, pulling a pad out of his back pocket. The team called these slips of paper "parking tickets," and O'Doul assessed them anytime somebody was out of line. He gave out parking tickets for petty offenses like leaving a mess in the locker room or making the team look bad. At the end of every season, the whole kitty went to charity. Last year they gave over ten grand to a Brooklyn homeless shelter.

"Want to get some barbecue for lunch?" Trevi asked O'Doul. "The Katt Phone says there's a good ribs joint nearby."

"I'm in," Castro volunteered.

"I wish," O'Doul said. "I have to get a fucking massage."

Castro exchanged a glance with Trevi. "And the problem is . . . ?" Castro asked.

"Eh," O'Doul said, hating the sound of irritation in his voice. "Not my favorite way to spend an hour."

"I'll take it!" Trevi volunteered. "I like it when Ari does that thing to the base of my skull. With her thumbs?" He held up his hands and wiggled his thumbs like a loon.

"Aw, hell yes," Castro agreed. "And when she does my feet, I always propose. How many marriage proposals do you think she gets in a week?"

"Let's see," Trevi said, grabbing his duffel bag off the sidewalk. "She works six days a week during the high season, six massages a day. So probably thirty."

"Six times six is thirty-six, moron," Castro said, shouldering his own bag.

"No kidding?" He gave Castro a playful nudge. "I passed the third grade, too. But not everyone proposes. I wouldn't do that to Georgia."

"I propose twice," Castro said. "Once for each foot."

"Oh, shut it, will you?" O'Doul hefted his own bag and turned toward the revolving doors.

"Come back in a better mood!" Trevi called after him.

Fat chance.

Ten minutes later he knocked on the door to a hotel room, the number for which had been texted to him by the bots who ran Bruisers' travel.

A startled-looking Ari opened the door a minute later, her own Katt Phone pressed to her ear. She held up one finger in the universal sign for *this will only take a minute*.

He walked past her into the room where her massage table had been set up in the space where a bed should have been. Everything else about the room was standard-issue hotel fare—there was a shiny desk which looked unused, and your typical bathroom. He kicked off his shoes and wondered whether it would be weird if he just stripped off his clothes, or whether it would be weirder if he waited to be told to.

"That's why I called a locksmith," Ari said into her phone. "It's not that complicated. Remove the lock that's there, and install a different one." She paused. "Well, the deed isn't in my name. But last time I used your services I didn't need it. Could I please speak to the manager? Yes,

I'll hold." She looked up at him. "You can change in the bathroom if that makes you more comfortable."

Busted. He went into the little bathroom and closed the door. But he could still hear her conversation. "Please look up my account. I've used you for years. The lock on the basement door is . . . What? *You* installed it? Seriously? *No,* I didn't authorize it!" She was almost shouting. "He *lied,* okay? Men do that sometimes."

O'Doul felt like a dick for listening. But the hotel door was thin and he had no place else to go. He removed his clothes—all of them this time—wrapped a towel around his waist and waited for her to finish up.

"Just *remove* the lock and give me another one. I didn't authorize it. And he is no longer a resident at that address."

A moment later she ended her call, and he counted to thirty and then left the bathroom. Ari had parked her backside against the edge of the massage table and buried her head in her hands. "Everything okay?" he asked stupidly. Clearly it was not.

She looked up fast. "Fine. Thanks." She spun around and went over to the desk. From a duffel bag she hurriedly drew out a sheet and several bottles of massage oil. But her hands were shaking, and the bottles began to knock into one another and tip. One of them crashed over her wrist and dove toward the floor.

He lunged forward to catch it, and he did. But his towel fell to the floor. "Shit."

She laughed suddenly, and the low, smoky sound of it seemed to brush across his bare skin. He grabbed the towel off the floor. *Hell.* Surely Ari had seen his ass before—she was in and out of the locker room on game night. But he felt like a bumbler.

"Sorry," she breathed. "But that was excellent comedy, and I needed a laugh right now."

He adjusted his towel. "Thank you very much, I'll be here all week."

Ari smiled, but she still looked a little strung out. She

stacked the last bottle onto the desk beside the others. "Just let me put a sheet down on the table." She grabbed the linens and shook out the sheet, her slim arms extending like a dancer's. She flung one end toward the head of the table.

Holding his towel more carefully in one hand, he caught the sheet in his other hand and helped her tuck it around the ends.

She gave him a grateful look and smiled again. "Thank you."

"No problem."

When she moved past him to pick up her phone off what should have been a bedside table, her long hair brushed his bare shoulder. This was exactly what he didn't like about getting a massage. It was weirdly intimate.

"Want to pick a playlist?" she asked, wrapping her hair into a ponytail.

"I liked what you played before." When she looked away to fiddle with a pair of wireless speakers, he got onto the table and spread the towel across his midsection.

"I'm sorry you were scratched from last night's game. Wasn't my idea, I promise."

"Okay." It hadn't even occurred to him to blame her. "It happens."

She turned her potent smile on him. "You say that so convincingly."

"Don't I?" He found himself smiling back.

Ari patted his arm. "I'm going to try to warm you up for a few minutes. After that we'll go back to the same active release technique as last time, because I think it was starting to work for you. How does that sound?"

"Fine," he said. Because what was the alternative, really?

Standing at his side, she adjusted the towel, keeping his crotch covered, but allowing access to his hip. There was something precise about her motions that made everything a little less weird than it should have been. Her strong fingers began kneading the muscle of his upper thigh and his waist. She moved slowly, firm hands squeezing, fingers sliding . . .

Goose bumps broke out on his chest.

Christ.

He wasn't a prude. But it was just *weird* having her hands on his body. Nobody ever touched him—*really* touched him. Sure there was sex, but that was entirely different. When he was horny enough to go home with a fan or a girl in a bar, it was because they both wanted something from one another. It was a fair trade. And the promise of release—and a drink or five—was enough to get him past the awkwardness.

This was a completely different experience, and he didn't know what to do with it. The intimacy made him wary. Usually he found Ari's lavender scent appealing. But he was too aware of it at such close range. And sometimes when she applied an especially firm grasp to his larger muscle groups, he could hear her exhale through the effort. The closeness made his skin prickle.

Her strong hands relaxed all at once. "You're fighting me, Patrick," she whispered. And the sound of his own name brought the goose bumps back.

"Sorry." He made an effort to relax, but she moved around the table until she was at his head, looking down. He couldn't avoid her gaze.

"I know this isn't your favorite thing. I get it."

He admired the shape of her big brown eyes and tried to imagine what was going through her head. "You must think I'm a total nutbar."

"Not at *all*," she said vehemently. "I could give you a sermon about how I'm a professional and this is just business, yada yada yada. But that would be bullshit."

"It would?" He couldn't help enjoying the shape of her sweet mouth as she said *bullshit*. "You're not a professional?"

She rolled her eyes. "Of course I am. But when you walk into this room, you don't just bring your muscles and your bones. You bring your whole history as a human being. You bring your *soul*. And when someone touches you, they're touching all of that, too."

"Okay . . ." He'd never thought about it that way.

"Did you ever stop and wonder why we shake hands?" She extended one of hers and shook hands with the air. "It's a cultural thing. But do you know why?"

"Can't say I did very well in social studies in school," he admitted, wondering where she was going with this.

She grinned. "I haven't the faintest idea where the tradition came from. But I have a theory. We touch someone we meet because it establishes trust. Maybe it's only a tiny little bit of trust. But if I shake your hand, I have to get close to your body. There's a brief exchange of heat and sensation. Give me your hand."

He reached up, and she took his hand in both of her smaller ones, and he forgot to hate being touched for a second because his palm tingled under her touch. "See—this is just a *small* extension of trust. But when you're on my table, the trust you extend to me is a lot greater than that." She released his hand, but not his gaze. For a second their eyes were locked together, and he saw boundless compassion there.

That made him just a little uncomfortable, too. Damn it.

With quiet deliberation, she put a hand on his bare shoulder. "Patrick, people have all kinds of reactions to massage. I think you'd be surprised. Some guys get chatty and tell me a hell of a lot more than they would if my hands weren't all over their naked bodies. Some guys fall asleep right away. This is all completely normal. Some people even start crying when I touch them."

O'Doul barked out a laugh. "Seriously? Do I know these people?"

Ari lifted her regal chin. "I wouldn't tell you that. *Never*. Just like I wouldn't tell another soul what reaction you have to being on my table."

"Sorry." Now he just felt sheepish. "I know."

She squeezed his shoulder. "I'm not giving up on you. But any ideas you have for making this easier on you, I'm all ears. I don't know if you're a fan of meditation, but that's something we could try."

"Eh."

She laughed. "Fine. Lie back now. And tell me this— where and when do you feel most relaxed?" She moved around the table to stand at his head, and then began to rub both his shoulders. That felt pretty good.

Though answering her question wasn't easy. He really didn't want to get into it. "At home. In my bed. Just like anyone."

He'd managed to live alone every year since that first apartment over the garage. And he didn't invite people into his home. These days he lived in an expensive loft in the same converted warehouse where some of his teammates lived. But he'd bought a one-room condo, because the sales-person had said that the other units were "perfect for enter-taining." He didn't want to entertain. His place was his sanctuary, and nobody else was allowed inside. Once in a while one of his teammates would say, *how come we never watch the game at O'Doul's?* He told them he was a terrible housekeeper and changed the subject.

Ari's hands moved down, kneading his biceps for a moment. That felt pretty good, too. "When I need a really relaxing thought, I think about the beach."

"Which beach?" he asked. She moved down to his hip again, which he didn't like. But maybe if they kept talking he could avoid worrying about his sore spots.

"Any beach." She smiled. "But, okay, not Coney Island, because it's crowded. When I was a little girl my grandmother had a place on Fire Island, and I used to stay the whole sum-mer there with her because school was out and Mom was at work. I like the way things sound at the beach. Like they're farther away. And the surf has a nice even rhythm."

He closed his eyes and pictured it. "Yeah, I never spent much time on a beach."

"What do you do during the off season?"

There wasn't much of it. Six or eight weeks. "Last year I went golfing with Beringer."

"You like golf?"

"No," he admitted, and she laughed. "But it was on my bucket list, I guess. To see why all the rich guys liked it."

"Aren't you a rich guy?" she teased.

"On paper. But where I grew up, nobody golfed. There was hockey and football. Even baseball was for pussies." He cleared his throat and realized that Ari's fingers had worked their way closer to his groin. The woman was smart. She'd distracted him.

"Where'd you grow up? Wait—Minnesota?"

"That's right. But not the nice part." And *that* conversation wasn't going to make him relax. "How about you?"

"Brooklyn. I grew up on Court Street, about two miles away from where I live now. I'm an Italian girl who teaches yoga in Brooklyn. I've got all the clichés working together at once." She patted his hip. "Roll on your side for me. Let's do this thing. Can you handle it? How's your pain?"

"I'm looser today than yesterday." He rolled.

"Maybe that night off wasn't such a bad plan?"

"What—you sure you don't want the credit?"

She laughed, adjusting his towel to cover his ass. "I never take credit. My job is to help you get out of your own way and then hog the limelight. Bend your knee. Are you working this muscle today?" She tapped his groin muscle once. "Or am I allowed to do it?"

"I wouldn't want to put you out of a job. Go ahead." What the hell, right? Yesterday she'd forced him to admit that he didn't want hands on his injury because it made him feel weak. But how counterproductive was that?

"Put your palm down on the table. I want you as stable as possible. Remember—don't use your back. We want a gentle extension, so if anything hurts, don't push it. Ready?" She dug into his hip and his groin with strong hands. "Extend."

He did. She worked her fingers into his groin muscles,

and he breathed through it. This was fine. She had surprisingly strong hands for such a small person. Her grip was confident, as if she were holding him together.

Really, things could be worse.

"Good!" she enthused after their eighth rep. "Let's leave it there for now. Roll onto your stomach if you wouldn't mind. I'm going to work on your lower back and ask you a few more questions."

He rolled, thinking to himself that he kind of liked the idea of her hands on his lower back. The questions were less appealing.

"Your goal is to avoid overcompensating with your back and quads," she said, kneading the muscle above his ass. "The nerves attached to your hip flexors stretch down your leg and around to your lumbar spine. Here." She stopped massaging to run two fingertips along his lower back. The light touch made his skin tingle. "So when you skate the warm-up tomorrow . . ."

". . . *If* I skate the warm-up tomorrow."

She patted his back. "Let's be optimistic, big guy. *When* you skate the warm-up, I want you to think about keeping the form of your stride all night long. When you're tired, don't change your stance to activate your back."

"I can do that." He'd been perfecting his stride his whole life. Keeping his form wasn't the issue. "The fight is the hairy part. But if I can knock that out in the first period, it's easier to keep things stable for the rest of the game."

Ari's strong hands worked his back for a moment in silence. "Can I ask you something? And I don't mean this to sound judgmental."

He snorted. "That's what people say right before they say something judgmental."

She laughed, and he registered the husky sound in his belly. "That is sometimes true. But I never saw a hockey game until I applied for this job. And I want you to explain the fighting to me. Why do you do it?"

That was the multimillion-dollar question, wasn't it? He'd

been asking himself that same thing lately. "There's a code. Most of the time when I fight, it's because someone broke that code or someone needs a refresher. I fight to protect my guys."

Her hands wandered up the center of his back, her thumbs finding aches to smooth out that he didn't even know he had. "Okay," she said thoughtfully. "But then who protects *you?*"

His eyes closed. The question seemed impossibly complex at the moment, especially as her palms warmed him from the outside in. "I guess I do. I dunno."

Maybe she picked up on the fact that he'd become too boneless to talk just then. Ari got quiet, too. He stopped tracking her exact movements. His hands unclenched, and his feet went slack.

All right. So this is what massage was supposed to feel like. His mind took him elsewhere. Behind closed eyelids he glimpsed fresh sheets of ice, and his teammates at practice. His subconscious ran a few drills—perfectly executed. Ari's hands kept time with a rock ballad. Her pleasant lavender scent enveloped him, and he stopped listening to the sound of her breaths. They were just there, keeping rhythm in the background. Everything was fine.

Until she worked on his lower body.

At first he didn't even notice the problem. Having allowed himself to feel some pleasure from the massage, he let his guard down. It was only when she asked him to turn over that he realized it wasn't a good idea. His body had gotten a little *too* comfortable with the pair of warm hands on his naked thighs.

He was hard.

There were no end of petty humiliations this week.

"If you turn over I can work on your quads," she reasoned, patting the back of his calf.

Nope. He could only imagine the tent he'd be raising in the towel then. "I have to run," he said. "I appreciate it, but there are some calls I need to return."

Ari's expression went from serene to defeated in two

seconds flat. "And here I thought we were getting along so well."

"We are." *Too well.* "Really. I'll show up tomorrow and everything."

"Good man." He received another one of her pats on the back. "Let me wash my hands and then the bathroom and shower are all yours. You don't want massage oil all over your clothes."

As soon as she disappeared, he hopped off the table and tied the towel around his waist as discreetly as possible.

Ari emerged from the bathroom drying her hands on another towel. "Take care of yourself," she said. And even though he still wasn't a big fan of her services, there was no doubt in his mind that she meant it.

FOUR

Ari watched the Detroit game from a seat behind the visitors' bench. O'Doul was back in tonight, and she spent much of the game watching him. *I need to know how he uses his core muscles during a game*, she told herself. But if she was truthful, the more she knew of O'Doul, the more compelling he was to watch. On the ice he was flashy and confident. But up close in person he was one of the more cautious souls she'd ever met.

Maybe it was none of her business, but she wanted to know why.

Tonight he exhibited his usual defensive brilliance. Wherever the other team needed to go, there he was, skating backward, blocking every impulse with his muscular bulk and his fast feet. His stick was an extension of his body, always in the way of his opponent's puck.

By the middle of the third period, there had been no fight. Yet. Ari hoped he could have a night off from brawling.

But with five minutes left on the clock, a Detroit player flattened Castro and was given two minutes for high sticking. It looked ugly as Castro went down, but he popped back up again and skated to the bench.

"Aw, hell," the fan beside Ari said to his buddies. "Crazy rookie was looking for a fight right there. That's what that was."

Ari tensed. And sure enough, after the power play, O'Doul circled the youngster who'd drawn the penalty. He argued with him for a moment and pointed at the home team's bench.

The kid's response was to throw off his gloves. The second they landed, every Motown fan stood up at his seat.

O'Doul stared the kid down and shook his head. Then, with what looked like a sigh, he threw off his own gloves, too.

The fight lasted about five seconds. The kid got two swings in before O'Doul grabbed him by the jersey and punched him. Ari closed her eyes. The stadium made a noise of unhappiness. When she opened her eyes, the guy was lying on the ice holding his face, and O'Doul was shaking out his fist, looking sour.

After that, the Bruisers scored twice more, finishing the game five to two. Ari had mixed feelings that became even more mixed as she made her way through the locker room. Most of the team was either showering or celebrating. Someone blasted the team's win song—"No Sleep Till Brooklyn" by the Beastie Boys—from a set of portable speakers. The new publicist, Tom, and a journalist were interviewing Beringer in a corner, but the room was in happy chaos.

Castro, who had been jabbed by the rookie, had a bruise on his shoulder. But it couldn't have hurt much because he was dancing—in his towel—with Trevi. And smiling.

That was the vibe—except for O'Doul. He was seated on a bench in the corner, his hair damp from the shower, wearing a towel and a don't-talk-to-me face.

"Is he okay?" Ari asked Henry with a nudge to his elbow.

The trainer cast a glance toward O'Doul. "Sure. He just gets like this some nights. Kinda withdrawn. He likes to be left alone."

She didn't leave him alone, though. She made her way

over to the captain and put a hand on his shoulder. "How are you?"

He looked up with deadened eyes. "Fine."

No, not so much. "What hurts?"

He shrugged, then shook out his right hand.

Ari grabbed it and smoothed his fingers between her hands. The knuckles were bruised. "Are you injured?"

He shook his head. "No. But I broke that kid's jaw."

She jerked in surprise. "Really? How do you know?"

"Felt the pop." His voice was flat.

"Come here," she said, tugging on his hand. "I want to get a look at your hip."

"It's fine," he said, but he allowed himself to be guided around the corner into the alcove where her table had been set up just in case.

She grabbed a towel off the shelf and flung it onto the table's surface. O'Doul climbed on without argument, flattening himself onto his stomach, turning his face toward the wall. She went to work on his shoulders first. He was tight. But when she worked her hands up into his hairline, he closed his eyes and sighed.

"Tell me about the fight," she said, expecting to be ignored.

"It was stupid," he muttered. "I told the kid he'd been a dick, and that his enforcer had better come out and answer for that bullshit on Castro. But he says, *I'll fight you myself.* I told him that sounded like a stupid idea."

"And . . . it was?" She worked her hands down his spine, aiming for his lower back.

"I spent hours watching their enforcer's fight tapes." He lifted his head. "We all do that."

"Of course," she said quickly. But she hadn't thought about it before. Made sense, though. If you had to fight a guy, you'd want to know his habits.

O'Doul dropped his head back onto the towel. "But this kid wanted to do it himself. And now he's gonna be having lunch through a straw for a month." The weary tone of his voice gave Ari a shiver.

She almost said, *it's not your fault.* Except it really was. "I'm sorry," she said instead.

"It's not *my* break," he growled.

Ari wanted to call bullshit on that, but she knew better than to say so here in the testosterone tank. The fight had hurt two people tonight. There weren't any winners. Maybe one guy had gotten all the visible injuries, but the one on the table was suffering, too.

She worked her hands up and down his back, then moved down to his hamstrings. He lay perfectly still on the table, more cooperative than he'd ever been. He was ill positioned for her to work on his hip, but she decided not to disturb him. She slid one hand beneath his hip and did the best she could. "How is this tonight? The same as after your last game? Or different?"

He shifted to give her better access. "Not as bad," he grunted eventually.

"Well. There's a shred of good news." She kept up her ministrations while he stared at the wall.

"Doulie!" someone yelled from around the corner. "Hockeybrawls.com has you at ninety-nine percent!"

O'Doul said nothing.

She left his hip and went down to his feet, pulling off the flip-flops he wore and dropping them on the floor. This was all she had left to give. If a deep tissue foot massage couldn't cheer a man up, then it couldn't be done. She dug into the ball of his foot, and he actually moaned.

Finally. Victory was sweet.

She worked in silence for five or ten minutes, and the set of his shoulders began to look more relaxed, and less haggard. She had already gotten used to the silence when he spoke up suddenly. "Does Castro really propose to you every time you touch his feet?"

The question was so unexpected that she let fly a peal of

laughter. "Yes, he does. We could be married a hundred times over by now."

His back rose and fell with a chuckle. "God. Tell him to get in line behind me."

"Why, Patrick O'Doul"—she gave his calf a pretend slap—"I'd almost think you *liked* this."

"It's tolerable," he grumbled.

And that's how she knew he was feeling better.

FIVE

Standings: 3rd place in the Metropolitan Division
15 Regular Season Games Remaining

O'Doul didn't go out with the guys after the win. They were in third place again, but celebrating felt premature. And Ari's impromptu massage had relaxed him enough that he thought he could sleep, which he did.

The jet was wheels up at eight thirty the next morning. Everyone on board looked a little hungover, but O'Doul felt refreshed. Although he should have faked a nap because Tom, the new publicist, decided to sit next to him and review the burgeoning interview request list.

Good times.

When they landed at LaGuardia, O'Doul was just musing over where he might eat lunch. He planned to skip the optional skate and take a rare afternoon off. But—damn it—Henry corralled him at the baggage claim with a bunch of questions about his hip.

"And you have a massage this afternoon."

"I had two yesterday!" he complained.

"Good work." Henry clapped him on the shoulder. "But you're due in Ari's treatment room at two. Don't be late."

So much for an afternoon alone.

He kept the massage appointment like a good Boy Scout. But this appointment was his least favorite so far. In the first place, Ari was wearing a soft pink shirt that somehow managed to emphasize her chest. It wasn't revealing, but the fabric draped in such a way that the pleasant swell of her breasts was hard to ignore. And he was all too aware of the soft sound of her humming along with the Stone Temple Pilots as she worked on his hip.

Now that he'd decided Ari was no longer a threat, his subconscious had apparently decided it approved of her. A lot. In order to keep his body under control, he spent the whole hour thinking about upcoming hockey fights. Occasionally he made himself picture Sister Odegerde, the unfortunately vile-breathed nun who'd looked after him at the group home where he'd spent his teen years.

The result was a less-than-relaxing hour. "You're so tense today," Ari kept saying, clucking her tongue.

"Sorry," he apologized, wondering what to do. He might ask the trainer if the team had any other massage therapists on call. But that would make Ari look bad, wouldn't it? *Christ.* It wasn't personal.

When his hour was up, they were both relieved.

O'Doul gathered up the personal items he'd dropped onto Ari's counter and got the hell out of there, stopping for a sixty second shower before donning jeans and a sweater and beating it outside again. It was three thirty, and his evening off could finally commence.

The practice rink was on the very edge of Brooklyn's Dumbo neighborhood, so he pointed his feet down Front Street. The sun was out, and the ever-present breeze off the river was warmer than he'd felt in months. The pleasant weather had brought out the stroller brigade. There were young families rolling babies down the sidewalk, diaper bags draped over the handlebars. Not one of them spared him a glance.

The anonymity of Brooklyn was perfect for him. While Nate Kattenberger and his fleet of marketers and publicists spent serious coin to try to raise the team's profile in Brooklyn, O'Doul was happy to go unrecognized. Sometimes people approached him in bars, especially if he was accompanied by other players, or wearing the team jacket. But to most of New York City's eight million people, he was just some dude walking down the street.

As it should be.

He crossed under the Manhattan Bridge as the subway train rumbled overhead on its way into Manhattan. In addition to the women and children on the sidewalks, there were couples admiring paintings in the windows of the art galleries he passed. That made it a weekend. It was Sunday if he wasn't mistaken. Professional hockey was a seven-days-a-week job during the season. He played three or four games a week, and the other days were dotted with meetings and weightlifting and charity events. It was disorienting. But it was all he knew.

He claimed a stool in the tavern on Hicks Street and ordered a cheeseburger. The place was mostly empty due to the odd hour.

"Good game against Detroit," Pete, the bartender, said when he delivered O'Doul's Diet Coke with a wedge of lime. O'Doul didn't drink during the day, and this guy remembered. It was a perk of being a regular, not of being semifamous.

"Thanks, man," he said, taking a sip. He set his Katt Phone on the table. The guys had talked about heading into Manhattan tonight to celebrate Castro's birthday at some new Asian fusion restaurant. In a couple hours the texts would start rolling in with the plans and the challenges. Who'd be drinking the most. Who'd be paying for it. And they'd goad the married guys who didn't want to leave their families into yet another night with the team.

He'd probably go along with the plan, whatever it shaped up to be. What else was he going to do?

His phone was oddly silent, though. O'Doul ate his burger and watched some college basketball on replay. He drank another soda and finished his fries. The afternoon slipped peacefully into evening. When his phone finally began to light up with texts, he was watching the last two minutes of a surprisingly close Kentucky game.

"Good game, right?" Pete asked, wiping down the wooden surface.

"Yeah. Their record is something else." He picked up his phone and scrolled to the top of the text stream. But these weren't texts from his teammates at all. In fact, he didn't recognize the sender's name. Somebody named Vince. And the dude was seriously pissed off.

YOU FUCKING CUNT, was his opening gambit. GET DOWN HERE AND OPEN THE GD DOOR.

Yikes.

He pressed the home button on his phone, then laid his thumb on the verification spot. But it didn't unlock.

DENIED the screen insisted.

Weird.

The screen lit up again with another diatribe, so he tried again to unlock his phone. He tried several more times, but the damn thing wouldn't unlock. Meanwhile, the texts came thick and fast. SLUT, I WILL FUCK YOU UP. DON'T PULL THIS SHIT. NOT SMART, BITCH.

Christ. And each time a new text came in, the phone made an irritating, audible ding. He'd changed the phone's settings so that it would never do that.

Oh.

Oh, fuck. This wasn't *his* phone. He was holding someone else's Katt Phone. Everyone on the team and on staff had the same model.

He stared at the thing in his hand, and then a chill climbed right up his spine. *Ari.* These texts were for her. "Pete!" he barked. "I need a phone."

"You do?" The bartender raised an eyebrow, probably because O'Doul was *holding* a phone.

He dropped it on the bar as another irate text came through. "I switched mine with someone by accident. And she's in trouble. Quickly, please." He stood up fast, as if that would somehow get him to Ari faster. He didn't have a clue where she lived, or whether she was at home at all.

Pete handed him a phone, unlocked.

O'Doul tapped in his own phone number and then jammed that sucker up to his ear. It rang once. Twice . . . too many times. Then went to voice mail. He heard his own stupid voice say, "Leave a message."

Fuck.

Maybe she wasn't home. She might be in the middle of a massage, without a clue she'd switched phones. That was the best case scenario. He could try to reach her at the practice rink. But he didn't have the Bruisers' numbers memorized because Nate had passed out the Katt Phones before they'd even moved to Brooklyn. He tapped the browser and then began tapping the team name into the tiny window with his fat fingers. Fuck. "Pete, does that computer have Google? I need to know the clubhouse office digits."

The bartender didn't ask questions. He just brought up a browser and began typing on the bar terminal. "Try this," he said and began rattling off a 718 number.

It went to a goddamn voice mail. *Press one for ticket sales. Press two for the stadium.* "Fuck!"

"I've found the admin page," Pete said, still bent over his computer. "Who do you need?"

"Uh . . . Becca. Rebecca Rowley."

Pete gave him another phone number to try. And all the while it rang in his ear, more threatening texts kept rolling through. Fuck. His next move would be to just run for the rink and hope she was still there.

"Hugh Major's office, this is Rebecca."

"Becca, it's O'Doul," he said quickly. "We have an emergency. We need to find Ari—she and I switched phones. Is she still in the building?"

"Nope!" Becca dashed his hopes. "Saw her leave about forty minutes ago."

"Fuck. Okay listen—some dick is texting her really threatening things. Sounds like he's at her house."

"No!" Becca gasped. "Her ex is a real douchewhistle."

"Where's her place?"

"Vinegar Hill. Right on Hudson Ave in one of those little brick houses, across from that restaurant."

"Address?"

"I'm looking . . . Seventy-one!"

He hung up, tossed the phone onto the bar and ran outside and up Hicks Street. After sitting still for a couple of hours, his hip flexors complained at the sudden burst of activity. But fuck it. It was less than a mile to Ari's house, and he was wearing sneakers.

This time he wasn't quite so invisible as he streaked down Front Street. People got out of his way, either cursing or staring. "Where's the fire?" someone yelled. But nobody stopped him. So it didn't take long before he was slowing down to make the turn onto Hudson, forcing himself to breathe deeply. He didn't want to be out of breath if he was about to face off against some crazy jackass. Becca had called him a douchewhistle, and he'd have to be to send threatening texts to a woman like Ari. Or *any* woman, for that matter.

He forced himself to walk the last half block, and to listen.

It wasn't hard to find the guy. There was only one asshole peering up at a Hudson Avenue address from the side of the building, holding a brick in his hand and screaming. "If you don't get your slutty ass down here I'm breaking another window!"

When the guy turned his head at O'Doul's approach, the situation got even worse. Because O'Doul *recognized* this particular asshole. The guy worked at a nightclub in lower Manhattan—the same club where he'd made an unfortunate and illegal purchase a month or so ago.

"What do *you* want?" the guy spat. "I'm not taking orders right now."

"Yeah, you are," O'Doul growled. "Put that shit down." He took a step forward, chest first. Somewhere above him—in a window maybe—Ari gasped. But he didn't take his eyes off the prick with the brick.

The guy's eyes widened a little at O'Doul's aggressive stance. "Get the fuck out of here."

"No. That's what *you're* going to do." He took another step closer.

That was the moment when the dick's synapses fired completely, and he realized that O'Doul was serious. "Fuck *off.*" He turned his body squarely towards O'Doul's in the universal signal of matched aggression.

At least now they were on the same page. "Go on. I'll give you five seconds to get the fuck out of here. One. Two . . ." He held the man's dark eyes, but his subconscious was focused on the brick in the man's hand. The guy's fingers had tightened on it. But his arm was still hanging there. And a brick wasn't the world's handiest weapon. It could be thrown, but not quickly. "Three, four . . ." O'Doul said. And then he lunged forward and swept the guy's feet out from under him, dumping him on his ass on the pavement, which was littered with a lot of glass shards.

"FUCK!" the asshole shouted from the ground. He scrambled up to a kneeling position and then readied his brick hand to swing at O'Doul.

But not fast enough. O'Doul used his left leg to ruin the arc of the guy's swing, then landed a punch to his opponent's jaw with his right hand. The asshole hit the ground a second time.

"You chickenshit," O'Doul spat down at him. "Don't you ever threaten a woman again or I will *end you.*"

"*Man on!*" Ari yelled from above.

O'Doul whirled and then immediately ducked, avoiding the large fist on a trajectory toward his head. Later he'd marvel at Ari's perfect use of hockey terminology in the clutch. But for now he was too busy sidestepping the young goon who'd entered the brawl to avenge his buddy's humiliation.

His focus narrowed to the two men and their movements. Boss man was still seated, looking shaky. But the new goon circled. Not for nothing had O'Doul been in a thousand fights, both on the street and on skates. His voice was steady and commanding as he addressed them both. "Just beat it. Both of you. How many neighbors do you think are watching right now?"

The goon's lip curled.

"You bangin' her?" the older man asked, using the brick wall to ease to his feet. "I knew it."

"Is that what you think?" O'Doul laughed. "That's what's got you breaking windows like a punk?" He stepped slowly around in a backward semicircle, avoiding the goon and putting his body closer to the front door of Ari's house, and closer to the street. If these morons had any sense at all, they wouldn't want an all-out brawl in broad daylight. But the new opponent tracked toward him.

O'Doul moved, watchful, waiting for his opening. The youngster had long arms like a gorilla. He'd have to quickly inflict some pain to put this guy out of commission.

Then one sound changed everything—the chirp of a police cruiser.

"Shit," the older man spat. He moved surprisingly quickly, taking off down the alley, away from the street. After a beat of indecision, his thug followed him.

When he heard the sound of an engine starting up, O'Doul jogged after them just in time to see an unmarked burgundy van peel away.

He recited the license plate number out loud twice, then noticed his own pounding heart. He had fight night adrenaline coursing through his veins. He turned around and walked slowly back through the alley, noticing everything, looking up to check out the broken window above. Ari's face wasn't in it. So he went onward to the street just in time to see a cop car pass slowly by without stopping.

"*Patrick*," someone gasped. He turned to see Ari in the doorway, her face pinched and white as a sheet.

"Hey," he said, closing the distance in two paces and jumping up onto her stoop. Then he did something completely out of character. He wrapped an arm around Ari and pulled her to his chest. "He's gone. Took off in a van."

Her whole body was shaking. "Are you okay?" she stammered.

"Yeah. Sure I am." His eyes scanned the street, looking for trouble. He was still locked into fight mode, hyperaware of everything.

"You'd tell me if you weren't?" She sagged against him.

"I'm fine, I swear. But I think you need to sit down." He lifted his gaze to see her living room just beyond the hallway. There was a comfortable-looking velvet sofa with big green pillows all along the back. It was very Ari. He steered her toward it. "Come on."

She sat down heavily on the cushion in the center. "C-c-close the door?" she asked.

He did, and locked it, too, hoping to make her feel safe. Her front curtains were drawn, and he parted them slightly. But there was nobody out there. "He's gone, sweetheart." That word had never come out of his mouth before, but Ari looked so wrecked that the situation required that he treat her gently.

"That bouncer," she said, swallowing roughly. "That guy is usually packing."

Ah. "That might account for their allergic reaction to the cops cruising by. Did you happen to call 911?"

She shook her head violently. "I *tried*. But my phone wouldn't log on. I almost threw it across the room I was so frustrated."

Oh, fuck. "Ari, that's my phone. We traded by accident at my appointment today."

"What? Really?"

He pulled hers out of his pocket and held it up. "I'm sorry. We have the same case." The blue and green one. They came in a dozen styles, so this had never happened to him before.

She took her phone out of his hand and unlocked it with her fingerprint. It flashed to life right away. "Jesus." Her eyes snapped up to his. "You saw these texts?"

He nodded slowly.

Her face reddened, and she looked away. "Sorry."

Sorry? "Shit. Don't be sorry." He slid closer to her on the couch and pulled her into his arms again. She came willingly. He took a deep breath of her lavender scent and sighed. "No landline?"

She shook her head against his shoulder. "Nope. My phone wouldn't work, and I couldn't think what to do. He started shouting, and I was upstairs trying to e-mail my neighbor from the laptop. Then he put the brick through the window right next to me. Scared me half to death."

No wonder she was shaking like a leaf. Sitting there, no way to call anyone, a violent dickhead outside trying to blast his way inside in. "I think you need to do some of that yoga breathing you're always forcing on us. In for a count of eight, and out for four."

"If you're trying to calm down, it's the reverse."

"My bad."

She laughed shakily, her hair tickling his chin. "God, I'm so *pissed off* right now! My window is broken. And that asshole made me feel unsafe in my own house. And I can't even fix it because we're off to Montreal tomorrow."

"One thing at a time, okay? There's no reason to be afraid right now," he said, hoping it was true.

She pulled back and gave him a look. "He'll be back. I had the locks changed on the storage room, because I think he was using it for some kind of dodgy business."

O'Doul kept the flinch off his face. He had a pretty good idea what dodgy business it could be. "Do you want to call the cops?"

She hesitated. "Maybe? Do I have to decide right now?"

"No. But why wouldn't you? Are you keeping him out of trouble?"

"He can *hang* for all I care. But if the cops arrest him, he'd get out on bail, pissed as hell at me. I'd rather find a way to just be rid of him. I shouldn't have locked him out. That was stupid of me. But I needed a way to motivate him to leave for good!"

She was getting all worked up again, her small body tense in his arms. "All right." He thought about it for a moment. "Let me take a look at your broken window. Can you call the super?"

"I am the super."

"Ah." He chuckled. "We need a piece of plywood, then."

With a sigh, she untangled herself from him. "I have one already, because the kids in the neighborhood have broken windows before. With baseballs, though."

He followed her upstairs to have a look at the damage. There was broken glass all over the floor. "You're not wearing shoes," he pointed out. "Let me do this."

She opened her mouth and then closed it again. "I'll get the broom and some damp paper towels."

Luckily, the room had hardwood floors instead of carpeting. It didn't take them long to sweep up the mess and fit the board into the window. But O'Doul hated the look of dismay on her face as she stared up at it. "God, if I replace it, will he just break it again?"

"It's too late to worry about it tonight, anyway. Are you packed for Montreal?" he pointed at a suitcase against the wall.

"Yes."

He picked it up. "Let's go. You can't stay here tonight. And in twelve hours you'll be on the way to the airport."

"Where are we going?"

Good question. "Anywhere you want. But unless you have a better idea, my place. I'm just on Water Street." The freaked-out look on her face was having a strange effect on him. He'd do anything to get rid of it.

"Okay," she said. "I . . . God, I'm *such* an idiot." She was staring at the boarded-up window again, as if trying to figure out how it got that way.

"Come on now," he said softly. "It's going to be all right." He carried her bag down the stairs and told her to gather her coat and handbag. She did these things as if in a trance, and then she followed him outside.

SIX

When they got out to the sidewalk, O'Doul stopped to take a look at the building's exterior. Ari followed his gaze, wondering what he saw. The first-level windows were guarded by decorative iron bars. That's how it was done in Brooklyn. There was a fire escape on the rear corner of the building. The ladder didn't reach very close to the ground, and Ari had never worried about it before. But if Vince were angry enough, he might use it to gain access to the second floor.

"Who lives up there?" O'Doul asked, pointing to the third level.

"Maddy, my tenant. That's her entrance," she pointed at the door beside her own. "I'll e-mail her tonight and give her a heads up. She already knows that Vince is a loose cannon, though. She won't even be surprised."

So why am I?

Two months ago, she'd lived with the man. She would have even said she loved him. Now he was calling her awful names from the street and throwing a brick through her window.

She followed O'Doul down the sidewalk, trying to wrap her head around it.

"Vince is your ex?" O'Doul asked eventually.

"Yeah. Long story."

"I've got time."

Sigh. "I threw him out six weeks ago. But we were together for eight years, since I was twenty-one, and a waitress at his club in Manhattan. I was young and stupid."

"Weren't we all."

She gave him a grateful look. "In my defense, he used to treat me really well. He was an older, successful man—he's thirty-nine now. I was attracted to his confidence. He treated me like a queen for years—until things stopped going well for him."

"And then?"

This part wasn't easy to tell. "He became overextended. When I met him he owned a club and had an interest in another. But over the years he tried to expand his empire, and it was harder than he thought it would be. I think he got into business with some people he shouldn't have trusted. I'm pretty sure they screwed him over. Every year it got a little worse. One of the clubs recently had a bunch of drug busts, and they lost their liquor license. And I think Vince owes a bunch of people money. But to listen to him, it's always someone else's fault. This past year I tried to ask more questions, and he didn't like that at all."

This story was interrupted by their arrival at the front door of O'Doul's building. A uniformed doorman opened the door for them. "Evening, Mr. O'Doul. Will you need a car tomorrow morning?"

"Yeah, thanks. Flight leaves at eight. So . . . seven?"

"I'll take care of it." The doorman gave them a friendly wave, and they proceeded through the grand lobby toward the elevators.

Ari had been to this building once before with Georgia, who had recently moved into Leo's apartment. The turn-of-the-twentieth-century warehouse had been stylishly renovated into high-end condos. Several players lived here because it was close to the practice rink and a full-service building.

It was also expensive as hell.

This was the new Brooklyn. The old one—kids playing kick-the-can in the streets, and the funny little Italian men's clubs on Court Street—it was disappearing fast. She was the last Bettini living in Brooklyn now.

In the posh elevator, with its brass button panel, O'Doul chose the fourth floor. When the doors opened, he gave her a funny smile. "I don't usually have people over. So it's . . ." he hesitated.

"A messy bachelor pad?" she guessed.

"Not exactly."

When he opened the door, though, it was beautiful inside. The ceiling was high, and the exposed bricks glowed with a rosy hue against the lights he flipped on. There was no mess at all. The place hardly looked lived in.

"It's all one room," he apologized. "But you can have the bed."

"You don't have to do that." His place *was* all one room— but that room was the size of Grand Central station. "Your couch could seat a family of six. I'm just happy to . . ." she turned to him with a sigh. "Thank you. For chasing him off. This has been the most embarrassing night of my life."

"Why?" He tossed his jacket onto a coat tree and reached for hers, which she shrugged off. "You didn't throw a brick through your own window, right?"

"I just never thought I'd be *that* girl." She let him remove her coat and hang it up. Then she crossed the big room and sat down on his sofa. "The one who needs a restraining order."

"We need a drink, I think," he said, and then smiled. "I don't entertain. So there's either Diet Coke or hard liquor. Scotch is my drink of choice. I'll bring you both, and you can decide." He moved toward the kitchen.

"I don't drink diet sodas. That shit can kill you."

O'Doul laughed. "If you feel the same about Scotch, don't tell me." He returned a minute later with a tray, two glasses with ice, a bottle of Macallan 18 and two bottles of water.

He sat down beside her and poured Scotch into one of the glasses. "You're in, right?"

"Hell yes."

He handed her one of the glasses, and she took a deep breath of its peaty perfume. "God, I love that smell. So good."

O'Doul gave her an approving nod. "I wouldn't have picked you for a Scotch drinker."

"Why? You think yoga teachers sit around drinking shots of kale juice?"

He snorted. "No. Okay, maybe. But you drink wine with Georgia."

"I drink wine with Georgia because Georgia likes the company. And because it's a habit. My ex didn't think a lady should drink Scotch. He never offered me any of his." *Hell*. The more she said about her relationship with Vince, the worse it sounded.

O'Doul shook his head, then held up his glass for a toast. "To your health, and to your ex taking a long walk off a short pier."

She touched her glass to his and then took a nice deep sip.

He kicked off his shoes and propped his long legs onto the stylish coffee table. "So what made you finally kick him out?"

Ugh. This was even more embarrassing than the brick through the window. "He stopped being nice to me. But I hung on a long time hoping things would get better. He'd supported me when I wanted to go to school for massage therapy. So I told myself that I should be there for him even during the rough times, you know? I wanted to be loyal. It was my idea to let go of his high-rent place in the city and move into my uncle's house when Uncle Alberto moved to Florida."

"Nice house by the way."

"Thanks. I pay ridiculously low rent in exchange for keeping the place up. But after we moved there, Vince just got mean. At first it was just petty criticism. He started insulting me in front of people we knew." Another drink of Scotch helped wash the taste of that memory down.

O'Doul grimaced, as if fighting off the urge to make a comment.

"Then I got the job for the team, and he *seemed* happy for me. At first. But I was gone a lot. He *hated* that. He started questioning my whereabouts and acting like a jealous freak. I thought maybe things would turn around for him and he'd just ease up." But it hadn't happened. As she pictured their last night together, her throat began to close up. She took a gulp of Scotch. How long would it take before she stopped feeling so upset over this?

"Hey," O'Doul whispered. "You don't have to tell me."

"It's . . ." she cleared her throat, and a single tear shook loose and ran down her face. "He got a little physical one night, and I left him the next day."

Concern lined his forehead. "Is that what happened to your foot?"

She nodded. "But please don't say anything. I didn't tell anyone the truth about that, except for Becca. I'd go over to Becca's tonight, but she and Georgia went wedding dress shopping and then out to dinner. Shit." She sat up straighter, still a jumble of nerves. "You probably had plans, too." A single guy with a night off? Of course he did.

He crossed his feet and took a sip of his drink. "I'm pretty sure the team can get drunk without my help for once."

Ari yawned suddenly. The alcohol was turning her bones to liquid.

O'Doul picked up the bottle and held it over her glass, then hesitated. "Did you eat dinner?"

"Yes. I was just throwing away my takeout box when the shouting started."

He poured. "Good. I could probably dig up some crackers, but that's about it. My fridge is nothing but ketchup and old leftovers."

"Well, you're on the road half the time. And in New York, nobody needs to cook anyway. I wonder what players do in the flyover states. Starve, I guess."

"I wish. They'd be easier to beat." He sipped his drink,

and she yawned again. "If you think you're going to crash, help yourself to anything in the bathroom. I'll make up the bed for you."

"I *really* don't want to put you out." A new wave of embarrassment warmed her face.

"Naw," he said, standing up. "Been a while since I've been to a pajama party. We can braid each other's hair and tell ghost stories."

Now that was a funny image. Smiling, she got up and crossed to her duffel bag, where her silk pajamas were. How handy to have a packed suitcase. It made fleeing her own home that much more convenient.

O'Doul's bathroom was spotless. She washed her face and dried it on one of his pristine white towels. Then she changed into her PJs. When she emerged, he was just finishing up changing the sheets on the giant king-sized bed.

The sight of this muscle-bound man changing the sheets on his bed for her did odd things to her tummy. For a second there, her subconscious offered up an appealing idea—that they were about to strip each other naked and roll around together on those sheets.

Yowza. That was just the whiskey talking.

"Did you furnish this place yourself?" she asked, just to force herself to focus on the reality of the moment.

He turned around and gave her a crooked smile. "Not hardly. I bought the apartment from a married couple— David and Dexter—who were moving into an antique house in San Francisco. They had bought all this Scandinavian stuff and were fretting about how it wouldn't match the new place." He laughed out loud at the idea. "So I bought, like, all their stuff. Even the dishes. Didn't have to set foot in a store. Best deal ever."

"That was very pragmatic of you. David and Dexter have lovely taste."

"I know, right? But I probably would have bought it even if everything was mint green. I hate shopping."

"And you don't entertain very much? Your place is nice."

He tugged a pillow into its case. "It took me a long time to get my own place. I'm not used to sharing."

Not for the first time she wondered about this man's childhood. "What do you mean it took you a long time to get your own place?"

O'Doul shrugged, avoiding her eyes. "Didn't get any help, that's all."

"From your parents?" she pressed.

"Don't have any of those." He chucked the pillow onto the bed. Then he grabbed a pair of flannel pants off the dresser and disappeared into the bathroom before she could ask another question.

She went over to his big couch and sat down. The TV was on now, tuned to a sports commentary show which was just ending. So she flipped channels with the remote on the sofa, choosing an action movie with Nicolas Cage. She tucked herself into the corner of the big piece of furniture and sipped her whiskey, and he joined her on the couch a few minutes later.

"Is this *Face/Off*?"

"Yeah." He made himself comfortable in the other corner of the couch, and Ari couldn't help but admire him. That broad chest looked like a fine place to rest her head. He looked over to catch her staring. *Whoops.* "Do you like this movie?"

"Of course. Nicolas Cage has the coolest money clip. A golden dragon head. Totally badass." He gave her a more relaxed smile than she'd ever gotten from him, and it made him look almost boyish. And *hot*. Was she crazy, or did his gaze linger a little longer than necessary, too?

None of that, she chided herself. It wasn't polite to perv on her rescuer, even if he was more attractive by a factor of ten than any of the Hollywood actors on the screen.

And anyway, she was feeling drowsy again. It had been a shit day of epic proportions. Her asshole ex had proven himself to be even more dangerous than she'd expected. But here she sat, drinking whiskey with Patrick O'Doul, feeling perfectly safe.

Weird.

Vince might make trouble again. No—he *would* make trouble again. But at least for tonight she wouldn't have to face him. This sofa was like an island of calm in the chaotic sea of her life. And she really did appreciate it.

She grabbed one of the water bottles off the coffee table, opened it and drank half. After she set it down again, she began to feel sleepy. *Drunk* and sleepy. She closed her eyes to the sounds of an on-screen car chase and drifted off.

SEVEN

O'Doul watched the rest of the movie, occasionally sneaking looks at Ari's sleeping face. The anxiety she'd worn for the last couple of hours was gone now, and he'd been a part of that. Satisfaction settled like a warm blanket on his chest, and the sensation was completely unfamiliar.

He'd never had a sleeping woman on his couch before, and he let himself wonder for a moment what it would be like to have someone in his life.

He glanced around his apartment, wondering what she saw. It was a huge space for one person. He was always here alone. What would it be like to live with a woman like Ari? To put his key in the door and find her at home, making a drink or sitting on the sofa, waiting for him? It was almost impossible to imagine. He'd been a loner so long that the condition was probably permanent.

After the credits rolled, he shut the TV off. He got up to brush his teeth and turn out a few lights.

Ari didn't stir or wake. He knew he could cover her with a blanket and let it go at that, but her head was angled onto the arm of the sofa in a way that didn't look comfortable enough to last eight hours.

Okay, then. He'd just have to do a little better for her.

"Come on, sweetheart," he whispered, kneeling in front of her. "Time to hit the hay." He patted her hand.

Nothing.

Welp, all right, then. He got up and slipped his hands underneath her back. When he lifted her slightly, a pair of sleepy arms came around to clutch his neck. "There you go," he said encouragingly. He carried her over to the bed. Luckily he'd turned down a corner of it when he'd made it up for her. So it wasn't too difficult to slide her into bed.

When her head hit the pillow, Ari rolled onto her side, toward the center of the bed, and let out a sleepy sigh.

Mission accomplished.

He walked around the big bed to turn off the lamp and remove the other pillow. He'd need it on the couch. But when he leaned over to reach for it, Ari mumbled something to him. He put a knee on the bed to try to hear her. "What's that, sweetheart?"

One warm hand emerged from the covers and clasped his. He slipped her smooth fingers between his rougher ones, his thumb tracing her wrist. "You're going to be fine, you know that, right?"

Her hand closed a little tighter on his, and she sighed. Her eyes were still closed.

Unsure what he should do, O'Doul sat down on the side of the bed, just holding her hand. His body felt heavy and tired, but in a good way. As he sat there in the dark, the day's strange events replayed themselves in his mind. He'd been in a scuffle tonight—the first one in years where he wasn't wearing skates. And that wasn't the only odd thing about the fight. It was also the only one in years he was certain had a real purpose to it.

Ari continued to hold his hand, and he let her. He knew he ought to get up and take his weary self over to the couch.

Although Ari had told him once that when two people touch, they touch with their whole soul. And her soul was clinging pretty hard to his right now, her long fingers clasping his hand as if her life depended on it.

Fuck it.

Still holding her hand, O'Doul stood up again and lifted the covers on his side of the bed. He slipped between the sheets and positioned himself carefully on his own side of the generously sized mattress. This would be a hell of a lot more comfortable than the sofa, anyway.

He closed his eyes, thinking that it should feel so strange to have Ari in his bed where no other woman had ever been. He'd always imagined he wouldn't be able to sleep if he brought someone home—that an unfamiliar presence would disturb the sanctity of his private space.

It didn't, though. The soft sound of her breathing only kept time with his own.

He drifted off to sleep without trouble. But when the low beep of his phone's alarm chimed seven hours later, he was a little disoriented. An arm had been flung across his chest in the night, and a slender knee was propped onto his.

O'Doul fumbled one hand onto the nightstand to silence the phone, then he took stock. In the first place, it was warmer in the bed than he was used to. But the weight of her hand on his chest was pleasant, as was the softness of her breasts pressed against his biceps.

All in all, having another sleeping person in his bed was less odd than he would have thought. But the contact of her sweet body gave his own a few ideas. If he ever did have someone in his life, maybe they'd wake up slowly together like this, pressed together . . . That happy thought made his cock begin to grow nice and heavy.

It was time to cut that idea off at the knees, obviously.

In one cautious motion, O'Doul rolled toward the edge of the bed and out of Ari's grasp. He ducked into the bathroom to take a leak and brush his teeth. When he came out, Ari was sitting up in his bed, looking sheepish. "Hi," she said sleepily.

"Hi yourself. You a coffee drinker?" Did yoga instructors approve of caffeine?

"The stronger the better," she said.

"I knew I liked you. I'll make some. We have about thirty minutes until the car comes. The shower is all yours."

"Thank you," she said, scrambling out of bed, then straightening the sheets.

He left her to it, heading into the kitchen to grind the coffee beans. He found a package of English muffins in his refrigerator. Splitting two of them, he set them into the toaster, then rooted in the refrigerator again to find a stick of butter in its sleek, modern Scandinavian butter dish.

When he heard the shower running, he took the opportunity to open his closet and pull on his shirt and trouser pants. Flying in a suit and tie wasn't his favorite part of the NHL lifestyle. But a guy had to do what a guy had to do, and after more than a decade in the NHL, he was pretty used to it. He grabbed the first tie off the rack and slung it around his neck.

The coffee was done and the toast was buttered when Ari emerged from his bathroom in a soft knit dress, towel-drying her hair. "You have the most amazing shower," she said with a shy smile.

"It's my favorite thing about this apartment," he agreed. "I don't know why the builder decided to put in three separate sprays, but I like it. Milk for your coffee?"

"If you have it."

He reached into the fridge and brought out a carton. "Always." He poured a dollop into both mugs.

She picked up one of the two plates he'd set out and took a bite of English muffin. "Patrick, thank you."

"It's nothing," he said, ducking into the refrigerator again.

"Not true," she insisted, waiting for him to meet her gaze. "Yesterday was a total shit show. I know it was just a coincidence that you were the one to witness it. But I really appreciate all the help. You have no idea."

"Well." He cleared his throat. "Don't mention it. Just glad I got there when I did." His Katt Phone buzzed in his pocket, and he pulled it out. "Our car is downstairs. You need anything before we go?" He took a bite of his toast.

"I'll just need another minute to grab my things."

A few minutes later they were on their way down to the lobby. O'Doul wondered who they'd meet down there, and what they might say. Anyone who saw them together this morning would get the wrong idea. He couldn't imagine that Ari needed to add gossip to her list of problems. But there was nobody in the lobby except a sleepy concierge.

Outside he opened the car door for Ari, then lifted both their bags into the driver's trunk. Just as he was sliding into the car, he saw Leo and Georgia emerge from the building's entrance, heading for another hired car parked just behind theirs. Leo was distracted by their luggage, but Georgia gave him a wave. And then he watched her eyes widen in surprise when Ari slid across the seat to make room for him.

The last thing he saw before the car slid away from the curb was her amused smile.

EIGHT

"I'm not buying it," Georgia said. The two of them had taken seats in the largely empty Canadian stadium. While the team sweated through practice on the rink below them, they ate dumplings from a food truck outside the stadium.

"Suit yourself, but it didn't happen," Ari insisted, nibbling a dumpling from her chopsticks. "These are really good, by the way. I love spicy peanut oil."

"You're changing the subject," Georgia accused.

"If you say so." She finished the dumpling, leaving Georgia to gape at her.

"Wait. *Really?* You didn't hook up?"

Ari shook her head. "I was having a rough day. My, uh, ex was giving me a hard time."

"Oh, no!" Georgia's face filled with sympathy. "What did he do?"

"He was just being a dick. Yelling at me." *Trying to break into my home*. She'd outlined her tale of woe to Georgia last month on a road trip. But today she didn't care to elaborate. "You and Becca were dress shopping, and O'Doul was in the neighborhood. So I went home with him. No sex happened. But I got drunk and passed out on his couch in front of *Face/Off*."

"Bummer." Georgia shook her head. "I like my version of events better. More hot sex. Fewer terrible exes."

"I know, right? But it's not like that."

"Could it be, though?" Georgia picked at her last dumpling. "I was kidding a second ago, but I'm serious now. I used to think O'Doul was an ass. But now I think he's just really lonely. My gut says that if the right girl softened him up a little, he'd be the most loyal man who ever lived."

Ari thought the idea had merit, but whoever finally got through to O'Doul would not be her. "Someone else will have to win that prize. I haven't been single since I was twenty-one. I need a break from men." Looking back on the last year with Vince, she didn't like what she saw. Did she stay so long out of loyalty? Or was she afraid to be alone?

Only one way to find out.

"Was he awful? Your ex?"

Yes. "I don't even know how to answer that. I put up with too much from him. I was like a frog sitting in the water on the stovetop. The water got hotter and hotter, and I didn't jump."

"But then you finally did," Georgia pointed out.

Too late, Ari chided herself. She hated being out of town right now, wondering what trouble Vince would stir up. How crazy was he willing to get? She should have left the storage room locks alone. But then he'd *never* have left. God, would she ever extricate herself from this asshole?

It was time to execute an emergency change of subject. "So, don't keep me hanging. Did you find a dress last night?"

Georgia laughed. "I found a dozen of them. Becca made me try on so many they've all blurred together in my mind."

"Ah. You overshopped."

"I did! Becca has some serious stamina. I swear to god, she has a special notebook just for my wedding, with dividers and sections, and a place to put pictures she's clipped. No wonder she's such a good office manager. But it's killing me. I can't wait to marry Leo. But the ceremony is twenty minutes, right? Is it awful that I'm way more interested in making it to the play-offs than in flower arrangements?"

"It's fine. But you do need to choose a dress."

"I think I did. Hang on—you can tell me what you think." Georgia dug into her purse and pulled out her Katt Phone. She flipped to a photo and handed the phone to Ari.

"Nice. Wow." The dress was sleek and strapless, and showed off Georgia's athletic body to a tee. "Did you buy it? That's kind of perfect."

"Not yet, but I will. In fact, I'll call them today and ask them to put it aside for me. Becca has this idea that we're going to look at some other shops. But I don't see the point. I'm going to wear it once. Why shop twice?"

Ari loved this about Georgia—her pragmatism. "It really suits you, too. It's not fussy."

"Thanks. I had no idea just how fussy those suckers could be. I put my foot down when Becca wanted me to try one with beads on it. Beads!"

"The horror," Ari teased.

"I know, right? I made the mistake of asking Becca if she thought I could get away with a dress that wasn't so weddingy, so I could wear it again. The poor girl almost had a coronary. So I tried on a dress with lace on it just to make her feel better."

"I don't see you in lace," Ari admitted. "Buy the one in the picture. You look amazing." She handed back the phone. "When I was a little girl I did that thing where you put a white T-shirt over your hair and pretend to get married. I couldn't wait to plan my wedding."

"Hmm . . ." Georgia said, her eyes on the guys skating drills below. "I didn't play wedding. But I did practice standing on the podium at Wimbledon, and curtseying for the queen. So I can't claim to be any less vain. And that Wimbledon thing isn't happening for me, so I might as well throw a wedding."

Ari watched the younger woman with fondness, and once again had a moment's appreciation for the new friendships her upheaval had brought. "When I was twenty-two years old, I was sure that Vince and I would get married. And even as things sort of fell apart with him, I still hoped he'd pull it together so we could plan our future. God, that was stupid."

Georgia turned to her with a soft look. "I'm sorry. But there are better men out there."

"Yeah." She cleared her throat. "Last night I was trying to explain to O'Doul why I stayed with Vince for so long. Everything I said sounded lame. And I didn't even tell him the worst reason."

Georgia's eyebrows rose. "What's that?"

"I want a child. I'll be thirty next year, damn it. I was hoping things with Vince would get better so that we could start a family."

"But you're still young!" Georgia squeezed her hand. "Five years from now you could have a husband and *two* kids. Lots of people don't have kids until their thirties. This isn't 1950."

"I'm just so annoyed with myself. When I teach a yoga class, I'm standing there asking everyone in the room to become mindful of their surroundings. But it turns out I wasn't doing such a great job of that myself."

"I don't know," Georgia said kindly. "You got the hell away from him the moment it mattered most."

"That's what Patrick said." Below them a whistle blew on the ice, and another drill started. Ari watched the captain skate. There was no hesitation when he powered down the rink. Were his strained muscles better? Or was the man just stubborn?

"So, wait," Georgia said, nudging her. "Back up a second. You stayed with Doulie *in his apartment*?"

"Sure? Where else would I stay with him?"

Georgia's eyes danced. "See, this *is* gossip! Nobody has ever been to O'Doul's apartment."

"What do you mean, nobody? I have."

"I know! But he's never invited his teammates over. Ever. What was it like in there? Castro has this theory that O'Doul has a sex dungeon that he doesn't want anyone to see. They tease him about it sometimes, but he doesn't react."

Ari laughed for the first time all day. "That's ridiculous. O'Doul's place is lovely. It's a loft space, though. All one room. Maybe that's why he doesn't like to entertain? The bed is right there in the room."

Georgia tossed her chopsticks into her empty carton and frowned. "Maybe the secret chamber is hidden behind a bookshelf. There could be a special brick—push it and the wall swings open."

"That must be it," Ari joked, and Georgia gave her a smile. Hell, she was pretty sure there were secret places—in O'Doul's *mind*. He seemed to keep a pretty tight lid on himself, and again she wondered why.

Today wouldn't be the day she learned, though. O'Doul was not on her schedule for massage that afternoon. Maybe the trainers believed he was recovering. That was good news for the captain, but as she worked through a long afternoon treating five other players, she found herself thinking about him, anyway.

"You're marrying me someday, right?" Castro asked as she massaged his instep.

"Mmm?" she asked, shaking off her private thoughts.

"Just my usual proposal," her client said. "But you seem distracted today. I'm gonna get offended."

She patted his calf and asked him to flip over, which he did without hesitation. All her clients were easier to treat than O'Doul. But none were as interesting.

After a long afternoon at work, Ari spent a few minutes texting with Maddy. She told her about the brick through the window, and apologized profusely for any drama that might come her way. *Please be vigilant*, Ari begged. *I'm trying not to be paranoid, but the man is pissed at me.*

I'll keep my phone charged, Maddy promised. *Don't worry about me.*

She did, though.

That night, Ari fell asleep easily in the hotel, safely three hundred miles away from Vince. The next morning she conducted an eight o'clock yoga session in the hotel health club.

Every yoga class had a different rhythm, and that morning the players seemed to bring a lot of nervous energy with them into the room. It was game night, and they were under so much pressure to make the play-offs.

As she paced the front of the room asking for different poses, they watched her with intense eyes. So she gave them an ambitious yoga experience to feed and center all that energy, with a fast flow including lots of chaturangas. Then she brought them into eagle pose and made them hold it for several minutes.

When it was over, she had two dozen men dripping with sweat, lying in corpse pose for their final breathing exercise, and probably cursing her name.

As they shuffled out afterward, Patrick gave her a wink. "Trying to kill us today?"

"That wouldn't be good for my job security," she pointed out. "I'm only trying to make it possible for you to rest before the game."

"I think it worked."

"Go right upstairs and nap," she ordered.

He gave her a warmer smile than she'd ever seen on his face. And then he went.

The game that night was down and dirty. Players on both teams began racking up penalties right away. She sat beside Georgia, who could barely keep still. She wasn't the type to yell at the ref, but she did a fair amount of screaming Leo's name.

Ari knew just from the sin bin stats that O'Doul would have to fight tonight. She was only surprised that it didn't happen until late in the second period, when he and another big guy from the other team began circling each other. She held her breath. And when they started swinging, she watched his movements closely.

He worked hard to keep his stance loose and his lower body out of the fray. But it made him tentative. She could see it all the way across the rink. A second later, that caution cost him. The Canadian player grabbed him in a headlock and started pounding on him.

Ari had to look away. She did *not* want to see Patrick at the wrong end of a bludgeoning fist.

The crowd made a satisfied noise, and she was afraid to look. On the ice, Patrick lay very still.

"Jesus," Georgia whispered.

Get up, Ari inwardly ordered him. *Right now.*

When he finally stirred some seconds later, she let out the breath she hadn't realized she was holding. Relief only lasted a little longer, though. Because moments later she happened to see Maddy's name light up the screen of her phone.

Honey, I'm so sorry, the message began.

NINE

O'Doul didn't remember picking himself up from the surface of the ice. As he skated toward the bench, his ankles wobbled in an unfamiliar way. He sat down heavily, and was vaguely aware of people talking to him. The trainer hovered, asking him questions.

It's just that he wasn't ready to take questions just yet. Someone handed him his helmet, and only then did he realize he wasn't wearing it.

"Let me see your face," the trainer said.

O'Doul turned his chin to allow it because that seemed easier than arguing. He heard the sound of the velcro giving way on his neck guard. Hands probed his skin, and he gritted his teeth.

"That hurts?" Henry asked.

"No." *I just don't like your hands on me.*

"Doesn't look too bad. We'll need to check for concussion symptoms. How's the hip?"

"Fine." And it was. He'd protected his hip, and gotten slammed onto the ice for his trouble. *Fuck.* He hadn't even seen it coming. That's what he got for fighting scared.

"Come on. The doc needs to evaluate you." Henry beckoned.

"I'm not leaving the game."

Henry looked at the clock. There were two minutes left. "You need to be evaluated. If the doctor is impressed, you'll be back when the overtime period starts."

He was not back when the OT started. The doctor found his concussion exam inconclusive and kept him off the ice.

What happened next was open to interpretation. According to the news stories that would run the next day, their opponents got a lucky bounce off of Beacon's leg into the net, winning the game 3–2. But O'Doul saw it differently. When he lost that fight and then left the game, he handed all the momentum over to the other guys.

Two hours later he boarded the jet for the short flight home. His head ached a little, but his ego hurt worse.

"Can't win 'em all," Coach Worthington had said about the fight. That's how he knew it looked bad. Words of pity from the coach were scarce.

The first open seat on the jet was next to Ari. He took it because she wasn't likely to update him on his score at HockeyBrawls.com. "Hi," he said with a sigh.

"Are you . . . ?"

He held up a hand. "I'm fine. Really."

"Looked like it hurt."

"I've had better days."

She laughed, but then her face sank into her hands. "Yeah. Do they have whiskey on the jet?"

"Why?" He reached up and pulled her hands away from her face. "What's wrong?"

"Nothing." She shook her head, but her eyes darted nervously to the side.

"Sweetheart," he warned. "Come on. You look freaked." Her eyes were red, too.

"I'm tired of being freaked."

"Sing it, sister. But we don't always get what we want. Just tell me what happened."

She pointed at her phone. "My tenant had to call the cops earlier. Vince showed up to saw the basement door off its hinges. I thought he might try something. All he had to do to know I wasn't home was read the game schedule."

"Shit. I'm sorry."

"He was removing stuff from the storage room when the cops showed, but Maddy thinks they didn't catch him. So now I have a broken window *and* a broken door. I need to follow up with the police. And my first appointment is supposed to be at nine in the morning and I just . . ." She put her head in her hands again.

"Hey, don't worry. Henry will understand if you need a couple extra hours tomorrow. There's no single-malt on the jet, but . . ." He waved down the flight attendant. "Jill, how are you?"

"Excellent, Doulie! What can I bring you?"

"Everyone in this row has had a shit day. We need something fun to drink."

"Like a margarita?" the young woman asked. "That's what I drink when I need more fun in my life."

"How do you feel about margaritas?" he asked Ari.

"I'm a lifelong fan," she said.

"Two of those, please." O'Doul passed the attendant some cash.

"Thank you," Ari said. "I say that a lot lately. But I mean it."

"I know," he said lightly. "This too shall pass. And in the meantime, there's tequila."

It was after midnight by the time the cab pulled up in front of Ari's house on Hudson Ave.

"Thank you for dropping me off," she said, looking with trepidation up at her house, her hand hesitating on the door's lever.

O'Doul paid the driver and got out, removing both their bags from the back.

She pointed at the cab just as it began to pull away from the curb. "Don't you need him to wait for you?"

"Nah. It's just a couple of blocks. I want to make sure you're okay here."

The look of relief on her face was pretty hard to miss. "Well, thanks. It's not like I expect to find him lurking in the shadows, but . . ."

He could be lurking in the shadows. Even though Ari had sworn her ex had been a good guy at some point, now he was acting like a desperate guy. Desperate guys did stupid shit. Ari was right to be cautious. "Do you want to take a look around back, first?"

She swallowed hard. "Sure."

He used his phone to give them a little extra light, and followed her around to the rear door. The door—such as it was—had been leaned back into place. It was currently sealed with police tape. A note stuck to the door read: *Do Not Enter by Order of the NYPD.*

"All right," Ari said, her voice shaky. "I guess I'm not looking in there tonight."

They walked back to the street. "The door can be fixed pretty easily," O'Doul offered uselessly.

"I know," she sighed.

He walked her through the nighttime silence to the front door, where she took out a set of keys with shaking hands. He was pleased to see that she had two dead bolts on her door. That would slow down an unwelcome visitor for sure. After the second lock clicked open, he followed her inside.

She flipped on an overhead light, her eyes darting around the room.

"Look okay?" he asked.

"So far, so good. I don't think anyone was here."

"Let's just have a look." He stepped around her into the tidy living room. If her ex had broken in here, he hadn't left a trace. Aside from a paperback book face down on the coffee table, there was nothing out of place. He walked toward the back of the house, past an old-fashioned dining table, into a small kitchen. There was nobody there.

"Is there access from the basement into your apartment?"

"Yes and no. I'll show you." She led him over to a six-panel wooden door at the juncture between the dining room and the kitchen. It had an old-fashioned metal sliding-bolt lock on it. "This is the basement door. I never open it because there's no light over the stairs."

"Okay. And nobody came through here tonight. You'd know."

"Right. I'd have *another* broken door. So it looks like he didn't try to get inside the house. Or he didn't have enough time." She turned and walked toward the front of the house, still looking warily into every corner.

He followed her, catching up to where she stood eyeing the stairs to the second floor. "You hear anything up there?"

She shook her head.

He stepped around her and climbed the stairs, flipping on a light switch at the top. He scanned each of the two bedrooms and the generous en suite bathroom with the old claw-foot tub. Ari's room was just as they'd left it two days ago—the board still in place at the window.

"Does it look okay?" she asked, coming up behind him.

"Sure, sweetheart." He scanned the corners. "Except we missed this chunk of glass." He set down both their travel bags for a second to fetch a rather large shard from against the baseboard. Then he tossed it into the same wastepaper basket they'd used to clean up the first time. The action of straightening up again gave his head a stab of pain, damn it. He scrubbed his forehead.

Ari's face fell. "Are you all right?" She reached for his head as if on instinct, and a second later her massage-therapist's fingers were smoothing his brow line.

I'm fine. The words didn't quite make it out, though, because he was suddenly overwhelmed by how near Ari was, and by her big brown eyes looking right into his.

Her hand stilled, the palm warming his face.

The moment yawned open between them, and it suddenly seemed as if everything had already been decided. When he leaned toward Ari, she didn't even look surprised. As he lowered his lips to brush against hers, he had the sensation that the first kiss had been planned sometime between his fall on the ice and the pouring of their drinks on the plane. And that the sweet little gasp she made now had been decided the minute she'd lifted her bag into the taxi they'd decided to share at the airport.

He pressed his lips against her softer ones, leaning in to deepen the kiss. She tasted like lime juice and sweetness. Her hands slid down from his achy head to the back of his neck, her body pressing closer. He parted her lips with the force of his kiss, and she opened for him immediately.

The moan she made when their tongues touched was better therapy than anything she'd ever done for him on a massage table.

TEN

Yoga was all about living in the moment, and focusing one's attention on the body. Ari found herself suddenly *very* motivated by both the moment and the body.

Two bodies.

All the pent-up stress of the last few hours was like dry tinder for the sudden spark of Patrick's kiss. She gripped the lapels of his jacket and dove right in. He was warm and solid against her. A sudden thunderclap of lust blossomed between the two of them. She ran a hand down his chest, over the buttons of his shirt, wishing she could touch more of him.

When her palm came to rest on Patrick's tight stomach just over his belt buckle, he shivered. When he softened their kiss, she found herself holding her breath, waiting to find out what he'd do next. For a moment, they stared into each other's eyes, their foreheads tipped together. Then he palmed the back of her head and began kissing a path down her jaw and onto her neck. When his tongue touched her collarbone, chills rose up on her chest. And there was nothing on earth she wanted more than his hands and his mouth on her body.

There was no doubt in her mind that they'd be naked and on her bed before she could say *impulsive much?*

Not all impulses were bad.

Patrick's hands skimmed down her back, cupping her derrière. He yanked her hips against his body. Then his mouth was back on hers, kissing her so deeply that she tasted only him. He made a needy, hungry grunt from the back of his throat, and the sound caused her pulse to jump again.

"Tell me to stop," he said between kisses. His hand traveled downward still, lifting her thigh and tucking it against his leg, opening her body to him. That naughty hand slipped under the hem of her dress, the heat of his palm searing her as it traveled across her bottom. "Tell me to stop," he repeated.

She did not tell him to stop.

Instead, she took a half step back, then hooked two fingers in his belt and towed him toward the bed until the backs of her thighs hit the mattress. She sat down, lifting her eyes to check his expression.

The heat in his gaze as he shrugged off his suit coat could burn the little house right down. "So I'm staying?" he asked, his voice pure gravel.

Instead of answering, she grasped the fabric of her dress and lifted it over her head, leaving only a lacy black bra and the tights she was wearing.

His lustful expression said, *challenge accepted.*

He tossed his jacket onto a chair without a glance, then leaned over to kiss her, his hand landing on her breast. The rough pad of his thumb stroked the sensitive skin just above her bra.

She wanted more, and she wanted it right away. With hands made shaky by eagerness, she tugged at the knot of his necktie, loosening it. When it went slack, she went to work on the buttons of his shirt.

He broke their kiss to help her. And those icy blue eyes bored into her own as he whipped the tie off, then wrestled the shirt off of giant shoulder muscles.

Wow. Patrick O'Doul removing his suit, ladies and gentlemen. It was not a sight to be missed. She stared at his eight-pack as thick fingers flicked the shirt to her bedroom floor then moved to his belt buckle. Slowly he unhooked it. His gaze was weighty on hers, asking for her permission. But there was no way in hell she was going to change her mind. She wanted *that* body on top of hers. Right now. And if tomorrow it all seemed like an awful idea, she'd just deal with the consequences then.

The sound of his zipper lowering sent a fresh zing of excitement fizzing through her belly. And when the trousers fell away, all that was left was a pair of black boxer briefs, stretched to their limits by a generous erection straining against the cotton. He reached one weather-beaten hand into his briefs just to adjust himself, straightening the thick column until the tip was visible above the elastic.

It was as good as an invitation. Ari leaned forward, her nose brushing the surprisingly soft skin of his belly. Closing her eyes, she took a deep breath of him, filling her senses with the scent of recently showered skin, tinged with the salty tang of desire. Nuzzling in, she brought her lips to his tip and kissed him softly. He tasted as good as he looked.

"Fuck." The contact made his breath hitch, and one big hand came around to the back of her head, tangling in her hair. She leaned in for another kiss, but two hands scooped her under the arms and tossed her backward on the bed instead. "Lie down," he ordered, and she rushed to comply, scooting backward on the bed.

Then his body was on hers, his knees forcing hers apart. His eagerness was like gasoline on flames, spiking her arousal again. His mouth covered hers, firm and demanding, and she opened for him right away. It had been so long since she'd felt like this—ready to make an offering of herself, willing to submit to something they both craved.

Their tongues tangled, and she let her hands wander over his muscular back. He yanked her tights down on one side, and cool air met her bottom. There were too many clothes between them still. Her breasts felt full and achy. She reached between their bodies to fiddle with the center clasp on her bra, but couldn't get to it until Patrick pressed up on his elbows, nudging her hands out of the way and then nosing along the lace cups. A hungry sound emerging from his throat. He unhooked the bra and then groaned, leaning down to pull her nipple into his mouth.

"Oh," she gasped, arching her back. She could hear her own ragged breathing, each shaky exhale a mockery of all those times she'd ever counted out a breathing exercise in a yoga studio. But it couldn't be helped. His mouth on her breast sent a rush of slickness between her legs. He shaped her nipple into a slick point with his lips and then bent over to repeat the torture on the other side.

She closed her eyes and ran her fingers through his thick, short hair, its texture unfamiliar against her palms. It had been eight years since she'd had a first time with anyone. She wished she could slow down time and appreciate each new sensation.

Slowing down wasn't really an option, though. The scent of need in the room was too strong. And she craved his weight on her body—all his muscular bulk pressing her down into the bed. So she lifted her feet to his waist. Using her toes, she caught the waistband of his briefs and pushed them down his hips.

With a groan, he raised himself above her, then yanked her tights down and off her body. That was it—the last scrap of clothing vanquished. Cool air prickled her heated skin while he just stood there for a moment, looking down at her, his gaze landing everywhere.

"What?" she asked suddenly.

He grinned. "Just enjoying the view. Is that so wrong?" He turned away from her, showing her his magnificent ass, and bent down toward his duffel bag on the floor. She heard a zipper and the crinkle of a wrapper. Then he stalked toward her again, powerful muscles popping as he moved, and it was her turn to stare, especially at the thick erection pointing straight up in front of him. A quiver of nervous excitement ran through her core. Were they really going through with this?

While she watched, wide-eyed, he put a condom in her hand and then positioned himself right in front of her on the bed. Maybe he sensed her split-second of indecision, because he dropped a hand to her chin and tilted her face up to meet his gaze. He didn't say anything, but his cool eyes asked her which way it was gonna be.

She swallowed roughly, then tore open the packet. He hissed when she curved her hand around his shaft and rolled down the condom. When she was done, he put one of his big knees on the bed and nudged her back. She lay down against the pillows again, and he came down on top of her, his mouth just beside her ear. "You ready? Because you are going to get it so good."

The moan she let out could probably be heard all over Vinegar Hill.

He began to kiss his way down her neck, and she squirmed under his ministrations. The anticipation was killing her now. He propped his elbows on the bed, kissing his way down her chest, her stomach. As he neared her sex, goosebumps broke out on her chest. And then his mouth was right there, his lips skimming her mound, his big hands wrapped around her thighs. He spread her legs wide and flattened his tongue right where it counted.

Ari couldn't help it. She let out a happy cry, which was answered by a deep moan from Patrick. And the vibration of his voice against her body only intensified the sensation. "So fucking sweet," he murmured against her clit. The sight of his strong neck bent in concentration over her body gave her shivers. And then he lifted his eyes to hers while dragging his tongue right down the center of her.

Just like that, he had her hovering on the precipice. She gripped the quilt with two hands as his tongue continued its wicked work. Someone was begging, and she was pretty sure it was her.

For a split second everything paused. Ari sucked in a much needed deep breath. But when she bore down again, seeking release, exquisite resistance was provided by a thick cock filling her in one smooth stroke. His name flew from her lips as his big body came down over hers, his hips pumping in time to her own desperation.

His tongue filled her mouth and his big hands gripped her own and everything was fast and rhythmic and head-spinning. She moved in time to the wicked pace he'd set, while her heart thumped out a mantra: *oh yes oh yes oh yes*.

Release came like water overflowing a pool—first a shimmer hovering at the edge, and then a flood. She sobbed into his mouth, tightening her legs around his body, tightening *everything*.

Before it was even over, Patrick began to curse. Then he moaned and then flattened her into the bed, his big body shuddering against her.

Silence descended a moment later. Patrick rolled to the side, taking her with him. Then he took a very deep breath and eased himself out, shivering once more as he left her. "Fuck," he whispered. "Now I know how people get religion."

She let out a nervous laugh. "What religion is this?"

He pulled her against his chest and buried his face in her hair. "Dunno. Can't string a sentence together right now."

Ari couldn't either. She'd thought sexual energy was a concept she'd already understood. But what had happened on her bed just now was more like combustion.

They lay there breathing hard, their limbs entwined. Ari let her thoughts drift out over the Brooklyn skyline, away from the madness of the last week. She relaxed in Patrick's giant arms and refused to think about anything important.

"So this is a problem," he mumbled eventually.

The first prickle of reality trickled down her back. "Can't we put off the regrets until daylight at least?"

"What regrets? I have none," he rumbled. "The problem is that I *already* get boned up on your massage table. Next time you put your hands on me at work I'm gonna start moaning like a porn star."

"Might have to get out a gag for you," she teased.

He let out a sleepy groan. "Doubt it'll work. Probably just turn me into a submissive."

Now there was a giggleworthy idea. And since when was Patrick O'Doul *funny?* Note to self—give a man an orgasm and learn his secrets. She ran her fingers down his spectacular chest and smiled.

ELEVEN

Patrick was not usually a cuddler. At all. But it was surprisingly comfortable to lie with Ari's head on his shoulder, letting his fingers sift through her soft hair. It didn't hurt matters that they'd just had *spectacular* sex. He felt both relaxed and spent in the best possible way.

This was the first time in years that he'd gotten naked with someone he'd known for more than an hour. *Note to self: Fucking someone you actually like is fun.* He already trusted Ari, and didn't feel as though he needed to live up to any weird celebrity expectations with her.

No wonder he didn't have the usual urge to make an excuse to bolt for the door.

Eventually he had to get up and deal with the condom, though. So he kissed Ari on the forehead and took his tired body into her bathroom for a few minutes. Washing up, he took a look at his bruise in the mirror. A big greenish blotch was already spreading across his eye socket.

Just another day at the office.

When he walked back into Ari's bedroom, she was sitting up, one hand clutching the sheet at her kissable breasts, watching him warily. "You can stay." She cleared her throat. "I mean, if you want to. It's pretty late . . ."

He settled the question by flipping down the covers on one side of her bed. "Not leaving you here alone, sweetheart. You don't know if dumbass is going to try to break in again, and it's too late to talk to the cops." He climbed in. "So it's your place or mine. And yours is closer." He stretched out on his back and closed his eyes. The second he got horizontal again, the exhaustion returned. It had been a long fucking day.

Ari got out of bed and padded into the bathroom. He heard the water running and a toilet flush. Then she tiptoed to her side of the bed and slid in. The bed rustled as she arranged the covers. But she didn't come closer.

Sleepy now, he reached for her hand, finding it on the sheet beside him. He raised it to his lips and kissed it. Then he fell asleep.

"Patrick."

"Mmh."

"Patrick." A warm hand rubbed his chest.

"Mmh?"

"There are cops at my front door."

His eyes flew open. "Really?"

"Someone's knocking, and there's a cruiser out in front."

"Fuck." He woke up fast, swinging his legs over the side of the bed. He looked at Ari and found her looking back at him. They were both still stark naked, and after last night's festivities, their clothes were still strewn everywhere around the room.

And there were cops knocking on the door.

He grinned suddenly, and she laughed. "Good morning. Welcome to chaos."

"Right."

"I'll tell them I need a minute to get dressed." She threw on a bathrobe and ran downstairs to deliver this message through the door, while he dug a rumpled T-shirt and a pair of athletic pants out of his suitcase. Then he went down to let them in while Ari went back upstairs to change.

"Good morning," he said to one uniformed and one plain-clothes officer on the doorstep.

Mr. Plainclothes showed his badge. "I'm Detective Miller of the eighty-fourth precinct. Looking to speak to a Mr. Alberto Bettini." The dectective squinted at him. "But that's not you. Hey—aren't you Patrick O'Doul? Am I crazy?"

"Couldn't say if you're crazy, man," Patrick said, trying to keep it casual. "I'm O'Doul, though."

The detective barked out a laugh, then extended a hand. "Nice to meet you. Saw the Rangers game last month."

"Patrick?" Ari said from behind him. "Is everything okay?"

Detective Miller looked past him to Ari, who was now dressed in jeans and a sweater. "I need to speak with the owner. Is Alberto here?"

"I'm his niece, and I look after the house. Uncle Alberto lives in West Palm."

"Ah. Well, we have a warrant to search the property, miss." He passed her a sheet of paper.

"Search it? For what?"

"Your neighbor who called in the B&E—she identified the burglar as Vincent Giardi. He's under investigation by law enforcement, and this is his last known address."

Ari clutched the sheet of paper, her eyes bugging out. "Investigation for what?"

"We can't disclose the details of our investigation. But we believe—and the judge believes—that Mr. Giardi was conducting illegal business activities from this property."

O'Doul's gut clenched. He had a pretty good idea of those illegal activities.

"He doesn't live here *now*," Ari spat. "I've been trying to get rid of his stuff in my basement for weeks."

"I hear you," the detective said apologetically. "But the warrant is valid. Do you mind answering some questions while Officer Brock takes a look around?"

Ari scanned the sheet of paper in her hand, then lifted frightened eyes to Patrick's. "So I just *have* to let them in? That's it?"

He put a hand to her lower back and rubbed. "Sweetheart, I know I'm supposed to be the heavy in this relationship. But I've only seen warrants on television."

The detective laughed, but Ari only gave him a look intended to demonstrate just how unhelpful he was.

"Call Rebecca," he suggested. "Tell her that you need to talk to a lawyer, stat."

She turned away and ran upstairs.

The detective watched her go, shifting his feet, looking uncomfortable. "She's not supposed to leave my sight. I was trying to be helpful by not asking you two to leave."

"Ari!" Patrick called up the stairs. "Can you make your call down here?"

She reappeared, Katt Phone in hand. Giving the cop a dirty look, she walked past them both to the sofa and sat down. "Becca! I've got a situation. Can you pull out whatever file you keep lawyers in? The douchewhistle has struck again. There are cops searching my house for unlawful activities." She paused to let Becca express some outrage. "I appreciate it. You, too, honey. Later." Ari hung up, looking miserable. "Shouldn't you be at practice?" she asked him.

O'Doul pointed to the big bruise on his temple. "They weren't going to let me skate this morning anyway. I'll check in a bit later." He crossed to the sofa and sat down beside her. "How about I order some egg sandwiches and coffee? We might as well eat while you wait out the long arm of the law."

She rubbed her temples. "Okay. I mean, you probably need to get going. So I'm good either way."

He squeezed her knee, aware that the policeman was watching them. "I'm going to call the deli."

He took her Katt Phone out of her hand, because his was still upstairs. "Unlock this for me?"

She did, handing it to him with a briskness that bordered on pissed-off. Hell, maybe she hoped he'd just get lost. But he wasn't going to leave until he heard what the detective wanted from her. And having your house searched by the cops was a pretty fucked-up way to start the day. She probably wasn't thinking straight. So Ari would be enjoying just a little more of his company, whether she wanted it or not.

He ordered food and watched the uniformed cop make a cursory sweep of the home's interior. "When was the last time Mr. Giardi was inside this portion of the house?" the detective asked.

"January 28th," she said immediately. "I threw him out that night, with my tenant's help. We moved all his possessions into the storage room, because it has separate access. I changed my locks that day, but not on the basement."

"Why?"

"Because I was not going to put his fancy clothes on the curb! I was trying to be civilized. But he didn't get lost like I asked him to. Instead of just removing his stuff, he kept hanging around the place. These past few weeks I kept seeing him out the window, more times than you'd need to take care of some clothes."

"When's the last time you saw him go in there?"

"Last Thursday. I was on my way to the stadium for the game against D.C. I saw him out the window, and there was another man, too. They were talking. The other guy left first, and then Vince left. On my way to the stadium that afternoon I went outside to try to figure out what he was up to. And I saw that he'd locked *me* out."

The agent raised an eyebrow. "Yeah? Then why did he have to saw open the door last night?"

"Because I retaliated!" Ari was all fired up now, her cheeks pink. "I had the locksmith remove his locks and add mine. I knew he'd be pissed off, but I didn't know how else to make my point. He doesn't answer my e-mails. I've asked him to get his things out of there for weeks."

"Would you show me those emails?"

O'Doul didn't like the direction this was taking. Maybe he'd watched too much TV, but he had to say something. "Do you want to wait and talk to a lawyer?"

She gave him a glare. "I don't have anything to hide. I just want this cleared up. And I need a restraining order against him."

"Now there's an idea I can get behind," he said.

The agent grinned at him, so he put a protective hand on Ari's knee. Maybe she'd be pissed off later, but this cop liked him. The whole fame thing was pretty useless most of the time, and if it helped Ari get out of this mess, he didn't mind exaggerating their relationship.

Ari found the outgoing e-mails on her phone, and let the cop read them.

The doorbell rang, which had to be the food he'd ordered.

"Hey, man," he asked the cop. "Mind if I grab my wallet from upstairs?"

"Go ahead. I think my guy is done up there."

O'Doul paid the delivery kid then set the bag down on Ari's coffee table. "Coffee?" he invited the detective. He'd bought four cups for this very reason.

"Thanks," the guy said. "Appreciate it."

O'Doul gave Ari a smile and dug into the bag for sugar packets and cream. "Honey," he said. It was too familiar sounding, but he wanted the cops to know he was watching over her. "You want me to get plates? I don't want to get crumbs on your couch."

Ari got up and went to the kitchen, returning with two plates.

O'Doul passed her a sandwich. And when she actually began to eat it, the satisfaction it brought him was something he'd have to examine later.

The detective began to pepper her with more questions. Why had she kicked Vince out? What did she know about his business?

"Not as much as you'd think," she said with a sigh. "Three years ago he had several clubs. But I'm pretty sure he's down to just one. And I think he owes some people money. He never told me his troubles directly, but I heard him on the phone sometimes, and his mood has been really foul since the fall. And that's all I can tell you."

"How long were you together?"

"Eight years."

The cop raised an eyebrow. "Eight years? And you don't know more about his business?"

O'Doul opened his mouth to express his displeasure at the cop's tone, but Ari beat him to it.

"Look, I have my own job, okay? And Vince didn't like that so much. And he had a big chest-beating macho streak. When things went wrong, I was the last person he'd tell. We didn't do a lot of *tell me about your day at work, honey.* Besides—his club has a business office. It's not like he was running the whole show out of my home. I showed his ass the door, and we have not had a conversation since."

"Okay." The detective rubbed his chin. "Then can you tell me who he worked *with?* You must have heard names, or answered calls."

She cleared her throat. "The co-owned clubs were with the Pryzyks. They were brothers, I think."

Pryzyk. O'Doul thought he'd heard that name on the news before.

"You ever meet them?" the detective pried.

"Once. Maybe a year ago? I met Vince at his office because we were going to the opera. And they were there. Not the most friendly people. I didn't feel the urge to see them again."

"So you never socialized with his colleagues?" the detective pressed.

O'Doul did not think Ari should have to answer all these questions.

"When I was young and working in Vince's first club, I knew everyone," she said. "They were my second family. But when I left to do training in yoga and massage therapy, I wasn't around anymore. And the turnover in nightclubs is pretty high. All my favorite people moved on."

"Okay," the detective said, tapping his pencil on his pad of paper. "Can you tell me if Vincent ever said anything about drugs in his clubs?"

O'Doul felt his gut tighten, but he kept his face impassive. Buying pills in that club was the stupidest thing he'd ever done in his life. The buzz he got from them lasted a couple of hours each time. And now he'd be worrying about this shit for the rest of his career.

"Vince told me once that every club had problems with drugs—that it was hard to keep the dealers out. And then, sure enough, one of his clubs kept getting busted and they lost the liquor license. But he didn't share specifics, and I didn't ask because he was such a grumpy bastard all the time about it." Ari looked the cop straight in the eye as she said it, and O'Doul hoped he would just leave her the fuck alone.

"To your knowledge did Vince Giardi ever decide to use the flow of drugs as an opportunity rather than a problem?"

Ari's eyes widened again. "You mean . . . encourage the dealing?"

"Did he take a cut?" the agent asked point-blank.

As O'Doul watched, she went through about seventeen emotions. Disbelief. Fear. Disgust. "God, I don't think so," she said finally. "I mean, he'd never tell me if he did. But the thing about Vince is that he isn't really a schemer. He'd rather pour you a drink and take a spin on the dance floor. Even when he was trying to build up his empire, it was all about the clubs themselves—which A-list celebs were going to show up, which DJs he could book. He got into the business because he wanted to party for a living." She shook her head. "I don't think he was the best businessman, honestly. I know he had money problems after the one club was shut down. He owed the Pryzyk brothers money, I think. Either that or he owed somebody else money, and he was trying to get the Pryzyks to help him."

"Why do you think so?"

She shrugged and looked up at the ceiling. "His phone

would ring with their name on the screen. He'd disappear into another room and argue for a while. I got the impression he wanted their help. But I never heard both sides of the conversation. That's really all I can tell you," she finished.

The cop took notes on a pad, writing furiously. "Okay. Thank you." He looked up. "Have you ever heard the name Andre Karsecki?"

"Um . . ." Ari's brow wrinkled. "No? Who's that?"

O'Doul had heard it. "I saw it in the newspaper—an unsolved murder in a nightclub."

The cop nodded, and there was an awkward silence.

Ari crossed her arms over her chest. "Look, I told you everything I know about Vince's work. I wish I'd never met the guy."

"We're going to inventory the items from your storage room downstairs, and remove the computer we found there. Did you keep any valuables in that room?" the detective asked.

"Depends who you ask. The collection of vinyl albums is my uncle's—they're valuable to him, but I have no idea if they're worth any actual money. Aside from a few pieces of old furniture I didn't want, nothing else in that room was put there by me."

He scribbled another note. "Any files? Any notes?"

"All Vince's," she said firmly. "When I looked through the window the other day, I saw a computer I'd never seen before. I have no idea how he was working out of that room. I changed the Wi-Fi password after he left, too."

"There was a splice," the cop said, still writing. "A direct line running from your cable connection."

"Damn it!" Ari yelled. "That *asshole*."

O'Doul reached for Ari's hand and rubbed her palm. "When can she fix the lock again?" O'Doul asked. "It isn't safe to leave that open. Someone could take advantage."

"We'll call you when we're finished with our investigation," the detective said, standing up. "Shouldn't be more than a few days."

"Like, maybe tomorrow?" O'Doul pressed. He didn't mind being an asshole on Ari's behalf.

"Maybe." The guy was noncommittal.

"Uh-huh. And how does she get a restraining order against him?"

The detective offered a business card to him. "That's not my specialty, but call my office line and ask my assistant to e-mail you the forms. She'll need to go to the courthouse on Jay Street."

Ari was the one to stand up and take the card from his hand. "Thank you. I'll do that today."

When the detective was finally ready to leave, O'Doul walked him out the door. The second the door shut, he turned to face Ari. "Are you okay?"

"Fine." But her expression was closed off, like a door slammed shut. "You'd better report to the trainers' office. They must wonder where the hell you are."

She wasn't wrong. But still. "Did Becca e-mail you some lawyers?"

"I'm sure she did." Ari hugged herself. "Thank you for chatting up the cop. I know you were trying to help, but"— she traced a pattern on the wood floor with her bare toe—"I can take it from here."

"Okay," he said, because what was his choice? He took two steps and put his hands on her shoulders. "Be well." He kissed her forehead. But, fuck. That wasn't good enough. He wrapped his arms around her, wanting to feel her soft body against his one more time. She was kind of addictive.

She gave him a quick hug in return, but then pulled back. And he had no choice but to release her, fetch his stuff from upstairs and go.

So he did. But he knew he'd be thinking about her the rest of the day. No—the week. Whether she liked it or not.

After a quick stop at home, O'Doul headed over to the practice facility. The doctor did another concussion examination, thankfully clearing him to play. He didn't even have to argue.

That done, he hit the weight room for an hour or so.

But on his way out that afternoon, Coach Worthington and the GM—Hugh Major—stopped him in the hallway. "Got a second?" Coach asked.

As if he could say no. He followed Coach into his office like a well-behaved player would. "Is there a problem?"

Coach shook his head. "Just wondering what you think of something."

"Shoot."

"How do you like the idea of Crikey fighting tomorrow night?"

O'Doul's chin snapped upwards. "Why?"

"To take some of the pressure off you," Coach said immediately. "Give your strain a little extra cushion."

"I can handle it," he said, sounding defensive as hell. But he didn't want anyone easing off his duties. When the team started taking it easy on you, it was the beginning of the end. He was thirty-two, not thirty-eight.

"The kid wants to fight, though," Hugh said, speaking up. "This guy Falzgar used to beat the crap out of him in juniors."

"So we're just gonna let him work out his vendetta in the middle of the game? That is not a strategy. And Falzgar is a leftie. Has Crikey fought a leftie?"

Frowning, the two people in charge of O'Doul's life exchanged a loaded glance.

Fuck.

"We need you healthy," Coach said. "You can take tomorrow's fight. But only if you are a hundred percent sure you're up to it."

"I am," he insisted.

He thought he'd be dismissed, but Hugh stroked his chin thoughtfully. "The salary cap means this team won't ever have another dedicated enforcer. Every player is here for his skills."

"I know," O'Doul insisted.

"If the fighting gets in the way of your skills, it's bad for the team."

"True." He grit his teeth to keep from saying more.

Finally, Hugh stood. "Rest up tonight."

"Thanks, I will."

He walked home, considering all the different options for resting up. He could go to the bar on Hicks and have a cheeseburger. He should check up on Ari to be sure she was okay.

Or he could go home and watch five dozen of Falzgar's fights on YouTube.

Two of those things were fun and one would make him into a dreadful wreck of a human. And he already knew which option he'd end up picking.

TWELVE

14 Regular Season Games to Go
Kattenberger Model Predicts: 74 percent chance of a
play-offs spot

After a two hour wait, Ari received an order of protection from a graying judge in a windowless courtroom. She spent some quality time on the phone with a lawyer Becca found for her. It was all quite boring and terrifying at the same time. Then she made a call to Uncle Alberto and confessed that his storage room had been broken into, and he made some anxious noises about his Brubeck on vinyl while she tried to reassure him.

Fun times.

She didn't make it into work at all that day, and since Becca had told the trainer she'd taken a personal day, nobody said anything. But the team's pain and injuries needed tending to, and she hated not being there to do it.

That evening Becca called, claiming that her live-in sister and baby nephew were driving her crazy, and asked if she could come and spend the night at Ari's place. "I'll bring a movie and some takeout," she promised.

Ari accepted this thin ruse because she was still a little freaked out about her last two visits from Vince. So, after hanging up the phone, she charged upstairs to change the sheets on her bed. Although Becca would stay the night on the twin bed in the guest room, she still felt the need to banish any evidence of last night's lapse in judgment.

Like the condom wrapper under the bed.

Her face began to burn as she plucked it off the floor and threw it away. She and Patrick must have had a *lot* of frustration to burn off last night, because it had been the best sex of her life. Her stomach shimmied just at the memory of the moment when he'd put his mouth . . .

Gah. She wasn't going to tell *a soul*.

The doorbell rang, and Ari had a moment's hesitation. What if it was Vince at the door? She tiptoed down the stairs. It rang again.

"Ari?" Becca's voice called through the wood. "I have Indian food and a DVD of *Magic Mike*!"

She opened the door. "Well, step right this way." *I will not confess. I will not.*

Becca walked in, handing Ari a bag of food. She kicked off her Dr. Martens and wrinkled her nose. "You look guilty. Why?"

"I do not!" Ari gasped.

"You so do. What happened?"

Damn it. "Patrick and I attacked each other like horny rabbits last night," she blurted out. "But it's never happening again."

Becca's eyebrows shot up, which was especially distracting because there was a barbell through one of them. "Wait. Patrick? As in . . . O'Doul? You call him *Patrick?* Nobody calls him by his first name."

"Really? *That's* what you find shocking about this?" She carried the food into the kitchen, trailed by Becca. "My life is a train wreck, and I just made it worse by screwing a client."

"Let's not be hasty. Was he good? Maybe it's worth it."

"It was epic," Ari admitted, taking out plates and silverware. "Then again, for the past few years I've only had sex with someone who resented me half the time. So maybe my viewpoint is skewed."

"God." Becca let out a dreamy sigh. "These days, even a night with someone who resented me sounds appealing. Why do you think I own Channing Tatum on DVD? Because I get no action. All day I'm surrounded by hard bodies at work, and yet my vibrator is always on the charger." She carried two dishes of curry to Ari's table.

"You could hook up, though," Ari pointed out. "It would be less scandalous for you to get busy with a player than for me. You don't have to touch their bodies in the line of duty."

"You'd *think* nobody would care," Becca said, tearing a piece of naan bread in half. "But once when Castro was having a shitty day I got him drunk in a hotel bar. Nate saw us all cozy and laughing in a booth at the bar and got the wrong impression. He was cold to me for a while after that. So I'm not going there."

A chill crawled up Ari's back. "Seriously? Nate got mad?"

"Hell yes. I swear I didn't imagine it. He was kind of a dick to Castro, too."

"Shit," Ari breathed. "I can't risk my job. I'm going to swear Patrick to secrecy."

"He's a decent guy," Becca said, helping herself to the lamb curry. "He puts up an asshole front, and he's kind of an egomaniac. But he's got that whole macho honor code thing working. So I think you'll be fine."

"Ugh." If she'd been using her brain at all last night, she wouldn't be in this predicament right now.

"How did it happen, anyway? Did he give you that overconfident squint and say, *hey, baby, wanna bang?*"

"No! Geez. We didn't talk about it first. He got out of the taxi here and helped me make sure the house was secure. And then we just looked at each other and . . . it was like someone pulled the pin on a grenade. *Kapow.*"

Becca pinched the front of her shirt between two fingers and fanned herself. "Oh, man. Just once in my life I want to feel like that. I had so many bad first dates last year." She stabbed a piece of lamb and laughed. "Nothing went *kapow*."

Ari scooped up a forkful of buttery rice and tried to figure out why her encounter with Patrick had been so hot and frantic. It was just happenstance, probably. A loaded moment when they both had the same outrageous impulse, and a week's worth of tension needing an outlet.

Instead of beating herself up about it, Ari would use the advice she gave her yoga students—acknowledge it and move on. It happened. It was spectacular. Now she would just let it go.

Letting it go meant ice cream, Channing Tatum, and Becca's laughter. Ari was grateful for the companionship, and she forgot to worry about freaking Vince until her Katt Phone began chirping with text messages on the coffee table in front of her feet.

Becca paused the movie. "Should you check that?"

"Oh, I suppose." But she was feeling too relaxed and happy to worry. And bad news from Vince—while there was plenty—tended to arrive via bricks and yelling. She scooped her phone up and checked.

Hi, sweetheart. I'm thinking about you tonight. Can you let me know you're okay? She could practically hear Patrick's gravelly voice when she read his words. A warm sensation settled just below her belly button.

"Omigod. Did O'Doul text you? You should see the look on your face right now."

Ari's chin snapped up. "He's just making sure I'm okay."

"Uh-huh." Becca rolled her eyes. "If he's on his way over here I'll make myself scarce."

"No! That is *not* happening. Start the movie. We're just up to the good part."

"It's all the good part," Becca pointed out. "But you'd better reply or he'll be knocking on your door five minutes from now."

Hell, he might be. So she did. *Watching a movie with Becca and she's staying the night.*

Nice. Are you going to have as much fun with her as you did with me?

Oh, boy. She was just about to text *stop it* when Becca grabbed the phone out of her hands.

"He's flirting with you!" she squealed. Then she started typing.

"This is so high school," Ari complained, grabbing for the phone. Becca dodged her and managed to press send before relinquishing the phone. "What the hell did you do?" Becca's text said, *Want to wash?* "Wash what? You're going to get me fired."

Becca giggled. "It was supposed to say *watch*. Damn autocorrect."

Her phone chirped with a new text and Ari groaned. "I'm afraid to look."

"I'll look!" Becca made a grab, but Ari didn't fall for it. She held on tight and read the text.

Becca got your phone, huh?

Ari snorted with laughter. *Yes and now I shall beat her with it.*
Tell her she's got me thinking about shower sex now. And you've seen my shower. Ari's stomach flipped over.

"You've seen his shower?" Becca asked, blatantly reading over her shoulder. "I thought he didn't let people into his apartment?"

Gotta go, she typed speedily. *See you tomorrow.* It was abrupt, but she needed to end this conversation.

Night, sweetheart, came the quick reply.

Becca made a motion like stabbing herself in the heart. "I can't *even* with this. Who knew O'Doul was a romantic?"

Ari picked up the remote and aimed it at the TV with the

eager grip of a cop show criminal holding his gun. "More Tatum. Less talking."

The ten thirty time slot on Ari's treatment schedule the next day belonged to Patrick O'Doul.

By the time his appointment approached, Ari was ready. She had the stereo switched off and her game face on. Before she began his massage therapy, she would greet the elephant in the room, acknowledge its presence, and then show it the door.

At ten thirty sharp he sauntered in wearing nothing but a towel, his hair damp from the shower, his skin glowing with a life force which she'd experienced the other night at *very* close range . . .

Focus, Ari. "Good morning," she said with the same firmness she greeted all her clients. "How are your hip flexors feeling today?"

Before answering, he shut the door and faced her. She was keenly aware that nothing separated her from the potent look in his eye except a not-so-wide massage table and a towel. It was as if he'd failed to hear the cool, businesslike tone of her greeting. He studied her the way she looked at the cupcakes in the case at One Girl Cookies—like she was a well-deserved snack he was about to gobble down. "Hi, sweetheart," he said slowly. "You doing okay?"

Gulp. "I'm doing well," she said, trying to remember what it was she had rehearsed saying. "I got an order of protection, and hired a process server to track Vince down to serve it. And the lawyer Becca recommended is ready to step in if the cops try to tie me to any of Vince's shady dealings."

"That's good," Patrick said, never breaking her gaze. His intensity made her knees feel squishy. Eventually he dropped his towel and slid onto the table, releasing her from that laser stare, thankfully. "No Pearl Jam today?"

"Um, I can turn it on." She tossed another towel over his

midsection before it became tempting to stare. "After we have a quick chat."

His eyes lifted to hers again, and he looked almost amused. "What's on your mind?"

"It's about the other night. We can't have a repeat performance."

"Of course not," he said, letting out a wolfish chuckle.

For a split second she was actually disappointed at how quickly he'd agreed. But then she caught herself and remembered to be relieved.

". . . I mean, not an *exact* repeat," he added. "I like to mix it up a little. The shower sounds good. Up against the wall."

"Patrick," she warned. "I'm not joking. We obviously have a bit of chemistry . . ." She rubbed a bit of oil onto her fingers and then started in on the muscles just above his knee.

He snorted. "We have a *bit of chemistry*. And hockey has a bit of violence. We practically burned down your bed together."

Did we ever. "Be that as it may, I need this job. It's the only part of my life that didn't just implode."

He reached down to squeeze her wrist before releasing it. "I would never jeopardize your job."

"Thank you."

"But I call bullshit. If you want to give me the brush-off you're going to have to do a little better than that flimsy excuse."

"It isn't flimsy! I have it on good authority that Nate doesn't like his staff, um . . ."

". . . Making the players come so hard they see stars?"

"I would have put it differently. But yes."

He grinned. "And yet Georgia is marrying Leo. I don't see her looking for a new job."

"Her dad is the coach? Hello?" She rolled his towel toward his crotch and kept working. "You seem tight today," she said suddenly.

"It wore off, I guess. Your latest treatment."

"Well, it's been a few days since you were on the table."

"That's not the treatment I meant."

She let go of his leg. "Don't make that joke." It came out a little too sharply. "I'm not a prude, and I don't think it's all that big of a deal to, um, get carried away one night with a friend from work. But this here"—she indicated the room—"is my professional space. I wouldn't ever touch a client inappropriately. It would violate the trust that you give me when you climb onto my table. And I'm sorry if that sounds really nitpicky, but the distinction matters to me." When she stopped to take a breath, she realized what a rant she'd just spewed out, damn it. "Sorry."

But Patrick's eyes became soft and lazy. "I understand, baby. I won't tease you anymore."

"Thank you."

"Not here, anyway." She gave him a glare and he laughed. "Can I have Pearl Jam, at least? I'll be a good boy."

"Yes, you can." She tapped the iPod with her knuckle, to avoid getting massage oil on it. "Now tell me why you're so stiff, without using any innuendo."

"You take all my fun away. Fine. Tonight we play Buffalo and I have to fight this asshole Falzgar."

"And you're not looking forward to it," she guessed.

"Can't say that I am."

"Let's work those hip flexors, shall we? Roll to the side."

She noticed that this time he let her really probe the muscles that had been bothering him. He didn't even flinch. Either he was feeling better or trusting her more. Maybe both. She worked on both his hips and then asked him to flip onto his stomach.

Except for the music, it was quiet in the treatment room. In spite of the raging attraction she felt towards him, it really wasn't that difficult to stay in the zone and handle him with the same care and efficiency she'd show any client. The playlist rolled on in the background while Patrick relaxed under her touch. When she worked on his lower back he sighed with appreciation.

Then a song came on that she would rather not have heard. So she took a second to tap a knuckle against the iPod again. But instead of advancing the song, she paused the music entirely.

Patrick lifted his eyes from the face cradle. "Something the matter? I thought you liked 'Better Man'?"

"Eh. That song isn't my favorite right now."

His expression turning thoughtful, he balanced his cheek on the table. "It hits too close to home?"

It did, actually. And since he knew her torrid little story, there was no point in lying. "The girl in the song stays with a guy who isn't good to her. I never thought I was that girl, and then I was."

His eyes went all soft again. "This is a serious problem now. We can't let that asshole put you off a perfectly good Pearl Jam tune."

"I'll manage." Ari was pretty sure she'd put herself off it.

"No, babe." He propped himself up on an elbow, which ruined her work.

"Turn over if you're going to talk. You're wrecking your alignment."

He flipped over. "The thing is, I think you've misinterpreted the song."

"I really don't think so."

"That song is really about a girl who's making some toast."

"Toast?" Her hands paused on his shoulder.

His cool blue eyes twinkled up at her. "Yeah. See, she's standing in front of the refrigerator. And she"—he broke into song—"can't find the butter, man! She can't find the butter, maa-aa-aan."

"Oh. My god," she laughed. "That is the worst pun ever."

He lifted a hand and pushed a lock of hair away from her face. "You're smiling now, though. So I think I did okay."

Ari felt the moment stretch and take hold. His eyes smiled up at her, and a flush of gratitude filled her chest. Even if it had been a mistake to sleep with him, Patrick O'Doul was a valuable and unexpected friend.

He dropped his hand to his side, still smiling. "I think I'm getting the hang of this massage thing. You schooled me."

She moved behind his head and worked on his well-developed neck muscles. "You could teach a course on how to get a massage."

He snorted. "*Massage for Dummies.* Chapter one—how to lie on a table and let a beautiful woman touch your naked body."

She tapped his shoulder. "Don't do that—don't make fun of yourself for not liking it. Everyone is different."

His eyes slid closed. "But I do like it now. Don't even think about quitting this place, because I'm used to you."

"I have no plans to quit. It's too much fun making a room full of hockey players do sun salutations."

"Doesn't it bug you, though?" he asked quietly. "You teach us a whole lot of Zen shit, and then we use it to beat the crap out of each other."

"I want business cards with that title—*Teacher of Zen Shit.*"

His eyes rolled up to find hers. "You know what I mean."

"It doesn't bother me at all. In the first place, there's plenty I admire about your team. The dedication to success is impressive. And I like working with people who understand their bodies. I never have to convince an athlete that a mind-body connection exists. You guys all get it."

"But you still hate the fighting," he prompted.

"The fighting isn't my favorite," she admitted. "But I don't think it's your favorite either."

"Not all the time," he admitted. "The hours before a fight are the worst. I spend a lot of time worrying about how to make this guy my bitch without getting too hurt, while he tries to make me his bitch without getting hurt."

"So you get anxious."

He made a face. "It's more like dread."

"Okay, dread." Because macho men weren't allowed to experience anxiety. "Maybe we can find you a meditation for those hours. Something that redirects your energy in a more positive way."

His expression was skeptical. "I don't think I'm very good at meditating."

"Neither am I," Ari said. "But that doesn't mean it isn't helping. An old Buddhist monk told me once that the mind is like an untrained monkey. If you don't give it something to do, it will tear your house apart and smear shit on all the walls."

"Really?" On the table in front of her, Patrick's eight-pack shook with laughter. "I want to meet this monk."

"Really. He said meditation gives your monkey something better to do. Even if you think you're bad at it, the monkey is still busy."

Patrick reached up and gave her wrist a squeeze. "I like your style, sweetheart. But I can't always connect to the meditations you give us during yoga. It's like I can't shut off my cynical brain. You tell me to soar like an eagle, and I'm thinking, there aren't any eagles in Brooklyn."

"Uh-huh. So you need the Brooklyn version of a guided meditation? More trash on the beach? Fuhggeddaboudit?"

"Yeah."

"I can do that. Close your eyes."

He closed them.

She lay both hands lightly on his shoulders. "I want you to listen to my voice," she said, using a soft voice and a nice, even tone. "Do your best to follow my instructions. Take a deep, slow breath and will yourself to be fully here, inside the moment."

His belly began to expand with breath.

". . . Make a calm space inside yourself for your breath. Let the inhale fill you with strength. On the exhale, I want you to gradually expel all the bullshit of the external world."

He opened one eye and looked up at her, then closed it again.

"That's it," she urged. "Center your awareness on your breathing. If you find your mind wandering to other thoughts, simply acknowledge that all is *fucking horseshit*. Let it go. Listen to your inner stillness. Breathe in calm. Exhale bullshit."

His belly was shaking with laughter now.

"You think I'm not serious? Meditation can sound however you need it to. It's your show, big man." She patted his shoulder.

He opened his eyes and smiled up at her again. "You are priceless. I hope you know that."

"Thank you," she stammered, his compliment hitting her right in the chest, landing with an unfamiliar warmth. "And now unfortunately we are out of time."

But his words, spoken in that gravely, masculine voice she'd gotten so used to hearing, would stick with her for hours. *You are priceless. I hope you know that.* She hadn't thought too highly of herself lately. It was nice to know that someone else did.

THIRTEEN

Standings: 3rd Place
13 Regular Season Games Left to Go

Crikey took the damn fight after all.

O'Doul didn't know whether to laugh or punch something. After all the preparation and the usual hours of mental anguish, Crikey skated up to Falzgar in the first period and challenged him to throw down. They went at it like a couple of schoolyard bullies until they both landed on the ice where the refs broke it up.

Crikey needed five stitches in his mug, but Brooklyn won their game that night. They were back in third place, too. And now the stupid punk kid was ordering shots all around at the Hicks Street bar and beating on his fool chest.

"Hey!" Beringer crowed. "You have fifty-one percent on HockeyBrawls.com! I call that a win."

"I see fifty-one point four!" Beacon, the goalie, slapped the table. "Another beer for the point four!"

O'Doul gave Beacon a pat on the back and took the bar stool next to him. They were both veterans, and since

Beacon didn't get many nights out at the bar, O'Doul tried to hang with the merriment and stupidity around him. But it took effort. After two rounds he was done. "Pete." He handed his platinum card to the bartender. "I want to take care of whatever these assholes drink tonight. Can you run it now and just cash me out later? I'm sneakin' out."

Pete waved off the card. "I'll e-mail the bill to Rebecca. That's what we did last time."

"Good man."

He made a stop in the men's room, then went out the side door. On the sidewalk ahead of him walked a familiar form. So he put his fingers to his mouth and made a loud catcall.

Ari turned her chin to give him a glare, then did a double take. "You ass."

He laughed. "I answer to that all the time."

Arms folded, she waited for him to catch up. "Had enough scotch?"

"Had plenty."

She studied him a little longer. "You okay?"

"Course I am." He put a hand to his hip. "Didn't even have to take a punch tonight, so I'm solid."

Ari touched his face with one finger, at the side of his mouth. "This muscle looks unhappy, though."

He put a hand to her back to get them moving down the sidewalk. "It's a weird night, that's all."

"Are you pissed at Crikey for fighting?"

Women's intuition wasn't just a myth. "I was. But he seems pretty happy with the outcome. I used to be just like that."

"Like what?"

"Sort of incredulous about the whole thing. I was young and stupid and they paid me a half million dollars a year to do something that used to get me thrown out of school. I thought I'd cracked the secret code of the universe, you know? People wanted my autograph, even though I was really just a thug trying to smash his demons for high pay."

She gave him a sidelong glance. "But it got old?"

"Fuck yeah. It's hell on your body. And then it's too late—you're already that guy who fights. So you have to fight everybody for the rest of your career. I can't just stop."

"Why not?"

He was quiet for a moment, trying to explain it. "There's no shame in being a player who doesn't fight. A lot of guys just don't know how, or they're too valuable as snipers. If Bayer or Trevi fucked up his hand, it would be a scoring disaster. But if I start refusing to fight, I'm a guy who backs down. They'd say—*look at that poor old fucker. He can't take it.* If people don't see me like that I can still have another few years in the league."

"Maybe Crikey wants to take some of the pressure off you. If there're two enforcers, neither of you has to do it all."

He chuckled. "Like a job share. If some hammerhead challenges me on the rink, I can just say, *talk to Crikey. I don't throw down on Thursdays.*"

"It was just a thought."

He put an arm around her shoulders, giving her a quick squeeze, a gesture he would never have made a month ago. "I know. I appreciate it. And Crikey has no idea what he's getting into. Maybe it seemed like a big adventure tonight. But next month maybe he hurts somebody really bad. Or he loses a fight and people jeer and throw food at him. He doesn't know all the shit that can happen. He doesn't know to wonder if some asshole fan goes home drunk after the game and tries to imitate your signature left hook on his wife."

"Jesus."

"You asked." It came out sounding really defensive, but this fucking topic got him all worked up. "Sorry."

"No, I want to know what's in your head."

"Why?"

She gave him a furtive smile, but said nothing.

"I think you like me, Ariana. S'okay, though. You don't have to admit it. It can be our little secret."

"You passed your street," she pointed out suddenly.

"No kidding. I'm walking the lady home. It's late."

Another furtive glance from Ari. "I appreciate it. But I'm going in alone."

"Of course you are," he assured her. Not that he wouldn't like to come in, but he knew how to play the long game. He could be patient when he needed to be.

Hell, he liked her so much. He hadn't felt this way about anyone in a long time. Maybe ever.

Her little building came into view. They crossed the brick street together, mounting Ari's porch. He waited while she fished out her keys. "Good night, sweetheart."

"Good night." She looked up at him with a shy smile. "Thanks for walking me home."

She hesitated, and he didn't miss it. Anyone who'd played pro hockey as long as he had could spot an opening like that. So he leaned in and gave her a kiss. It was meant to be only a tender one, because tender was how he felt toward Ari tonight.

But the moment his lips brushed hers, she made a soft sound of happiness. Her lips were even sweeter than he remembered. She tasted of white wine and sweetness. He cupped the back of her neck to perfect their connection, and her arms wrapped around his body.

Yes. This was everything. The whole fucking league could burn to the ground as long as her lithe arms held him tightly. He slicked his tongue across the seam of her lips, because he couldn't help himself. She gasped and opened immediately.

Their tongues tangled. All he wanted was to lose himself in her kiss all night long.

But she'd said no.

Not tonight.

Goddamn it.

It took every shred of his willpower to ease up. He slanted his head one more time. One more kiss. One more perfect taste. Then, panting, he stepped back, careful to hold her by the ribcage until she stood on her own two feet again.

Breathing hard, Ari blinked up at him.

"Good night, sweetheart. Sleep well."

For a split second, she looked at the keys in her hand as if she'd never seen them before. Then she shook them out and turned toward the lock. "Good night, Patrick."

His chest gave a squeeze. Nobody ever called him Patrick. Not since he was eight and lost his mother. "Let me hear you lock that door behind you."

She pushed inside, gave a quick wave and shut the door. He heard the deadbolt a moment later.

There was nothing left to do but walk away.

FOURTEEN

After locking the door, Ari peeked through the curtains to watch Patrick retreat toward Water Street.

Tonight she'd be staying alone in her house for the first time since Vince's breaking and entering. She could have asked Patrick to stay, but she knew exactly where *that* would lead. It wouldn't be his fault, either. She did not trust herself at all around that man. Even if she'd asked him to stay in the guest bedroom . . .

Right. Too much temptation.

There were other options. She could have slept on Becca's couch, or Georgia and Leo's. But she was determined not to let Vince drive her out of her own home. So she flipped on a lamp in the living room and took stock. Everything was just as she'd left it. There was no reason to believe that anyone had broken into her home, but she had a good look around just to make herself feel sure.

Then, even though it was silly, she brought her Katt Phone upstairs with her. She put it on the charger right beside her bed, just in case. After getting ready for bed, she locked her bedroom door for perhaps the first time ever. But maybe it would help her sleep to know that there was one extra barrier between herself and trouble.

It took her a long time to fall asleep, but she managed. Two times she only woke up to listen to the sounds of her old house settling. To ease her mind, she replayed Patrick's big, steamy kiss on her front stoop. God, that man was a maddening study in contrasts. Nobody had as cool a facade as Patrick O'Doul. He didn't like to be touched. But he kissed like he was starving for it. Thinking of him made her toss and turn for different reasons.

It wasn't the most restful night's sleep, but she did it. Vince hadn't won, and he wasn't going to.

The next morning was an easy one, thankfully. She sat through a staff meeting with Henry and the other trainers. And she didn't happen to bump into Patrick at the practice facility, thank goodness. She would need to put on her game face before seeing him again. That kiss had scrambled her brain.

After the meeting she went home to pack for the team's four-day trip to North Carolina and Philly. It was a mid-day flight this time, and, she made sure to hire a car which would get her to the airport early. Missing the team jet was one of the more embarrassing mistakes an employee could make. Her boss Henry had actually managed to get himself left behind in Dallas once last year when he lost track of time. His Katt Phone had run out of batteries, too, so the team couldn't raise him. His punishment had been twofold: a very expensive plane ticket and a whole lot of ribbing.

Ari arrived at the airport an hour ahead of time, because she didn't *ever* want to make that mistake. A woman's errors would always be counted differently. Her mother was right about that.

As a result of her promptness, she was the first one on the jet. And when Patrick O'Doul boarded a while later, he gave her a solemn nod before moving down the aisle. *Do not turn and admire his ass*, she ordered herself. And she didn't. Maybe it was all the meditating she did, but will-power was one of Ari's strengths.

At least she used to think so.

When the jet had reached cruising altitude, Trevor, one of the office assistants, tapped her on the shoulder. "Hugh Major would like a word with you in private."

Ari closed her book with a startled slam. "Thank you," she said, rising from her seat. It was *not* an ordinary occurrence to have the general manager asking for a meeting—let alone on the jet. *Hell.* What had she done wrong?

One recent sin leapt to mind.

She ran a hand through her hair. Then she stood up, straightening her skirt and heading for the back. The players she passed were relaxing in their seats, earbuds in, listening to music or watching movies on their Katt Phones. Many were sleeping. Athletes were good at taking advantage of downtime. Their overworked bodies demanded rest, and they knew to give in.

Patrick O'Doul was not one of the players she passed, and it should have been a clue.

She rapped lightly on the office door.

"Come in!"

When she slid the door aside, her heart sank. There sat Patrick, a grim look on his face, beside Hugh Major. "You wanted to see me?"

"Sit down, Ariana. We have a bit of a situation."

Shit! As she slid into the booth on the opposite side of the table from the men, her palms began to sweat. She *knew* it had been a mistake to sleep with Patrick. She just hadn't known how huge.

But when she was seated, Hugh said something completely different than she'd expected. "Ariana, it seems you have a stalker. O'Doul brought it to my attention, but I do need you to know that you can always ask the organization for help with any security issues you're facing."

Ari opened her mouth and then closed it again. What the hell?

Hugh opened a file folder on the table in front of him and slid a photograph toward her. She felt nauseated as soon as she realized what she was looking at. A perfect shot of

Patrick's goodnight kiss. The resolution of the photograph was crystal clear. It demonstrated in all too much detail everything she'd felt about that kiss, and everything she'd never wanted the GM of the team to see.

"Turn it over," Patrick said softly.

She flipped the photo onto the desk and saw a hasty scrawl in black marker on the back.

YOU STUPID FUCK.

Her mouth was as dry as the desert. Ari pushed the photo across to Hugh, afraid to look up. But when she did, there was nothing but worry in his eyes. "Where did it come from?"

Patrick laced his hands together and squeezed so hard his knuckles were white. "It was delivered to the Bruisers offices this morning in an unmarked envelope. But it's not hard to guess who sent it."

No, it wasn't. "My ex," she said, the word almost choking her. Before now she'd never felt *toxic*—like everything she touched became tainted with scandal. "I'm sorry."

"No, Ari," Hugh said. "Don't apologize. This isn't your fault. But we're really good at security around here. You can tell us if there's a problem. I'm going to ask our security team to make you a panic button." He held up his thumb and index fingers, about an inch apart. "It's a little device this big. You can wear it around your neck. If you push the button, Kattenberger Technologies routes the emergency to law enforcement and our private team, too."

Yikes. "That's really not necessary," she said. Knowing her luck, she'd push it by accident while stretching in child's pose and summon a battalion to her door.

Hugh chewed his lip. "I think it is. I hear you have an order of protection against this asshole?"

"I got one," she cleared her throat, hating that her personal troubles were now being aired at work. "But it hasn't been served to him yet. The process server I hired can't find him."

There was a deep silence while the GM probably questioned her judgment for getting involved with a jerk like Vince. "I want you to keep me apprised of the situation, okay? This guy involved my organization when he sent the photo to O'Doul."

Ari flinched. *So this is what complete mortification feels like*.

"The reason we employ such an excellent security staff is that our athletes draw all kinds of unwanted attention. That's not your fault," Hugh said again. "The moment you joined our organization, your security needs changed. There will always be assholes who want to try to use your access to the team for their own ends. That's why we're equipped to handle situations like this."

"I understand," she said, if only to hurry the discussion along.

Hugh made a note on his legal pad. "Would you mind providing my security team with a copy of your order of protection?"

"Sure," she said. *Anything. Let's just stop talking about it*.

"Thank you. I'm turning this over to the security team when we land. But I'll need you to report the photo to the police who opened the file after your break-in. I'll email you a scan of the front and back. If they want the original, they can have that in two days."

"I'll send it to them," she promised.

Hugh reached across and squeezed her hand. "Hang in there. Nobody's gonna let him near you."

"Thank you." She slid out of the booth to make as fast a getaway as possible.

"Ariana, I'm sorry," Patrick said quietly as she reached for the door.

She couldn't look him in the eye. *You should be*. Why the *hell* had he shown the photo to Hugh before discussing it with her in private?

Instead of answering, she beat a trail back to her seat, sat down and closed her eyes. A wave of nausea rolled through her stomach. Hugh hadn't said a word about the kiss, of course. But that didn't mean he had no opinion. Now he would see her as *that* employee, the one who fooled around with players. Would he tell Henry, too? *Ugh*. She could just *kill* Patrick for sharing that picture.

She spent the flight glued to her seat, hiding from everyone. Then she spent the afternoon in the bowels of the rink in Raleigh, avoiding people in general and Patrick specifically. He wasn't on her therapy list that day, which helped.

There was a team dinner at an Italian joint that night, but Ari didn't go. She slunk off by herself and took a hot yoga class at the health club adjacent to the hotel. After a quick shower, she treated herself to dinner at a falafel joint.

Back in the hotel lobby, she intended to go right upstairs and avoid the team. But no such luck. The players were milling around the glitzy fountain, discussing their plans for the evening.

"Let's pick a place with dancing this time," Castro suggested.

"Curfew is in an hour and a half," Beringer said. "Let's just pick someplace close."

Ari skirted them all and headed for the elevator bank. Where Patrick O'Doul stood waiting. *Crap!*

"Hi, sweetheart," he said, his eyes kind.

Don't call me that, she almost snapped. "Hi," she said instead. She was still mad at his breech of their private business.

He was worried, though, her conscience whispered. But still! He could have handled it differently.

The elevator doors parted and he waited for her to step inside. She pressed the button for her floor. "What floor?" she asked him.

"Seven."

She dropped her hand because seven was already lit. "I guess we're going to the same place."

Were they ever. While Ari was letting herself into room number 709, Patrick was swiping into 710.

"We're neighbors," he said.

"I see that." It came out a little more abrupt than she'd meant it to, and his face fell.

She went inside and hurled her bag at the bed and then climbed onto it. A minute later she heard a tap on the door adjoining the rooms. "Ari?"

Oh, boy. She got up and opened her side, but she didn't step out of the way to let him in. "What is it?"

"I'm sorry about the picture." He reached forward and squeezed her hand. "I know you hate that Hugh saw it. I think it's fine, but . . ."

"It's not *fine*. I don't want to be everyone's gossip nugget."

"I get that," he said quickly. "I'd never have shown that photo to Hugh without your permission."

She just stared at him. "Then why *did* you?"

"I didn't. This envelope got dropped off at the office with my name on it—no return address. We get that shit sometimes. Instead of passing it to me, they gave it to the security team. They opened it and showed it to Hugh."

"Oh."

Oh.

Hell. She felt stupid now.

Patrick's eyes went soft. "I'm sorry if you're embarrassed. But I won't apologize for kissing you. I can't, because I'm not sorry."

And, damn him, he stepped into the cramped space between their doors and kissed her *again*. His lips were soft and firm, and he tasted like mint and sex. She wished he didn't taste so freaking good. It just wasn't fair.

Ari made an unhappy noise, and then kissed him back.

With a chuckle, Patrick caught her chin in his hand. "Can I come in?"

"Absolutely not."

"Why? Nobody will know."

"That's what I used to assume, too."

He ruffled her hair. "The horse is already out of the barn, sweetheart. Why do the time if we can't do the crime?"

"It's just not a good idea."

He pulled her close and wrapped his arms around her. "I think it is," he purred into her ear. His fingers rubbed up and down her back. "You feel tight."

"It's been a stressful day."

"Too many massage appointments?"

"Too much shitty news."

"Mmm," he said, rubbing her back. It felt inconveniently marvelous. "Who massages *you?*"

She snorted. "Nobody."

"Uh-huh. Want a massage?"

"I don't know. Would it be a prelude to something else?"

"Is that a deal breaker?"

She smiled into the shoulder of his dress shirt. "Depends. How skillful is your massage technique?"

"For a guy who doesn't like to touch people, I'd say I'm pretty decent."

She laughed. "What the hell am I going to do with you?"

"I'm gonna let you find out." He backed her into the room, and she let him. He felt so *good*, though. The backs of her legs collided with the bed and she sat down fast.

"Wait here. Where's your table?" he asked, looking around. "Oh. There it is."

Amused, she watched him struggle with unfolding her massage table. It took him a couple of minutes, but he did it. Whistling, he went into her bathroom and returned with four towels. Two of them went onto the table. Two he chucked onto the bed. Then he came back to stand in front of her. "Okay, sweetheart. Time to strip."

She stood up and met his hungry gaze. "Really? You're going to massage me? Or are we, like, writing a porno flick right now?"

He grabbed her top in two hands and tugged. "A little of both. Just work with me." He lifted her shirt away, and she didn't miss the appreciative look he gave her breasts in their lace bra. "This is going to be so much fun."

Ari felt a sizzle right where it counted, and had to agree.

Did it matter now that Hugh knew about them? Would it even help if she stopped getting carried away with Patrick?

Those were questions for later. Because he'd reached around her body to unzip her skirt. She let it fall, then swept her tights down her body and all the way off.

He growled when he realized there was nothing underneath them.

Ari grabbed a towel off the bed and put it in front of her body. She lay down on her own massage table for the first time ever, letting the towel cover her lap and thighs. "Let's see your technique, big man."

"All right, miss. Are you comfortable on the table?" he asked. "Do you have any pain or trouble spots I need to know about?"

She laughed. "I'm fine, thanks."

"Good." He rubbed his hands together, warming them. "Let me know if you feel too much pressure at any point. Massage doesn't have to hurt to do good."

"Some smart person must have taught you that."

"The smartest." He came to stand beside her left thigh, then gently rolled the towel to expose her leg, just the way she would have done. Warm hands landed atop her quadriceps and began working their way down her leg with firm but gentle strokes.

How bizarre to be on the receiving end of a massage from him. She spent the first five minutes grinning.

But then, somehow, she forgot that this was sort of a joke. His hands moved in a soothing rhythm, and her mind began to drift. She thought about the yoga class she'd teach in the morning, and a new pose she wanted to try with the players.

He switched legs, and then moved down to her feet. "Omigod," she said as he rubbed her left foot in his big hands. "Arrrgh, that feels so good."

"Not too much pressure, miss?"

"Oh-hell-no," she stammered. "Don't stop."

"That's what all the ladies say."

She closed her eyes and sank back into the table. So this

was how it felt to be her client. The foot massage would be even better with oil, but she didn't want to stop him to fix that.

"Why don't you turn over now," he said softly, squeezing her ankle.

"Mmkay." She grabbed the towel and rolled. Her bra dug into her skin, though, so she reached down and unclipped it, then tossed it aside.

Patrick put the last towel across her legs to keep her warm, just as she might have done. His big hands landed on her back. First, he stroked both hands down her lats, fingers spread. Then he reached up to her shoulders and began to work them both at the same time.

A happy groan escaped from her throat. She remembered giving Patrick a speech about touch, and how it wasn't ever purely clinical. How true that was. She felt so *cared for* right now. This was blissful. His hands were warm and wonderful, and she never wanted it to end.

He swept the hair off her neck. And then—even while his hands continued to massage her shoulders—soft lips brushed her nape. His kiss was so light that she shivered. "Arms over your head," he rasped.

Ari complied, draping her arms up and letting her hands fall off the table. His hands began to stroke her sides, now. His fingertips dipped down to tease the edges of her breasts. "Oh," she sighed again. That felt delicious.

He kept it up, his fingers stroking down her ribcage, after reaching inward to tease her breasts with whisper-weight strokes. Wow. She squirmed against the towel. He'd barely touched any erogenous zones, and she was already turned on. There was something about lying here while he did all the work. *Biggest turn-on ever.*

He bent over her again and began to drop soft, open-mouthed kisses in a line down her spine. Goosebumps rose up on her skin, and she found herself holding her breath. A towel was whisked away, and broad hands landed on her bottom. He stroked over the sensitive skin, making her shiver. Then his mouth landed on the back of one thigh, and he kissed and licked his way into the seam between her legs.

"Oh . . . geez," she panted into the crook of her arm.

She heard a chuckle, and then a zipper unzipping. She kept her eyes shut, because the mystery of what he'd do next was half the fun. Though the sound of a condom wrapper opening gave her a happy throb.

He put a hand on her ass. "Checking in here, miss." His gravelly voice was at odds with the too-polite words. "How are you feeling?"

"Pretty great," she said honestly.

"Hmm." He kneaded her ass with both hands. "So I should continue?"

"Absolutely."

"Very well, miss."

Two hands wrapped around her knees and parted them suddenly, and Ari's breath caught in her chest.

He massaged his way up the backs of her legs, halting just at the juncture with her bottom. At first, his fingers just teased the sensitive skin of her buttocks. But then his thumbs swept into the slickness between her legs.

Ari mewled and gripped the edge of the table as he touched her, his fingers sliding over her clit and circling. Her legs twitched with the effort it took to stay reasonably still. She closed her eyes and buried her face in the towel underneath her. If he kept that up another thirty seconds she was going to come.

But just as she processed that thought, she began sliding—he'd grabbed the towels she was lying on and pulled. Slowly, she slid down the table until her toes touched the floor. He went back to work massaging her—working his hands at her hips, smoothing his fingers up the backs of her thighs. She tried to keep her breathing deep and even, but the anticipation was killing her.

All at once he lifted her hips an inch or so into the air and then filled her with his cock.

"Oh!" It was so unexpected and wonderfully dirty that she let out a shuddering moan.

For a moment, he didn't move at all, except to smooth his thumbs across her ass. Then he lowered her hips to the table and bent over her, elbows on either side of her body. His mouth hovered over her ear. "I'm going to fuck you, miss. Nice and deep."

"Y-yes," she stammered, waiting.

"Like this." He gave his hips a roll, and she could swear she saw stars.

She sank into the rhythm as he began to piston his hips. She was so helpless in this position—spread out for him, her toes barely touching the ground. There was no way she could really contribute, except to lie there and let him fuck her. His lips landed at the back of her neck, and he began to suck gently there. Meanwhile, his breath became more ragged.

"Turn over," he grunted after a time. "Want to watch you come."

She nodded, and he pulled out and flipped her over as if she weighed no more than one of the towels. Then he was looming over her, shrugging off his shirt and tossing it aside. That wall of abs and pecs rippled above her and she liked what she saw. He shoved his jeans and underwear down and kicked them off.

First he lifted one of her ankles onto his shoulder and then the other. Hers was a vulnerable position—her legs straight up in the air. But she forgot to feel ridiculous as he slid inside again, biting his lip and giving his head a shake. "Fuck. I'll never get enough of you." He picked up the pace right away, pistoning his hips, folding her body in half to lean in for a kiss.

"Harder," she demanded against his lips, just because she knew he'd listen.

He gave her a big, shit-eating grin. But this display of ego lasted only a few seconds. As he picked up the pace, he began to groan. Watching him inch closer to climax was the best sight in the world. His eyes were heavy lidded, and rough breaths sawed out of his chest. His big hands curled around her thighs. "Mmm," he grunted. "Fuck." One hand slid slowly down her leg until he reached her sex. He lowered his big head and focused on the place of their joining, licking his lips at the sight of his shaft moving in and out. Then he squeezed his eyes shut as his thumb began to circle her clit.

"Ohhh." Ari moaned and arched her back. It was coming, and it was going to be good.

"Miss." Patrick panted. "Touch your breasts."

She didn't need to be asked twice. She used both hands to cup herself, fingering her nipples.

"Fuck," he ground out, his blue eyes gleaming with appreciation. He swallowed roughly, his Adam's apple working, and he tipped his head back, as if the view was too much.

Hers was, too. The sight of his hard body pumping away over her was more than she could withstand. An electrical charge of pleasure shot down her body, tits to toes. With a greedy moan, she surrendered to waves and pulses of pleasure. Above her, Patrick shuddered and came, bending forward to grip the table, as if his legs might not hold him.

He gave a lengthy groan, and then all was still except for their heavy breathing.

"Wow," Ari said. There really were no better words.

Patrick said nothing at all. He pulled out, which seemed a pity. Then he scooped her up off the table and set her down on the bed. She lay there catching her breath for a second while he visited the bathroom. And when he came back, he nudged her, urging her over. Then he climbed into the bed, pulled the covers over both of them, and covered her with his body.

"Hi," he said.

"Hi." She stared up at him.

"I have a future in massage therapy, right?"

"Uh-huh. Your technique is nonstandard, but highly effective."

"You feel relaxed?"

"Yup."

He kissed her. It wasn't just a friendly kiss, either. He slanted his head and built the kiss slowly from a press of softened lips to a deep press of tangled tongues and mutual sighs. When they came up for air, he rolled onto his back, taking her with him.

They were silent for a few minutes. Ari lay still, trying not to let the day's earlier events back into her consciousness.

"I know you hate it that Hugh wants to get involved," he said. "But I think you should let him."

She groaned. "I know you're all just watching out for me. And it's not like I don't think he's a threat." *I can barely sleep in my house alone anymore.* "But now I'm the girl who fools around at work *and* the girl with the crazy ex."

"I know you worry." He gave her a squeeze. "But I don't think Hugh cares if we're together."

"We are not together," she said immediately. But the credibility of the statement was somewhat undermined by the fact that she was currently lounging on his big, naked body.

"Uh-huh," he said, too polite to call her on it. "But we should be."

"Why? Besides the outrageously good sex."

He smiled into her hair. "That's not a good enough reason?"

"Fuck no."

He laughed, and she bounced on his chest with the motion. "Because you're funny and smart. You're the coolest chick I know, and I like you a lot."

Whether she was ready to admit it or not, those words warmed her everywhere at once. "That's really nice of you to say, but I can't be *with* anybody right now. I haven't been single since I was twenty-one years old, and my only ex is on a crime spree. The universe might be trying to send me a message."

"I'm not that guy, Ari," he said, his voice low and serious all of a sudden.

"I know that," she whispered. But the truth was she *didn't* know Patrick O'Doul very well. And there wasn't any room in her life for romance. A girl had to bail all the water flooding into the boat before she could set a new course.

"Then you should also know that it's not like me to tell someone how much I like her. In fact, I want you to guess how many times I've done that."

"Wait, you keep track?"

"Guess so."

"I can't guess."

"Fine. One."

That shut her up. "One other time?"

"Nope. One including right now."

"Oh." Could he even be serious? "I'm honored."

He stroked her back. "You should be."

"We still can't date, though."

"Okay."

She lifted her head. "Okay?" She'd expected him to argue.

He palmed her head and brought it back down onto his chest. "I'll take what I can get, sweetheart. Now get some sleep. I've got a game tomorrow."

And even though she'd rather not give him the wrong idea by obeying his every whim, it was late, damn it. His body was warm and comfortable. So she slept on it.

FIFTEEN

Standings: 3rd place in the Metropolitan Division
13 Regular Season Games to Go

O'Doul woke up curled around Ari's body, amused with himself. Who knew that sharing a bed with a woman was so easy? Like rolling off a log.

He spent a couple of minutes just admiring her in the morning light which filtered through the hotel drapes. But he had an early morning skate to get to. So he eased away, tucking the covers behind her back, so she wouldn't be cold. He tiptoed into his own room to start the day.

Forty minutes later, at the rink, he stretched his hip flexors carefully. His body had an easy looseness which was either attributable to a good night's sleep or intense sexual gratification. Or both. When it was time to hit the ice, he skated as hard as he dared.

"You look good this morning," Coach said after the final whistle blew.

"Feel good," he agreed.

"You okay to fight tonight?"

"Sure," he said automatically. He'd have to be.

But on his way down the tunnel toward the visitors' locker room, he passed DiCoda, Carolina's enforcer, on the way to his own team's ice time. "Hey, man!" O'Doul greeted him. DiCoda was one of the good guys in the league—the kind of guy who'd beat the shit out of you and then buy you and your whole team drinks. People came to fighting all different ways, but whatever DiCoda's reasons, the man did not seem to be brimming over with excess aggression.

"Hey!" DiCoda grabbed him into a backslapping hug. "Got a sec?"

"Sure. What's up?"

DiCoda winced. "My jaw is acting up again." He raised a hand to his face. "Might need surgery, actually. Can't fight you tonight."

"Fuck, I'm sorry."

"Yeah, thanks." The other man made a grim face. DiCoda was a true enforcer—he was really only on the roster to fight. The guy had something like ten career goals in as many years. The awkward truth hung between them. If DiCoda couldn't fight again, his career was finished.

"So . . ." O'Doul cleared his throat. "Are your guys gonna stay in line tonight? I don't want to have to throw down with some kid who doesn't know any better."

DiCoda grinned. "I don't think any of 'em have plans to take you on, so I'll tell 'em not to piss you off."

"Good man," O'Doul said, squeezing the guy's elbow through his pads.

"Later," DiCoda said, giving him one more smile.

O'Doul trudged on toward the locker rooms, worrying about all the ways the earth kept shifting under his feet.

Staying healthy in a fight no longer looked to be today's top problem. But there were other issues. And one had a name—Vince Giardi. The guy was only going to make more trouble. Forget his strained hip flexors—that guy was his most likely career-ender.

That fucking photograph had been meant as a warning to both him and Ari. The words on the back—YOU STUPID FUCK—made that very clear, even if neither Hugh Major nor Ari understood their significance.

O'Doul was willing to stipulate that Vince was right. He'd been a very stupid fuck indeed the night he'd bought pills from that guy. The message on the back of the photo was like a bill coming due. One that O'Doul couldn't pay. If Vince thought he could get Ari back by threatening him— it was never going to happen. She was done with Vince whether they went on to become a couple or not. He'd do whatever it took to keep that rat away from her.

Though he got a chill just wondering what the hell Vince wanted. Hush money? Maybe. Though anyone with half a brain could tell you that paying a blackmailer was pointless.

In the visitors' locker room, he pulled off his skates while trying to imagine the worst-case scenario. So far as O'Doul could tell, Vince was a man with nothing to lose. He'd already lost Ari. And it sounded as though the police had found evidence of the man's involvement in drug dealing in that storage room. He was probably desperate. And a desperate man was the most dangerous kind. He might do anything.

If Vince told the cops that O'Doul had bought pills, he'd be questioned for sure.

Sitting there on the bench, he had another thought, one that made him feel guilty. The cops had already met him the other morning at Ari's door. If he told the detective that Vince was only trying to smear him out of jealousy, he'd sound *very* believable.

Only an asshole uses his fame and his favorite girl as a cover for the dumbest mistake he'd ever made. But without a doubt, he'd lie if it came down to it. *What? Who? Me? Never heard of the stuff.*

So there was a happy thought.

He showered and hopped onto the bus back to the hotel with his teammates. They were greeted in the lobby at nine thirty by Jimbo, one of the roadies who helped lug gear around on their road trips. "Hey man. Where's breakfast?"

The kid jerked a thumb over his shoulder. "In the conference room behind me. That's why I'm standing here like an idiot, to make sure you guys find it."

O'Doul grabbed Jimbo's shoulders and turned him toward the breakfast room. "Come on, then. Let's eat. Anyone misbehaving today? Do I have to knock any heads?"

"Nope. The charter company didn't even lose anyone's luggage. But the day is young."

At the buffet, O'Doul filled his plate with scrambled eggs and sausage. He chose two grapefruit halves and poured himself a cup of coffee. When he sat down with Jimbo at the center table, he noticed Ari hovering by the buffet, picking up a cup of yogurt and a plastic spoon. She looked up to catch him watching her.

Busted. He gave her a smile and pointed at the empty seat next to his.

She gave her head a little shake and dropped her eyes to her portable breakfast. A moment later, she exited the room.

We are not together, Ari had said last night. The words didn't leave a lot of room for argument. He tucked into his breakfast, wondering how he might change her mind.

Leo Trevi took the seat that Ari passed up, and Beringer, Beacon, and Castro filled in the rest of the table. "How's tricks, captain?" Leo asked. "Didn't see you at the bar last night."

"Too tired," he lied. If Ari wanted privacy, he'd do his best. "Hey—college boy. I got a question."

"Shoot."

"What do you do if the girl you're meant to be with won't date you?"

Leo laughed and put down his fork. "Well, if you're me, you date people you really don't like for five or six years until she comes around."

"Huh." It was nice to remember that even College Boy didn't always have his shit together. But it didn't help with his problem. "Who has a better answer?" he demanded of the table.

"Well," Beacon said, pushing sausages around on his plate, "you can get her pregnant when you're both eighteen and clueless."

"Oh, man," Castro said under his breath.

Beacon's luck was widely acknowledged to be the worst on the team. He'd had an unhappy marriage to his high school sweetheart, then *almost* got divorced because both he and his wife were in love with other people. Before the paperwork went through, his poor wife was diagnosed with a really awful cancer that spent a long year killing her. Now, at thirty-two, he was a widower and a single father to a grieving thirteen-year-old daughter.

And one wondered why O'Doul had stayed single his whole life.

"Cap'n, *why* won't this girl date you?" Beringer asked. "You're not my type or anything, but I'll bet the ladies see a rich guy who's not *too* ugly. The world is full of women who'd make time in their schedule for you."

He snorted. "Thanks, B. My face isn't the problem. She just got out of a relationship that ended badly. Doesn't wanna go back there."

"That's cool, though," Castro argued. "You can just be her rebound guy. Plenty of sex, no commitment. Sounds good to me."

"Nah," O'Doul argued. "I want more."

"But why?" Castro wanted to know. "In Canada we have this saying—you don't need your own rink if you can get ice time for free."

O'Doul took a deep drink of his coffee and wondered if anyone on his team knew a single thing about women.

"So, she just got out of a bad scene," Leo Trevi said thoughtfully. "Maybe her ex had some bad habits. Maybe he didn't treat her very well."

You have no idea.

". . . I think the solution might be to turn on the romance

taps full blast, man. You have to woo her so she sees how different you are from the other loser."

"Like . . . with candlelight and shit?" he asked.

"Maybe jewelry," Castro suggested. "Chicks like bling."

"Not all of them," Leo pointed out. "My girl doesn't like jewelry, because it gets in her way when she feels like punishing me on the tennis court."

O'Doul considered and then immediately rejected the jewelry idea. Ari didn't wear anything flashy. She sometimes wore a simple silver chain around her neck. He'd often caught himself admiring the way it sat against her slender throat.

But bling it was not.

"Okay, listen." He slapped the table. "Jimbo!"

The younger man looked up from his pancakes. "Whadd-aya need?"

"Get out the parking tickets. Every player gets one."

"What? Why?" Castro griped.

"Everyone here owes me an idea. You all have five minutes to write down the best way to romance a woman. If your idea is decent, you don't owe anything to the kitty. If your idea is shit, it's a twenty dollar fine."

There were several groans. Beacon took out his wallet, peeled off a twenty and tossed it over to Jimbo. "Let's just save time." But everyone else took a ticket from Jimbo as he passed them out.

"Doulie," Castro complained. "We don't know this chick. How are we supposed to guess what she likes?"

"She's, uh . . ." He had to think of a way to describe her without giving her identity away. "Well, she's smarter than me." He held up a hand. "Don't say it—that's pretty much everyone." That got him some chuckles. "Okay, she's thoughtful. Classy. Not into bling."

Castro shook his head. "Bummer. It's easier when they're into bling. Expensive, but easier."

Pens were dug out of bags and shared. It was quiet for a moment while two dozen heads bent over their work. O'Doul finished his breakfast while his teammates wrote down their suggestions, and then Jimbo collected them.

"You have to read 'em out loud," Castro demanded. "We're entitled to a little entertainment for our trouble."

"I'll read 'em," Jimbo volunteered. He picked up the first card, which was Leo's. *"Buy her treats from her favorite bakery."*

"Not bad, College Boy," O'Doul said.

"Always works for me," Leo shrugged.

If only O'Doul knew what Ari's favorite treat was, it would be a winner. "Next."

Jimbo flipped a ticket. *"Write her a poem."*

"Christ, have you met me?" O'Doul grabbed the paper from Jimbo's hand. "Crikey puts twenty into the kitty."

When Jimbo read off the next ticket, O'Doul almost fined Bayer for suggesting that he *sing her a song.*

"But you always do okay on karaoke night," the other player argued. "And I saw it in a movie once. Chicks dig that shit. Doesn't matter if you do it well. Only that you do it."

There were murmurs of agreement. "Someone pass me a piece of paper," Castro announced. "Some of this shit might be useful later. I'm gonna take notes."

"Buy her shoes," was the next suggestion Jimbo read. *"Chicks love shoes."*

"No," Leo argued. "They like *shopping* for shoes. Would you like it if somebody else picked out your shoes? I wouldn't."

"Good point," O'Doul agreed, tossing the idea aside. A whole room full of dudes, and not a clue among 'em. "Next!"

"Sully says, *Take her ice skating,*" Jimbo announced next.

"Gosh, how ever did you think of that?" he asked the backup goalie dryly.

"Dude. Your skating is better than your poetry. And if she can't skate, she'll have to hold onto your hands."

"Awwwwww!" the whole room chorused. Several wadded-up napkins were hurled at Sully, but O'Doul filed the suggestion under maybe.

The next card said: *"Cook her dinner."*

"Not bad, Massey," O'Doul had to admit. "I can do linguini with clam sauce." Then again, Ari was Italian. Maybe his linguini wouldn't stack up so well. Another maybe.

Next Jimbo read off two travel suggestions. *Take her to Europe. Take her to Disney World.*

"Those are fine ideas—three months from now," he growled.

"Have some patience," the contributing player urged. "Not my fault it's play-off season. Don't take my twenty bucks."

Jimbo read *lingerie* off the next card.

Just as O'Doul was picturing Ari in a smoking hot negligee, Castro began shaking his head violently. "Bad idea, man. Seriously *dangerous*. I got into so much trouble for buying my girl size large once when she was a medium. If you're not a hundred percent sure of the size, you might not get any lovin' for a week."

Jesus. There was more risk in romance than he'd realized.

The next suggestion wasn't bad. *Get her a book. Shows you're thinking about her beautiful mind, and not just her beautiful tits.* And, hey, there had to be something in the bookstore she'd like, right? That was a keeper.

There were two cards left. The first one said simply: *Edible underwear.* "What the fuck?"

"Wait—" Castro held up a hand. "Who's eating whose underwear?"

He threw the card over his shoulder. "Jimbo—fine Smithy. Okay—last one. *Buy her birthstone earrings. Not only are they pretty but it shows that you know when her birthday is.*"

"Whoa!" Leo said. "Sneaky! I like it. Whose idea was that?"

O'Doul took the card from Jimbo's hand. "There's no name. Good idea, though. Anyone want to take credit?"

Slowly, Jimbo raised his own hand, his face reddening, and everybody laughed.

"Christ, kid. How old are you, anyway?"

"Nineteen."

There was more laughter, and somebody called out "Jimbo for president!"

"Wait," Castro said, bent over his notes. "What came right before the underwear? I might have missed a couple."

O'Doul gathered the cards into his hand. "Get your own ideas. It's been a pleasure, boys. We're watching tape in forty-five minutes."

He walked out of the breakfast room wondering if there was a bookstore nearby.

SIXTEEN

Ari had mixed feelings when she woke up alone. She'd promised herself to steer clear of men. And then she'd gone and had wild monkey sex on her massage table and clutched Patrick all night long as if he were her personal teddy bear.

It was glorious. And also a huge mistake.

Anyone would need a couple hours to herself to get her head on straight. That's why she'd avoided him at breakfast, choosing instead to head over to the rink to chat with the trainers and set up her table for her first massage appointments. It was going to be a busy day, too. She gave three massages in a row before it was time for Patrick to show up for his.

But before he appeared, Hugh Major stuck his head into her treatment room. Ari's anxiety level cranked up by several notches. "Good afternoon," she said weakly.

"Afternoon, Ariana. Can I see you for a moment?"

"Of course." For the second time in twenty-four hours she felt like a kid reporting to the principal's office. Or, in this case, a little cell of a room the opposing team had allocated for management to use while they were in town.

"Have a seat," Hugh said. "I just got a FedEx for you. It's a panic button. Have a look."

"Oh. Thank you." What else could she say? She would have preferred to live out her life without knowing that panic buttons existed.

He handed it to her. It was a little silver-toned oval with a sliding cover. She pushed the cover with her thumb, and it moved aside to reveal a bright red button.

"It's well designed, so that you can't trip it by accident," he said. "Press the button now—it's not activated yet."

"Okay." Ari pushed the switch, and it slid into its alternate position with a click. "I see. And I could clip this to my handbag."

"Exactly. Or your belt at home."

"Well . . ." she cleared her throat. "I'll carry it, if you think I should. But it seems like an unnecessary expense."

Hugh grinned. "One of my many jobs is buying all kinds of insurance for the team. And I buy a ton of it, always hoping that it's a complete waste of money. Welcome to my world."

It was hard to argue with that logic. "So what happens if I *do* flip the switch?"

"Several people will be alerted at once. Law enforcement at the precinct house. Also me, Rebecca—she volunteered . . ."

"Wow. Seems like a lot of trouble," Ari said, embarrassed.

"Not as much trouble as if something happened to you. Take it. Wear it. I know it's not something you wanted, but we can't have anyone using your position in the Bruisers organization as some kind of nasty leverage. If you push that button there are a few other people who will be notified, including whichever Kattenberger security team is on duty. And"—he cleared his throat—"Patrick O'Doul. If that's okay with you."

She felt her face pinking up. "If he doesn't mind."

"His idea," Hugh said. "He lives so close to your house. But it's totally up to you."

Ari took a deep breath. "Can I speak frankly, sir? If you would rather I didn't continue with Mr. O'Doul as my client,

I would understand completely." This was a speech she'd never wanted to give. By admitting her complication with a player, she'd just made herself a less valuable employee.

But he looked thoughtful, not angry. "Ari, give me a second while I figure out how to put this in a way that won't have the entire HR department on my ass." The manager crossed his beefy arms in front of his chest. "Okay, it's like this. Everyone raves about your work. They even show up for fricking *yoga* without complaint. I'm happy. The owner is happy. I don't need to change a thing. But if you notify me at any point that you're not comfortable treating a player on my team, other arrangements will be made. No questions asked."

"Thank you, sir," she said quietly.

He raised an eyebrow. "Do you wish to request a transfer of any player to another therapist?"

"Um, it's not necessary to make any changes on my account, sir."

He heaved a sigh of relief. "Good. Because Henry has been trying to get O'Doul to accept treatment for that hip for *weeks*. I need that player healthy and in fighting form. Whatever you can do to keep him showing up for therapy, I'm on board . . ." His eyes narrowed suddenly, and he tipped his face upward, toward the ceiling tiles. "You know, that didn't come out the way I meant it."

She hopped out of her chair. "I knew what you meant, sir."

"Fuck." He shook his big head. "HR hates me already. I just meant that using your professional skill, you'd . . ."

"I get it," she said a little too brightly. "And now if you'll excuse me, I have a whole list of players to keep in fighting form."

He gave her a salute. "Go forth and conquer muscle soreness."

When Ari slipped back into her assigned treatment room, she was startled to find Patrick stretched out on the table, hands behind his head, looking as relaxed as anyone ever had on her table. "Hi!" he called out as she entered.

"Hi," she breathed. Just the sight of his broad shoulders

gave her an inappropriate shimmy through all the, er, lower chakras. It was only hours ago when he'd loomed above her as they . . .

Yikes. *Focus, Ari.* "You feeling okay this morning?" she asked. "How's your pain?" A flush touched her neck now. In her own questions she heard an echo of Patrick's faux massage therapist queries last night.

"I feel like a million bucks, honestly. Skated well this morning. Had a good breakfast. No complaints." She braced herself for a joke or an innuendo referencing the other reasons he might be feeling good, but none came. "Go ahead— do your worst," he said instead. "I'm ready."

"Good," she choked out, rolling up her sleeves.

"Oh—don't forget the music," he said. "Got any Clapton?"

"Sure." She was flustered now, and for absolutely no reason. Patrick was behaving like a perfect gentleman. She grabbed her battered iPod and scrolled to a Clapton playlist another player had sent her last year. "Wonderful Tonight" came on. Getting down to business, she rolled back Patrick's towel a few crucial inches and found bare skin. She oiled up her hands and put them to his thigh. "We only have thirty minutes," she said. They'd given her a bunch of short sessions this afternoon. "So I have to get right to the trouble spots."

"That's fine, sweetheart," he said, his voice low and happy. As she worked, he let out a sigh. Her hands traveled over his tensor fascia muscle and down his lower quads. She knew this body so well now. Not just its form—she was well acquainted with the muscles and tendons of much of the team—but its responses. She felt an unexpected tenderness when he took another deep breath and then relaxed.

It was totally normal to feel all gooey inside when one of your clients was feeling better, right?

"Let's have you on your side," she said eventually. "Let's work that hip."

He rolled for her. She worked his adductors without a flinch from him. Although he seemed to be . . . counting something to himself?

"Does that hurt?"

"Nope," he said cheerfully. "Just distracting myself with some hockey stats."

"Why? Because of pain?"

He chuckled. "My body has other reactions to your hands besides pain, sweetheart. Just trying to keep things professional."

"Ah. Roll onto your stomach for me." When he was face down, she made sure his backside and legs were covered, and she went to work on his lower back. "Remember when I gave you that speech about how everyone has different reactions to massage? Some people fall asleep, some people cry . . ."

He spoke into the circular face cradle. "Uh huh."

"There's probably a dent in my table from all the boners."

His back shook under her hands as he laughed. "Whose? I'll have to kill them now. Shame, too, right before play-offs."

She gave him a playful pat on the back. "Don't say that. Sexual response is one of many possible results of muscle relaxation. It only means that the client's subconscious trusts me. I pretend not to notice, and life goes on."

"My subconscious has a little more to go on than the rest of your clients," he pointed out, his voice muffled.

"I know. That's why if you wanted to switch to another therapist, Hugh said he'd make other arrangements. No questions asked."

Patrick picked his head up and craned his neck to look at her. "*Fuck* no. You're the only one who gets to touch me."

"Okay," she said, pressing on his shoulder, asking him to lie flat again. "It was only a suggestion. I was trying to make you more comfortable."

"Not possible," he muttered. "I only want you, Ari. For this and all things."

Surprise made her hands go still for a moment. Her poor, battered heart warmed at his words, even if she didn't know what to do with that sentiment right now. After a moment she remembered to breathe, and to finish up Patrick's massage. She ended at his neck and shoulders, kneading the muscle there while he made a happy groan.

When she had to announce that their time was up, he peeled himself reluctantly off the table, towels around his waist. "Thank you, sweetheart," he said quietly.

"You're welcome, as always. See you for yoga later," she reminded him.

He gave her a wink and was gone.

What am I going to do with you? she'd asked him last night. Today she was no closer to an answer. She shut off the Clapton playlist and removed the linens from her table, wiping it down and fitting a fresh sheet over it for the next client on her list. It wasn't until she picked up her printed schedule that she found the shiny little book hiding underneath it.

Ari grinned the moment she saw the cover. *Yoga Cats* was the title. And the photograph was a tabby cat in warrior pose. She flipped it open. Each page was a different kitty in a different pose. Hysterical. And how funny that Patrick had left her a *gift*. The whimsical, lighthearted gesture surprised her.

Still smiling, she tucked the cat book into her knapsack just as her next client walked in for his appointment.

That night, the team won the Carolina game. And two nights later they picked up another point by taking Philly into overtime. Even though their home-bound flight was late, the team was jubilant. Ari fell asleep in her seat to the sound of happy smack talk and play-off predictions.

At the airport at midnight, she made sure to jump into a cab before Patrick had a chance to offer to drop her at home. Not that his company wasn't appealing. But she needed to show a little self-restraint.

Before her taxi made it off the highway, though, she found a text from him on her phone. *Can you let me know when you make it home safely?*

I'll be fine, she replied. *And I have this fancy new panic button just in case.*

Humor me?

She did that far too often.

When the cab dropped her off in front of her building, she paid the driver with her corporate credit card and then marched boldly inside. "Hi, honey, I'm home!" she called into the stillness.

Luckily, nobody answered.

She took her panic button with her upstairs, but it seemed silly. She was all the way in bed before she remembered Patrick's texts. She grabbed her phone off the nightstand and sleepily replied. *Home and safe in bed.*

Can I come over and verify?

Nope.

Bummer. Sleep well, sweetheart.

As she read the words, she could hear his gravelly voice pronouncing them in her ear. The man had bad timing, but he was more appealing than she'd like to admit.

She fell asleep with a smile on her face.

SEVENTEEN

Standings: 3rd Place
11 Regular Season Games Remaining

O'Doul spent much of his downtime that week working on his list of romantic ploys to get Ariana to agree to date him.

She'd once told him that meditation would prevent him from worrying about fights—that it would give his monkey something to do. Fortunately, his mental monkey also enjoyed pestering Becca for inside information.

"Which cookie place?" he prodded on his third phone call to her.

"One Girl Cookies. That place on Main."

"What's the best thing they have?"

"Look, Doulie—I have a meeting. All the cookies are great, and the whoopie pies are awesome."

"Huh. Don't know what that is, but I like the name."

"I'll bet. The corner of Main and Water, buddy. Her birth month is August and she's a size small. But I've got to go, okay?"

She hung up on him, but he had the ammo he needed. Thanks to Google, he learned that the peridot—whatever the fuck that was—was the birthstone for people born in August. So his mental monkey got busy searching the web for peridot jewelry.

Not that he was an expert, but a lot of jewelry on the Internet was really freaking ugly. He'd have to dig deep. But he liked a challenge.

At any rate, he didn't expend the usual amount of energy worrying about his upcoming fight against Columbus. And who knows—maybe three hours of YouTube review wouldn't have changed the outcome.

But the outcome was pretty painful.

Late in the second period, Leo Trevi tripped over an opponent. The guy's glove fell off and his hand was sliced by Leo's skate. It was a fluke, O'Doul had never seen anything like it. There was blood all over the ice. No penalty was called against Trevi, but the other player left the game.

Their guy challenged O'Doul to a fight immediately. And he accepted just as quickly. That's how these things were done.

O'Doul won the fight. Sort of. But their guy was a leftie. He got a champion grip on O'Doul's sweater, and the blows rained down faster than he could weather. The tunnel of silence that always descended on him during a fight had a different quality tonight. It sounded like a high-pitched screech. He didn't think he could hang on anymore under the assault. So he wound up one more good punch and let it fly.

When he watched the tape later, he'd see himself get up off the ice a few seconds after they both went down, and stagger off. But that's not how it had felt at the time. O'Doul didn't really come to until he was sitting on a table in the medical bay, while the team doctor stitched his face back together.

"Ow, fuck." Those were his first truly conscious words.

"I'm almost done," the doctor said.

Somebody's hands—Jimbo's as it would turn out—tightened on his jaw, helping him hold still.

"What's the shcore?" he slurred.

"Dunno," the doctor said. "Doesn't really matter at the moment."

He disagreed. He almost never left the rink after a fight, but here he was for the second time this month, sitting on his ass while the game went on. *We'd better not be losing* was all he could think.

They did, though, damn it. Columbus sank one right before the buzzer, so they couldn't make it into overtime for the extra point, either. His face throbbed and his hip throbbed and his team had needed this win.

And since Boston—still their closest points rival—won a game tonight, Brooklyn was back in fourth.

O'Doul took a tediously awkward shower while trying to keep the spray off his face, dressed his aching body slowly, and fought off all the lingering attention of the training team. "I'll ice it at home," he said a dozen times. It was late and he was too beat to listen to any more advice.

He was tying his shoes in the coat room when someone put a hand on the back of his head. His old reflexes kicked in, and he jerked upright, knocking the hand away.

"Jesus," Ari said, jumping a half step back.

When he looked into her startled eyes his stomach fell. "Sorry. Didn't know it was you." *Hell.* He never wanted to *scare* her.

She laughed, but it sounded nervous. "Wow. Only one of us is allowed to be jumpy at a time, okay?"

"You're jumpy?" He stood up. "Is something wrong?"

She crossed her arms protectively across herself. "I'm fine. I thought I saw a certain van in the neighborhood tonight on my way here. I'm probably just paranoid, but I was going to ask you to walk me home."

"Of course I will." He threw his suit jacket on. "Did the asshole get served with his restraining order yet?"

"Nope. They still can't find him. I'm trying not to feel so paranoid, but the whole situation just creeps me out."

"You're not paranoid," he said. "That guy is *scum*." His head gave a fresh stab of pain, thanks to Mr. Vince de-Scumbag. That guy was like a cockroach. He had both O'Doul and Ari in his sights, and he wasn't going away unless O'Doul stomped him like a bug. If he ever got the chance, he would take it. Gleefully.

Funny how he could look forward to the one fight that could get him in serious trouble, while he dreaded all the ones he was paid two million a year to take.

"Let's go," he said, with a hand on Ari's shoulder.

There was nobody else around by now. They'd all moved on to the bar. His phone was full of teammates' texts asking if he was all right, and whether he was coming to the bar. He'd just have to catch up with them in the morning.

When he and Ari got out of the stadium, it was raining. And here in downtown Brooklyn they were a mile from home, as opposed to the couple of blocks they walked home from the practice rink in Dumbo. But the taxi gods smiled. A lit roof light swung into view and Patrick darted for the curb and threw his arm in the air. And, *fuck*. His neck spasmed. One of the joys of getting a drubbing was slowly discovering all the secondary pains as the night wore on.

The taxi came to a halt in front of him. Gritting his teeth, he opened the door, waving Ari across the wet pavement and into the back seat.

After she slid inside, he carefully folded his body into the car and shut the door. Everything throbbed. It was time for more ibuprofen or a nice glass of Scotch. Maybe both. "Can you take us to the corner of Front and Hudson Ave, pal? Thanks."

"What's wrong with your neck?" Ari asked.

"Nothing." Though the palm he had clamped on it made him a liar. He dropped his hand and sighed. "Did you see that mutual ass kicking we gave each other?"

"I didn't watch the whole thing."

"No?"

She looked away, out the rainy window. "Don't like to see anyone hit you."

"Aw, Ariana! Careful, sweetheart. I might start thinking you like me." He gave her knee a squeeze.

"I do like you. Never said I didn't." She put her hand on top of his.

"But you don't want to date me. Guess I didn't get any prettier tonight."

She turned to look at him, and her expression gentled. "It's not you. I'm not *dating*. Period."

He flipped his hand over to catch her softer one. He rubbed his thumb across her small palm and smiled. "Are you going to come upstairs with me and look after my neck?"

"Do you need me to?"

"No." He picked up her hand and kissed the palm. "But I want you to."

"Aren't you exhausted?"

"Yeah." He kissed her wrist. "Never too tired for your company, though."

She turned her head quickly, hiding her face from him. "Okay."

"Pal." He leaned forward to speak into the hole in the driver's plexi partition. "Can you stop at Bridge Street instead?"

"Sure thing."

The rest of the short trip passed in silence. O'Doul paid the fare and held the door open for Ariana. "If you change your mind I'll walk you home." Hell. She'd asked him for an escort, and he'd dragged her back to his lair.

"I'm good. Don't worry."

The doorman welcomed them home, and Ari glanced around the lobby. "Who else lives in your building, anyway?"

"Hugh Major, Coach Worthington . . ."

"*What?*"

"I'm kidding, yogi. You clearly don't want to be seen with a guy who has eight new stitches."

"Eight?" she gasped.

He waved a hand, dismissing her concern. "Leo and Georgia. Massey. Castro. I think that's it right now. This building is convenient as hell. But nobody has as short a commute as you."

"My commute is a New Yorker's dream," Ari agreed. "When I heard about this job opening up I thought I'd never get it. Everything about it was too perfect. When Henry called to tell me I could have it if I wanted it, it was really hard not to start squealing like a preteen at her slumber party."

O'Doul laughed, and it made his ribs hurt. He escorted her out of the elevator and down the hallway to his door. The sound of his key unlatching the door was the best thing he'd heard all day. "I'll get the Scotch," he said. "You're in, right?"

"Sure," she said. "But let me get it. You sit."

He hesitated. "I didn't invite you up to wait on me."

"God, I know. Just sit down already. My own neck hurts just looking at you. Your gait is off."

She stalked into his kitchen, and his eyes followed her. "The Scotch is . . ."

"Over the refrigerator," she finished.

Right. He took off his suit coat and hung it up in his bedroom closet.

"You have tequila, too," she called.

"Uh-huh. There are limes in the fridge."

"How would you feel about a margarita?" she asked. "I do good work."

"I'm in," he said. "If you're mixing it, I'm drinking it." He dropped trou and stepped into a pair of sweatpants. He took off his damn tie and finally began to feel like a human.

She was pouring their drinks from his cocktail shaker over ice when he joined her in the kitchen. How odd to see a woman standing there, humming to herself in his space. He liked it. A lot. He put a hand to the back of her neck.

"Thank you, sweetheart. Are you hungry at all? I could order something from the twenty-four hour diner." He usually ate at the bar after a home game.

"I'm good, but you go ahead."

He decided to skip it. "Let's sit." He picked up both cocktails.

"Hang on." Ari stopped him so that she could add a wedge of lime to the rim of each glass. "There." She was so freaking cute.

He hid his smile by turning away, carrying their drinks toward the sofa.

She sat beside him. "Here's to the end of a shitty night."

"We drink to that a lot, you and me." He touched his glass to hers.

"Truth." She took a sip, and then another one. "Let me work on your neck." She handed him her glass and got up, skirting the sofa to stand behind him. "Put your elbows up on the back of the sofa."

He did it, a glass in each hand. "This's just so you can reach your drink, right?"

"Exactly." She removed the glass from his hand, took a sip and put it back. "Okay, incoming."

Her hands landed at his shoulders. With sturdy pressure, she loosened him up. Then she began to work closer to his sore neck. He felt himself tighten up automatically.

"Come on, O'Doul. Not this again."

"Sorry." He sighed. "I'll be a good boy."

The next thing he felt was a single, soft kiss below his ear. "I know you can't stand having weak spots," she whispered. "Just work with me."

Her breathy voice made his cock stiffen immediately. "Okay," he said.

He closed his eyes and focused on Ari's presence behind him. He listened for the soft huffs of her breath as she worked. And he paid attention to the warmth radiating from her body. He let himself remember that night in her hotel room. Both of them naked . . .

Everything above his waist began to relax, while every-thing below his waist began to firm up. He'd invented a new relaxation technique—Horny Meditation. He leaned into her touch, and bit by bit his muscles were smoothed into submission by the heat and friction of her touch.

"We'll leave it there for now," she said, patting his neck.

She sat down in the distant corner of the sofa. He had to stretch to hand over her drink. Ah, well. He pointed the remote at the TV and put on a late-night talk show. He drained his margarita and then lifted her feet into his lap. "Your turn."

"Mmm," she said as he squeezed the ball of her foot. "That is nice. But I didn't strain anything tonight. Watching hockey isn't very tiring. And the owner's box has these warm Brazilian cheese puffs. I think I ate a dozen of them . . . Mmm."

"What's it like in the box with Nate Kattenberger?" he asked. He'd always been curious about that, and Nate in general.

Ari offered him her other foot with a smile. "It's great. Some nights he gets all quiet and broody, but we can never tell if it's the game or if he's busy reinventing the Internet in that big brain of his. Tonight he was in a fun mood, joking with Becca and Georgia and taking bets. We only wager pretzels, though. Georgia won the pot by guessing that Leo Trevi would be the first to score. Then she screamed her lungs out when he did. Nate says he's deaf in one ear now."

"Sounds like fun. I guess I thought he'd be all crazy intense up there. He's got more money invested in the team than the GDP of a developing nation."

"He *is* intense," Ari said, leaning her head back against the sofa arm. "About everything. But so are sports fans everywhere. Walk past any sports bar and there are guys screaming at the TV. Do you feel like Nate is more entitled to his intensity?"

"Sure he is. He signs my checks." He rubbed the arch of

her foot. "We're all just hangin' by a thread, babe. It's not just you who worries about job security. It's every guy on that team. Every day."

She flashed him a sympathetic smile, and he felt it in his belly.

"What else does Nate do on game night?" he asked. "Is he superstitious? Does he carry a rabbit's foot or rosary beads?" Hockey was sick with superstition. Every player had something—Massey took one specific route to the stadium on game night. Castro ate a peanut butter and strawberry jam sandwich before every game. (It had to be strawberry. Nobody knew why.)

"Let's see. He turns off his phone during the games. Does that count? He seems like the kind of guy who never unplugs. Oh—and he never has a drink until the third period, and only if we're losing."

O'Doul snorted. "Bottoms up tonight, then."

"The man can drink, too. And after four Scotches he's still sharp as a tack." Ari grinned.

"I've noticed that. Crazy." He gave a giant yawn.

"You're beat. Let's go to sleep."

"Sorry," he said, scrubbing the uninjured side of his face. "I'm not a fun host. I'll walk you home if you want me to."

"It's almost one in the morning," Ari pointed out. "Let's crash." She got up and collected their empty glasses.

He came up behind her in the kitchen and gave her a little squeeze. Is this how it felt to be half of a couple? "Thanks for working out my kinks."

She turned her head, amusement on her face. "Patrick, you are still full of them."

Smart girl. She had his number. "Leave those," he said, referring to the glasses in the sink. "Borrow anything in the bathroom. There are probably a couple of those airplane toothbrushes in the medicine cabinet."

Ten minutes later he switched off the lamp beside his bed and slipped between the sheets. Ari was already dozing on the other pillow, curled up in his *Brooklyn: Fuhgged-daboudit* T-shirt. It had draped practically to her knees when she put it on.

"Good night, sweetheart," he whispered. She made a soft, indistinct noise of agreement. He leaned over and kissed her temple, just because he could.

Then he hooked her feet between his and fell asleep.

EIGHTEEN

Standings: 4th Place
10 Regular Season Games Remaining

Ari didn't begin to wake up until the room was flooded with natural sunshine. Keeping her eyes closed against the light, she took stock.

Her back was pressed pleasantly against a hard, hot chest. And a broad hand was sliding slowly up her body, inside the big T-shirt she was wearing, past her panties, over her belly. Then Patrick's fingers rose further still until he cupped both of her breasts in one big hand.

Goosebumps broke out everywhere on her body. She took a big breath and sighed.

"Morning, sweetheart."

"Mmm," she agreed, pressed back against him. An ambitious erection was tucked against her panties. She stretched a hand back and met the bare skin of his hip.

He was here, he was hard, and he was naked. *Good morning*, indeed.

"You sleep okay?" he whispered, fingering one breast.

"Yeah," she breathed as her nipple hardened between his fingertips. "You?"

"Like a brick."

"How's your pain?"

Instead of answering, he trailed two fingers down her chest and abdomen, then dipped into her panties.

"Ah," she gasped as he teased her with light, glancing touches. The moment shimmered with promise. There was sunlight on her eyelids and heat at her back. Soft lips brushed her neck and then began to nibble their way toward her ear. Her body was caught between the weight of sleep and the anticipation of sex.

Heaven.

Patrick lowered her panties with one quick tug. She kicked them off.

Then he clasped her knee and lifted it a few inches. He slid his cock between her legs and rested it there, lowering her knee to trap himself. She tightened her legs together around him and he groaned and rolled his hips.

"Sure like waking up with you in my bed," he rumbled into her ear. He took her hand and brought it down to her mound. "Touch yourself while I work your tits." Her pulse kicked up a notch, and then another when he reached under both her arms and cupped her breasts, thumbing her nipples. "Get yourself ready for me."

She took a deep breath and pushed her fingertips down, touching both his firm cock and the soft folds of her own body, already growing slick for him. She grasped him and rubbed his shaft against herself.

"Fuck," he growled. "Want you."

"Have me," she said immediately. But the tone of her quick and utter capitulation nagged at her a little. "But this time we're doing it my way."

"Fair enough." He slid one of his big hands down her body and tucked a fingertip between her legs, landing right on her clit. "Tell me how you want me."

He swirled his finger and she almost forgot what they'd

been discussing. *God*, this man. He played her body like a fiddle, and it always made her lose her head. Biting her lip, she let him torture her. He thrust his hips, reminding her just how good it was going to be. "Mmm," she sighed. "Sit up. Against the headboard."

A low grunt of approval came from his chest. But when he withdrew both his cock and his finger, she almost regretted the decision.

He did as she asked, and when she rolled to face him the sight made her mouth water. That muscular body sat propped against a pillow, thick, long erection jutting upward, the plump head pointing at his belly button. Even with a big bandage covering part of his face, his cocky grin was irresistible as he tore open a condom packet. She couldn't stop watching the muscles in his forearm move as he rolled it down, covering himself.

Yowza.

Feeling shaky with anticipation, she straddled his thighs, walking her knees up toward his body. Cool blue eyes watched her approach. And when she lined him up beneath herself, he stopped breathing.

"We're going to go slow," she warned.

"Okay." He exhaled.

"Slower than you've ever gone."

"Show me, sweetheart. Wherever you lead, I'm following."

She lowered her body an inch, his cockhead breeching her, but just barely. "You know what tantric is?"

He shook his head. "Don't know my own name when you're on my cock."

"Think—yoga sex." She slid down another inch and his eyes went half-mast. "Look at me," she prompted. His eyes opened again, and she rewarded him by filling herself completely with him.

He groaned. She gave him a quick kiss. He tasted minty. Somebody had already gotten up and brushed his teeth. "Breathe with me," she demanded.

"I'm breathin'."

"Purposefully. Like in yoga class."

He grabbed her face and kissed her. Then he took a deep, slow breath.

She rubbed his chest. And when he exhaled, she inhaled. And vice versa. He held her gaze, and they fell into a natural enough rhythm. Slowly, she leaned forward and kissed him between breaths. Then again. And again.

He made a lovely noise from the back of his throat. While he met her breath for breath, she stroked his pecs and then his arms. She trailed her fingertips over his face and through his hair.

Breath. Breath. Kiss.

Breath. Breath. Kiss.

Ari could feel all the effort it took him to hold back, and a fine sweat broke out on his shoulders. His fingers dug into the flesh at her bottom, and his hips twitched with pure need.

She dug her knees into the bed and began to ride him slowly. His eyes fell shut with gratitude. But she wanted that eye contact. She wanted to know if he could withstand so much intimacy. So she held still and waited for him to rejoin her.

His eyes flickered open. "You like it slow." It was a statement, not a question.

"Sometimes," she whispered. "I like it *all.*"

He touched his smile to hers. "Go out for dinner with me," he said against her lips.

The demand caught her by surprise. "Right now?"

"No," he laughed, and she could feel his cock jump inside her. "But I want to see more of you, and I figure right now is as good a time as any to ask."

He pushed his hips forward and the sudden contact made her groan. "I'll think about it."

"She'll *think* about it." He leaned down to kiss her neck. "What does a guy have to do around here to get a date?" He grabbed the T-shirt she wore in both hands and eased it over her head. "Is it still tantric if I play with your tits?" Roughened hands cupped both her breasts, and Ari felt her control slip a little. So she took a deep, slow breath and kissed him again.

No matter how torturous she made this, he smiled at her, breathing through the rhythm she'd set. She'd meant to challenge him, but now it was her own desire that would not be contained. With every slow movement she made, her body tightened around him. And every time she bottomed out onto his lap, he gave a sexy groan. The tendons stood out on his neck as he strained to hold himself in check.

"You're very patient with me," she whispered against his lips. "But I don't want to be patient anymore."

"Enough of your way?" he asked with a grin.

"Yeah."

"On your back, girlie." But then he didn't even wait for her to move. He rolled them both over, pinned her hands above her head and gave a good, hard thrust. They both cried out from the pleasure of such wonderful friction after the lack of it. And there was no holding back after that. He unleashed himself, attacking her mouth, pumping his hips.

Her climax approached like a storm rolling in—first it was merely a heaviness on the horizon. Then came an overwhelming crash of sensation, blotting out the rest of the world. She groaned and pressed herself into the bed, letting gusts of pleasure sweep through her.

Patrick moaned her name, low and deep. Then he gasped and shuddered and thrust into her one more time.

Wow. She put a hand on his sweaty back and took a deep breath. She felt wrung out, the same way she'd feel after an hour of bikram yoga.

But better.

Patrick rolled onto his side, hauling her with him. "I swear," he said, his voice husky, "gets better every time."

Her pounding heart skipped a beat. "That's just because we did it my way," she teased.

"Liar." He pulled her face in close and kissed her. "But I'll take you any way I can get you." He kissed her again.

"Are we late for work?" she thought to ask.

He lifted his head to see the clock, then dropped it again. "Don't think so. It's just eight o'clock now."

"Good. Because I don't think I could hurry anywhere right now. How's your face?"

"What face?"

She laughed. "Should I ask you later?"

His smile made his eyes light up. He looked almost boyish when he smiled. "I got up earlier and took some ibuprofen. I feel okay."

"You going to practice?"

"Yeah, sure. Unless they keep me back for another concussion evaluation."

All the mirth drained out of her. "Do you think you have a concussion?"

He shook his head. "But every time I take a beating they need to check."

"I don't like it when you take a beating." She cupped his good cheek in her hand.

He rose up on an elbow suddenly. "Is that why you won't go out to dinner with me?" His cool blue eyes waited for an answer.

And, damn it, she'd walked right into that one. "I already told you why I can't date. You don't really want to start something with me, anyway."

"Yeah, I really do."

She shook her head. "The next man who has the pleasure of starting a relationship with me is getting a cynical girl with trust issues and a ticking biological clock. How's that for sexy?"

"Ari . . ." he whispered, trailing the back of his hand down her naked abdomen, "in the dictionary under sexy, there's a picture of you in the warrior pose. And—hell—nobody has more baggage than I do."

"Awesome. Then we should definitely become a thing."

"That's what I've been trying to tell you." He leaned over and kissed her, in spite of her sarcasm.

She wrapped her arms around his neck and sighed. "I'll go out to dinner with you on one condition."

"Anything."

"You tell me how you started fighting, and why you don't like to be touched."

He stiffened in her arms. "Why would you want to hear about that?"

"Because I'm interested in you."

He rolled onto his back, out of her grasp. "It's not a nice story, Ari. No need to go there."

"Your call," she said, sliding out of bed. "I'm going to use your fancy shower."

She thought he might follow, but she showered alone.

NINETEEN

"March, man. Fucking March." Castro set the barbell back down on the squat rack with a grimace. "It's the month that killed Julius Caesar, and every year I think it's gonna kill me, too."

"Tell me about it," O'Doul said. His body ached everywhere. A day off just wasn't enough to repair the damage.

"Sixteen games in thirty-one days," Castro said, wiping off the bar with the towel. "Batter up."

When Castro moved out of the way, O'Doul adjusted his weight belt for his set. "You know who are a bunch of pussies?"

He hefted the weight, and Castro moved in behind him to spot. "Who?"

O'Doul hefted the weight three times before he answered. "Football. Players," he huffed, guiding the bar back into its restraints. It fell with a clang, and then he could speak again. "One game a week," he said, sweat pouring off him. "And average time on the field is eleven minutes. You believe that shit?"

"No, I do not," Castro agreed. "Let 'em try to skate forty minutes in a game, three and a half nights a week. They'd curl up in a little fucking ball."

"Your turn," O'Doul said, giving Castro the weights. He

wasn't going to do another set, either. His hip felt tricky after last night's beat down, and he was trying to take it easy. "Need a spot?"

"I got it."

"Okay." O'Doul wiped off his face with his T-shirt and went over to the mat to stretch his hip.

"How are you today?"

He looked up to find Nate Kattenberger watching him. "Good, sir. You?"

"Can we talk for a second?"

"Sure." As if he'd ever say no to the owner. It was kind of weird to find Nate here on a weekday, wandering through the weight room. The man should be at his Manhattan skyscraper, changing the world or whatever. He held the stretch for another sixty seconds, then followed Nate into an alcove outside the training office.

"I want to show you this chart," Nate said, pulling up a file on a gleaming tablet the size of Brooklyn.

"Okay." He squinted at the screen, where bubbles of different colors floated on an axis. "What am I looking at?"

"Ten years of history. Each dot is a team in a given year. They are plotted like this: injury days versus wins. Do you see the pattern?"

O'Doul hated this little exchange where he was supposed to answer the questions correctly. Nate stood in front of him, arms crossed, squinting at O'Doul the way teachers used to look at him. As if he was measuring him and finding he came up short.

He didn't see the pattern. And then he did—the dots massed along a diagonal line. "Okay—yeah. The teams that had more injuries have fewer wins."

"*Exactly.* And that's just logical, right? But look how *strong* that correlation between healthy teams and winning is. Do you think they're just smarter—their GMs somehow chose players that don't ever get injured?"

"No." He pointed at the chart. "They don't have a fucking crystal ball in Dallas."

"Right," Nate agreed. "But they've realized that doing everything under the sun to keep people healthy is going to pay off. That's what we're going to do, too. I think winning more games isn't like the sports pundits like to make it. We have the skills. We just need to keep everyone in rotation."

"Okay."

Nate turned to him and lifted his smug chin. "That's why the club needs you to do less fighting."

This again. "That's a nice idea. But exactly how do you think I could avoid it?"

"Let Crikey take some," Nate said immediately. "Coach asked you to, and you pushed back. I'm asking you to stop pushing back."

The billionaire always had a way of saying these things that sounded irrefutable. The tone got under O'Doul's skin. He pointed at the chart. "But are you trying to tell me your fancy stats don't apply to Crikey, too? He hasn't scrapped much up 'til now. He could fuck up his body immediately. And every player counts, right?"

Nate's eyes widened, and there was humor in them. As if he was surprised that O'Doul would argue at all. "Every player counts. Of course they do. But he's a young kid. If he gets hurt he'll bounce back faster."

"Is there a chart for that, too?" Hell, he shouldn't be a smartass to Nate, but it just slipped out. Any time anyone made him feel old, it got his back up.

Nate actually laughed. "Probably. But we don't need another chart to know which of you has played almost a thousand NHL games. That's you, not Crikey. The next ten games are going to be the most important of the year. We need *experience* on that ice. Don't sacrifice your body over some macho code. Skate more, take fewer punches."

"'Some macho code,'" O'Doul repeated. "Why did you buy a hockey team if you don't like fights?" *Weren't the Knicks for sale?*

"Fights are a sideshow, and you know it," Nate said, all the humor gone from his face. "If they keep butts filling some of our seats, that's their only value to me. The game is so much bigger than fighting. And I know you agree with me."

Maybe he did.

"In fifteen years, fighting will be gone from the NHL," Nate continued. "The Canadian juniors teams are already leaning away from it. Concussion research will condemn it. If you step back now, it's not a failure. You're just trendy. This is Brooklyn. Be a hipster. More yoga. Fewer stitches." He picked up the tablet and slid it into a sleeve. "Gotta run. You and Coach had better teach Crikey a few things so we can stay in the right corner of that chart."

Without waiting for a response, he left the O'Doul standing there, trying to process everything the owner had just said.

Then he went to find Crikey.

TWENTY

Ari's day had started out well. First there was tantric sex with the hottest man in Brooklyn. Then, after her first massage appointment, a deliveryman showed up out of the blue to drop off half a dozen whoopie pies from One Girl Cookies.

"I didn't order anything," she told him.

"If you're Ari, these are for you," the kid insisted. "Sign here."

Inside the bag, she found a card. *A little bird told me you liked these. They must be good if they're called whoopie pies.—P.*

Ari ate one of them and set the others out of eyesight so she wouldn't be tempted.

But her good fortune didn't last. She checked her messages on her lunch break, and that's when everything went sideways. She had a voice mail from Detective Miller asking her to stop by the precinct and drop off the hard copy of the photograph Vince had sent to Patrick. She'd been ducking this errand for days. But now she rescheduled her 1:30 massage—Castro didn't have any injuries, he just liked having a rubdown—and headed over there.

When she tried to drop off the photo with the desk

sergeant, they asked her to wait a moment. When Miller came out and asked her to stay for coffee, her stomach sank. "I just had one," she said.

He smiled. "Come on back for a minute anyway. We have a couple more questions we need to ask you," he said.

"All right." Uneasy, she followed him into a messy office and sat down in the visitor's chair.

"Were you able to serve your ex-boyfriend with his order of protection?" he asked immediately.

She shook her head. "The process server can't find him. I don't know where he's staying."

"I see." The detective made a tent out of his fingers. "I need to show you a document and ask you if it's your signature on the bottom."

"Okay?" Her voice quavered, because that sounded bad. There couldn't be many documents with her signature on them in the world. Except for tax forms, and anything she filled out for the Bruisers.

He opened a folder and slid a photocopy of what looked like a check in front of her. "Does this look familiar?"

She squinted at the document—a cancelled check drawn from a bank she'd never heard of, in the amount of nine thousand dollars. In the lower right-hand corner, someone had signed *Ariana Bettini*. "Oh my god. What is this?"

"That's what I was hoping you could tell me."

"I certainly don't write checks for that amount. And I don't know this bank."

"I see." The detective passed her a form. *Signature Verification* it read. "Would you mind filling this out, please? In the middle section, sign your name five times."

Her fingers shook as she first printed her name in the space at the top. "What the hell is going on? Why are you asking me to do this?"

"I can't comment on the investigation," he said.

Ari took a deep breath, but the pen was sweaty in her hand. "There's a bank account with my name on it somewhere? What does that mean?"

He just shook his head.

Ari signed her name five times in rapid succession. Then she passed the paper to the cop and stood up.

"Hang on—I have a few more questions."

"Too bad," she said, hefting her purse onto her shoulder. "I'm going home to call my lawyer. You can clear your questions through him."

The cop didn't bother arguing as she got the hell out of there.

When she got back to the practice rink, she called her lawyer. When she was finished filling him in, there were twenty minutes left before Massey's appointment. So she walked through the gym to see if he wanted to get started early. There were voices—lots of them—echoing from the stretching room.

She stuck her head through the doorway to see what all the fuss was about. Players lined the room, watching Patrick and Crikey in the middle. The two players were wearing protective gear and circling each other on the mat.

"Keep your chin up," Patrick prompted. "Yeah." They were both sweating profusely. They must have been at this for a while. "Your reach is better than mine, so stay loose and don't let me get near you until you're ready to grab the sweater. Ready?" Patrick moved in, trying to grab Crikey. Crikey dodged him and then made his own grab.

"Yeah!" players cheered. "You got this!"

Nobody was working out. They were all just standing around, enjoying the spectacle.

Crikey punched Patrick (with a boxing glove) and Patrick pounded on Crikey. The younger man went down, and Jimbo blew a whistle. They rolled apart from each other, panting.

"You're gettin' the hang of it," Patrick said, sounding tired.

"Dude. What a rush," Crikey breathed from his back. "Where'd you learn to fight, anyway? Who taught you?"

"When I was ten I started hanging out at a boxing gym. You never heard this story?"

"No. Ten? Fuck. You're a prodigy."

Patrick reached his arms over his head and stretched out his rib cage. "Eh. It was necessary. The older kids at the group home where I lived kept stealing my food . . ."

Ari stopped breathing.

". . . I hung around the boxing gym because I needed to figure out how to shut that shit down. The guys in there thought it was funny that a kid wanted to fight, so they taught me."

"Jesus." Crikey sat up. "Did it work?"

"Sure. Eventually. I'm here now, right? Didn't starve. You want to go one more time?" He planted a hand on the mat and sat up.

Ari didn't react quickly enough and his icy gaze landed right on her startled face. His mouth got tight and he looked away.

Even though he'd told this ugly little tale to a room full of people, she had the guilty feeling of someone who'd just eavesdropped. "Is . . ." she cleared her throat. "Massey? Are you ready for your appointment?"

The defenseman high-fived both Crikey and Patrick, then followed her out of the room.

That night she was restless. She paced her bedroom, a nervous wreck. The lawyer had just instructed her not to speak to the police again without counsel. If Vince had involved her name and social security number in any shady dealings, she would have to prove her innocence.

Lawyer bills could sink her. This week she'd bought a new window and a new basement door. Those costs paled in comparison to a lawyer's fee. Moonlighting might be one solution. If she fit some private massages into her schedule on the evenings she wasn't traveling with the team, the extra money would help.

But she didn't want the team to know she was moonlighting, so she'd have to keep it a secret.

More secrets. Yay.

Her Katt Phone rang. The number read PRIVATE CALLER. She hesitated a moment before answering. But it could be the lawyer. "Hello?"

"Ariana." After eight years, it was easy to pick out Vince's voice at just one word. "Don't hang up."

"Why shouldn't I?" she yelped. "What the *hell*, Vince. You got yourself mixed up in some bullshit and now the cops want to talk to me."

"That will all go away," he said quickly. "But you have to do this one thing for me."

"I don't have to do *anything*."

"Yeah, you do. It will take you fifteen minutes, and you'll never hear from the cops again."

She wanted to hang up. She really did. But she also wanted to be rid of this hassle. "What is it? No promises."

"I need to get into the house."

"Why? I put all your things in the b . . ."

"*Listen* to me, girl. If you don't want your boyfriend's ass hung out to dry. *You. Will. Listen.*"

He's not my boyfriend, her brain offered up. But she already knew that arguing the point was a bad idea.

"We'll set a time," Vince said, his voice low. "You'll exit from the front door and leave it open behind you. Take a walk around the neighborhood for fifteen minutes. There's something I need to retrieve."

A chill snaked down her back. "What is it?"

"Never you mind. It's nothing you can find without my help. And if you touch it, everything turns to shit. I promise you do not want any part in this."

She shivered. "What the hell have you done?"

"*Nothing*," he said vehemently. "And I aim to prove it. You screw this up for me, and your boyfriend will regret it."

"Don't *threaten* me. A judge gave me a restraining order with your name on it."

"Leave it on the coffee table for me," he snarled. "I need in there. Fifteen minutes. After eight years, you can give me fifteen minutes."

"I'll think about it," she said.

When he spoke again it was between clenched teeth. "I don't have time for you to *think about it*."

"Yeah? I'm done being bullied by you." Feeling absolutely crazy, she ended the call.

It rang again a moment later. She tossed the phone onto the bed as if it was a venomous snake.

If she thought she'd been tense earlier, she'd been wrong. There was nothing like wondering what awful thing Vince had hidden in her home.

She did the obvious thing and began ransacking closets. Standing on chairs, she reacquainted herself with everything on the top shelves of her few closets. But there was nothing terrifying to be found. She turned up nothing more interesting than the term paper she'd written while studying anatomy for her massage therapy certificate.

By nine o'clock she felt both paranoid and irritated. Maybe a better woman would have plopped down on her yoga mat and meditated, but she didn't think she could relax in this house. That asshole had ruined her peace *again*.

Ari put on her coat and tossed a toothbrush into her bag. Then, feeling paranoid, she left an upstairs lamp on and tiptoed down her own stairs in the dark. In the kitchen she grabbed the pastry bag full of whoopie pies off the counter. Then, in the living room, she peered out onto the street, taking care not to ruffle the curtains.

No van. No Vince.

Quickly, she left by the front door, locking the place securely behind her. Walking fast, she headed for the more populous part of her neighborhood, stopping at the liquor store on Jay Street. She bought a bottle of good tequila and her favorite margarita mix. Then she called Becca from the checkout counter.

"Hi," she said while handing over her credit card. "Can I come over? It's an emergency."

"What kind of emergency?" Becca asked over the sounds of a baby crying in the background.

"The kind that needs a margarita. Not a bail bondsman."

"Whew. You had me worried there. It's, uh, not that relaxing here. Meet me across the street in the lobby of 220. We'll go to Georgia's."

"Okay."

It was a two minute walk, so she got there just as Becca was exiting her little building across Water Street from the pricey converted condo building where Georgia, Leo, (and Patrick) lived. "Hey!" Becca said, giving her a hug. "Is this latest news going to piss me off?"

"Probably."

Becca looped her arm in Ari's. "Come on then. You can tell me while we're drinking."

In the lobby of Georgia's building, Becca began to explain to the doorman where they were headed. "We're going up to . . ." she began.

But the doorman nodded, waving them up without a phone call upstairs. "Have a nice night, ladies."

"I'm here a lot," Becca explained.

When they knocked on Leo and Georgia's apartment door, there were voices and TV noise inside. "Hey!" Georgia said when she pulled open the door. Then her face fell. "Tequila and a bakery bag? And Becca has her pedicure satchel? Oh, crap. Who died?"

"Ari is having a bad day," Becca explained. "And my nephew is teething. So we came to your place."

She looked over her shoulder and wrinkled her nose. "March Madness is on, and half the team is here to watch it."

"Fuck," Becca said.

"Well . . ." Ari cleared her throat. She looked past Georgia to count the players in the room, and did not find the one she was looking for. "I have an idea. Come with me."

She led them to Patrick's door and knocked. He opened up with a look of utter surprise on his face. "Ladies? Everything okay?"

"No, but Ari hasn't given us the update yet," Becca said, pushing past him. "We need your apartment. You can go watch basketball with Leo."

Ari lifted her eyes to Patrick's and found amusement there. "If you were going to stay in tonight, I can drag the girls back to my place. But I didn't want to be alone there."

His eyebrows lifted. "Dare I ask why?"

"Don't tell him before us," Becca argued from the kitchen area. "Doulie, do you have martini glasses? Hey—you *do!* I'm astonished."

Without comment, Patrick opened the door wider, ushering Ari and Georgia inside.

Becca rooted around in Patrick's freezer, filling his cocktail shaker with ice. "Okay, Ari. Do your magic. I'll open the tequila. You bought the big bottle. Damn. Is it that bad?"

"It's pretty bad," she admitted. "Can you check the fridge for limes?"

"I'll do it," Georgia volunteered.

Across the room, Patrick had taken a seat on a leather club chair, feet propped onto the coffee table, hands behind his back. He was watching the three of them as if they were a show put on just for him.

"Found one!" Georgia said. "Knife?"

Becca opened a drawer and handed one over.

"Cutting board?"

"Men never have cutting boards," Becca explained.

"Not true!" Patrick called from the chair.

"No way," Georgia said, opening cabinets until she came up with a lime green cutting board. "After Patrick leaves we're going to discuss his ridiculously civilized apartment."

"Who says I'm leaving?"

"You can stay," Becca offered. "But everyone who stays is having his or her toenails painted."

"Hmm," he said. "That's not really my scene."

"Exactly," Becca agreed.

"You'd better have four glasses out over there, though,"

Patrick threatened. "I'm not leaving until someone gives me a margarita."

"Fair enough," Becca sighed, reaching into a cabinet for one more. "I guess you can have a drink, since we invaded your home and everything."

"She guesses," he muttered.

Ari put ice water into the glasses to chill them down, then she mixed the drinks. It took two shakers-full to serve everyone. She brought Patrick's drink over to him and bent down to whisper in his ear. "You are very patient with us."

"You are very amusing to me," he whispered back. Then he kissed her neck.

When Ari straightened up again, she found a stunned expression on Georgia's face. She felt her face begin to heat. "Okay, kids. Drink up. Because I need you all nice and loose to help me guess what my douchewhistle ex has done this time."

Ari plopped down in the middle of Patrick's thick wool rug. The texture was like that of a sheep skin. She folded her legs into Sukhasana position and then told them everything about her awful day—from the check with her supposed signature on it to the creepy story of Vince's call, and ransacking her closets. "Then I just had to get out of there. Now I feel *watched*."

Patrick hadn't said a word while she spooled through all the day's events. But his expression had darkened with each new revelation. Now he drained his drink, a stony expression on his face. "Sweetheart. Don't leave here before I get back, promise?" He stood up, fixing her with his icy blue stare.

"Where are you going?"

"Basketball down the hall. 'Cause my nails are fine the way they are." He carried his glass over to the shaker on the sideboard and poured himself the dregs. "Just don't go home alone, please."

"Okay," she said quietly.

He gave the three of them a wink, then strode out of his apartment, margarita glass in hand.

The second the door clicked shut, Georgia got up off the couch and sat down on the rug in front of Ari. "Omigod. You need to *spill*."

"I just did."

Georgia rolled her eyes. "No, honey. Not about your ex. About Doulie. You told me—and this is a direct quote—*it's not like that.*"

"Well, it's sort of like that now. I assumed Becca told you."

"I am a *vault*," Becca crowed. "You told me to keep my trap shut."

"And I thank you," Ari said quickly. "I don't want the team to know."

"I won't tell a soul," Georgia promised. "Not even Leo. But I don't know why you're so worried. The team is nice to me," Georgia pointed out. "Hell, I think they like me better now."

"But you don't touch their naked bodies every day." Ari didn't even want to know where her clients' minds would go if they knew she was sleeping with Patrick. "I don't want anyone imagining sex with me on the massage table."

Becca gave a little moan and flattened herself onto the sofa. "I hear where you're coming from. But maybe you should give massage table sex a try with Doulie. That sounds extraordinary."

"It was," Ari whispered and the other two burst out laughing. "But we didn't do it at *work*. God."

"God," Georgia echoed. But then she turned red and put both hands over her face.

Becca sat up fast. "Wait. What did *you* get up to at work?"

"I didn't mean it to happen," Georgia said from behind the wall of her hands. "But Leo came to find me in my office one day last week . . ."

"And?" Becca prompted.

Georgia peeked out from behind her palms. "He discovered that my office door locks. We did it on my desk."

"Omigod." Becca grabbed a copy of *Sports Illustrated*

off Patrick's coffee table and began to fan herself. "I'll never eat donuts on your desk again."

"We were very tidy," Georgia insisted, her face pink. "And anyway, we're getting off the topic. Is Doulie a good boyfriend? I'll bet he is."

"He's not my boyfriend," Ari insisted. "I can't have one of those right now. I think I need to remember how to be alone."

"I remember!" Becca cried, raising her hand. "And it blows. So forgive me if I don't think your argument holds any water."

"Even if I wanted to date someone right now, I don't think we're a good fit. I always fall for the bossy macho men, and then I can't figure out why they want to control my life."

"Hang on," Georgia said, running a hand over the bumpy nap of Patrick's sheeplike rug. "Macho can take many forms. They aren't all bad. Does Doulie push you around?"

Ari shook her head. "He's bossy, though." *Usually when we're naked.* But was that even fair? "Ugh. He shouldn't press me for a relationship, anyway. I'm a freaking wreck. My ex is trying to break into my home, and even worse . . ." She cut the sentence off. Some things were harder to admit.

"What could be worse than a violent ex?" Becca asked. "I mean, seriously. You've got no place to go but up."

"Bec!" Georgia scolded. "Everyone makes mistakes."

Mine last for eight years. "I can't afford to make another mistake," she admitted. "Because I want a child. And Patrick told me once that he's never having kids." Even as the words came out, she recognized how important it was to her. The truth was that she liked Patrick a lot. He was a good man, and she didn't really doubt he'd make somebody an awesome partner.

But she wanted kids. And he wasn't the type.

Georgia pointed at Becca. "Maybe it's time to move on to the nail-painting portion of the evening. Before we're too drunk to do a good job."

"Good call." Becca peeled herself off the couch. "I'll set

up the footbath." She disappeared to rattle around in Patrick's kitchen.

"Let's pull the coffee table out of the way," Georgia suggested. "We need the whole rug."

They set that up, and then Ari remembered the bakery bag. "Hey—I have baked goodies."

"Yesss!" Becca yelled. "Let me guess—whoopie pies from One Girl Cookies?"

"How did you know?"

Becca's laugh was evil. "I may have been consulted."

"You *helped* him?" Ari yelped.

"Who wouldn't?" Becca asked, carrying a tub of soapy water and a dish towel toward the rug. "He's adorable. You know—in a really rugged, panty-ripping kind of way."

Georgia arranged the towel and the tub. "Take off your shoes, Ari. You're going first. Becca's theory is that everyone thinks better with her feet in a tub of warm water."

Ari didn't argue. She stripped off her socks and put her feet in the bath.

"Oh—and Becca likes to choose the polish. She's bossy like that."

"Only for you, sweetie," Becca said, opening up a big bag full of nail polish and poking through the bottles, which knocked together like marbles. "Because you aren't vain enough to get it right."

"Well, damn," Georgia said. "Just for that I'm going to warn Ari that you screw with the travel reservations sometimes. Don't be too shocked if Doulie ends up in the adjoining room when you go to Ottawa tomorrow morning."

Ari almost swallowed the wedge of lime she was sucking on. "Omigod!" she said, setting the glass down on the floor just off the rug. "That was your doing in Raleigh?"

Becca grinned, and passed the bag of nail polishes. "Did it work?"

"Good lord. Hottest night of my life," Ari admitted. She *still* caught herself thinking about the way it felt to slide down the table toward Patrick's waiting . . .

Gah.

"You're blushing," Becca pointed out.

"You would, too."

Her friend sighed. "Always the wingman, never the target. Somebody better make me another margarita."

"I'm on it," Georgia promised.

Ari passed Becca the bag of whoopie pies. "We still have to figure out what Vince left in my apartment. What could it be?"

"His heart, honey," Becca said softly. "I think he's just jealous. Sometimes men don't know what they have until it's gone."

Ari wished that was the answer. "That's a nice idea, but I think he's serious. I'm going to have to go to the police again, aren't I?"

"Probably," Becca agreed. "I'll go with you if you want. But tomorrow we're going to Ottawa, so you have a reprieve."

"And your drink is ready!" Georgia called from the kitchen.

She looked from one of her lovely friends to the other and wondered how life could be so beautiful and so troubling all at the same time.

TWENTY-ONE

O'Doul had taken some heat for waltzing into Leo's apartment with a fancy drink in his hand.

"This is our captain on his night off," Castro teased. "He probably wears a silk smoking jacket around the house."

"What's a smoking jacket?" Zac Sullivan asked. "Maybe I need one."

But Castro just shook his head, as if he couldn't be expected to explain shit to the masses. He was another smart guy, like College Boy over there on his sofa. O'Doul studied their relaxed faces. None of his teammates were dumb enough to get caught up in the bullshit Ari's ex wanted to rain down on him.

If he got out of this mess with his dignity intact, he swore he'd never be so stupid again.

"Who's winning?" he asked the room. "Louisville," someone said with a sigh. "We're all losing our bets tonight."

"You can't *all* be losing," O'Doul pointed out. "Who has Louisville in the bracket?"

"The kitty!" Castro complained. "The charity kitty has Louisville. I think Jimbo put that in, the little smartass. It sucks because the winner is supposed to buy us drinks after the Final Four! You'll never let us dip into the kitty for drink money. I know this."

Hysterical. "Buy your own damn drinks, asshole. You're pullin' down more money than most people can make in years."

"It's the principle of the thing," Castro said, beer bottle pointed at him like a weapon.

"The principle of the thing, huh?" O'Doul grinned. "Put twenty bucks into the kitty just for being a boob."

"Fuck." He reached for his wallet. "Who do I pay?"

"I'll tell Jimbo you owe him."

"What's in your glass, captain?" Beringer asked. "Doesn't look like Scotch."

"Maybe a lady friend made it for me."

There was a chorus of "whoa!" and other interested noises.

"So it's all working out for you?" Leo asked. "Do we ever get to meet her?"

"Dunno," O'Doul said, trying to picture a future where he and Ari were an honest-to-god couple in public, and coming up blank. He'd never had a girlfriend before. But he'd never wanted to be with anyone the way he wanted Ari. "Your bakery thing was a hit. They even delivered it for me."

"Never underestimate the power of baked goods," Leo said, nodding like a prophet.

"My next ploy will be Jimbo's birthstone thing," he said, sipping his margarita. "Found something, but it took a while. There is some fugly jewelry in the world."

"Next time, ask a chick where to shop," Castro suggested. "Who has nice taste? Georgia, of course, but she doesn't seem like a shopper. Rebecca, maybe. Or—I know—ask Ari."

Oh, Christ.

"Or how about Lauren?" Leo suggested. "She's always dressed to kill."

"With Lauren, that's not a metaphor," Castro said. "Say the wrong thing to that chick and she'll cut your balls *right off*. No sense of humor on that girl."

Nobody else in the room was willing to touch that, even if Castro was right. The veterans understood that Lauren had her reasons. "Hey," O'Doul muttered, moving around the sofa to try to find a place to sit. "Castro, I need that ottoman."

"My feet need this ottoman."

"It's either that or we're snuggling together on your part of the couch."

Castro sighed and removed his big feet from the foot-stool. "Take it. I don't want a love triangle with your lady friend."

"What a gentleman." He sat down to watch Louisville win the basketball game.

Two hours later O'Doul paused in front of his apartment door. He heard female laughter coming from inside.

"That is bullshit," Georgia giggled. "Matt Damon is so much hotter than Ben Affleck."

"He can't pull off a beard, though," Ariana argued. "Admit it."

"Or a ponytail," Becca added.

He shook out his keys and let himself into the apartment. "Hi, ladies. Miss me?"

All three of them were stretched out on his rug, throw pillows under their heads, looking up at the TV. The coffee table had been moved aside. Their bare feet were pointing straight up, and there was . . . paper towel? Something white was strung between their toes. It was the weirdest thing he'd ever seen.

"Hey." Ari sat up fast. "Whoa." She seemed to sway, though she wasn't even standing up. "Wow. We had a lot of tequila."

"Indeed!" Becca sat up, too. "Ran out of margarita mix. Had to do some shots."

O'Doul bit down on his lip to keep from laughing. "And how'd that go?"

"Pretty good!" Georgia slurred from her cushion. "But I can't really feel my face right now."

"Is that right?" he asked as laughter threatened again. There were three women on his floor, and they were *wasted*.

"I think I can get up by myself. Let's give it a try." She rolled over and got to her hands and knees. "So far, so good."

Becca stood up, then leaned over Georgia. She seemed to be faring the best of any of them. "Come on, babe. Let's pour you back into your own apartment."

"M'kay." Georgia staggered to her feet.

"Come over here and hold onto the door while I get my stuff," Becca coached, leading her friend toward the door.

"I can walk her home," O'Doul suggested. "And you, too."

"We're fine!" Becca said cheerfully. She tripped over the edge of the rug, though. "Whoops!"

"Don't worry about the . . ." Ari made a sloppy waving motion at the crumb-covered plate and the margarita glasses. "I got those."

A couple of minutes later Georgia and Becca were on their way. O'Doul watched Becca walk Georgia down the hall toward her own door. They seemed fine, so he locked his door and turned his attention to Ari.

She was seated in the middle of the rug, knees to her chest, forehead in her palms. "I'm drunk," she said, as if this was news.

"I know, baby. It's okay."

"I've had more drinks this month than in the last"—she paused to hiccup—"*year*."

"Is that bad?" he asked, walking over to her and sinking to his knees.

"Maybe? I think my chakras are out of alignment."

"You can work on that tomorrow," he suggested. "Let's put you to bed."

"I brought a toothbrush in my purse. I thought I was going to crash at Becca's."

He got up and found her bag and brought it to her. Then he picked her up in his arms and carried her to the bathroom, steadying her in front of the sink.

"I can do this," she said, nudging him away.

"Please don't fall down and hit your head."

She made a noise of displeasure. "You do sometimes. They pay you for it."

Women. They outargued him even when they were drunk. "Just humor me and stay vertical. I'll find you a T-shirt to sleep in."

After spending a few minutes in the bathroom, Ari shuffled out and sat on the edge of his bed.

"Here," he said, handing her two ibuprofen and a glass of water. "Do you think you could take this? How's your stomach?"

"Fine," she said. "Thank you." She swallowed the pills and drank the water.

O'Doul set the glass aside. "Let's get this off," he said, lifting her shirt over her head.

"Mmm," she sighed, and reached for his fly.

He let her fumble with his zipper because it kept her busy. He had her changed into his T-shirt just a couple of minutes later. "There you go," he said, pulling the covers back. "Hop in there."

She didn't hop, exactly. It was more like a military crawl. He pulled the covers up to her chin and she sighed. "Come to bed?"

"In a few minutes."

He spent some time putting the glassware in the dishwasher and shutting off lights. By the time he finished getting ready for bed, Ari was curled up on the pillow, breathing softly. Sleeping.

But when he got in on his side (and since when did he start thinking of his bed in halves?) she rolled to face him. Ari put her hands on his chest and sighed. So he pulled her closer. "The room is spinning," she complained.

"I got you," he whispered, laying a hand on her head, enjoying the silky softness of her hair.

"Not supposed to like you so much," she murmured.

"Uh-huh," he said. "Tough luck, because I'd be an awesome date."

"So humble," she said into his T-shirt. "Thanks for letting us get sloppy on your parket." She hiccuped again. "I mean *carpet*."

"Totally worth it." He chuckled, trying not to bounce her head around with his laughter. "You girls are very entertaining when you're drunk."

"Don't know why you like me," she slurred. "I'm a pain in the gluteus maximus."

A month ago this whole scene would have been unfathomable—margaritas in his living space and cuddling in bed. He was getting comfortable with this. It made him feel useful in a way he wasn't used to. "You're not so bad," he said, cradling her closer.

"It was not a good day. I have to hire the lawyer for more hours."

"I'm sorry, baby."

"I should have *become* a lawyer. Two hours of private massage equals one hour of lawyering."

He petted her hair. "But then you'd only live half as long because lawyering sounds boring as shit." And he'd pay for her fucking lawyer if she'd let him.

She giggled. "I don't know if *lawyering* is a word."

"It is when you've drunk a lot of tequila."

Ari sighed against his chest, and he thought she was done talking for the night. But a couple of minutes later she spoke again. "I heard you telling Crikey how you learned to fight."

His hand froze on her head. Fuck. "Yeah. It was a long time ago."

"Where were your parents?"

He resumed stroking her hair, and tried to decide how much he was willing to say. Not much.

"Just tell me, Patrick. You want me to trust you, but everything is on your terms."

Fuck. She sounded a lot more sober all of a sudden. "You know, you're the only one who calls me Patrick since my mother died. Since you want to know so bad, I was eight when it happened. I watched my father shoot my mother in the head."

"Oh my god." Ari lifted her face off his chest.

He did not want to have this conversation. Not ever. But here it was. He tucked her head back down, because it was easier to talk without looking her in the eye. "Obviously my father went to prison. I went into the state's care. For a couple of years they found foster homes for me. But foster parents are usually people without a lot of stability, too. When I was ten they sent me to a group home, and it was a disaster. I was the youngest kid there. Never got enough to eat because the teenagers would take my food, my school supplies. Once they sold my shoes to buy beer. I started trying to fight back but they outweighed me by a hundred pounds."

Ari gripped his wrist, as if trying not to react. His shitty childhood wasn't her fault. And if he could have avoided talking about it, he would have.

The next part of the story was sort of fun, though. "That's when I found that boxing gym in the neighborhood. I passed it every day after school. I started staring into the window watching these guys train. And I was just a kid who had nothing to lose, so I started imitating them—right there on the sidewalk. I'd shadowbox in front of the plateglass window. They must have thought it was hysterical. So after this goes on for a while the owner invites me inside. His name is Rick, and he's got tattoos covering like ninety percent of his body. I thought he was so big and scary and so badass. I wanted to be just like him so I could scare the shit out of the guys who keep taking my stuff."

This got a small smile out of Ari. But still, her body language went all stiff and weird.

"'What are you doing, kid?' they asked me. 'Do you have to train for a fight?' So I told them yes. And Rick asked, 'When's your fight, kid?' And I said, 'Every morning at breakfast and every night at dinner, but lunches are at school and the big kids can't steal my lunch except for Saturday and Sunday . . .'"

He'd known right away that he'd said something weird, because all the men stopped grinning and just stared at him.

". . . So, anyway, Rick put some protective gear on me and let me kick off my shoes and get into the ring. And I just about pissed myself with glee."

Ari wrapped her arms around him. Tightly.

"Those guys taught me to fight for real. How to punch, and how to keep my head up, and how to move. I went there every day and they didn't kick me out. I didn't always get time in the ring, but there were bags to hit, and people standing around to tell me what to do. And then I decided I'd learned a lot, right? So one night when this high school kid decided he was going to eat my piece of meatloaf I socked him right in the eye. He still weighed twice as much as I did, so he picked me up and threw me into the bookcase face-first . . ."

He hated remembering this shit.

"I had bruises all over my face and a broken tooth. When I went to the gym the next day, the guys were so fucking mad. They wanted me to tell them who did it, but I was afraid to rat the guy out. So they started teaching me to fight dirty. How to stomp on feet and pull ears and knee somebody in the nuts.

"It only took about two more weeks for the bigger kids to figure out that I wasn't worth the trouble anymore. They stole other kids' food instead of mine. But I never stopped going to that gym. The owner gave me a job. He let me clean all the mirrors in the bathrooms, and put away all the free weights and equipment. He'd slip me a couple of dollars for a couple of hours work. This went on for a couple of years. Then, one Friday when I was fourteen, I told Pete that I wanted to play hockey, but I couldn't because you had to have skates. On Monday afternoon, the guys gave me my first skates. They tried to say that somebody had an extra pair, but they were brand-new out of a box." He cleared his throat. "So it wasn't all bad, you know?"

He waited for her to say something. But maybe it would be better if she didn't. If she fell asleep right now, she might not even remember this conversation tomorrow.

"That's just about the shittiest childhood I've ever heard of," Ari said quietly. "That's why you don't like to be touched."

"Probably," he admitted. "Spent a lot of time trying to keep other people's hands off me. Whenever they got close enough to touch me it was never good. They'd do *anything*, too. No violence was too much. No line was too far to cross. Every kid there had nothing to lose."

She slid a hand clumsily up his chest, onto his neck, cupping his jaw. "Thank you for letting me touch you. I like it a lot more than I wish I did."

That awkward endorsement made him grin into the darkness. "Sure like touching you, baby. Don't ever make me stop."

"We'll see."

"You are a tough sell, Ariana." He removed her hand from his face and kissed her palm. "I don't know what I have to do to win you over. But I'm gonna keep trying. You hear me?"

She didn't, though. Ari had finally fallen to sleep.

TWENTY-TWO

Standings: 4th Place
10 Regular Season Games Remaining

The next morning had a rough start.

Ari had woken up in Patrick's bed with a pounding headache and a mouth the texture of old burlap. "Just kill me already," she'd moaned into his pillow.

"How about I buy you a bagel and coffee instead?"

Later, at the rink, she gave massages to four players, including Patrick. He grinned at her every time she gave a little groan.

"I'm never drinking again," she said more than once.

"You're hot even when you're hungover," he insisted.

The liar.

Then it was time for a quick stop at home to pack for their overnight to Ottawa. She gave her house what was sadly a familiarly critical inspection when she went inside. But nothing was out of place. There was no sign of Vince, or of trouble. She threw some things into a bag and carried her portable massage table to Water Street, meeting Georgia,

Leo, and the limo they'd hired to take all three of them to the airport.

"Does your head ache?" Georgia asked as they slung their bags into the trunk. "Mine is killing me."

"We overdid it," Ari agreed. "Thanks for helping me drown my sorrows, though," she whispered, mindful of Leo, who had his phone pressed to his ear. "Who's he talking to?"

"His mom. And we can't leave for another minute, because we're waiting for Becca."

"Really? I didn't know she was coming on this trip."

"Me neither," Georgia said, sliding onto the stretch limo's leather seat. "But she sent me a text ninety minutes ago asking if she could bum a ride with us. So Leo upgraded the car."

Ari patted the seat. "Nice. If my head weren't killing me, I'd enjoy the trip."

"Why'd you girls get so lit last night, anyway?" Leo asked, stashing his phone.

"Ari had a bad day," Georgia explained.

"I'm here! We can leave," Becca said, leaping into the car. She tossed her bag at their feet and slammed the car door.

Leo rapped a knuckle against the driver's window, and it slid down. "We're ready when you are," he said.

"Yes, sir."

The big car glided away from the curb, and Ari pulled out her water bottle, willing herself to feel better. Flying with a hangover sounded pretty miserable. "How's *your* head?" she asked Becca.

"Never better. Why?"

Georgia gave her friend a feeble smile. "Just ignore her. She's one of those people who doesn't get hungover. Why are you going to Ottawa with us, anyway, Bec?"

Becca blew out a breath. "Nate decided to go last minute, since he's all stressed out about making the play-offs. And I had a total panic attack, because my sister has a midterm exam today, and I'd already told her I'd stay home with the baby. My nephew can't go to daycare because he had a fever last night, and they make you wait twenty-four hours. Or something. I don't know. But I was supposed to babysit, and then Nathan called and said, 'pack a bag.' So I did the unthinkable."

"What's that?" Ari asked.

"I called Queen Lauren and asked her to go to Ottawa in my place."

"She'd never agree to that, right?" Georgia asked. "She hates traveling with the team."

"I *know*, but she hates failing Nathan more. I really didn't want to owe her a favor, because she'll lord it over me. But I didn't want my sister to miss her test. So I told Lauren why I was in a bind. Since Lauren is getting a business degree at night school, I knew she'd understand about the test."

"Wait, really?" Georgia squeaked. "She's getting a degree while she works for Nathan? Where does she find the time?"

"I know, right?" Becca shook her head and the stud in her eyebrow flashed. "She clearly is not as caught up on the trashy TV shows as we are. But she understood my issue, although her solution was not what I predicted."

"What was it?" Georgia asked. "Let me guess—she hired some fancy nanny service to come and stay with Matthew?"

"Nope!" Becca sang. "Lauren is in my apartment right now taking care of the baby herself."

For a couple of seconds, Ari and Georgia just stared at her. "Seriously?" Georgia's voice had a hushed tone. "You left your nephew in the care of Queen Lauren?"

"I did. He looked very happy, though. They were cooing at each other."

Georgia cleared her throat. "Do you have a photo? I can't reconcile the idea of Lauren in her Chanel suit holding a drooly baby. And no offense but . . ."

". . . He drools like a fire hose. Trust me, I know. And, yeah. I think she likes babies. After they'd bonded for a moment she looked up at me with that Lauren face and basically dismissed me."

"Whoa," Georgia said. "Fascinating."

"I know! My sister is going to come home in an hour and say, 'who the hell are you?' So now I'll owe Lauren *and* my sister. What a week."

Leo shifted in his seat. "Nate is freaked about our play-offs chances? Great." He thumped his head back against the wall of the car. "So am I, then. Coach switched up the lines again last night. I wondered if Nate was pressuring him."

"Dad wouldn't take coaching tips from Nate," Georgia pointed out. "That's just weird."

"I hear you," Becca said. "But Nate has this way of arguing a point until you're either won over or ready to kill him."

"Nate's not so bad," Georgia said. "I like the guy. I can never tell what he thinks of me, but my gut says he's a good man."

"He is a good man," Becca agreed. "As long as you like 'em wildly opinionated, stubborn as a mule, and really smug. Even as I'm saying this, I'm pretty sure I'd lay down in the road for him. The thing about Nate is that he understands where everyone's boundaries lie. It's like—he has godlike abilities but he understands that it's special, and he can come down to your level and work with you anyway."

Ari rubbed her temple, wishing she had the godlike ability to make a headache disappear. "Don't sell yourself short, Bec. The way you handle tequila is rather extraordinary."

"If only it were a marketable skill," she sighed. "I could really use some extra cash right now."

Couldn't we all, Ari agreed privately. Maybe when her head stopped aching she would look at her schedule and try to find a sliver of time for some moonlighting.

They got to the airport in plenty of time. Some of the players were already gathered in the little waiting area in the charter terminal.

"Hey, Ari." Patrick waved at her. "How are you?"

It was a friendly greeting, but not overly familiar. He was

respectful of her need to appear professional, and she really appreciated it. "Afternoon, Patrick," she replied. "I'd like to say that I'm fine, but my head is killing me."

His blue eyes twinkled. "Did you go out drinking last night, Miss Bettini?"

"I did. And I learned my lesson."

He patted his pocket. "Want an aspirin? I always carry them."

"I have some with me," she said. "But can I leave my carry-on with you for a second? I need to refill my water bottle."

"Of course."

She made a trip to the ladies' room where she took an Advil and splashed water on her face. *Tequila is not the answer*, she told the tired-looking woman in the mirror. Maybe she'd get some sleep on this flight. That wouldn't hurt.

When she came back they'd begun to board the plane. Patrick bent over and picked up her bag off the floor, tucking it over her shoulder. "All set?" he asked.

"Yes, thank you." She gave him a wink. As she boarded the jet, she felt his warm gaze on her back.

The man was tempting. That was for damned sure.

Georgia waved her into a seat in the middle of the plane. Across the aisle, Castro and Becca were sitting together, laughing about something already.

"You do *not* have the entire play memorized," Becca insisted.

"Do so! Since the ninth grade. I was a kick-ass Romeo. Which bit do you want to hear? I'll prove it."

"Fine. The balcony scene."

"Act II, scene II." Castro rolled his eyes. "Everyone picks that bit. I'm bored of it."

"Maybe you don't really know it."

"Girl, I do! Listen." He cleared his throat. "But, soft! what light through yonder window breaks? It is the east, and Rebecca is the sun."

"Oh, lordy," she said, laughing.

"Arise, fair sun, and kill the envious moon, who is already sick and pale with grief, That thou, her maid, art far more fair than she. Be not her maid, since she is envious; her vestal livery is but sick and green and none but fools do wear it; cast it off." He took Becca's face in his two hands. "It is my lady, O, it is my love!"

"Wow," Becca breathed. "You must have made all the ninth-grade girls swoon."

"That's right, baby."

"*Rebecca*," a stern voice cut through the silliness. All eyes lifted to find Nathan, messenger bag slung over his shoulder, eyes narrowed in irritation.

"What?" she squeaked, pulling her face out of Castro's hands. Her cheeks were tinged with pink, probably because Nathan's tone was so scolding.

He stared at her another moment, raising the awkwardness quotient into the stratosphere. "Bring this month's attendance numbers back to the conference table, please. We'll start in two minutes." Then, finally, he moved away.

"Yikes," Georgia said under her breath.

"What crawled up his ass and died?" Castro whispered.

Ari couldn't help but turn around in her seat to watch him stomp down the aisle toward the back of the jet. Her gaze snagged on Patrick, who was also watching the big boss storm away from the awkward little fit he'd thrown. When Patrick turned his chin, their eyes locked.

Ouch, said his gaze.

You see why I worry? hers replied.

The flight attendant began to make security announcements. So Ari buckled her seatbelt and pulled her phone out of its pocket to shut it off. She'd avoided looking at it all day.

Seventeen. That's how many text messages Vince had sent, asking her to call him. And that wasn't counting the voice mails and the missed calls.

Jesus.

She shut the phone off, knowing that she really ought to tell the security team instead. The flight taxied and took off.

While they were climbing to a cruising altitude, Ari searched her brain for a solution to the Vince problem. For the hundredth time, she came up short. So when the flight attendant announced that it was safe to move about the cabin, she did what she had to do.

Getting up, she walked carefully to the back of the plane. She passed Patrick in his seat, headphones on, eyes closed. He looked younger when he slept. Peaceful. It was nice to see.

She found Hugh Major in the last row, reading something on his Katt Tablet, scribbling notes on a legal pad.

"Sir?" she said. "Do you have a minute?" It really didn't appear that he did, though.

Hugh looked up. "How can I help you, Ari?"

This was going to be incredibly embarrassing. "You said I should tell you if I had any more security issues."

"Yeah," he nodded. "I want to know."

"Well . . ." She cleared her throat. "My ex-boyfriend is demanding access to my home, claiming he left something behind. And I really don't like the sound of it." She told him about Vince's call, and everything he'd said. "I wonder if your security guys could refer me to a private investigator. My lawyer suggested it, and I didn't want to listen. But now I think I just need to know what he's involved me with."

Hugh nodded. "Right. I've already green-lit an investigation."

"You've . . . what?"

"I've already asked the PI we use to look into it. That picture he sent to Patrick was awfully . . ." He stroked his chin. "*Personal.* I decided it wasn't going to go away on its own. So my team is looking into the perpetrator. I'll call them when we land and see what the PI turned up. We can set up a meeting for later this week. We'll all sit down and have a status update."

Ari's cheeks burned from the knowledge that the team was expending resources to investigate her ex. She could only imagine what Hugh was thinking right now. *If only we hadn't hired this chick* . . . She pushed her hair out of her overheated face. "Thank you, sir. I sure am sorry that's necessary."

"Me, too, Ariana. It's a shame you're dealing with this. I wish all my team members had trouble-free lives as the play-offs approach. And yet . . ." He grinned. "I've been doing this twenty-five years, and haven't had an easy season yet. You'd think I'd get used to it."

She tried to return his smile, but the effect was probably more like a cringe. "Thank you, sir."

"We'll talk more after I hear from them," he promised, pulling his work closer to him on the tray table.

Ari slunk back to her seat once more, wondering what on earth the PI would say to explain Vince's craziness. The flight to Ottawa was only ninety minutes, and Ari dug into the duffel bag at her feet for her book. But when she lifted it out, she saw an unfamiliar glint of color there. Leaning forward, she plucked a small box, wrapped in purple paper with a white bow.

"What's that?" Georgia asked, peering over her own book.

"I don't know." Ari pulled one end of the ribbon, untying the silky thing. She slid a thumb under the paper's edge and freed the unmarked box.

Inside, on a little velvet pillow, lay a green crystal pendant, roughly faceted into a cushion shape and set in a hammered silver bezel.

"Pretty!" Georgia breathed. "That's so . . . *you*. Is that a note?" Her seatmate pointed at a little square of paper in the lid of the box.

Ari unfolded it to reveal a brief message. *This is a peridot, and I thought it would look good on the chain you wear.—P.*

"Aw," Georgia said. "Somebody really likes you."

"It's awfully nice," Ari agreed, fingering the stone. It was the size of her thumbnail. And, damn it, it *was* her taste— more like an earthy crystal than a flashy jewel. "He makes it hard to stay single."

"No comment," Georgia said, a smile in her voice. "But let's put that on your chain, because it will look nice there. Here, turn your head. I'll take it off you."

Ari lifted her hair, but then dropped it again. "I can't," she said.

"Why not?"

She blew out a breath. "He's great, and I really like him. And all the things he's done for me are so sweet. But my life is a mess right now, and I'm giving him mixed signals. I have to cut that out."

Georgia made a sad face. "I think you guys would be really great together. And I've never seen Doulie go after someone before. I think he really cares."

That just made Ari squirm. "He asked *you* out, right?"

"Once. Barely. But I've never seen him like this." Georgia tapped the box in Ari's hand. "And forget the present. The way he looks at you is so sweet. He's softer when you're around. Like his rough edges are worn away."

Last night she'd gotten a better glimpse at Patrick's rough edges. The story of his childhood was so harrowing it had given her chills. But that just made her decision even easier. Patrick deserved someone who could love him without reservations. And she was not a good candidate for the job.

Reluctantly she put the pretty little box back in her bag and zipped it up tightly. She wouldn't string him along. It just wasn't fair.

TWENTY-THREE

There were certain places that always made O'Doul feel like a punk kid again, and the hotel in Ottawa was one of them.

The team frequently stayed at the hundred-year-old Chateau, probably because Nate Kattenberger liked it. On the outside it looked like a stone castle, complete with turrets and towers and a peaked copper roof. The river swept by, a ribbon of gray in the fading twilight.

Inside the lobby, the team gathered beside one of the oak-paneled walls, waiting for rooming assignments. Even in his thousand-dollar suit, O'Doul felt like an imposter. Fusty, old-guard places always made him ill at ease, even in a room full of hockey players who didn't care which fork he used at the fancy restaurant later.

He just felt *off* today. They needed this win, but the game had him on edge. They were ranked higher than Ottawa, but there were no guarantees. And it was still unclear whether he or Crikey would take tomorrow's fight.

None of that had him so ruffled, though, as the fact that he'd spilled his guts to Ari last night and then slipped a gift into her bag. O'Doul thought he knew what it meant to be vulnerable. Usually it meant letting a giant on skates swing his fist into his face. But the toughest fight in the NHL now paled in comparison to laying his heart—and his awful history—at Ari's feet.

She hadn't brought up their midnight trip through his horrible childhood this morning. They'd gotten up late because of Ari's headache. And when they finally did rouse themselves, she was in such pain that conversation—aside from her profuse apologies for getting wasted with her friends in his apartment—didn't happen.

Now she was only ten yards away, but it might as well have been ten thousand miles. Sitting on a velvet sofa with Georgia, her dark, wavy hair gleaming under the soft light of the chandeliers, the sight of her was like a low-grade ache in his chest. He'd always made fun of his teammates who'd lost their heads over a woman. But he got it now. There'd been a lot of things he'd yearned for in his life. A quiet place to sleep, where nobody would jump him. A fine meal. A good glass of Scotch. And winning—he'd always wanted to win.

Wanting Ari wasn't like any of those other wants. It was far more terrifying. In the first place, there was too much that was out of his control. He'd always been able to say: *if I just work a little harder, I can have this. If I just put in the hours.* That wasn't the case with Ari. Even as he dreamt up the next romantic thing he might do for her, he knew it might never be enough. She could decide that a punk from the wrong end of Minneapolis wasn't what she needed in her life.

There wouldn't be a damn thing he could do about it.

Jimbo came over eventually and passed out room keys. "Bayer. Beacon. Trevi . . ." He handed them over, and one by one the players headed for the elevator banks. "O'Doul."

He took his key with a glance at the velvet sofa. The women were already gone. He went upstairs, his footsteps hushed by thick carpets beneath his feet. He let himself into a room with a four-poster bed piled high with ornamental pillows. He set his bag on a fussy upholstered bench and walked over to the heavily draped window to peer out at the city lights. The first eighteen years of his life had been lived within a thirty mile radius of the hospital where he was born.

The first time he was ever on a plane was when the Long Island team had invited him to participate in a training camp. He'd been busting his butt for an ECHL team, making five hundred dollars a week. In the summer he worked for a landscaping company, mowing lawns and planting hydrangeas.

Then all of a sudden he's on a jet to LaGuardia.

"Where's your suit and tie?" Hugh Major had asked him when he'd stepped off the plane. Those were the first words Hugh ever spoke to him.

"I don't have one," he'd had to say.

Hugh had gotten one of the office assistants to drive him to a Brooks Brothers. In the store, the salesman had asked him questions about how he wanted to be fitted. All the words were unfamiliar. "Break" and "spread" and "flat front." He didn't have any idea what they were asking him. He'd bought the suit, and he'd had to use both of his credit cards to pay for it, all the time praying that he'd make the roster, if only to pay off his suit.

The team put him up in a cheap hotel right under the JFK airport flight path, and his dreams were filled with sonic booms.

Fast forward a decade, and he was wearing a three-hundred-dollar shirt and peering out the window of a five-star hotel. He'd been to each of the thirty NHL cities, and then some. But there were days when it all seemed like some kind of cosmic joke, where he was sure he was the punchline.

There was a tap on the connecting door. "Patrick?" Ari's voice was muffled from the other side.

He crossed the room in four paces. "Ari?" He opened his side of the door, and there she was. "Hi, sweetheart. You're my neighbor again."

"Becca has fun deciding who's next to whom," she said, not quite meeting his eyes. "Can I talk to you for a second?"

His stomach dropped a notch. "Of course." He stepped

back and she entered the room carrying the box he'd slipped into her bag, and a worried expression. His stomach dropped all the way to the soles of his expensive dress shoes.

"This is beautiful," she said, finally lifting her soft gaze to his. "But I can't take it. When I told you that I couldn't be in a relationship right now, I wasn't kidding. My life is messy."

"I know, baby." He took a half step forward, meaning to pull her into his arms, but something in her expression stopped him. She reached forward, offering the box. He took it reluctantly. "Sit down a second," he said.

She hesitated. "Okay."

He turned, removing his suit coat and tossing it on the bed. Then he sat down at one end of a smallish couch with carved wooden legs. Ari took the other side. He tapped the box. "This isn't a fancy piece of jewelry. I wasn't trying to buy your affection. It's your birthstone, and it was just a gimmicky way to show you that I was paying attention. It doesn't have to be a big deal."

Her eyes were a little shiny by the time she spoke again. "It's the classiest gift I've ever gotten. But I already knew you were paying attention. You show me that every day." She swallowed hard. "The thing is, what I really need in my life right now is not a relationship, but a *friend*. Can you be that?"

An hour ago he would have thought it would be devastating to be rejected by the only woman he'd ever really wanted. But there she sat, two feet away, needing him to understand. So while he wished her decision were different, it wasn't hard to agree. Sliding down the sofa a foot or so, he gathered her into a hug against his favorite tie. "I care about you too much to say no."

"Thank you." She took a deep breath and wrapped her arms around him. "I'm sorry."

"Don't you be sorry. I'm a big boy. But can you do me a favor?"

"What?"

"Keep the pendant, unless you don't like it."

"I love it."

"Then wear it sometimes, and remember that your birthday is coming. Because by the time August rolls around, I'm betting a whole lot of the bullshit in your life will be finished. You'll be out to dinner with your girlfriends and thinking, *hell, that year sucked. But things are looking up.*"

She smiled against his cheek. "God, I hope so. I'll be thirty—a new decade. One where I don't cohabitate with any criminals."

"Aim high, honey." She laughed. At least he had her laughing.

Ari straightened up, flicked a single tear away from her cheek and smiled at him. "You always cheer me up."

"Back atcha, babe." He offered her the box again. "Here. Wear it in good health. Start the countdown." She took it from his hand and opened it. "You've got . . . four or five months until the big three oh. That seems like enough time to let it all blow over."

She reached behind her neck and removed the silver chain she wore. Then she opened the box and threaded the pendant through it. "Would you . . . ?"

"Sure."

She pulled her hair to the side, swiveling to turn her back, and he carefully lowered the pendant over her head, securing the chain with clumsy fingers around her slender neck. The urge to kiss the back of her neck was so strong, but he did the right thing and abstained. He stood up instead. "We should get downstairs. Dinner will start soon. It's in that fancy dining room with the curved ceiling."

Ari stood up, straightening her skirt. "You say that like other people would say, *dinner will be served from the garbage can in the subway station.* What do you have against the Chateau?"

"Eh." He grabbed his jacket off the bed and put it on. "It's stuffy." He smoothed down his lapels (a word he'd managed to learn while shopping for his second or third suit) and joined her in front of the door.

"Thank you," she whispered, her hand on the knob.

He didn't have to ask what she meant. It sucked that she didn't want everything he wanted to give her. But if she wanted to be friends, he'd do it. He'd do anything she asked. He bent down and kissed her forehead. Just once. It was enough to fill his head with her lavender scent, and he had to hold back a sigh. "You're welcome. Now let's go eat rich food and rub elbows with the owner."

Downstairs, they reached the dining room together. Trevi and Beacon stood there, practically tapping their feet. "I'm starving," Beacon complained. "They're not quite ready to seat us."

"Hey, guys," Castro said, catching up to the group. "Hey, Ari. I hope I'm on your schedule tomorrow morning. Nobody has rubbed my feet in ages."

"You poor thing," Ari said. "Coincidentally, nobody has proposed marriage to me in ages." She smiled at the silly young forward, and O'Doul noticed her fingers flutter up to her breastbone and touch the pendant that hung there before falling away again.

"Hey, that's pretty," Castro said. "That color suits you."

O'Doul had the sudden urge to yank Castro's chin upwards, removing his eyes from Ari's chest. Who knew there was a downside to buying your girl something pretty to wear?

"Thank you," Ari said, touching the pendant again. "It's my birthstone."

"*Reeeeally*," Castro said slowly. "Your birthstone."

"Right. August."

Castro's eyes—plus a few other pairs—cut to O'Doul's. *Hello, awkwardness.* Slowly, and with great deliberation, O'Doul gave a single, sad shake of his head.

Maybe hockey players weren't known for being the most subtle bunch of guys in the world, but not one man said anything about it until later. After the official team meal they were allowed to ditch their suits and slink across the street to a bar.

"So. Ari?" Trevi asked, grabbing the stool next to his. "You and she are a thing?"

"Damn," Bayer said, rubbing his hands together. "Didn't see that one coming. We'll all stop proposing marriage to her on the massage table if that makes you uncomfortable."

"Not sure it matters, champ," he said, tossing back his Scotch. "She told me quite firmly today that it isn't gonna happen."

"So I do have a chance," Castro joked, nudging O'Doul's shoulder.

O'Doul made a growling noise. He couldn't help it. He was willing to accept the fact that Ari wouldn't date him. But if anyone else started hitting on her, they'd better brace for some trouble.

"*Joking*," Castro said. "Jesus."

"How do you get over someone?" he asked suddenly. He'd never had to do that before.

Trevi chuckled. "If you pass out tickets and make us all turn in suggestions, you're just gonna get twenty-four pieces of paper back that say *get very drunk* on 'em."

"Not necessarily," Jimbo put in. "I'd write: *Listen to sad music and play a lot of Xbox*. It's cheaper than drinking, and a better distraction."

"You really are wise for a nineteen-year-old," Trevi said.

"And would you believe that the legal drinking age in Ottawa is nineteen?" the kid asked with a smile.

"Drinks for Jimbo!" Trevi called, pulling his wallet out of his pocket. "Who's with me?" He let Jimbo pick the beer, and ordered another pitcher. Then he slapped O'Doul on the back. "So what's your strategy?"

"My strategy?"

"Wait her out or find someone else?"

But I don't want anyone else. "I'm just going to give her some space. I'd be lying if I said I wasn't hoping she'd change her mind. Pretty sure it won't happen, though."

Trevi looked thoughtful. "You still have a chance. Women are complicated. Let me give you an example. My girl doesn't like to shop. But in a store, she still takes a long time, evaluating all the pros and cons of the features or what-the-fuck-ever."

"What are you trying to say?"

"Women make decisions differently. How do you choose a coffeemaker?"

O'Doul shrugged. "I point to one that looks good. Then I just buy it."

"Exactly."

"So? What does that have to do with Ari?" He hated it when College Boy got all metaphorical.

"Maybe she already found the model she wants, but she has to walk out of the store one time just to be sure she knows her own mind."

O'Doul grunted. "I don't know. If I walk in to buy a coffeemaker, I'm leaving with a coffeemaker."

"That's my point. You're leaving with a coffeemaker because you have a dick."

"Wait—" Castro held up a hand. "Who left his dick in the coffeemaker?"

"Check, please," O'Doul said, lifting a hand to the barkeep. Trevi burst out laughing.

TWENTY-FOUR

With Becca and Georgia, from a seat behind the penalty box, Ari watched every minute of the Ottawa game with her heart in her mouth.

Late-season tension gripped the crowd, and the game seemed to happen at top speed, the puck flying with even more velocity than normal.

Her eyes followed Patrick everywhere. She could pretend her interest was based on concern for his iliopsoas muscles, but that would be a lie. He'd gotten under her skin. As she watched him fly by on the ice, looking as fit and energetic as she'd ever seen him, she felt a tug.

I just told him no, she reminded herself.

In the third period, Ari had the thrill of watching Patrick score against Ottawa. It was a beautiful shot, too. A wrister that Trevi had passed backward to keep it away from the other team's defenseman. It flew right to the tape on Patrick's stick. A nanosecond later he'd sent it flying over the goalie's knee pads straight into the corner of the net.

Leaping from her seat, she screamed, as both Becca and Georgia grabbed her into a hug.

The score was 3–1 in favor of Brooklyn, with the clock winding down.

The other team's response was to use their time-out, of course, and then to pick a fight. Ari tensed when she saw the other team's enforcer getting chippy during the next two face-offs. But it was Crikey who ultimately threw down his gloves. His tussle with the other guy wasn't flashy or even decisive. But it didn't last too long, and Crikey seemed to only shake out his fist before the refs finally pulled them apart.

Ari let out a sigh of relief, and wondered if Patrick did the same.

"We are going to have to celebrate after this is over," Becca said, collapsing back into her seat.

"There are still three minutes on the clock," Georgia chided her. "Don't you dare jinx us."

"It's going to be fine," Becca argued. "We've got this."

Georgia clamped a hand over her mouth and yelled toward the rafters. "She didn't mean it, god! Don't punish us."

Ari snickered. Her two friends were a walking dialectic about superstition. Ari didn't know which camp she was in, either. Could fate be tempted into smacking you down? She hoped not. Because that would mean she had seriously pissed off fate somehow lately.

Whether fate gave a damn or not, the clock still read 3–1 when the final buzzer sounded a few minutes later. Brooklyn had two game points to take back with them on the jet tonight.

"Now can we celebrate?" Becca whined.

"Sure," Georgia said. "I'll spring for overpriced drinks at the airport bar before takeoff."

Two hours later they were sipping wine out of plastic cups in front of a fake fireplace in the charter terminal of the airport.

"So let me get this straight." Becca held her cup up. "You told Doulie you wanted to be friends, and he was okay with that?"

Ari took a slow sip. "He was really nice about it," she

admitted. "So nice that I suspect he has a secret plan to change my mind. He knows that each time he tries to remove my clothing, I always shed it like a long-haired cat on a pair of black velvet pants."

Georgia giggled. "You sound like you *want* him to change it."

"I've made up my mind, but my body didn't get the memo," Ari confessed. "When I told him I needed a friend, he hugged me. And he smelled so freaking good I just wanted to climb into the collar of his shirt and stay there forever."

"That would get weird eventually," Becca said, draining her cup.

"This from the woman who slept with her knees against my butt last night," Georgia teased. Since Becca's addition to the trip had been so last-minute, the travel department didn't make her a reservation. Becca had roomed with Georgia, and Georgia's room had one king-sized bed.

"You loved it," Becca insisted. "It was just like old times. We watched trash TV and whined about how hard we work. Although, in ye good old days, we were *both* sexually frustrated."

"Sorry, toots. I still have my moments," Georgia said. "Leo has always had a NNBG rule, even in high school. But lately the time span is getting ridiculous."

"What's NNBG?" Ari asked.

"No Nookie Before Games," Georgia said. "He used to only mean *hours* before. But as we approach the play-offs, he says he likes to save it up for afterward." She got a dreamy look on her face, then. "I don't really mind, because afterward is pretty great. After that win tonight? I'm going to be extra tired at work tomorrow."

Becca groaned and flopped back in the airport chair, hands raised into a prayerful pose. "Lord, hear my prayer. Just one hot night! That's all a girl needs, god! Just send me one."

"You and Castro seemed pretty cozy the other day," Ari pointed out. "Anything there?"

"Nah." Becca waved a dismissive hand. "We're just buddies. He's fun, and we just kid each other."

"Nate didn't think it was fun," Georgia said, checking over her shoulder to make sure there was nobody nearby to overhear. "I've never heard him so grumpy."

"I know, right?" Becca crossed her feet and sighed. "He's just out to ruin a good time. He thinks I ought to actually *work* for my paycheck. The nerve of that man."

"Bottoms up, girls." Georgia pointed at the screen of her Katt Phone, the rim of which glowed red. "The jet is boarding." She leapt up, grabbing her bag.

"Look at her hurrying," Becca whined. "She's going home to a sextravaganza." She poked Ari in the elbow. "Your plan to stay single just baffles me right now."

"I have my reasons," she insisted. If she could only manage to keep her clothes on, she might even remember what they were.

TWENTY-FIVE

Standings: 3th Place
9 Regular Season Games Remaining

B ack at home in Brooklyn in the wee hours of the next morning, O'Doul's bed felt uncommonly empty. Which was ridiculous, because for years nobody but him had slept in it anyway. They'd won the game, which made him happy. But there was nobody to talk to. For years he'd looked at his married teammates and wondered how they balanced it all. Some guys made it sound like trying to keep a wife and kids happy was another full-time job.

He got it now, though. Having someone to come home to suddenly made sense. The stats lighting up his Katt Phone predicted a 91 percent chance of making the play-offs, and he had nobody to celebrate with.

In spite of his brooding, he slept well and woke up feeling optimistic. It helped that he was busy as hell. They had a play-off spot to clinch, so he rose early and went to the optional morning skate.

Naturally, the next thing on his schedule was a massage with Ari.

"Good morning," he said, entering the treatment room with as much of a smile as he could muster. He'd promised her once already to keep things professional in the treatment room. And he'd told her that she was the only one who was allowed to touch him.

That was all still true.

"Hi there," she said, patting his arm as he relaxed onto the table. "I sure enjoyed watching you skate last night."

"I enjoyed it, too," he said truthfully. See? He could do this. He could be Ari's friend and make small talk.

She began to work her magic on his muscles. "How's your hip today? Any new soreness?"

"Feeling pretty flexible, actually. I had some pain by the end of the game last night, but on balance it's less than it was ten days ago."

"Awesome," she said, and he felt her smile even with his eyes closed. "Was it okay with you that Crikey took the fight?"

"Yeah." He'd admit it to Ari, but maybe nobody else. "He and I are gonna train together some more. We both need to stay injury free. We'll work something out."

"I know you will," she whispered, and the sound of her breathy voice brought goose bumps to his chest. He'd wondered if it would sting to see her today and to have her hands on his body. It did a little. But it would sting more not to see her at all.

Life had had fewer ups and downs when he had been happy to be a loner.

"Turn over for me?" she asked. "I'm done with your hip."

"Already?" How odd that he hadn't noticed. It wasn't so long ago when the idea of her touching the injury at all made him tense. These days he forgot to worry at all. He rolled, and she adjusted the towel.

He let his mind drift as she worked over his hamstrings. Trevi's wisdom about the difference between women and men floated past his consciousness. "Let me ask you a question," he said, almost slurring the words because he was so relaxed.

"Anything."

"When you need to buy something, do you take a long time thinking it over?"

"Hmm. It depends what it is, and how much it costs."

"Say I needed to buy a coffeemaker." Her sweet hands moved to his lower back and he sank a little further onto the table.

"They all just push hot water through grounds, right?" she said, running a hand up his lats. "No point in dragging that out."

"Fucking Trevi," he chuckled into the face cradle.

"What's that? Am I hurting you?"

Only my heart. "No. That feels great."

O'Doul left his massage whistling. He had a shower and got dressed. But those were the last easy minutes of the day.

Hugh Major appeared as suddenly as a storm cloud, his phone in his hand, his expression full of doom. "O'Doul," he growled. "Step into my office. We have a situation."

O'Doul had always wondered what the end of his NHL career would look like. He'd hoped it would end with his jersey hoisted into the stadium rafters, and a plaque on his wall. But as the manager led the way down the long corridor from the treatment rooms into the corporate suite, he knew all too well it could end exactly like this. A long walk to the boss's office. A door closing with a quiet click. The G.M. crossing his arms, looking both angry and disappointed.

"What's the problem?" he asked when they finally reached Hugh's office. As if he didn't already know.

"There's a journalist from the *Post*." His lips made a flat line. "She says she can prove you bought drugs in a nightclub. Apparently that's not enough of a story for her, either. Sounds like she's going to try to spin this thing into some kind of big doping scandal."

The same quiet, focused calm descended on him that he felt during a fight. He played back the manager's words in his head, and they weren't what he'd expected. O'Doul had predicted that Vince might try to leverage his dirty secret via law enforcement. But reporters? That might actually be worse. "Hugh, the team doesn't have a doping problem," he said. "That's ridiculous."

"Yeah," Hugh said, folding his arms and looking up at the ceiling. "It is. But that still leaves us with a problem."

Here it comes.

"She says there's a picture. You in some nightclub's back room, making a buy."

Pictures, fuck. This was bad. "What is it that I supposedly bought?" he asked as calmly as possible.

Hugh huffed out a sigh. "Don't play it that way, Doulie. Just tell me what the hell happened at that club. I can't help you if I don't know what I'm really dealing with."

O'Doul hesitated. Hugh had been good to him for more than ten years, but the man's responsibility was to the team as a whole and to Nate, his boss. It didn't matter if Hugh was a good man, and he was fair. He had a job to do, and that job was not to save O'Doul's ass. "I have to speak to my agent," he said.

"Seriously? After all this time?" Hugh shook his head. "Just *talk* to me. You think I'm going to just toss you to the wolves?"

Yeah, if you need to. "I'm calling Tommy. We'll speak later." He walked out of the office suite then, just leaving Hugh behind to stew. He crossed the lobby, where a video of him scoring in overtime played in a continuous loop.

Outside, the air blowing off the river was cool and damp. He turned his face into the wind and took a deep breath. He'd been a hockey player long enough to understand that everything could change in an instant. One minute you might be flying down the ice, the puck under your control. The next second you might be smashed into the boards like a bug on a windshield.

Bad news worked in just the same way. It didn't give any warning.

Quick strides ate up the two blocks between team headquarters and his apartment. The concierge swept the door open for him and he strode into the ridiculously fancy lobby of his building.

If this was it—if it was all really over—he'd probably leave Brooklyn. There'd be no point in staying two blocks from the team that had ended his career.

Where would he even go?

He pushed that worry away and unlocked his apartment. He tossed his jacket on the couch and took out his Katt Phone. His finger already hovered over his agent's name when he realized his mistake.

Shit.

O'Doul shut down his Katt Phone. Then he carried it into the bathroom, placing it on the counter top. For good measure, he turned the bathroom sink on to run water noisily down the basin. He left the bathroom, closing the door behind him. He went to the landline phone—so underused there was dust on it—and dialed Tommy's number from memory.

"Doulie?" Tom answered immediately. "Hey, man. Everything okay?"

"Not really."

"Sorry to hear that," Tom said. "What's up?"

O'Doul carefully relayed everything Hugh had just told him.

"When were you at this club?" Tom asked. The man was smart enough not to bother asking if it was true.

"January."

"What did you buy?"

O'Doul said "uppers," without hesitation. But that didn't mean he wasn't burning with shame just hearing the word come out of his mouth. Dumbest thing he'd ever done.

"Okay," Tom said quickly. "When's the last time you took one?"

He thought back. "When did I play at Denver?"

"Hang on." He heard the clicking of a keyboard. "February second."

"That's the night. We went to Phoenix after that, and my stash was fresh out."

Tom sighed. "So that's . . . more than six weeks."

"Yeah."

"You're sure?"

"Absolutely."

"Anything else in your bloodstream that you wouldn't want written up in the *Post*?"

"No sir. Unless they're testing for Scotch whiskey."

His agent was quiet for a moment. "Okay, man. Here's what I need you to do—deny this completely. Whatever the picture looks like, it's not you in it. Or it *is* you, but you're paying for a lap dance or some shit. Just deny anything to do with drugs."

"You think that will work?"

"That stuff is only testable for a few days. A week, tops. But, *shit* Doulie. Buying at a *nightclub?* Worst idea I ever heard. Those places thrive on blackmail. They don't make all their money selling overpriced martinis."

Jesus. "Not exactly skilled at breaking the law, Tommy. Only bought the one time."

"Once?" His agent made a noise of pain. "Then you are one unlucky bastard. You can't trust anyone, okay? There's something you think you need, you tell *me*. I'll find a guy to get it to you."

Oh my fucking god. Now his agent was offering to be his dealer? That was not what he expected to happen. "Are you positive I can't be nailed on a drug test? Should I just offer to take one to clear the air?"

"If you're sure you've got the timing right. And if you're sure your club won't just lie about your results."

O'Doul flinched. If they wanted to put him out to pasture, he'd just made that really easy for them. "Hugh won't do that," he decided. "He's not an asshole, and it would make the team look bad. I think Hugh wants to help me."

"Careful," Tom said. "The only person you can trust is me, because our interests are completely aligned. But Hugh doesn't have the luxury of being loyal. Give your team a flat-out denial, and offer a test. They might not even test you. In the first place, there're more recreational drugs in hockey than you can shake a hockey stick at. And Hugh doesn't want to start a real witch hunt. Nobody will end up looking good."

"All right. But forget Hugh for a second. What can the league do to me?"

"Nothing, except test you if they feel like it. But they can't test the whole team until the postseason, no matter what the newspaper prints. Now let me go so I can call Hugh on your behalf as soon as we hang up. Don't forget the party line—whatever they think those pictures show, they're crazy. And that's all we have to say on the subject."

"All right."

"Stay strong, man. We'll get through this. They'll be offering you a contract extension in July like we need 'em to."

"Thanks."

They hung up. O'Doul went back into the bathroom and shut the water off. But he didn't turn his phone on. Whatever it was that people had to say to him, he wasn't ready to hear it. He needed to cool his heels while Tom dealt with Hugh and the team.

It was lunchtime, so he went into the kitchen and opened the refrigerator. Then he caught himself just standing there, staring.

Don't trust anyone, Tommy had said. The man was right, too. His whole life he'd been fending for himself. No family. Even though it sometimes felt as though the team was his family, it wasn't really true. If he let them down, he'd be out on his ass.

He slammed the fridge and went to lie down on his sofa.

It was so fucking quiet in his apartment. The silence had never bothered him before, but now it seemed oppressive.

Naturally his thoughts went to Ari, as they so often did lately. Today or tomorrow she'd hear about this. She'd see the story in the newspaper or hear it whispered at work. She'd think, *What an idiot. There's a bullet dodged.*

And she'd be right.

TWENTY-SIX

Ari slept uneasily in Brooklyn that night. Georgia had tried to convince her to spend the night in their spare room, but she hadn't agreed.

Instead, she kept her panic button close by, and spent half the night listening for trouble, before finally falling into a deep sleep around three thirty.

She woke up with a start when her alarm went off, and felt immediately uneasy.

Given all that had occurred in her life lately, that wasn't terribly unusual. But as she came to consciousness alone in her own bed, it wasn't Vince she was worried about. This morning she woke with an image of Patrick in her mind, and a tickle of worry at the base of her skull.

Maybe it was just uncertainty about the gift she'd bought him. Yesterday after her massage appointments ended she walked Atlantic Avenue until she found what she was looking for—a dual coffee and espresso machine, the same model as her own. It made good coffee and it had never let her down. She'd figured she could save him the hassle of shopping and just gift it to him.

But was that weird? Friends could buy friends a coffee-maker, right?

She ate a small breakfast in her pajamas at her kitchen table. An hour from now she'd be up in front of the team, teaching a yoga class at the practice facility. Usually she used this time to meditate on what she wanted to accomplish with them.

But the prickle of unease wouldn't leave her. It persisted while Ari drank some water and changed into yoga clothes. Before she left her house, she picked up the pendant Patrick had given her. It was so pretty, but she felt a twinge of guilt at keeping it. So she put it back down on the dresser. But that didn't feel right either. So she picked it back up again and put it on.

The home screen of her Katt Phone glowed with her schedule for the day. *Yoga class in twenty minutes*, it said. *Studio B*.

She slung the shopping bag containing the coffeemaker over one shoulder and left the house. It was a cool morning, and on her short walk to work, she felt the chill all the way to her bones. So when she reached the Bruisers' headquarters, she stashed her gift in her treatment room, then went straight to the yoga studio to bump up the thermostat.

Ari loved teaching in this bright, modern room. It had high-tech sprung flooring and soft natural light. She hooked her iPod up to the sound system and straightened the stack of yoga blocks in the corner. Sometimes she looked around this lovely room and thought, *I can't believe this is really my job*.

Players began to trickle in one at a time, placing their mats on the floor facing hers at the end of the room. A yoga class was supposed to begin peacefully, without a lot of chatter, and they all knew the drill. So it was quiet while they assembled.

Too quiet, though. Today the silence was tomblike. At first she attributed it to the early hour. But one after another the players who unrolled their mats in the room sank down on them, eyes cast low, expressions grim. Ari looked up as Georgia entered the room in her yoga clothes. She always came into the room with a cheery smile. But today she looked tired and drawn. And—this was weird—she didn't make eye contact with Ari at all.

At one minute to eight she counted heads. Most every player was there, and members of the training staff. But Coach Worthington, Hugh Major, and Nate Kattenberger were all absent.

That was a little weird, too. Nate always tried to make her classes, usually scheduling his Manhattan appointments an hour later than usual just so he could begin his day with her vinyasa class. It was his favorite way of staying in touch with the team. Consequently, his management staff usually showed up, too.

Not today, though.

The very last person to enter the room was Patrick. Whoever is late to yoga class always ends up in the front row, dead center, and it was no different for him. He strode into the room purposefully, as if he'd shown up on a dare. But he didn't look anyone in the eye either. And when he took the last spot right in front of Ari, she could swear that she heard a crackle of tension in the air.

That was odd.

"Good morning," she told the class. Fewer than the usual number of attentive gazes raised to meet hers. "Let's open our practice in a seated position." She sat down on her mat, crossing her legs. "It's cold outside, and I really feel the chill." *Not just from the weather, either.* "So we're going to raise the temperature of our practice today, and sweat out our tensions."

A couple of the players shook their heads. Not everyone loved hot yoga.

Ari asked her students to close their eyes and relax. She walked them through a brief meditation on the subject of inner focus. Then she hit play on her iPod. A drum rhythm started up, lending the room its heartbeat. "Rise into mountain pose, please. On the exhale, forward fold. Hang there and gently roll your head for two breath cycles. On the next inhale, rise to Utkatasana . . . Good." She walked over to the thermostat and nudged it up to eighty degrees, just as an opening gambit.

". . . Arms up, offering the heart," she said, lifting her hands in the air. "On the exhale, dive into forward fold."

As a room full of bodies dropped forward in perfect sync, Ari was full of gratitude. The power she commanded in this room was only hers because her students gave it to her. For an hour every other morning, they handed her the reins, and she held them gently.

It was an honor.

"Inhale, rising to half lift, finding length in your back. Exhale, hands planted, feet float back to high plank." On their mats, she took them through a quick series of push-ups, and then into the basic vinyasa. "Exhale, rising into downward dog. Now walk it out. Stretch those hamstrings."

Butts in the air everywhere—that was her view. Two dozen guys warming up their powerful bodies. Just another day at the office.

Next, she took them through a long series of sun salutations and warrior poses. But there was still so much tightness in the room. And the tightest of all was Patrick. His shoulders were tense, and his movements short. He was the epicenter of the morning's stress. She could almost feel the others leaning away from him, as if his aura were poisonous.

She nudged the thermostat's temperature even higher. Maybe she could burn away the tension. There was no complaining, even as sweat began to drip off the players. One by one they shed their shirts, until the room was full of rippling abs. To think that they paid her for this.

"Well done," she encouraged them as their muscles began to shake in Ardha Chandrasana, or half-moon pose. "Balance is the key to all strength. Notice how your breath moves through the body in this pose. And at the bottom of the next breath, bring it back into a forward fold."

She guided them into pigeon pose next, a hip opener.

While they held it, she moved around the room suggesting corrections to make the stretch feel more natural.

"I never saw a pigeon do this," Castro muttered when she stopped beside him.

"Mmhhmm," she said, easing the position of his back leg.

Then she knelt beside Patrick, touching the fold of his hip. "Take it easy here," she whispered.

He turned his chin so she could see his sharp, blue eyes, and she almost wish he hadn't. That piercing gaze was unhappy. And even worse, it regarded her as a stranger.

"Are you okay?" She meant his hip, but it came out sounding like a bigger question.

"Sure," he grunted.

"Are you on my schedule later?" she whispered. She'd glanced down the list of names on her phone in the elevator and had been surprised when his wasn't there.

"Not sure it matters," he said cryptically. Then he dropped his chin toward the yoga mat and ignored her.

Yikes. She knelt there a beat longer out of confusion. Then got up again to resume the class.

By the time it was over, everyone was sweating fountains, yet they appeared no less tense or unhappy than beforehand. She didn't have many classes with the team that felt like utter failures, but this was going to go down as one of them.

"Namaste, class," she whispered at the end.

"Namaste," came the muttered response.

She'd hoped to catch Patrick and give him his present. But he bolted from the room immediately.

Ariana ducked into the empty women's locker room for a quick shower. She changed into clean clothes and then set up for her first massage appointments of the day. In the treatment room she set up her iPod and fetched a stack of clean sheets and towels.

As usual, before a massage, she pulled out her phone to shut it off. Right on the front screen she found a text from Vince. *Your boyfriend is in trouble now,* he'd written.

The hair stood up on the back of her neck. What the hell had Vince done? She unlocked her phone and looked at her texts. There was one more: *You think this is bad, just tell him I have video. I can make it look like the whole team is involved.*

There was a link to a newspaper article in the *Post*.

BROOKLYN BRUISERS CAPTAIN ADDICTED TO PILLS

Ari gasped. "What the fuck is this?" Scrolling down the story, her eye zoomed right in on the name of the club where Patrick O'Doul supposedly bought drugs. It was Vince's club. "This is *bullshit*," she hissed aloud.

But there was even a picture—sort of. It showed a man who might or might not be Patrick taking something from one of Vince's minions. She tried to zoom in on the man, but the resolution of the picture quickly went to seed.

"Ari?" Becca stuck her head into the alcove. "Are you okay?"

"No! This . . ." She held up the phone. "It can't be him. Where is Hugh Major?" She had to explain what was happening to the GM. Vince had drummed up a smear campaign to make Patrick look bad because of *her*.

She didn't even wait for Becca to answer. She ducked past the massage table and jogged through the players' dressing room. Pushing open the door to the hallway, she spotted Hugh and Patrick in a tense conversation. "Guys, this is bullshit," she said, holding up her phone. "He's making this up to get back at me. You can put me in front of that reporter. She should know that the owner of that club is just pissed off at Patrick because of me."

Neither man said anything. They both stared back at her with tight expressions.

"Am I not speaking English right now?" she asked, her voice sounding high and squeaky. "This is all my fault."

As if he hadn't even heard her, Hugh turned back to Patrick. "We'll talk in a little while." Then he walked away.

"What the fuck?" Ari hissed. "Let's just fix this."

"Ari, has he tried to contact you today?" Patrick asked, his voice low.

"He texted," she admitted. "But it's ridiculous."

"What did he say? Show me."

"*Why?*" she demanded. "It's just a smear campaign. He's using you to hit at me. That's not even you in the picture."

Patrick leaned back against the wall and sighed. "Ari." He looked over his right shoulder and then his left. "It's me in the fucking picture."

"You . . ." She tried to make sense of it. "Really? When? And what were you doing at Vince's club?"

His expression flattened. "I was there just randomly with a bunch of team members. It was Massey's birthday, I think. It doesn't matter why."

"The *Post* thinks it does! God, I'm so sorry. This is awful. It's all my fault."

He stood up to his full height and lifted her chin toward his face. Those cool blue eyes looked both tired and intense at the same time. "There is nothing about this that's your fault. That's all I can tell you."

"But . . ." Of *course* it was. First, that photograph of their kiss. Vince had practically advertised his capacity for jealousy and vengeance. The only way this wasn't her fault was if the drug buy was real.

Oh.

Oh, shit.

"Wait—seriously?" she hissed. "You went to a club to buy drugs?"

His eyes closed, as if he was in pain. He dropped his hand from her face and winced.

"Jesus, Patrick." Her mind tilted with panic. "So when you punched Vince at my house, you already knew him. He was your *dealer*."

"We are *not* talking about this . . ." he began through gritted teeth.

"Oh. My. God," she spat, taking a step backward. "This whole time you were sticking close to me because you needed to know what Vince was up to."

"NO!" he bellowed. "That is not what happened."

"Wow," she said, her throat constricting. "People told me that you never got close to anyone, and how unusual it was. Now I know *why*." She choked on the last word.

Patrick clenched his fists at his sides. He closed his eyes and forcibly banged his head back against the wall. "That's all the faith you have in me," he said to the ceiling. "At least now I know." He shook his head and started to move down the hall, away from her.

"Thanks for lying to me. When I asked you to be my friend, that's not what I had in mind."

He halted in his tracks, and she held her breath, wondering if he would turn around.

But he didn't. He just kept going, leaving her there, mouth open in shock, wondering what the hell had just happened.

TWENTY-SEVEN

Ari worked her way through four massage appointments, feeling absolutely numb.

The feeling was mutual, apparently. The men on her table seemed sad and subdued. A scandal was bad for everyone. And if O'Doul got thrown off the team, their chances at the play-offs suddenly looked grim.

At the first gap in her schedule, she decided to step outside. Maybe a walk around the neighborhood would steady her. When she grabbed her jacket, the coffeemaker in the corner mocked her. She and Patrick were never as close as she'd imagined they were. In fact, the entire scope of their relationship began to look dubious. The moment they'd started spending time together was the same moment Patrick punched Vince outside her house.

He'd chased her ex away, and then he'd brought her home and made her feel safe. And the whole time, he'd had entanglements with Vince, too.

Yet he had never said a word.

Walking down the sidewalk, she tilted her face up to the cloudy sky. "I am so done with liars in my life!" A mother pushing a stroller down the sidewalk in the opposite direction gave her the side eye on her way past.

Yay. She was actually frightening people, now.

She went home to her own kitchen and put the kettle on. Her mind was whirring with anxiety. She should call the lawyer and tell him this new development. She should call Georgia and offer to speak to the reporter anyway, just in case it helped the team stay out of the tabloids. She should meditate, or take an aspirin for the headache that was just starting up at the base of her skull. Or both.

But first, tea.

She was just turning off the burner under the boiling kettle when her Katt Phone rang.

Vince.

Shit.

She poured the hot water over her tea bag and considered her options. The phone stopped ringing, but then it started up again a minute later.

Feeling impulsive, she answered it. "Vince," she sighed. "This is no way to get what you want."

"Yeah, it is. And you need to hear exactly why."

Fear prickled at the back of her neck. "What are you saying?"

"I have video of your boyfriend making the buy. Check your e-mail. I sent you a clip."

Just as she was choking on the word *video*, he hung up.

With shaking hands, she opened her email inbox. The subject line of his email was,

Watch me make it worse.

She clicked on the Play button for the video. And the twenty-seven seconds of footage she saw made her angrier than she'd ever been. It was Patrick on tape, and although she had no way of knowing what it was that the dealer handed him in that little baggy, he *looked* guilty. Before he took it, he looked over one shoulder and then the other, his eyes darting around to check who was watching.

It made her want to shake him for being so stupid.

Her phone rang in her hand. The caller was Vince again. "Look," he said into her ear. "Sorry to be the bearer of bad news. I know you think the dicks you work for are the second coming of Christ. Maybe you think I'm a loser for getting mixed up with some drug dealers, Ari, but I don't *swallow* that shit."

She was shaken to the core but she wasn't about to let him hear it. "What do you want from me?"

"Give me my property and I'm gone. You'll never hear my name again. But if you don't help me, tonight I'm giving the reporter a bunch more material. Here's the thing—with a little creative editing I can also make it look like he bought the stuff to share with the rest of the team. They'll all know it's bogus, too. And they'll blame you for it. Bye-bye job. So open your front door."

"I'm not home right now."

He laughed. "Really? You have a twin I don't know about? Just saw you walk through your front door two minutes ago."

Fuck.

"I need to get into your house, and right now. One thing is all I need. It's smaller than a breadbox."

"*What* is? What are you after?"

He sighed into her ear. "A gun, babe. You want a handgun in your house? It was used in a crime scene."

"Jesus," she gasped. "Why the hell is there a gun in my house?"

"It's evidence, and it's protecting me from some grade-A assholes. I need it *right fucking now*, Ari. It will take ten minutes. Or less if you help."

"Help? You can't be serious." Someone knocked roughly on the front door, and Ari jumped a foot into the air.

"Let me in. We can do this the easy way or the hard way. Pick easy, babe. Ten minutes and it's done."

Later, she would wonder why she opened the door. Was it bravado? Stupidity? Being rid of him sounded awfully good, though. Even if she should have known better.

The first thing she realized when the door swung open was that Vince looked like shit. His hair was greasy, he hadn't shaved in days. *Yikes*. There were bags under his eyes as he looked past her to scan the room.

"There's nobody here," she said, her voice so flat that he didn't bother checking the truth of it.

Vince kicked the door shut with the heel of his shoe. "It's upstairs," he said, pointing up the stairway.

Ari felt nauseated by the idea of walking up that staircase with him again. The last time she'd done that, she'd ended up with a broken bone. "Where?"

"The bedroom. Go on."

She turned quickly away, if only to hide her stricken face. *Ten minutes*, she reminded herself. And then, finally having a moment of self-preservation, she snatched her purse off the bottom step and brought it upstairs with her. The panic button still clung on its discreet metal loop to the strap. Walking up the stairs in front of Vince, a tingle of fear clung to her spine. How many hours had she spent alone in this house with him? Thousands. But this didn't feel the least bit familiar. Not at all.

At the top of the stairs she went into the bedroom and paused in front of the dresser, waiting to see what he'd do.

"We're moving the bed," he grunted. "It's underneath."

Lovely. I've been sleeping above a weapon. Ari dropped her purse, knelt down and pulled her suitcase out of the way. Not much light shone underneath the hanging quilt, but there didn't seem to be anything at all under there.

What if it wasn't here? Would Vince flip out?

"Come on," Vince prompted. "We have to move this so I can get under the floorboards."

Jesus. During the last awful months with him, she'd worried about his bad attitude toward her job. When she really might have worried that he was *prying up her floorboards* to hide illegal activity. She put her hands underneath the crosspiece on the side closest to the window and waited for him to do the same on the opposite side.

"Ready? Toward me," he said. "Go."

Ari shoved the heavy bed toward him. "Don't lift with your back," she cautioned.

He raised an eyebrow at her. But it was just instinct that had made her say it—a yoga instructor's reflex to watch out for body strains. It wasn't affection, it was self-preservation. If he injured himself she wouldn't be rid of him as quickly.

As soon as they'd shoved the bed aside, Vince pulled a screwdriver out of his back pocket and wedged it under the molding along the wall. With a yank, he pried it up.

Ari stopped herself from protesting the destruction. She could fix it all later. If he'd only leave. She studied his profile as he frowned down at his work, prying the end of the floorboard up next. She looked at his haggard face and tried to feel something. There had once been a smiling Vince who called her "my girl" and liked to dance. That guy was long gone, though. And this one looked like a stranger to her.

Three boards were levered up before he reached into the darkness below and pulled out a ziplock bag with something heavy inside.

She turned her head away, as if it wouldn't be true if she didn't see it properly.

He gave a dry chuckle. "Yeah, I know. Stay in your Zen bubble, girl. You think you're better than me."

I'm not the one tucking a gun into my jacket. She was too smart to say that out loud, though. "I was loyal to you," she said instead. "Whatever attitude you think I have is in your head."

"ARI!" came a shout from outside. Goose bumps broke out across her neck because it was Patrick's voice. "Man on!" he yelled.

Still kneeling on the floor, Vince froze.

That's when she heard it—cautious, nearly silent footsteps on the stairs.

Terrified, Ari moved on pure instinct, slipping into the adjacent bathroom, shutting the door and sliding the hardware store latch lock into place.

"Fuck," she heard Vince curse.

The sound she heard next was the cock of a gun—*click-click*—just like in the movies. "You got something there for me?" a stranger's voice asked on the other side of the door.

Ari trembled. Sure, she was alone in the bathroom. But now she was *trapped* in here.

Without her panic button, of course.

Think, Ari. She edged toward the narrow little window over the toilet. It hadn't been opened in months, since the summer. Quietly, she lowered the toilet seat and then stepped up onto it, one foot at a time.

"Just take it out, nice and slow," the stranger's voice said.

"Let's make a little deal," Vince's voice proposed. She could hear his fear through the wall, and it fueled hers.

The other voice just laughed.

She put shaking fingers to the crosspieces of the window and pressed upward. Slowly, the window opened a little ways and then stopped. Two inches of sunshine was all she'd gained. But the cool air hit her face and she tasted victory. She braced her hands again and pushed. Nothing. So she relaxed for a second and then pushed *hard*.

A horrible wood-on-wood squeal filled the air as the sash raised another three inches.

"Who's that?" the strange voice demanded.

Ari inhaled sharply, terror streaking through her chest. She braced her arms again and pushed, but fear made her inefficient. The window didn't budge. *I need to break it*, she thought, her mind wheeling. And maybe that would have worked in the first place, but now it never would. The stuck window's wooden sash divided the escape route right in two.

The sound of footsteps outside the bathroom crawled right up her throat, and then the bathroom door rattled as someone tried to turn the knob. She froze, listening. Outside she heard another squeal, this one metal against metal. What the hell was that? She stuck her face into the six-inch window opening, getting an awkward view of the fire escape that ran past the bathroom and bedroom widows. A face popped into view at the far end of the fire escape, scaring her half to death until she realized it belonged to Patrick. He'd climbed the ladder.

Their eyes locked even as someone began to kick at the bathroom door.

Patrick pointed at the bedroom window, silently asking a question.

NO! she mouthed. The man with the gun was there.

He began to move, crawling across the narrow metal ledge, trying to stay beneath the sightline of the window.

Behind her the kicking got louder, and she heard the first splinter of wood beginning to give out.

Frantic now, Ari shoved at the window again. It moved a tiny fraction of an inch. And then all at once it gave way, slapping upward and out of her hands as Patrick forced it from the other side. Then his hands were reaching through the opening, grabbing her, pulling her through to the other side.

She made a terrifying headfirst dive toward the metal fire escape, which shook as Patrick caught her. There was a crash inside the building, and then loud cursing, and it was coming closer.

"Oh my G . . ." she started to say before Patrick's hand closed over her mouth. In this, the most jacked situation she could ever remember being in, that rough palm was actually calming. Then it moved to her shoulder, asking her to stay put.

The next two seconds seemed to take a year. Patrick crouched over her as someone moved through the bathroom. She tensed as the moment of their discovery approached. Except Patrick suddenly sprang upwards. There was the sick sound of his fist connecting with a face, and an enraged scream. And then breaking glass a few feet to the side of her head.

Apparently Ari wasn't the only one who'd thought of leaving the premises via a window.

But nobody came through the broken bedroom window, and Patrick was urging her toward the ladder at the end. "Stay low," he barked in her ear. He had her by the shoulder and by the waistband of her jeans. "Go."

She crawled on command toward the other end. When the ladder came into view she turned her body around and scrambled down it. As she moved, a single gunshot rang out, which was followed by a scream. Her feet connected with the asphalt, but she wasn't ready. She folded onto the pavement, bile in her throat.

Patrick landed on the ground a few seconds later. He scooped her up and parked her against his side, drag-carrying her to the front edge of the building. He peered around the corner while she tried to catch her breath. "That restaurant." He pointed across the street. "Run. Now."

She did it, because it was so much easier to follow his instructions than to think about what was happening. She ran, his footsteps right behind her. He threw open the door and they slipped inside, startling a skinny man in a waiter's apron who was rolling silverware into cloth napkins at a table just inside the door.

"Dial 911," Patrick ordered the man as he flipped the lock on the restaurant's front door.

The waiter's eyes got huge, but he slipped a phone out of his breast pocket and lit it.

Patrick must not have thought he was moving fast enough, because he grabbed the phone out of the guy's hands. A moment later he spoke rapidly. "Gunfire on Hudson Ave. Number seventy-one. Two or three men inside the house, at least one of them armed. Handgun. Shots fired."

Two or three men?

"No, I'm not inside the house. I'm at the restaurant across the street." He dropped his gaze to look at Ari.

She was seated on a wooden chair that she didn't remember pulling out from the table, her chest heaving. She was so disoriented. As if her mind had become jet-lagged by the last ten minutes. Looking up into Patrick's cool blue eyes helped a little. She found her center as he stared back, reminding her that they were both still here, and both okay.

Okayish. She couldn't stop shaking.

Patrick let out a huge breath and dropped the phone onto

the waiter's table. Then he knelt down in front of her and took her wrists in his hands. "Baby, you're bleeding."

She looked down to discover that he was right. Her hands had many vicious scratches across the palms and the undersides of her fingers.

"That's from the broken glass," he said quietly. "Are you hurt anywhere else? Anywhere at all?"

She shook her head. But the adrenaline which had gotten her through the last few minutes was starting to sour in her stomach.

"Breathe, sweetheart," he said. "It will pass. It always does." He set her injured hands palms up on her knee and reached around to rub the small of her back. "Shh," he said, even though she was still silent. "I know you're in shock, but it will be okay."

Would it, though? She'd heard a gunshot inside her house. Someone had screamed. She knew who it was, too. But she just couldn't think about that right now. She shoved that thought away.

Sirens sounded outside. She heard loud voices demanding access across the street, identifying themselves as the police. But surely nobody would answer her door.

Then she was lifted into the air. Patrick carried her further back in the restaurant, depositing her on a banquette. "Let them handle it," Patrick whispered. "They'll be asking you questions soon enough."

That turned out to be true, although she couldn't say for sure how much time passed. There were more sirens outside, one of which would prove to be an ambulance. Police knocked on the door of the restaurant and were admitted by the waiter, who began snapping pictures at some point, his phone pointed through the plateglass windows.

It was all a swirl of confusion, really. She put her head on Patrick's shoulder as he whispered to her and gently picked at little shards of broken glass in the heels of her hands.

"What can you tell me?" a cop finally demanded of her.

She took a drink from the glass of ice water that someone had provided. "I was home alone," she said, trying to keep the detective's face in focus. She was suddenly so tired. "He demanded to come in and get something that was his . . ."

Ari told the story slowly, limping through the details. A paramedic worked on her hand at the same time, bandaging the cuts and using tweezers on the bits of glass. The cop began probing her history with Vince, and Ari sighed. She'd spoken of almost nothing else lately. And she was so, so tired.

"That's enough," Patrick insisted. "You need Detective Miller. He has all this history already, and she isn't ready to repeat it right now."

"I'll call him." The cop flipped his notebook closed. "Just don't go anywhere."

They didn't.

Patrick didn't leave her side until Rebecca turned up, showering her with hugs and making concerned noises. "Nathan is on his way to Brooklyn," she said.

"Geez," Ari breathed. It was only starting to sink in that she and Patrick had escaped from *gunfire*. "Is there going to be ugly publicity?"

Becca just shook her head. "Let Georgia worry about it, okay? Sweetie, I have to tell you something."

"What?"

Her friend let out a breath. "Vince was shot in the chest, and he didn't make it."

"Vince . . ." Did she even hear that correctly? "He *died*?"

"Yeah, he did." Rebecca rubbed her arm. "I'm so sorry. I know you spent a long time with him."

"Wow," she said stupidly. She could still picture Vince as the laughing, dancing guy who owned a club because he liked to party. That Vince that hadn't shown up at home in years, but it didn't make his death any less surprising. Somehow he'd taken such a terrible turn, and she hadn't been paying enough attention to notice exactly when. He'd stopped dancing and started dealing with people who had murder weapons.

"What a *waste*," she said aloud.

Becca murmured comforting sounds while Ari tried to get her head around this news. Vince had woken up today—somewhere—not knowing that it was his last. He'd had a double espresso, probably. His favorite.

Now he was just *gone*.

Ari burst into tears.

"Oh, sweetie, I'm sorry," Becca said, hugging her.

Ari sobbed. But it wasn't grief in the simplest sense. That was simply the moment her consciousness picked to put all the pieces together. It was *terrifying*. You could love someone and they could change until they were unrecognizable. You could sleep over a handgun in the floorboards and not know it. You could be trapped in your bathroom while someone tried to break in. And you could escape from the mayhem while your ex-lover died within earshot.

It was all too much. She hugged Becca tightly and cried like there was no tomorrow.

TWENTY-EIGHT

It would be hours before O'Doul could finally shut the door to his apartment on the last visitor. Friends, cops and members of the Bruisers organization had buzzed around all evening, asking questions. The police had an investigation to carry out, and Nate's team was preparing to handle the mess in Ari's house. And as soon as the police had finished their investigation, Nate's people would hire a company to clean away any evidence of struggle or death. They'd secure the place, fixing broken windows and doors.

Now that everyone was finally gone, it was up to him to do what he could for Ari. She still hadn't said much. After ushering out the last visitor, he locked the door and made up a bowl of soup for her. Someone—probably Becca—had had the presence of mind to order takeout and leave it there for the two of them.

He brought her a tray on the sofa. She thanked him at a whisper and then began to eat the soup. But the look in her eyes was glassy. He had the impression that the slightest breeze could knock her over. As soon as she'd finished the bowl, he took the tray away. When he returned, she sat hugging her knees to her chest, curled in on herself.

He stopped himself from asking, *are you okay?* There

was no point. Of course she wasn't okay. She was grieving the man with whom she'd spent her twenties. And she was traumatized by the way it had all gone down.

If he weren't so busy taking care of her, he might be traumatized, too.

Sitting down close to her now, he pulled her into his lap, which was more for his benefit than hers. All afternoon his gut kept clenching at the memory of two men entering Ari's front door—one with a gun drawn. Nothing had *ever* scared him so much as those assholes disappearing into her house, shutting the door behind them.

Panicked, he'd sprinted toward the door. As he reached it, he heard the sound of the deadbolt clicking into place.

Dread had clawed at his insides as he snuck around the outside of the building, looking for another way in. The whole thing had been like a nightmare brought to life. All he could do was call out a warning at the top of his lungs and hope they didn't point the gun out the window and shoot him for it.

"Why were you there?" she asked suddenly, as if she'd been listening to his thoughts. "How did you know something was wrong?"

He cleared his throat. "When Nate's people gave you that panic button, they also programmed your phone to pick up anything suspicious from Vince. I was just leaving the rink when I got a call from security saying you'd had two phone conversations with him, and an email with a threatening subject. They could see that I was only a block and a half away, and they asked me to check on you."

"Oh. Wow."

He gave her a squeeze. Their gazes connected for the first time in an hour. And he felt the same thing he always felt when she looked at him—hope. Only this time, the hope wasn't for sex, or even that she'd somehow agree that they should be a couple. The hope was that she'd be okay.

"I should never have let him in," she said, her voice flat. "He might still be alive if I didn't open that door."

"That was *not* your fault. It was never going to end well for him. I heard the police say the Pryzyk brothers had been hunting for Vince and that gun. He stole it from them for some kind of leverage, I think. That wasn't ever gonna end well."

"I'm sorry you got dragged into it. Wish I could make it up to you."

He wrapped her into a hug and sighed against her shoulder. "Christ, Ari," he whispered. "You don't have to do anything but keep breathing, okay?"

She put her arms around him, too. He'd never felt anything better. "You got me out of there. I can't even believe . . ." He heard her swallow hard, the sentence sticking in her throat.

"Shhh." He hadn't meant to scare her all over again. "You would have been okay either way."

She shivered in his arms. "It's finally done, right? It's over. That guy got away, though."

Unfortunately one of them had. Just one Pryzyk had been apprehended under the Manhattan Bridge while trying to dispose of the gun that had killed Vince, and the other one was still on the loose.

But nobody believed Ari was still in danger.

"It's over, sweetheart," he said. "You've got nowhere to go but up." He held the woman he loved a little more tightly. Christ. He'd never used that word on anybody, even in his head. On any other day he'd probably have found it terrifying. But today he'd known really terror. Admitting to himself he loved Ari was suddenly as easy as breathing.

She pressed her face into his neck, and he closed his eyes. He brought himself fully into the moment and focused on the way her soft lips felt against his skin. With his whole body, he measured all the places of their connection. The weight of her curves in his lap, and against his chest. The texture of her soft sweater against his forearms. He rubbed her back and took it all in.

He'd always been terrible at meditating in yoga class, but that's because he hadn't been meditating on this.

"I'm cold," she said, curling closer.

Poor baby. "You haven't eaten much today, and your body is off-kilter. Shock is tricky. We could tuck you into bed under a pile of blankets. Or you could have a bath." He smoothed down her hair with one hand.

"That sounds nice."

He kissed her forehead, then deposited her on the sofa. "I'll run it for you. Be right back."

The giant tub in his killer bathroom could fix her right up. It always helped him after an especially brutal game. He started the tap—it was a big slot in the tiled wall, so that there'd be no pointing faucet to get in the bathers' way. Then he found some big fluffy towels in his linen closet and turned the heat up, so she wouldn't be cold when she got out.

But when he returned to tell Ari that all was ready, he realized the bandages on her hands could be an issue. "You'll have to keep your hands out of the water."

She stood up. "Good point. But I still want to soak right now. I just want to wash it all away."

"I know, baby. Go ahead. I'll bring you a mug of tea, too?"

Ari gave him a weak smile. "I have no idea what I'd do without you today."

He kissed her cheek and nudged her toward the bathroom. The truth was that there were a lot of people standing by to help. Her mom and her great-uncle in Florida had already bought plane tickets to fly up tomorrow to stay with her. And Becca and Georgia would have happily taken her in.

The reason Ari was here with him was because *he* needed it, and she'd allowed it. If she'd gone to stay in the guest room at Leo's he'd probably be camped out on the floor right now, just watching over her.

Even if they weren't a couple, he still had it bad for her.

After her bath he'd tucked her into his bed. He'd killed the lights, hoping she could sleep. Then he'd taken a long, hot shower. Twelve hours ago he'd thought his life was over. And maybe his hockey career was still about to swirl down the drain, but that problem seemed a hell of a lot smaller than it had first thing this morning.

Taking care to be quiet, he put on flannel pants and a T-shirt and climbed into bed.

Ari rolled immediately, closing the distance between them, laying her head on his shoulder. He welcomed her in with a sigh.

"Are you okay?" she asked sleepily.

"I'm fine," he said automatically.

"Earlier today we were shouting at each other."

"I remember," he sighed. "But that conversation can wait."

"You'll tell me the truth?"

"I will," he promised.

They lay there together a while longer, and he began to feel drowsy. Her head was a comfortable weight on his body. It held him in place. He felt grounded by her presence.

"I got you a coffeemaker," she said suddenly.

"What?"

"A coffeemaker. You asked me if they were easy to shop for, so I just bought you the same model I have at home. It's in my treatment room. I didn't get a chance to give it to you today."

Oh my fucking god. He smiled into her hair. "Thank you, sweetheart. That was nice of you. Now go to sleep."

She did.

TWENTY-NINE

Standings: 3th Place
9 Regular Season Games Remaining

W hen Ari woke up the next morning she was alone. But there was a note on the pillow beside her.

Sweetheart—

I had to go to practice this morning because I cannot afford not to show my face. Georgia is waiting to walk to work with you this morning. Could you please give her a call and walk with her? We're all just trying to make sure you're okay.

—P

Fine. She dug her Katt Phone out of her handbag that had been fetched from her house by one of the cops working the case.

Georgia answered on the first ring. "Hey! How are you feeling?"

Ari really wasn't sure. "I'm okay. I'll try to go one day in a row without being the team drama llama."

"Aim high, girl. I'll be ready to go in about a half hour. Is that enough time for you?"

"Sure. I'm just going to use Patrick's amazing shower, in case I'm never invited back."

"Why wouldn't you be?"

"If you have time to stop for coffee on the way to work, I'll tell you."

Even though it was the opposite direction from their workplace, Georgia and Ari went to One Girl Cookies for lattes and pastries. And then—because you don't have armed psychos storming your house just every day—they sat down at a table to eat and talk, even though it made them both a half hour later to work than they'd planned.

"So I gave him a lot of grief right before everything happened," Ari said, stirring the foam in her cup. "And I still don't know what to think. It doesn't square up in my mind that Patrick likes to buy drugs. He just doesn't strike me as the type. But he didn't deny that it was true."

Georgia folded the square of wax paper where her chocolate croissant had just been. Then she folded it again. "I'll admit that he doesn't seem the type, either. He's awfully serious. And nobody has ever whispered about substances in connection with Doulie. Not to me, anyway. And yesterday, before all the mayhem began at your house, he submitted a voluntary drug test."

"Yeah?" Ari's heart leapt at the idea.

"But I'm told that most street drugs clear your system pretty fast."

"I don't know what to think," Ari admitted. "I'm completely weirded out by the fact that he and Vince had met before. And that he bought drugs. Jesus. I should have gotten involved with a nice tax accountant who enjoys golf."

Georgia made a face. "Then you'd die of boredom instead of gunfire."

"True." Ari's feelings about Patrick were a confusing swirl of contradiction. "It's weird how much I still *trust* him. That's pretty much a summary of all my interactions with Patrick. My heart trusts him, but my brain is always screaming *wait a second!*"

Georgia smiled and shook her head. "You kill me."

"Why?"

"Because you're flawed, just like the rest of us. I used to be intimidated by you and all your yoga wisdom. Now I know you're just as nuts as I am."

"Oh, goody," Ari said with a sigh. "Will you at least tell me how I've been nuts this morning?"

"Sure." Georgia pushed her empty plate away. "In every yoga class you always ask us to observe how we feel, and to notice it from a place of curiosity . . ."

". . . Not judgment," Ari agreed.

"Exactly," Georgia said with a little eye roll. "But every conversation we have about Doulie has you saying—I like him so much, but it's wrong. Wrong time. Wrong guy. Wrong to meet someone at work. See, I don't think you're observing from a place of curiosity, yogi. I think you're Miss Judgie McJudgerson when it comes to how you feel about him."

"Oh, hell," Ari breathed.

Georgia patted her hand. "I know."

"But, God. It's like I can't *afford* to be curious just now. Because I had my eyes entirely closed for the last couple of years, and that's still blowing up in my face."

"I get it. Except I wonder what your favorite yogis would say to the idea that you're too busy to be curious."

"They'd say it was bullshit," Ari admitted. "That I'm just using fear as an excuse to withdraw. That I've let fear triumph over the heart's natural inclination to explore." She groaned. "The truth hurts."

"The truth requires a cookie for the road, don't you think?" Georgia got up and took their empty dishes to the bussing station so they both could get to work.

On the way toward the Bruisers headquarters, Ari checked her phone. Then she checked it again.

"Something wrong?" Georgia asked.

"There's no schedule for me listed—no yoga class and no massage appointments. But there's a meeting in the C-suite."

"They're just looking after you. No need to panic."

When they walked into the offices, Rebecca looked up from her desk. "It's about time you girls made it into work. Which one of you brought me a cookie?"

Georgia's eyes went wide. "You *spied* on us? You tracked our Katt Phones?"

Becca pointed at Ari. "Hers is on the top security setting right now, so the GPS is open in a window on my desktop. I saw two blue dots having pastries while I was alone here, toiling at my desk."

With a frown, Georgia pulled a paper sack out of her purse. "Here. This is for you. Oatmeal raisin."

Becca's pierced eyebrow hiked higher. "That's your favorite."

"No kidding. But take it because I love you. And no more questions." Georgia turned on her heel and went into the office suites.

"So," Ari asked, feeling a little uneasy. "What's this meeting where I'm needed?" The club wouldn't *fire* her this morning, would they? God knows she'd been the world's most bothersome employee these past few weeks. But even if they'd had enough of her, it was bad form to fire her on the same morning that police were performing a murder investigation in her home.

"It's with the private investigator," Becca whispered. "Jay's coming in to share the findings of the investigation."

"Uh . . ." Ari felt her stomach roll. She'd been successful all morning at trying not to think of Vince's death. Until now. "Isn't it a little late to hear his findings? I'm not worried about Vince anymore."

Becca shrugged. "I don't know, honey, because Hugh wanted you to hear this. And he wouldn't waste your time, today of all days."

Twenty minutes later Ari sat fidgeting in the conference room when a woman in khaki cargo pants, Chuck Taylor sneakers, and a blue sweatshirt walked in. "Hi. I'm Jay," the woman said, offering a hand for Ari to shake.

It took Ari an extra beat to reciprocate, because she was surprised to find that the PI was a woman.

"I know," the investigator said with a cheerful grin. "You were expecting a man."

"It's just . . . your name?" she stammered. But that wasn't quite the truth. Ari felt a wash of shame. Here she was, doing a job that was usually held by a man in the NHL, and her idiot brain had assumed that a PI would be a man.

Jay pulled out a chair and sat down. "Don't worry about it. I get that all the time. And it helps me, too."

"It does?"

"Sure. Your ex, for example"—Jay raised her eyes—"and I'm sorry for your loss."

"Thank you," Ari said quickly. It was going to be so odd hearing that from the people in her life. All she'd wanted was for Vince to *get* lost. But she'd never wanted him to *die*.

". . . He'd been very paranoid this past week, looking over his shoulders a lot. What do you think he did every time I walked through his line of vision?"

"Um . . ." Ari did not want to speak ill of the dead. But Jay would have been invisible to him. She looked like a soccer mom.

Jay smiled. "That's right, he ignored me. Makes my job easier, let me tell you." She pulled a folder out of a messenger bag and set it on the table. "Okay, what I've gathered comes too little too late. And I'm sorry about that. We don't have to talk at all, except Hugh Major thought it might give you some closure."

Ari was afraid of what she was about to learn. But she did want the truth. "Tell me what you found."

Jay opened the folder. "I got some of my information from tailing him, and some of it from policemen who will share certain things with me. But I don't have access to everything. So there's some guesswork involved."

"Okay."

"The police probably won't lay it out for you, either, because parts of their investigation will be ongoing. So my guesses might be the best you get for a while." She pulled a photo from the file. "This is where Vince was staying before he died."

"Yikes." It was a picture of a shady looking roadside motel.

"Things had gone sour with the Pryzyks. From what I gathered with a little help from my friends on the homicide squad, they think the Pryzyks might have been responsible for the murder of Andre Karsecki."

"That nightclub murder?"

Jay nodded. "It doesn't seem like Vince was involved, but he may have witnessed it."

"Okay." Ari didn't know how to feel about that. So she hadn't been living with a murderer. Yay. But it was still weird to realize how deeply he'd fallen in with bad people. How had she missed that?

"Maybe the Pryzyks asked him to dispose of the gun, or maybe he stole it as insurance. But he'd kept it at your home for safekeeping."

"I wonder . . ." Ari tapped her fingertips on the desk. "Why was he in and out of my storage room so much?"

Jay shrugged. "I didn't start tailing him until after that, but I can make a few guesses. Maybe the Pryzyks knew you'd kicked him out, so he thought they wouldn't look for him there."

"Or for the gun," Ari guessed.

"Right. At the very end they caught up to him, though. They tailed him to your house yesterday."

Ari shivered.

"There's something else you should know, though. When I was digging into Vince's motives for harassing you, I discovered there's a transfer of property happening regarding your Hudson Street home."

"A transfer of . . . What does that mean?"

She opened the folder and peeked at a page inside. "Mr. Angelo Bettini is executing a transfer of ownership of the house."

"To who?"

"To *you*," Jay said. "Unless there's another Ariana Bettini."

"Really?" she breathed. "I thought he wanted to cash in."

Jay tilted her head to the side. "He's eighty-four years old. Maybe he's realizing that you can't take it with you. Does he have children of his own?"

Ari nodded. "Two sons. They should inherit."

"Maybe they're inheriting something else. I'm sorry to drop this little mystery in your lap, but I dug it up by accident."

"Did Vince know?" Ari asked, then braced herself for the answer. Was he just hanging around the last year because he thought she was about to become rich?

"I really couldn't guess," Jay said softly. "Your uncle would have had the quitclaim deed notarized. Then he filed it with the state, where it became a public part of the tax rolls. But he'd have to have looked to find it."

Well. Ari would have to find a way to ask Uncle Angelo about this strange development. "Thank you for telling me."

Jay closed the file folder. "You're going to be okay. You know that, right?"

"Yes," Ari admitted. "I'm going to be fine."

"I investigate a lot of people, and some of them are pretty awful. To me, Vince just seemed really lost and scared. He made a lot of shitty choices during the last three months of his life. It happens. Good and evil are for movies, Ari. Nobody is ever that tidy."

She took a deep breath and let it out slowly. "Thank you. I think I understand." Ari had to stop beating herself up over her own stupid choices, because all the self-flagellation wasn't helping.

Everyone was flawed. Everyone was complicated. Some people were lucky enough to hold themselves together, and others ended up dead from their misdeeds.

Now there was something to think about.

She shook Jay's hand and then checked her phone, finding a text from her mother: *We'll land on time at three and take a cab into Brooklyn. See you soon, baby!*

"You okay?" Becca asked from the doorway.

"I'm good," she answered truthfully. "And I'm looking forward to the day when nobody asks me that anymore."

"I'll bet. I have some news—the police are done at your place, and the fix-it people are on their way over there."

"Thank you."

"Don't mention it. So keep yourself busy here for a few hours and then you can go home."

She couldn't wait.

THIRTY

After the morning skate, O'Doul's phone glowed red with an urgent meeting someone needed him to take.

With two doctors.

Fuck.

But, hey, at least doctors weren't the ones you'd see if they were about to throw you off the team. So when both Dr. Herberts and the team shrink, Dr. Mulvey, ushered him into a treatment room, he made his face as impassive as possible and followed.

If he'd failed his drug test, he'd be in Hugh Major's office right now, right?

Dr. Mulvey shut the door and hopped up on the treatment table, leaving the chair to O'Doul, who sat down and steeled himself for whatever discussion was forthcoming.

Doctor Herberts spoke first. "Your drug test yesterday revealed no banned substances, no narcotics and no recreational drugs."

O'Doul would have sagged with relief if they weren't watching him so closely. He didn't know what the right response was, either. He didn't want to be cocky, so *gotcha, suckers* wasn't going to work. "All right," he said instead.

The two doctors exchanged glances. "So let's have a

hypothetical conversation," Dr. Mulvey suggested. "Because Herberts and I get paid by the hour and we like talking."

O'Doul managed not to roll his eyes. "Okay. What hypotheticals do you feel like discussing?"

"Well, you're the captain of the team," Mulvey said. "So you should know a few things in case one of your guys ever needs the information."

"All right. Shoot."

Herberts took a shift. "If a player had a wrist injury earlier in the season, and was given some painkillers, he might become addicted to them through no fault of his own," he said.

Ah. Maybe the guy was just covering his own ass, then.

"Sometimes a player who has a wrist injury doesn't even fill his prescription after the hospital procedure because Vicodin made him throw up the one other time he took it," O'Doul said. He'd never forget the time a minor league physician gave him some Vics after a knee injury. The pills made him so nauseated he didn't eat for two days.

"All right," Herberts said thoughtfully. "From time to time a player might have use for other kinds of pills. Uppers, maybe. In that case, the team's doctors would still offer that player a treatment program to free himself of the addiction. And if the player doesn't feel comfortable telling his troubles to someone who works for the team, that player ought to know that there are other doctors in the city, and other ways of getting help."

O'Doul's throat became inexplicably dry. Shit. The fact that they were willing to play this silly game, pretending they weren't discussing him had to mean they really wanted to help. He hadn't expected this. Not at all.

He cleared his throat and decided it wouldn't hurt to keep the farce going. "That is encouraging. And I'll make sure my team knows it. But sometimes a player tries something, and even though the effects are awfully attractive, it's hard to get. And maybe after he burns through his ill-gotten supply, he quits because asking around for it is embarrassing."

"Okay," Herberts said slowly. "If that has been any player's experience, I'd like to point out how lucky he is." The man's eyes held his, and they were dead serious. "Your player should know that methamphetamine is highly addictive. And those who take it soon find they need more of the substance just to feel that same rush. Quickly they're needing two, three times as much to get by. And by now, the comedown is a bitch. Then a host of long-term problems start to kick in—heart trouble, high blood pressure, weight loss, increased risk of stroke, memory loss and severe tooth decay . . ."

O'Doul probably did a very bad job of hiding his discomfort then. "I get it," he said suddenly. "It's a bad idea."

"A disastrous idea," the doctor said quietly. "Everyone who gets hooked on that drug ends up wishing he'd never seen it before. Still, if that happens to anyone you know, there are people who would help a guy get off it."

He cleared his throat a second time. "That's good to know."

"Let's just take it in a different direction for a second," Mulvey said. "Somebody who took that drug before games might do so because he felt he had no other choice. Would you say that's a possibility?"

Oh, boy. Here comes the head-shrinking bullshit. "Maybe it just seemed like a good idea at the time."

"Maybe," Mulvey said slowly. "Or maybe he was in a rut and looking for a way out."

O'Doul shrugged. He really didn't want to get into it.

"But there's *always* a better way," Mulvey pressed. "If a guy found he couldn't keep going just the same way, there are people he could talk to about it. For example, you should know that your team psychiatrist enjoys complete doctor-patient privilege. The things a player says to him in confidence will never be repeated. Your team sports-medicine specialist," he pointed at Dr. Herberts, "is contractually obligated to tell management about health issues which affect an athlete's ability to play."

O'Doul nodded. He knew that.

"But one of the reasons Nate Kattenberger employs *two* physicians for his team, is to accommodate his players' health in a way which allows for privacy when strictly necessary." The shrink grinned.

"Interesting," O'Doul said slowly. That distinction *was* something he really ought to tell his guys, if indeed they were still his guys when the whole scandal had burned itself out. It was potentially useful information.

"In fact . . ." The shrink patted his pocket and drew out a business card. "I think it makes sense for the team captain and I to discuss it privately later this week. Just to be sure we're on the same page." He extended the card to O'Doul. They locked eyes.

He hesitated, but not very long. Talking about himself sounded like no fun at all. But if it kept his head in the game, he'd give it a shot. Once. He took the card and shoved it into the back pocket of his jeans. "Thanks," he said gruffly.

"Thank you for your time," Herberts said, rising. "If you have any further questions, my door is always open."

"But mine is opener," the psychiatrist said with a wink.

O'Doul remained in his chair until they had both disappeared. Then he let out a giant sigh of relief. He'd passed the drug test. It wouldn't make sense for the team to get rid of him now. They wouldn't do it right before play-offs unless the publicity was so awful they couldn't avoid it. Coach Worthington would have to let him play tonight, too, or there would only be more gossip on the blogs.

So that was one hurdle cleared. But there were plenty more. He needed to speak to Ari, to lay his sorry story at her feet and ask for forgiveness. She thought he'd gotten close to her only to preserve his good name. But that was exactly the reverse of what had happened. The moment he realized Vince and Ari were connected, a smarter man would have kept his distance.

He wasn't a smarter man, though. He was a smitten one. Convincing her that he was worth the trouble was going to be an uphill battle. But he'd do it. He'd do anything for more of her attention.

But first, it was game night.

After a rest at home, O'Doul walked to the stadium alone. The security guard at the players' entrance let him in as usual. So that was another hurdle jumped.

The first person he saw inside the door was Ari. She was trailed by an older version of herself—an attractive woman with long wavy hair shot through with gray streaks. And a very elderly man.

"Sweetheart," he called out before he could think better of it.

She turned around, surprise on her face. "Hi."

"Hi," he said a little awkwardly, wondering how friendly he should be in front of her family. Maybe she hadn't mentioned him to her mother.

Ari closed the distance between them, stood up on tiptoe, and kissed his cheek. "Mom, Uncle Angelo, this is Patrick."

Her mother beamed. "Thank you for all the help you showed our baby girl," the woman said.

"Mom," Ari warned.

But her mother cackled. "Sorry, love. But I still worry, no matter how capable you are."

Patrick shook both the visitors' hands. He was glad Ari had her family around her. "Are you back in the house on Hudson Street?"

"Just got back in this afternoon," Ari said, her eyes on her shoes.

He should have felt happy for her, but it meant she wouldn't be sleeping in his bed tonight. "That's great," he said with as much conviction as he could muster. "I'd better . . ." he pointed toward the locker rooms.

"Yeah," Ari agreed. "Have a great game. Take care of yourself out there."

"Thanks." He gave them a wave and moved down the hallway.

Ari's mother murmured something to her daughter as he walked away. It sounded like, "He's so handsome."

Her daughter's response was to shush her mother.

Smiling, he went to his locker to hang up his suit jacket and change into some practice gear. After that, he headed straight to the lounge area, which was packed with players. It was two hours until the puck dropped. Time for stretching, for last minute strategy, and for the taping of sore muscles and hockey sticks.

As he moved through the room, all the conversation dried up. He grabbed a bottle of water out of the refrigerator, and the silence was unnerving.

Slowly, he turned around to check their faces. Beacon looked grim. Castro stared down at his hands. Did they think he was a druggie? Or about to be cut from the team? *Christ.* He added two dozen names to the list of people whose trust he needed to win back. For more than a decade he'd given this team his sweat and his blood. He'd given everything he had. He'd watched their backs in every game in every corner of the continent. But it wasn't really enough to carry them through this ugly moment. As captain, he'd always thought it was his job to be a rock—to never show any kind of fear.

He'd overshot, it seemed. He'd never shown fear. But he hadn't shown anything else, either. These guys were his life, and they didn't even know it.

O'Doul cleared his throat. Some sort of gesture was necessary. But what? Ari would know, but she wasn't here. So he took a second to ask himself what she would do in a situation like this. She had so many ways of reaching people. Soothing words. Steady hands. What he'd learned from Ari was that there was always more than one way to touch someone.

"Guys? Before tonight's game I think we need to have an emergency . . ." He almost said meeting. But that sounded bleak. "Retreat," he said instead. "Let's get everybody in here, shut the door and have a talk."

"Okay," Beacon said slowly. "Who's missing?"

Jimbo texted every player who wasn't currently present, and one by one they appeared in the doorway, curious looks on their faces. When the last man had arrived, O'Doul asked the training assistants to leave. Then he went over to the door to close it.

But Coach Worthington was standing there, an ornery look on his face. "What are you playing at with your secret meeting?" he asked.

O'Doul stepped out into the hallway and closed the door behind him. Earlier today he'd been humbled to find the organization he'd worked for this past decade had had his back. But Coach was a new addition. Of course, he wasn't going to get the same breaks from this man who hardly knew him.

"Are you willing to trust me?" he asked. "It all comes down to that, right? Either I'm still your captain, and you'll give me this moment to apologize to my guys. If you can't do that, might as well demote me right now."

Coach squinted at him in that appraising way that he had. "You gonna do the right thing for us? Even when it's hard?"

"Yeah," he said without hesitation. "I am."

Coach nodded. "Go ahead then. But apologize fast. We've got a game to win."

"Thank you, sir."

When Coach turned to go, he went back into the lounge where two dozen pairs of eyes waited. There weren't any seats left anywhere, so he leaned against one of the high tables and studied the faces in front of him. They were all different shapes, different colors, and different ages. It's sort of a miracle that they usually got along so well, given they were united by one odd thing—the ability to play hockey at an elite level.

"Listen," he said, wishing he had a more elegant opening.

But he had to start somewhere. "My official stance on that picture in the *Post* is that it didn't happen. But off the record I just wanted to tell you guys that I'm sorry I embarrassed the team. It was a dumbass thing to do."

The silence was punctuated only by the sound of a coffee cup set down on a table. Nobody said a word.

"I'm pretty sure we've already seen the end of it, but I wanted to say that anyway," he continued. "I hope we can all get past it. In the meantime I want to tell you something I learned the hard way this week. If you think there's something about this job you feel you can't handle, there's probably a smart way and a dumb way to deal with it. Don't be like me. Take the smart way. Find someone in the organization to talk to. I didn't do that, and now my name—and the team's name—is in the fucking *Post*. If I'd gone to someone trustworthy, it all could have been avoided."

"Well," Beacon cleared his throat. "Some of us do stupid shit and haven't been caught. So not every guy in this room is hating on you right now. I'm not."

"Sucks, though," Castro said. "If we make it to the playoffs, someone's gonna say it's because we're all doping."

O'Doul had never wanted to have this conversation—with the whole team staring at him, wondering how he could be so dumb. Too bad he hadn't thought of that beforehand. "I sure am sorry for that," he said quietly. "Wish I could undo the damage."

Leo Trevi leaned forward on one of the sofas, his elbows on his knees. "Is there anything we can do? I mean—any way we can help you?"

O'Doul felt heat climb up the back of his neck. Now he had a brand-new regret—he was sorry he had ever been a dick to this kid. "No, man. I'm in a better place now. But I appreciate the question."

If he wasn't mistaken, his guys finally started to relax a little. They shifted in their seats again, and finished their drinks.

"Any questions for me?" he asked.

Nobody raised his hand.

"All right. I just want to add that if you are ever on the fence about asking for any kind of help, run it by me. I won't tell a soul." He straightened up and went to open the door again.

Crikey nudged him before he got there. "Who's fighting tonight—you or me?"

Hell. With everything going on, he'd missed his usual twenty-four hours of nervous preparation. "We can play it by ear?"

"All right. You and I didn't spar yesterday. I don't know if I have this guy figured out yet."

O'Doul squeezed Crikey's biceps. "I'll take him. I don't mind. He'll be looking for me anyway. You can get the next one, maybe." He opened the door, and players began to disperse to the dressing room or to stretch.

"Anyone wanna kick the soccer ball around?" Trevi asked. A few guys followed him out.

The room quieted down, and O'Doul took a newly emptied seat next to Beacon on the sofa.

"Can I ask you something?" The goalie ran a hand over his own jaw. "Was it the fighting that got to you?"

"Uh . . ." He'd never said this out loud. "It was a lot of things. But that's a big one. It sort of consumed all my focus, trying to figure out how to stay healthy and still do battle every night."

Beacon shook his head. "Don't know how you do it, man—ten years of stepping in front of somebody else's fist. I'm a bag of bruises just from the game itself."

"The things we do for money," he said, laughing it off. But the truth was that he liked hearing Beacon say it—that it wasn't easy. Maybe he didn't always have to pretend that it was.

All the rest of the pre-game chatter was about points and play-off standings. They were playing Boston again, the team which was their greatest rival for a play-offs spot. If they lost to Boston, they'd be knocked into fourth place again. So this game had double the usual weight. If they won, the play-offs were within reach.

Kattenberger's Statistical Model was throbbing with anticipation over this game, assigning it an importance rating of ten.

"This one goes to eleven," Castro joked as they walked down the chute and stepped onto the ice. Tonight was a sellout crowd, and they were loud as O'Doul and his teammates skated once around the rink and then lined up for the national anthem. Tonight it was competently sung by a pop star he'd never heard of. He found his thoughts drifting to Ari. She was probably up in the box, watching right now. Or maybe in some comped seats with her family.

Even if hockey had been kicking his ass this winter, he still felt that zing. Standing here facing the opposing team, ready to do battle. It was still the best kind of rush.

Tonight he was paired with Massey, and they started first shift. The other team's offensive line kept them busy from the first second. He slipped into the zone right away, his entire consciousness focused on the action at hand. His stick became an extension of his will—darting out to foil the other team again and again.

Midway through the first period, Leo Trevi scored an ugly goal right in front of the net, and the hometown fans went wild. O'Doul slapped the rookie on the ass as they skated back to the bench. The arena fizzed with excitement. The Bruisers picked up their pace even further, confident that it was possible to win this thing.

Hoping to turn the tide toward his own team, the enforcer—Trekowski, the same jackass who'd called him out on Twitter—challenged him to a fight two minutes later.

O'Doul actually smiled. "You wanna throw down now? Whatever floats your boat, man."

Trekowski gave him a weird look before dropping his gloves. "Gotta fight you before they fire your ass for doping."

"Uh-huh. Go ahead. I'm so looped up right now, I fucking *love* pain. You're doing me a favor." O'Doul tried on a wild-eyed stare. He skated in a lazy backward circle. When he was younger, he'd acted loopy sometimes when he didn't know what else to try.

Funny—he'd forgotten how it felt to be new at this. To make your own rules.

At that thought, he lunged forward and grabbed Trekowski's sweater. "This what you want?"

Trekowski swung but O'Doul got there first. They both landed punches but O'Doul's was harder. Just for fun he gave a deranged scream. His next punch connected so hard that Trekowski's helmet flew off.

He knew he'd win just from the look in the guy's eyes. That flicker of hesitation. O'Doul gave it one more good punch and the guy buckled, sprawling out on the ice.

The whole thing was over in seconds. O'Doul shook out his fist and picked up his gloves. On the way back to the bench, he probed his jaw where he'd been hit.

"You okay?" the trainer asked, opening the door for him.

"Never better."

As the night progressed, it was true. Boston couldn't catch them. Bayer got a goal, which Boston answered. But it wasn't enough. They won 2–1 during regulation play and walked back down the chute two points richer.

"Fire up the Katt Phone!" Castro howled. "I want my gold star. Nate can tattoo it on my ass after that game."

"Fuck, I'm tired," Trevi complained. "But it was totally worth it. Someone carry me to Grimaldi's. I need a slice and a beer."

"Tell you what," O'Doul heard himself say. "I'll order ten pies to my place."

"Your place?" Castro asked. "Like, your *apartment?* Does it really exist?"

"Yeah, smartass. There won't be enough chairs, but it'll work." Then he added, uncharacteristically, "I'd like you all to come."

There was a stunned silence. Then Leo Trevi said, "I'll bring a case of beer. And don't worry, Castro, I'll make sure there's a light beer in there for you."

Castro flipped him off, and everyone began stripping off their pads.

Before O'Doul hit the showers, he called Rebecca.

"What favor do you need now, Doulie?" she answered on the first ring.

He chuckled. "I need to feed two dozen players in my apartment ASAP. How would you do that if you were me? How late does Grimaldi's deliver?"

"Nice of you to give me some notice."

"Yeah, I know."

"Here's what I'm going to do for you," she said. "I'll call Grimaldi's myself and beg, because the team puts a lot of money in their pocket. The delivery will show up at ten fifteen because they close soon after that, but I'll warn your building's concierge in case it beats you home."

"I owe you," he said.

"No kidding, hot stuff."

"Do you need my credit card number?"

"I have it memorized. Anything else?"

"Just that you're a goddess, and feel free to come up and have a slice with us."

She snorted. "I will. But now let me go so I can grovel to the restaurant for your insta-dinner. Bye." She hung up on him.

There had never been *half* so many people in his condo since the day he bought it.

Trevi had shown up first, given that his commute was only down the hallway. When O'Doul opened the door, the rookie dragged in a beanbag chair in one hand and a case of beer in the other. "You said there weren't enough chairs," he said, surveying the big room. "But you're right—it doesn't matter. Nice rug. Nice everything."

"Thanks," he said a little stiffly, relieving Trevi of the beer. He wasn't used to this.

"Should I run out for paper plates and cups?"

"You don't have to. I have a lot of dishes."

Trevi dragged his beanbag chair over to the wall and plopped down on it. "Leave the door open for . . ."

"Hi!" Georgia said from the doorway. "I brought margarita mix. Because I can't visit this place without drinking tequila. Too bad Ari's not around tonight to mix it for me."

It really was too bad. But Ari would be with her family tonight.

The buzzer on the wall sounded. When O'Doul pressed the button, the concierge informed him that a handful of players were on their way up. "Thanks," he said. "There'll be more, too."

It was mayhem after that. There were jackets thrown onto his bed and players leaning on his kitchen counter, unpacking the pizzas. Rebecca had done a nice job of sampling the menu. Each pie had a different combination of toppings.

Players kept knocking on the door. Everyone took to yelling, "It's open!"

O'Doul handed out napkins and beer. Every guy who came through the door had a six-pack, and the collection of bottles on the counter looked like the UN of beers.

When everyone was finally served and sprawled around his living area like Romans at a banquet, he made a plate for himself. He thought he'd stand at the bar and eat it, but Castro moved down his sofa, opening up a space that was sufficient if not quite as roomy as he would have preferred.

He sat, though. If he'd gone to the trouble of inviting the whole team into his home, hiding in the kitchen area went against his message.

The message was hard enough to articulate anyway. He just knew he needed . . . more. More openness. More contact. Sitting there, wedged between his teammates, he wondered if it was too little too late. But Ari had shown him that some of his solitary habits were breakable. She'd speared through a number of them without even trying.

"Pizza and beer," Beacon sighed. "There's no better way to refuel."

"This is more relaxing than the bar," Castro agreed. "But the puck bunnies can't find me here."

"They're not looking anyway," Trevi teased him.

"Shut it, Mr. Engaged," Castro grumbled. "We don't all have the perfect girlfriend."

"How am I perfect?" Georgia asked from the kitchen. "Make it good or I'll whisper to the PuckeredUp blog that you have a tiny penis."

There was a roar of laughter, and Castro sputtered praise at Georgia, a terrified look on his face.

"Get over here, Castro," Jimbo called, waving the PS4 controller in the air. "It's your turn at *Call of Duty.*"

O'Doul got up, too. "Who needs a beer? I'm throwing you all out in ninety minutes, though. Got to get some rest before we fly to Tampa."

His guys began to gather up the plates and stack them into his dishwasher. It was the first time he'd ever heard a lot of male chatter and smack talk bouncing off the exposed-brick walls of his condo.

He kind of liked the sound of it.

THIRTY-ONE

Standings: 3rd Place
6 Regular Season Games Remaining

The team traveled to Tampa and Nashville without Ari. Her contract specified that she would travel with the team at least 85 percent of the time, and her average was already higher than that. So she spent a few days letting her mother fuss over her, and showing Uncle Angelo all the new things in the neighborhood.

The windows and door that had been broken during her scariest day on earth were all fixed. The fire escape was tuned up, and a newer model ladder was installed, one that was less likely to lead to a break-in.

On the first day of his visit, Uncle Angelo had told her that the house was to be hers. "It's yours already, honey."

"I don't know what to say," was her reply.

"Say you'll look after it, that's all."

She thanked him profusely. And after that, she began to look at the place with new eyes. The living room walls might look fabulous in a new color. A creamy yellow, maybe, with contrasting baseboards and molding.

"Maybe someday you'll be able to afford to renovate the kitchen," her mother suggested. "If you took out that wall, opening it up to the dining room, you'd have more light throughout the main floor."

"That would look spectacular," she agreed.

"When you have children you'll need a safety gate at the top of the steps," her mom added. "And maybe a carpet runner on the stairs. They're a bit slick."

"Doesn't seem like I'll be needing to worry about that anytime soon," Ari said.

Her mother patted her hand. "You never know. You and that Patrick fellow would make pretty babies."

"That's not really on the table," she said quickly, not wanting to encourage her mother's fantasy.

"I don't know," her mom argued. "He'd look pretty good on the table. Or up against a wall, or . . ."

"Mother!"

She laughed. "Sorry. But with a body like that, a girl could get carried away."

Ari blushed. She had indeed gotten carried away. Even now he was never far from her mind. She told herself it was because the team had so much at stake. It felt unnatural to be home in Brooklyn while they were doing battle in the south. She watched both games on television because she couldn't stay away. They won one and they lost one.

Every time Patrick skated onto the screen, she couldn't take her eyes off him. And when he fought a player on Nashville's team she stopped breathing.

When it was over he skated away with a bloody cut on his face. After the game she twice picked up the phone to call him and then set it down again. She didn't want to give him the wrong idea. They weren't together, and she was still mad at his betrayal.

But, god, I miss him, she had to admit. The war between her mind and her heart raged on. It should be easier than this when he wasn't even in town. She shouldn't care so much.

Yet she did.

"So tell me more about Patrick," her mother said at lunch the day before she left town again.

Ari set down her sandwich. She'd been thinking of him that very minute. Obviously she was so drenched in thoughts of him that she was now capable of beaming them across a restaurant table. "Patrick is complicated. He hasn't had an easy time of it."

"But is he a good man? Does he love you?" her mother asked. "Those are the important questions."

She was fairly sure that the answers to those questions were probably yes and yes. But it was too much, too fast. "Vince loved me once," she said. "And look how that turned out."

Her mother waved a hand, as if waving the idea away. "You were both young and foolish. You're wiser now. You can see past a man's quick smile. What do you see when you look at him?"

Even that answer was complicated. Lust was near the top of the list, and she worried that it crowded out all the other saner judgments. "He's sturdy," she began. "But troubled."

"We are all troubled sometimes," her mother suggested.

Ari speared an olive in her salad. "You are awfully supportive of a man you met once for thirty seconds. I know you want grandchildren but let's not get ahead of ourselves."

Her mother cackled. "You're right, I don't know Patrick. But I can tell he matters to you, and that's why I like him. My girl has excellent judgment. He must be worth the trouble."

"How can you say that? I mean—I appreciate the loyalty, Mom. But if my judgment were sound we wouldn't be sitting here together right now trying to recover from my ex's murder in my presence. This year my life has been like a television crime drama."

"Sweetheart," her mother said, and Ari heard an echo of

Patrick's voice in that word. "You do have good judgment. You've also made good friends like Rebecca and Georgia. You are well loved by an entire hockey team. You work hard and you live within your means. Just because it took you a little too long to leave Vince doesn't mean you shouldn't trust yourself again. Be kind to my Ariana. She deserves kindness from you and everyone else."

Ari's eyes felt suddenly hot. "Be kind to yourself" was something she taught her yoga students, too. Why was it so hard to do?

"If he's not the man for you, then you'll make the right decision," her mother said. "But if he is, don't fear it. I have faith in you."

"Thank you, Mom," she choked out.

"You're welcome. Now eat your salad because I see real Brooklyn cheesecake in that dessert case and I want some."

After Ari put her mother and Uncle Angelo in a cab to LaGuardia, she went to the practice facility for the first time in three days. She sat through a meeting with Henry and the trainers, where they went over the status of player strains and injuries.

"I'm putting O'Doul back on your schedule tomorrow morning," Henry told her. "He's doing pretty well but we have to keep that hip supple."

"Of course," she said as her heart tripped over itself. "Who else?" she asked with feigned nonchalance.

When the meeting was over, she was free to go home. Tonight the players would enjoy a night off, though she glimpsed many of them in a conference room with Coach Worthington. They were watching tape of tomorrow night's opponent.

Ariana sped by the conference room window. *Do not look for him*, she ordered herself. *You'll see him tomorrow.*

She'd almost made it to the door at the end of the hallway when a roughened voice stopped her. "Ari? Can I talk to you for a second?"

The sound of her name on his lips was like a sip of cool water after a hot yoga class. She hadn't even known how badly she'd wanted it. She stopped walking and slowly turned around.

He was still in his suit pants and a nice dress shirt, but his tie was askew. He leaned against the conference room doorjamb, looking like some kind of sex-tousled power broker. "Can we talk?" he repeated.

"Sure," she heard herself say. "But don't you have to . . ." she pointed into the conference room.

He pushed off the doorframe and walked toward her. "We're done in there."

She watched his approach, feeling helpless. The broad set of his shoulders appeared frequently in her dreams, as did the heated look in his eyes. "Where do you want to talk?" He'd better suggest someplace public. If the two of them went someplace private right now, not much talking was going to get done.

"How do you feel about linguini with clam sauce?" he asked.

"Hmm?" She shook her head to try to clear it of the sex haze that had descended on her the moment she saw him. His words finally penetrated. "Actually, I'm allergic to shellfish."

His eyes widened. "Figures."

"Why?"

He shook his head, smiling at her. "How do you feel about ice skating, then?"

"Skating? Me?"

"Yes you. You work at an ice rink. Two of them, actually." He grinned. "Have you set foot on the ice since you started working here?"

"I haven't skated since I was twelve."

He took her hand. "Come on, then. No time like the present."

She let herself be led through the locker rooms and toward the rink door. "I don't have skates," she pointed out.

"Not a problem—Georgia started giving free ice time to the Boys and Girls Clubs of Brooklyn. She has a whole stash of loaner skates now. I'll show you."

He wasn't wrong. The skates lined a set of shelves in a supply closet off the rink. Ari found a pair of figure skates in her size and swiped her thumb across the blade. They'd even been recently sharpened.

"Girly skates?" Patrick teased. "Don't you want to learn the right way?"

"These are what I'm used to," she argued. "You don't want me to fall down and break something, right?"

"Good point, rookie. Have a seat on the bench and I'll be right back to help you."

She sat down and began to lace up. It had been a long time since she'd done this. Right after she'd gotten the Bruisers job she'd had the itch to go skating again. She'd asked Vince if he would go with her to the rink in Prospect Park one weekend. But he'd turned her down, and she didn't ask again. *Stupid girl*, she chided herself.

Be kind, her mother's lingering voice reminded her.

Patrick returned with his own skates in hand and sat down beside her to lace up. He glanced at her tight laces. "You did that very well."

"I've been tying my own shoes since kindergarten, thanks."

He gave her a smirk.

"You're still wearing your suit," she pointed out.

"Well, you didn't get a chance to change, so I figure it's only fair. You can hold onto me if you feel shaky, okay?"

"Was that your plan?" she teased. If it was, he was about to be disappointed.

"The thought did cross my mind. But I really just wanted

to spend time with you." He turned to look at her with those cool blue eyes, and her pulse skipped a beat or three. "I missed you, Ari. The *only* reason I spend time with you is because you're important to me. You're everything that I want, and everything I need. You already have my heart, and I don't want it back. You understand?"

Slowly, she nodded. *I miss you, too.*

"Ready?" He stood up and offered her a hand, which she took.

Rising, she felt blades under her feet for the first time in more than fifteen years. "I forgot that I'd be taller," she said with a laugh.

"But so am I," he pointed out.

When she raised her gaze, she got another little jolt from those blue eyes. And it suddenly dawned on her how close together they were. His hand was warm around hers. If she took a small step forward, she'd be close enough to kiss him. "Let's skate," she suggested for her own good.

He grinned, as if reading her mind. "Right this way." He led her across the rubber pads to the door, which he opened by sliding the bolt. The bright surface gleamed back at her. She'd forgotten how magical it was to step onto a fresh sheet of ice. "We're going to scuff it up," she pointed out. "Will anyone care?"

"Not much. Come on, now." He turned around so that he stepped backwards onto the ice. He offered his other hand, too.

She took it and stepped out onto the slickness with her left foot and then her right. Patrick gave a tug on her hands and then they were gliding together effortlessly. He moved in a gentle backward rhythm, towing her.

It was like waterskiing, but the tow rope was the hottest man in Brooklyn.

"See?" he crowed. "You got it. You're really stable."

"Mmmhmm," she agreed. "Let's see how I do on my own." She let go of his hands.

Smiling, he did an easy crossover, curving around with the shape of the rink. God, he was beautiful, powerful muscles visible through his suit pants, strong forearms visible beneath the rolled-up cuffs of his shirt.

But she had to stop staring and start skating. The first couple of steps were a little shaky as she felt for the edges of the blades for the first time in years. Then she was able to lengthen her strides and find a natural gait.

"You're . . . wow," Patrick said, still skating backward, watching her. "Nice."

It was like flying. How had it taken so long to do this again? Although it probably lacked grace, she pushed forward on her right foot and lifted her back leg into the air, arms outstretched, then carved gently into a turn.

"Jesus."

Ari didn't spare Patrick a glance. She was too busy remembering how this was done. She flipped her hips around and skated a few backward crossovers. That felt graceful enough—on one side, anyway. Then she pressed out to the left and wrapped her right leg around, pulling herself into a spin. The rink flew by a few times in quick succession before she slowed herself to a stop.

And damn it, she was dizzy. That's what you get for not skating for half your life.

When her eyes could focus again, she looked over at Patrick. He was standing still, feet together, bent over to clutch his knees, and *laughing*.

"It wasn't *that* bad," she protested.

He straightened, shaking his head, his face red. He couldn't even speak he was laughing so hard. "Baby," he wheezed after a minute. "You kill me. I swear to God." He skated forward to wrap his arms around her. "All I do is try to impress you, and it's impossible. Because you're the most impressive person I ever met. I'm so screwed."

Even as she leaned into the hug, his chest bounced with laughter. He smelled so good, like clean man and icy air.

"I'm so gone for you," he ground out, still laughing. "I've got it bad. It might take me years to convince you I'm a good guy, but I'll never stop trying."

"The thing is . . ." She took a shaky breath against his warm chest. "I believe you."

Two big hands rubbed her back. "You do?"

"Yeah." She pushed her nose into his shirt collar and took a deep breath. Fighting him didn't make sense anymore. She didn't have to punish them both for all the scary near-misses of the past month. She could just *be* with him—take him home, make him dinner, and take him to bed. It didn't mean that she'd sacrificed all her principles, or that she couldn't stand on her own without a man.

It didn't have to be a statement. It could be just an evening with someone she liked. A whole lot.

She lifted her chin. His blue gaze waited at close range. They came together in slow motion. The first brush of her lips across his made him groan. She loved that sound. So she kissed him properly. His lips were just as firm and soft as she remembered. Strong arms pulled her in. He tilted his head to the side to improve their connection. She threaded her fingers through his hair as his mouth made a sweet, eager pull against her own, and she sighed.

Why had she been fighting this, exactly?

He kissed her again and again. Her libido sprang up and did a perfect sun salutation, her skin coming alive everywhere they touched. Maybe it was the ice skates, but the next kiss made her wobble.

Catching her, he chuckled into her mouth. "Easy."

She was breathing hard, and not from the skating. They couldn't get so carried away—not until they got home, anyway. "You dragged me out here," she said, trying to cool down. "Let's skate."

"All right. Show me some more of your fancy moves. You did some figure skating?"

"Yeah. In middle school. But then it got really competitive

and I stopped. I liked the skating more than I liked the pressure."

"Ah."

She grabbed his hand. "Come on, you can be my partner. Back crossovers."

His smile was amused as they began to cross the ice backward, hand in hand. "Do I get to hold your butt and hoist you over my head?"

"I don't think we're up to that."

"Skate with me, sweetheart." He gave her hand a tug.

She turned, allowing him to grasp her free hand. They were face to face, with him skating backward. She reached up to put a hand on his shoulder, mindful to keep her strides in synch with his so their feet wouldn't tangle. She'd never skated with a partner before. It was harder than it looked on TV.

"That's it," he encouraged, slipping a hand onto her waist. "I've got you." He kept his stride nice and even, and she discovered she didn't have to look down to know where his feet were.

"Fancy," she breathed as they glided past the penalty box.

"I'll show you fancy." He grabbed her hips and lifted.

Suddenly she was airborne, her hip on his broad shoulder. It might have looked cool, except for the fact that she hugged his head in terror. Laughing, he skated in a tight circle, spinning her until she let out a shriek. Strong arms slowly lowered her back toward the ice, and he came to a stop before setting her down.

"That was terrifying," she complained, although the dizzy smile on her face made her a liar.

He kissed her forehead. "I'm hoping for a ten from the Russian judge."

"Omigod!" a voice squeaked from nearly. "You guys are adorable. I could kill myself for not having my Katt Phone handy . . . Whoa!"

There was a small thud, and Ari looked behind Patrick to find Rebecca sprawled out on the ice. "Becca! Are you okay?"

She scrambled over to Becca just as her friend lifted her head. "Fuck!"

"Here." Ari offered a hand, but Patrick was quicker. He crouched down and scooped Rebecca up off the slick surface and set her on her feet.

"This is so embarrassing," Becca said, rubbing a hand along her jaw. "You two were having so much fun, though. I realized I'd never set foot on this ice in two years. But I should have gone for three."

"Are you okay?" Ari asked for the second time.

"Of course," her friend said.

But she was leaning on Patrick, and Ari didn't like the weird squint she was making. "Just humor me and sit down for a minute."

Becca grumbled, but she let herself be led off the ice and over to a bench where she sat down heavily. "I was just looking for you," she said, rubbing her temples. "Henry said he forgot to ask you in the meeting whether your hands are okay for a full slate of massage appointments tomorrow. He couldn't find you but your phone was still in the building."

"My hands are fine," she said quickly. "Did you hit your head?"

"No." Becca sat up straighter. "I'm fine, I swear. And I don't want to interrupt date night or whatever."

Patrick gave her a smile over Becca's head. He raised an eyebrow questioningly. *Is it date night?*

Ari supposed it was. She sat down and began to remove her skates. "We were just about done skating anyway," she reassured her friend. "Want to get some dinner?"

"Nope." Becca stood up slowly. "But I want you two to get some dinner. Together, in case that wasn't clear."

"Subtle," Ari murmured.

"I don't do subtle." Becca gave a wave and walked toward the door. "See you in the morning!"

Patrick waited until she was out of earshot to ask, "Want to get dinner?"

"Subtle," Ari said, and he grinned. "Sure. Let's do that."

He checked his watch. "It's only four thirty, though. Too early for dinner."

"Hmm." Ari put her own shoes back on. "How will we pass the time?"

When she looked up, Patrick gave her a slow grin. "I have a few ideas."

"So do I."

THIRTY-TWO

As it turned out, Ari's idea for how to pass the time was not the same as his. She dragged him to the grocery store. "It's been a while since I cooked a good meal," she explained. "I miss it."

Who was he to get in the way of that? Besides, she was really fucking cute as she inspected the tomatoes and bullied the fish guy into giving her the best salmon filets.

"Your kitchen or mine?" he asked, carrying the bags out of the store.

"Hmm. You have that awesome Wolf range that I covet. But do you have a good sauté pan?"

"Probably. David and Dexter liked to cook." *And my bed is bigger.*

"All right. I'll risk it. Hang on—we need a bottle of wine."

A half hour later Ari stood chopping tomatoes at his counter, singing along with Green Day. Patrick had changed into sweats and a T-shirt. His ass was parked against the refrigerator, a glass of wine in hand as he watched her cook. He'd never say it out loud, but he loved having her in his kitchen. Not because he was a sexist pig, but because nobody had ever cooked for him before. *Fed* him. Forget the seven-thousand dollar oven that was preheating for their dinner. Ari was the luxury here.

"Where did we put those olives?" she asked.

He set down his glass of wine and fetched them out of the refrigerator. When he brought them over to Ari's workstation, he lingered behind her, pulling her hair out of the way and kissing her neck.

"Mmm," she said with a sigh. "What's that for?"

Cooking for me. Being with me. Trusting me. "Do I need a reason?"

"No." Her voice was low.

"I just like you, that's all." He ran a hand down her elegant back, the lean yoga muscles resisting his touch. He cupped her bottom in one hand and kissed her hair.

Ari opened the tub of olives and began spooning them out onto the cutting board. "These get chopped a bit, and mixed with the tomatoes and garlic," she explained. "Then I add the breadcrumbs and douse it all with olive oil."

He lifted the column of her hair and leaned in again, kissing her neck. She smelled of lavender and fresh food, and he did not want to stop. Unbidden, his hands found her hips.

"That is . . ." She took a breath. "Really distracting."

His fingertips lifted her top, skimming her tummy over the waistband of her jeans. "Should I stop?" he asked between kisses beneath her ear.

"Um . . ."

Before she could answer, he caressed her, one hand cupping her breasts while the other unzipped her jeans.

"Ungggh," she mumbled, relaxing back against him.

"Put the knife down, sweetheart." He smiled into her hair.

"Good idea."

He heard it come to rest on the cutting board as his fingertips dipped into her panties. He teased the top of her mound and sighed. "I'm in the mood to spoil you."

"I'm in the mood to let you."

Grasping her hips, he turned her around, then dropped to his knees. She looked down at him with wide eyes as he took one of her hands in his. One by one he put her fingers into his mouth, cleaning off tomato juice and olive oil with his tongue.

"Oh geez . . ."

He took her second hand and repeated the treatment, lingering on each finger, sucking gently, staring up into her lovely face. She'd become flushed, with a soft, unfocused gaze that was just for him. "Put your hands on the counter, Ariana."

Immediately, she did as she was told.

He gave her jeans a tug, then pulled them all the way down and off. That left nothing but a tiny pair of panties. He leaned forward and began dropping kisses along their hemline, and down to the juncture of her legs. He paused, pressing his nose into her softness, breathing out a long, slow breath that was meant to feel warm right where it counted. He kissed the fabric once. Twice.

Above him, Ari whimpered.

With one finger, he tugged the fabric aside, exposing an inch of pretty heaven. He kissed that, too.

"You're killing me," she whispered.

He slid a finger between her legs, skimming her softness and enjoying the slickness that had begun to accumulate for him. "I'm too hungry to wait for dinner," he said, grasping her panties and sliding them down all the way, so she could step out. "I want . . ." He nudged one knee until she stepped her legs a bit wider apart. "An appetizer." Then he fitted his mouth against her body and began to kiss her in earnest. His erection strained against his sweats, and so he gave himself one slow stroke through the fabric. But that was all for now.

Two hands gripped his hair as he tongued her. "Patrick," she gasped. Then, "Oohhhh."

He buried his smile in her sweetness and kept up the torture until her knees began to shake. "You okay up there?" When he raised his chin, her eyes were closed.

"Take me to bed," she said, looking down at him.

"What about dinner?" he teased.

"Later." She reached down and tugged his chin until he stood up.

O'Doul picked her right up in his arms and carried her there, tossing her onto the big mattress. "Take off your shirt," he ordered.

Hastily she complied.

"The bra, too. Then I want you on your knees. In Bala-sana pose."

Ari's hands faltered at her bra strap. "Wow. Look at you, speaking Sanskrit!"

"It's the only pose I know." He whipped his shirt off. "Whenever you demonstrate it, I want to climb on top of you."

"I love hearing what's in your head." She reached behind herself, unhooking her bra. Then it fell away. She was sitting naked on his bed, dark eyes looking up at him. So trusting. "Right now?"

"God, yes."

For one long moment more, she studied him. Then she tucked her knees into her body and rolled onto them, facing away from him. He saw her chest expand with a deep breath. Then, exhaling, she slid her arms forward on his bedspread, elongating her upper body, sinking onto her folded knees until her forehead came to rest on his mattress.

"Whew," he breathed. At the beautiful sight of Ari stretched out and waiting for him, his dick hardening to the texture of an iron bar. He put a knee on the bed so he could press a palm to her lower back. "So beautiful. Even better than in my dreams." He skimmed his palm up her smooth back until his fingers sifted through her silky hair.

Then he gave into the temptation to kneel at her ass. He ran both hands up and down her sleek body, rubbing her ass cheeks, warming her everywhere. He curled his body over hers, bending down to press a kiss to her back. "Just like this," he whispered, bringing his eager dick against her ass.

He pushed his hips forward to show her what he meant. "You're open and ready for me."

She made a happy noise. "I'm not sure I get it. Demonstrate again."

He pressed his chuckle against her spine, kissing her smooth skin. "Stay there. I have to suit up." As much as it pained him to leave her, he slid off the bed and dropped his sweats. Then he headed over to the nightstand for a condom. She turned her head to watch him, her eyes tracking his hand as he rolled it down over his rock-hard length. "You see anything you like?"

She smiled at him. "A yogi doesn't fish for compliments."

"Never said I was any good at yoga." He climbed on the bed behind her again, nudging her feet apart with his knee. When he slipped a hand between her legs she gasped, and he groaned. "You missed me," he rumbled, his fingers sliding everywhere.

"Enough with the talking."

Well then. Grasping her hips, he pushed himself home.

They both let out noises of shocked pleasure. Watching himself, he slid in and out again slowly. The view was the stuff of porn films. But it wasn't exactly what he wanted. So he lowered his elbows to the bed, one on either side of her body. Fitting every inch of his chest onto her waiting back, and kissing her neck again, he began to rock.

Ari made an incomprehensible sound that may or may not have been his name. Rolling his hips, he gathered her even closer. It was probably a good idea that she couldn't see his face right now, because there was no way he could keep the look of devotion off of it. He had everything he wanted in this moment. He'd tell her straight up how he felt—he couldn't wait to do it. But he'd only had her back for a couple of hours and didn't want to freak her out. So he laved the sensitive skin under her ear with his tongue, and then sucked until she moaned.

"You . . . we . . . so good . . ." she said into the bedspread.

"I know," he whispered.

"Love the way you feel."

Love you. He slipped a hand beneath her arm and reached down until he could touch the place where they were joined. She gasped again, and pushed her hips back to meet him. He took a deep, steadying breath and bore down. This was everything. He moved inside her, listening to the rising sounds of her pleasure, knowing he'd never been so lucky a day in his life.

"Balasana is supposed to be a resting, restorative position," Ari told him afterwards as they lay on the bed, breathing hard.

"Well. I feel completely restored."

She laughed, and hugged him. They lay there a long time just holding each other. "Good thing I hadn't put dinner in the oven yet," she said eventually. "Shall we finish it now?"

They got up slowly, and Ari put the fish in the oven.

They tidied up the kitchen together, and he loved their companionable silence, and the way she touched a hand to his back when she moved around him.

"I still owe you an explanation," he said when the prep area was clean again.

She put a hand to his bare chest. "What do you wish to explain?"

"I already told you that I only met Vince once before he threw a brick through your window. I didn't know you two were connected. Didn't care, either. I saw those texts, and I didn't know who he was. When I ran over there and he was threatening you, I just wanted to shut him down, no matter who he was."

"Okay." She nodded slowly. "I understand."

"I mean, when he sent that picture to the Bruisers' office, he was telling me to back the fuck off. That he could damage me. But I wasn't going to listen. And it didn't have a thing to do with the . . ." He cleared his throat. "Junk I bought from him once."

"Why'd you do it?" she asked.

That was the really hard conversation, wasn't it? "Another player—a competitor—told me they'd make me feel invincible. And he was right. But buying them made me feel like a lowlife. And I spent my whole adulthood trying not to be that lowlife kid from the group home, right? So after that one time I didn't buy again."

"You're not taking anything now," she clarified.

"No, baby. I'd tell you if I was. But that's why I passed my drug test."

"Those things are easy to pass."

"If they are, I don't want to know."

A soft hand cradled his face. "Thank you for telling me. If we're going to be together, you can't take that stuff again."

"Aw." He gathered her up. "That's a hell of an incentive." He kissed her shoulder.

"Some people can't stop, though," she said softly. "Even if they mean to."

"The team doctors told me I was lucky not to get sucked in right away. They said to stay away from that shit because I might not be lucky again."

"And you're going to listen?"

"Yeah. I am. I'm doing good, sweetheart. I promise."

"Okay," she whispered. "I trust you."

His heart squeezed. "What else do you need from me? I want to know."

She rolled her head to face him, amusement in her eyes. "See, you're not going to like my demands. There's a reason I tried to stay away from you."

"Tell me why that is."

Ari put her cheek on his chest. "We need to be subtle at work. I don't mean secretive. But the job really matters to me, and I have to act like a professional. So no touching."

"Hmm." He caressed her breast in his palm. "Okay. I might need to do some extra touching in private to tide me over."

"That's not a deal breaker."

"What else, then?"

Ari opened her mouth, then closed it again.

"What is it?"

She just shook her head. "Nothing. I think I should get up and take our dinner out of the oven."

"All right," he said, uncertain about the change of topics. "Can I pour you a glass of wine?"

"I'd love one."

THIRTY-THREE

Ari woke up the next morning wrapped in Patrick's arms. And she woke up happy.

Then they shared a shower in his magnificent bathroom. It was a long and multiorgasmic shower, after which she had to go home for a change of clothes before work.

"Meet me out for coffee and a pastry," Patrick suggested as she got dressed. "You like that cookie place, right?"

"Okay," she said immediately.

"That was easy," he teased, kissing her cheek.

But it *was* easy. It was a relief to just give in to her feelings for him. To say yes instead of "it's a bad idea." Not only did she enjoy his company, but it was her nature to lean in rather than to pull away. By saying yes to him, she was saying yes to herself, too. "I'll meet you at One Girl Cookies in half an hour."

"I'll be there," he promised.

And he was. Her eye was drawn to his handsome, solid form even before she'd made it inside the door. Lola—the counter girl—was smiling at him with stars in her eyes while he inquired about the offerings.

"Hey," she said, approaching.

Lola looked up. "Hi, Ari!"

Then Patrick turned to greet her, and his whole face changed shape. His eyes lit up, and he smiled in a way that she was pretty sure he didn't show anyone else. "Missed you," he said.

"Well I'm back. Have you had the chocolate croissant? They're awesome."

"Two chocolate croissants," he told the young woman who waited with a plate and a pair of tongs. "And a large coffee."

Ari ordered a latte, and Patrick didn't let her pay. He hadn't let her pay for the groceries last night, or the wine, either. "I can buy my own food, you know," she argued after the girl moved away to make their drinks.

"Humor me." He shrugged. "I've never had anyone to spoil before now."

Her heart melted into a puddle approximating the chocolate inside the croissant that Lola was setting down in front of her. "Well, if you put it that way."

His hand found its way onto her ass. "I'm trying not to scare you, sweetheart. But you're it for me. There isn't anything I wouldn't give you, or do for you. So have a croissant on me." He pulled her in. And even though PDA was not Ari's style, the kiss she received was worth it.

"Ahem," Lola prompted. "Your coffees are ready."

They broke apart, and Ari picked up her cup, not quite meeting the young woman's eyes. "Thank you."

She turned around to scan for an empty table, and her heart stopped dead.

There sat Nate Kattenberger at a table with his assistant, Lauren.

She must have made a sound of dismay, because Patrick turned to look. Then he chuckled under his breath.

"Don't laugh," she hissed, turning her face toward Patrick and away from Nate. "I told you I wanted to be subtle. That was less than ten hours ago and we've already blown it."

His blue eyes regarded her kindly. "I'm sorry, baby. It's all my fault, but now I'm going to say good morning to Nate now. Come with me, okay? There's no point in acting guilty."

She knew he was right. But heat crawled up her neck

anyway as she followed him over to the table where the owner and his assistant had notes spread out. They were obviously in the midst of a morning meeting. Anyone who glanced at their table would be forgiven for confusing the corporate titan with the office manager. What a funny pair they made—Lauren in a killer suit, dark red with matching shoes—and Nate in one of his identical hoodies and a pair of his thousand-dollar designer skateboarding sneakers.

"Morning," Patrick said as he approached.

"Good morning Patrick. Ariana."

"Hi." He had to have seen that kiss. It wasn't subtle. She couldn't blame Patrick, either. It takes two to play tonsil hockey in a bakery.

Lauren lifted her regal chin and gave Ari the once-over. "Nice show you put on over there. I didn't know you were dating a player."

Just like that Ari's blood pressure doubled. *Thanks, Lauren. What have I ever done to you?* She wished the floor would open up and swallow her.

Patrick sighed. He set their tray down on a neighboring table and crossed his big arms. "Lauren, it's always a pleasure to see you."

She rolled her eyes.

". . . But Ari is about to kill us both right now, because she's skittish about spending time with a player."

"She should be," Lauren said, capping a fancy-looking silver pen. "Because that always ends so well. I'm heading into the office now. We're all set, right, Nathan?"

Ari's eyes cut to Nate, who nodded at Lauren. He wore the usual inscrutable Nate face—partly amused, a little smug, and only half present. "Have a seat, you two."

Oh, goody. Face time with the big boss just after he saw you making out with his star player. She pulled out a chair and sat down.

Patrick grabbed their tray off the other table and put it down in front of her. She picked up her cup to give her hands something to do.

Nate drained his own coffee and watched Lauren depart. "She doesn't pull her punches."

"Never has," O'Doul agreed calmly.

"She's a great office manager," Nate said. "Everyone has different methods, but Lauren rules through intimidation." He chuckled, then met Ari's gaze. "Try not to be too irritated with her. Lauren is out of sorts because I asked her to work in Brooklyn for the duration of the Bruisers season. She's not happy with me." He gave the famous Nate smirk. "But you should know that I don't share her pessimism for whatever relationship you have with our captain here."

"You don't?" Ari asked a little too quickly.

Setting his cup down, Nate shook his head. "The people I employ work some of the longest hours in New York. I don't mean just the hockey team right before play-offs—I mean everyone at my software company, too. What kind of asshole would I be if I discouraged my employees from finding a partner at work? Where else would my employees meet people? I'm not heartless, and I'm not stupid. If workplace romances were forbidden, I'd lose good employees to my competitors. Besides—the employees I want are the ones who know how to forge strong relationships."

"That is a good point, sir," Patrick said.

Ari studied the foam on top of her coffee. She liked the sound of Nate's words, but she didn't trust them. The rules for women were sometimes different than the rules for men. She'd seen the way he reacted to Becca's flirting. Speaking of Becca, Ari's consciousness stumbled over something. "Why did you ask Lauren to work in Brooklyn?" she asked suddenly.

Nate leaned his head in one hand. "Rebecca is going to be out for a few days, if not longer."

"She is?" Ari broke in. "Why?"

The owner's mouth formed a thin line. "She hit her head yesterday. She said it didn't seem like a big deal at the time."

"Oh god," Ari gasped. "I was there. She insisted she was fine."

Nate winced. "In the night she had a lot of pain, and felt really ill. Her sister took her to Brooklyn Methodist. They're running some tests."

She and Patrick exchanged a glance. Becca hadn't looked too bad yesterday. And she'd denied hitting her head. Poor girl was probably trying to save her dignity. "That is terrible. What can I do to help? Does she need anything in the hospital?"

"That is an excellent question. When we hear more, I'll let you know. In the meantime . . ." He turned his gaze to Patrick. "Could you let your teammates know that they need to take it easy on the office until she's back? I've asked Lauren to step in, because she's terrific in a crisis. But things won't go as smoothly for a little while."

"Sure," Patrick said. "Though I'm probably the worst offender. I'll tell my guys they have to take a little extra care with travel arrangements and receipts. To not make anyone chase 'em down."

Nate turned to Ari. "And how are you feeling? Do you need any additional time off?"

She shook her head quickly. "We'll be back to yoga tomorrow morning. No worries. You and the rest of your team have been extraordinarily helpful to me."

"I'm happy to hear that." He smiled. "All right. I'm heading into Manhattan, but I'll see you both at the game tonight." He got up and left the cookie shop.

Ari had two people to see in the Bruisers offices that afternoon. She had a message from Georgia asking her to swing by. And she needed to pick up her pay stub from Queen Lauren.

She went to Georgia first, of course, because she was still mad at Lauren.

"Hi, gorgeous!" Georgia called from behind her desk. "Thanks for stopping by."

"What's up?" She flopped down into the visitors' chair.

"I have a favor to ask."

"Anything."

Her friend folded her hands on her desk and licked her lips nervously. "Would you be a bridesmaid in my wedding? I know it's kind of a pain, with the fussy dresses and all the . . ."

"Yes," Ari said firmly. "I'd be happy to."

Georgia's face lit up. "Really? Thank you! I hate asking for things like this. Not everybody likes pomp and circumstance."

"It would be my pleasure. And do you need help with the planning?" It had just occurred to her that Becca's concussion was going to affect more than the Bruisers' front office. "I don't want you to worry because Becca is sick."

"I'm not worried about the wedding," Georgia said. "It will be fine. But I am worried about Becca. I'm heading over to her apartment right now, actually. Want to come with me?"

"Of course. I just have to swing through the GM's office to get my pay stub."

"Me too," Georgia agreed. She got up and tossed some things into her bag, and then grabbed her jacket. "Let's go."

When they entered the office it was Lauren who was seated at Becca's desk. She wore a sour face as she sorted through the stack of pay stubs with her perfect, shiny nails.

It pained Ari to see her sitting where Becca should be. "Thank you," she said as Lauren slid her document across the desk.

"So," Lauren said, handing Georgia's over, too. "Doulie, huh? Interesting pick. I always thought of him as a cold fish, but I think he likes you."

Ari realized she had a problem. She was supposed to work with Lauren for the next couple of weeks, even though she was horribly mad at her. The only thing to do was to clear the air. "Lauren, I didn't appreciate your making a big deal of it in front of Nate this morning. That was embarrassing to me."

Lauren rolled her eyes. "He doesn't care. Hell, that man loves gossip."

"Well." She cleared her throat. "In Becca's experience, even when she's just joking around with . . ."

Lauren laughed suddenly. "Stop right there. Rebecca's experience is *not* relevant."

"Why?" Georgia asked, her eyes flashing with curiosity.

Lauren leaned back in Becca's desk chair and smirked up at both of them. "Really? You haven't figured it out?"

Slowly, Georgia shook her head.

"Nate gets crazy when anyone flirts. *With Becca.*" Lauren snorted. "Wake up, ladies." She slammed the pay stubs folder shut. "Nate has it bad for little Miss Perky. I've been watching that little charade for years now. It never gets old. I just hope Rebecca recovers quickly, because I cannot *wait* to get out of this building."

Georgia's gaze collided with Ari's. A pair of startled eyes asked a question. *Did she really just say that?*

My god, I think she did, Ari tried to communicate.

Georgia's mouth opened and then shut. Then it opened again. "Lauren? *Why* do you hate hockey so much?"

Lauren's sneer deepened. "You *really* aren't up on your gossip, are you?" She gave both of them a look of irritation. "Thanks for stopping by. I'll see you both at the game tonight, unfortunately."

Ari and Georgia walked outside in silence, heading toward Water Street.

"What just happened there?" Georgia asked eventually.

"I don't know," Ari said slowly. "Maybe she's crazy."

They turned the corner, crossing the cobblestone street where Becca lived across the street from Georgia's new digs. "Let's order an early dinner at Becca's," Georgia suggested. "That way we can make sure she eats."

"All right."

But just as the words left her mouth, a black stretch limousine glided past them. It slid to a stop about a half a block up, in front of Becca's little building. The driver got out of the car and walked around to the passenger's side. He opened the door.

Nate Kattenberger got out, carrying a flower arrangement the size of a compact car. In his other hand, he carried a giant shopping bag from Dean and DeLuca, a gourmet food shop in Manhattan. The limo driver stepped up to the buzzer panel of Becca's apartment building and pushed a button.

Georgia and Ari halted in their tracks.

"Huh," said Georgia.

"Um . . ." said Ari.

"Early dinner elsewhere?" Georgia suggested.

"Good plan. My place?"

"Yeah!"

The two of them turned around and headed back in the other direction.

THREE MONTHS LATER

Patrick O'Doul had never been very interested in weddings.

College Boy's wedding reception was the good kind, though. It was outdoors, for one thing. And casual. O'Doul was wearing a suit, not a tux, thank god.

He was drinking a summery cocktail, watching lit up sailboats pass under a pink-streaked sky over the Long Island Sound. Beside him, Ari and Rebecca were having a conversation with Leo Trevi's college pal, a sweet young woman named Corey Callihan. They were discussing adaptive yoga, as Corey had a couple of physical issues which prevented her from doing some of the poses.

"Pilates works better for me, honestly," Corey said. "Since a lot of it takes place seated. I can't fall when I'm on my backside."

"I've managed it," Ari said, and the two women laughed.

It was a struggle not to stare at Ari all day and night in her sleek, strapless bridesmaid dress. The way the satin skimmed across her chest made him want to run a finger across her smooth skin.

After just a couple more hours, he could.

He looked around at all the happy people. Some were

chatting here beside the docks, some were dancing under the white tent. College Boy had a lot of friends. There was Hartley—the Boston forward he'd met a few months ago, and John Rikker, another player he'd matched up against during the season. And Rikker's boyfriend, the sports journalist Michael Graham.

"Oh, man, a *journalist*," O'Doul had grumbled, shaking Graham's hand for the first time. "Don't quote me."

"Don't worry." The big blond guy laughed. "The whole weekend is off the record. Unless you want to give me an exclusive on your team's final game of the season."

"New rule," Leo said, wrapping an arm around Graham's shoulders. "No talking about the play-offs at all. We're here to relax, right? Don't get my, uh, new father-in-law all spun up. He's likely to ask us to do some sprints just for fun."

"But wait," Rikker had argued. "If we can't talk hockey, what else is there to talk about?"

"You can talk hockey. Let's just not relive the most intense four weeks of my life. We're here to celebrate. I'm going to Hawaii tomorrow, where they don't even have skates."

O'Doul felt a zip of excitement himself. In a couple days, he and Ari were also headed for a vacation—to Mexico, because Ari said she wanted to try snorkeling.

Now he reached forward and took her hand, and she turned to him. The band was playing a slower jazz tune. "Dance with me?"

Ari's eyes widened. "Patrick O'Doul, you keep surprising me. I had no idea you danced."

"I don't," he said, leading her toward the dance floor. "But I want to hold you. And I doubt you'd let me throw you over my shoulder and haul you back to the hotel."

She made a happy sound as he pulled her in, bringing a hand to her slender waist. He inhaled her lavender scent and felt nothing but optimism.

"Did you like the wedding?" she asked.

"I liked watching you in it," he answered truthfully. "You?"

"I love seeing Georgia so happy, and seeing Becca healthy again." She looked around. "Where did she disappear to? Anyway—it wasn't a long wedding, either, so I didn't have to hold still for a long time in these shoes."

"Those are all good points," he said, guiding her around the dance floor slowly. The makeup that she'd worn today made her eyes look even bigger and more dramatic than normal. Had there ever been a man as lucky as he was? "What do you want to do on our vacation?" he asked. "Aside from the obvious."

"Aside from swimming with fish?"

"That's what I meant. Yeah."

She smiled at him. "I just want to lie in the sun with you. I'm bringing SPF 50 sunblock for you, though. Can't get you too sunburned. You won't want me to touch you."

"Oh, yes I will." He kissed her quickly. "Fish aren't the only thing I'm doing on this vacation."

Ari snickered. Then her eyes darted toward Georgia and Leo. "We'll have to start watching Georgia for a baby bump in the fall."

"Already?"

"You never know." Ari shrugged. "They might get carried away on their honeymoon."

O'Doul gave a little grunt of impatience for all the good times ahead. "I can get carried away anytime you're ready, baby." As the words came out of his mouth, he realized too late how it sounded—as if he was referring to baby bumps, not just sex. He chuckled. "Sorry, I meant . . ."

"I know what you meant," Ari said quickly. She looked away, studying the boats on the sound with a serious gaze.

Too serious, maybe.

"Ari," he said quietly. "Honey?"

"Mmm?" She still didn't meet his eyes.

The song they were dancing to ended, and everyone clapped.

They broke apart then. Ari stepped back, looking ready to walk away.

"Hey," he said, catching her hand. "Come here a second. Please?" He led her over to the side of the tent. "Did I say something wrong?"

She shook her head, but she looked uneasy.

Think, Doulie. Everything to do with relationships still came slowly to him. Although he was getting better. It helped that he was dating the best girl in the whole world. Ari always told everyone where they stood with her. She was honest to a fault.

Except for right now, apparently. Her wary gaze and obvious itch to exit the conversation was his only clue. Though if Ari were mad at him, she'd say so. That couldn't be it. So what, then?

The only times she ever avoided him were when she wanted something but did not want to trouble him about it.

Oh.

Oh, hell.

"Sweetheart," he said, cupping her chin gently. "Tell me what's on your mind."

"It's nothing," she said. Then she corrected herself. "It isn't the right time. Weddings make me irrational, that's all." Her dark eyes dipped. "They make you consider all the big questions at once."

He put his hands on her bare shoulders, his thumbs tracing the line of her slim neck. "I know what you mean." Watching Georgia and Leo declare their love forever made something go a little wrong in his gut. He'd never pictured himself as someone's forever until he'd started spending so much time with Ari. Though he'd assumed he'd need to put in a few more months of good behavior and staying out of the newspapers before he got anywhere close to discussing it with her.

But maybe he was wrong about that.

"Ari? You know I love you, right?"

Her eyes flew upward to his. "I love you, too."

O'Doul had to pause for a second to appreciate how easily those words had just rolled off of both their tongues. Forget weddings. This simple exchange was something he'd never imagined he'd do. He pulled her against his chest and sighed. "You make me so happy. There isn't anything I wouldn't do for you."

She laughed. "Careful."

But he didn't want to be careful. "No, I mean it. If having babies someday is on your to-do list, you can tell me sometime. I won't panic."

"You won't?" She sounded so skeptical it broke his heart.

"No." *Not much, anyway.* "There's a lot of things I thought I'd never do. Never thought I'd back away from a fight. Never thought I'd tell someone I loved her. But that was all before I met you. You can't scare me, Ariana. I trust you. If you want to have a conversation about babies at some point, I'll listen."

Her arms tightened around him. "I think about it sometimes."

"Next time you're thinking about it, I want to hear your thoughts."

"That's putting the cart before the horse, isn't it?"

"No," he said firmly. "You and I aren't on the traditional plan. We've both had some troubles, and now we know how to spot something good. We make our own luck, you and me."

She lifted her head and gazed up at him. "We do. You're right."

"I know it." He kissed her nose. "When do I get to peel this dress off you, anyway? Soon, right?"

Ari smiled. "Soon*ish*. They haven't cut the cake yet. We'll have to say good-bye to Georgia and Leo when their car comes. Georgia will throw the bouquet, and all that jazz."

He laughed. "How good are you at catching?"

Ari shook out her arm. "Decent."

"Like your skating?"

"Better," she teased.

"Oh, man." She laughed and he leaned in to kiss that smile right off her face.

"Get a room!" one of his teammates teased.

"They're cutting the cake!" someone else yelled.

But O'Doul hung on for one more kiss. And then just one after that. Then he finally broke it off, breathing hard. "You ready for cake?"

"I'm ready for anything."

"Love you, Ariana," he said again, testing it out again. It felt right.

"Love you, too, Patrick O'Doul." The words hit him right in the chest. Hard. And he liked it a lot.

Continue reading for a special preview of

Pipe Dreams,

coming out in May!

The first time Lauren Williams ever had a drink in front of her boss was the night the Brooklyn Bruisers clinched a play-offs berth for the first time since Nate Kattenberger bought the team.

But the moment team captain Patrick O'Doul buried a slapshot in the corner of the net, securing an overtime victory against Pittsburgh, Lauren walked straight over to the bar at the side of the team owner's private box and poured herself two fingers of scotch, neat. Lifting it, Lauren drained her shot.

Not that anyone noticed her sudden affection for whiskey. The rest of the VIPs in the owner's private box rushed over to congratulate her boss. This was a big moment for the young billionaire who owned the team. A *great* moment.

But not for her.

Lauren forced herself to look down at the rink where the players celebrated their victory. They'd convened into a knot of purple jerseys, rubbing helmets and slapping asses in the way of victorious athletes everywhere. There had been a time when this team was Lauren's whole life.

Until the sudden, awful moment when it wasn't anymore.

Somewhere in that clot of players down below was the

one who'd turned her entire world upside down. Not only had he broken her heart, but he'd made it impossible for her to feel comfortable in the organization where she'd devoted a decade of her life. For the past two years, she'd avoided this place and everything to do with hockey. She'd avoided the entire borough of Brooklyn, except when her boss's business brought the two of them over the bridge for a meeting. And the moment she was free to go, Lauren always hightailed it back to Manhattan where she belonged.

But not this month.

Nate had asked her to step in and manage the hockey team's office and travel during the play-offs. And unless she wanted to quit a job she'd worked her ass off to get, she had to do what the boss asked of her. Even though it stung.

The sound of a cork popping brought Lauren out of her grumpy reverie. "Did it!" cried Rebecca Rowley, the woman who was supposed to run the Bruisers' Brooklyn office. She held a magnum of Cristal in two hands, which she now levered toward the first of a row of shining glasses.

Lauren's eyes narrowed at this display of joy. Miss Perky was supposedly recovering from a rather freakish concussion she'd sustained by walking out onto the ice rink in her street shoes. What had seemed like a minor fall had resulted in terrible symptoms for the poor little idiot. She'd been absent from work for a week already, and was therefore the cause of Lauren's sudden craving for Scotch whiskey.

But now Becca passed around glasses as if nothing in the world were wrong with her. She poured another glass as her friend Georgia—one of the team publicists—skated into the room with a grin on her face. "Press conference in ten minutes, guys. Oh! Champagne."

"Have some." Becca handed Georgia a glass, then moved on to their boss, who gave her with a hundred watt smile. "I'm so happy for you," Becca crowed, stretching her arms around the billionaire and giving him a big friendly squeeze.

Nate looked a little stunned by the full-frontal embrace.

As usual, he did a poor job of concealing his reaction to Rebecca. His arms did what they probably always wanted to do, and closed around her back. His eyes fell shut, too.

Lauren had to look away. The yearning just rose off Nate like a mist. Hell—hugging Rebecca might be as exciting to Nate as the hockey victory itself.

Rebecca pulled back a moment later, as oblivious to him as she always was. She grabbed another glass of champagne off the table and held it out to Lauren. "Champagne? I know you aren't really a drinker but . . ."

Lauren took the glass from Miss Perky and took a gulp immediately. "Thanks."

"You're . . . welcome," Becca said, her eyes full of surprise. Then she took a sip of her own glass and moved off to serve someone else, her hips swaying to the victory music that was playing in the stadium—"No Sleep Till Brooklyn" by the Beastie Boys.

Lauren checked her boss's face, and found his gaze tracking Becca across the walnut-paneled room. Lauren had been witness to this little romantic farce for the past two years. It was like living in a sitcom that she could never shut off.

And yet, if Nate's pining for Becca was the most irritating thing about Lauren's situation at work, she wouldn't be drinking tonight.

Her problem wasn't with the job itself, either. Before Nate Kattenberger bought and rebranded the Long Island team, she'd spent ten years working in the Syosset offices. In fact, it had been Lauren who managed the team's office during its last three play-offs runs.

Heck, Lauren was the veteran and Becca was the rookie.

Then, two years ago, when the young internet whiz made a lot of changes to the organization, Lauren expected to be fired along with the rest of the casualties. In fact, her father—the team's General Manager—was the first person Nate axed after the purchase went through.

Lauren wasn't fired, though. On the contrary, when Nate

moved the team to Brooklyn, he stunned her by moving her even further—whisking her into the corporate headquarters of his internet company in Manhattan.

She'd been ecstatic about this change, since working for Nate's Fortune 500 company was exactly the sort of corporate leap she'd always hoped to make. Not only that, but the move away from the hockey team solved a lot of problems for Lauren all in one fell swoop, including the one huge problem that suddenly knocked her on her ass.

And that problem was down on the ice right now, draped in sweaty goalie pads, lining up to skate past the other team for the traditional handshake. For the millionth time this week, Lauren closed her eyes and prayed to be spirited back to Nate's office tower where there weren't any hockey players, and there weren't any reminders of the man who'd almost made her dreams come true.

But as long as Becca was unable to work, Lauren was stuck in Brooklyn. And now that the Bruisers had won their freaking play-offs slot, it meant a hailstorm of planning and administrative overtime. The NHL play-offs were not a quick affair, either. Four rounds of seven game series. It would be two *months* before the Stanley Cup winner was crowned.

And there would be *travel* with the very people she'd spent two years avoiding.

"Lauren." Nate's voice cut through her reverie. "Please call Becca a car. She needs to get home and get some rest."

"Omigod." Rebecca rolled her eyes. "I can just walk, or grab a cab. I'm fine. All I do is rest."

But Nate gave Lauren a look over Becca's head. And that look said, *get her a car.*

"No big deal," Lauren sighed, taking a healthy slug of her champagne. "I have cars waiting outside already." She'd dealt with transportation during the third period of the game, while everyone else was screaming encouragements toward the ice. "You should take . . ." She pulled her Katt Phone out of her bag. ". . . Number 117. It's parked at the curb outside the rink door."

Nate gave her a thankful nod. Then he went over to the coat rack in the corner and fetched Becca's leopard-print jacket. He eased it onto her shoulders until Becca set down her empty wineglass and shoved her arms into the jacket, an irritated look on her face. "Pushy," she muttered under her breath.

Lovesick, Lauren countered in her head. Did it make her a horrible person that she wanted to knock their heads together right now?

Probably.

"Let's go, Nate!" Georgia said, clapping her hands. "You can't be late for your own press conference." She grabbed his suit jacket off a chair and herded him toward the door.

The fact that their fearless leader was actually wearing a suit spoke of tonight's significance. Nate was a jeans-hoodie-and-800-dollar-sneakers kind of guy, even on game night.

Lauren followed her boss, the publicist, and Rebecca into the private elevator, wondering why she couldn't at least be happy for Nate. He'd wanted this so badly. But all Lauren felt was dread for the next few weeks. And a healthy dose of anger, too.

Bitter much? *Why yes, I still am.*

This was an unpleasant realization. Most of the time, Lauren was able to stay away from both hockey and Brooklyn. In Manhattan, she was able to focus on her excellent job, her tidy little Upper West Side apartment and the college degree she was just finishing up. She was too damn busy to feel bitter. But as the elevator slid lower, toward the locker rooms, so did her stomach.

The doors parted momentarily on the main level for Becca's exit. "Goodnight!" Miss Perky called, stepping off the elevator.

"Night, babe!" Georgia called after her. "Rest up! We need you back!"

Do we ever.

Becca gave them a cheeky salute and then walked away,

while Nate watched, a worried look on his face. When the doors closed again, he finally gave his attention to Georgia. "Okay, what's the scoop? I'm not used to giving victory speeches."

"Just don't sound smug," Georgia begged. "Try for grateful."

He smirked. "As in, Brooklyn should be *grateful* to me for bringing the team here?" She rolled her eyes and he laughed. "Joking! Okay, how about this—I'm proud of my team's success at landing a play-offs spot."

"I'm *humbled* by my team's inspiring efforts," Georgia suggested.

"Sure. I can be humble."

"No you can't," Lauren interjected. "But you can fake it when necessary."

Nate grinned. "You don't do humble either."

"That's why you have me working in the office and not in front of the camera," Lauren pointed out. "I'm going to start booking hotel rooms in D.C. in the morning. It's not jinxing us if I do it now, right?" Nate had refused to even consider travel plans before they were officially headed to the first round of the play-offs.

"Bombs away," he said. "But we need the whole organization in one hotel," he cautioned. "Coach will burst a vessel if the guys aren't all together. Team unity and all that. If you have any trouble call the league and ask for help."

"Got it," Lauren said. She'd done this all before, and not that many years ago. Although it felt like another lifetime.

The doors parted once again, and Georgia put a hand on the boss's arm. "Slap on that humble face, Nate. Here we go."

An entire corridor full of reporters swung their lenses in Nate's direction. They began to shout questions as he made his way past their camera lenses. "Press conference starts in five!" Georgia called. "This way, please!"

Nate led the way into their press room, which would be packed tonight. At the other end of the hall she spotted Coach Worthington and defenseman Patrick O'Doul. The team's captain was already showered and wearing his suit. The new publicist—Tommy—must have bribed the guy to get him camera-ready so fast. And he was *smiling*.

O'Doul was not a smiler. The whole world was turned on its ear tonight.

She followed her boss into the press conference where she spent the next half hour trying to appear joyful while avoiding eye contact with any of the players. Just another day at the office.

It was eleven o'clock before the room emptied again after speeches and Q & A. Lauren had reported to work fifteen hours ago already. That was life in professional sports. Now she faced a car ride home to midtown. At least there would be no traffic on the FDR.

She'd given away all the hired cars already, so Lauren found herself on the Flatbush Avenue sidewalk, tapping her Katt Phone to summon an Uber driver. The app gave her a four-minute wait. She used the time to compose a monster of a to do list for tomorrow. Not only did she need to play for the play-offs, but she needed to check in on the Manhattan office, making sure that the place wasn't going to seed in her absence.

And at some point during this fiasco she'd have to do a final revision of the senior thesis she was about to turn in. Thank God she'd only had one course left before graduation, and her work was almost complete. If the Brooklyn Bruisers wrecked her odds for receiving her diploma this June, she would not be responsible for her actions.

Nate wouldn't let that happen, Lauren's conscience whispered. Her boss had made every possible accommodation these past two years as Lauren struggled to get her degree. Nate, for all his quirks, liked to see his people succeed. She was still mad at him, though, for asking this of her. The man knew exactly why she avoided the team, and he'd put her in this position anyway.

"Hi," said a voice beside her.

Startled, Lauren whirled to find the very reason for her misery standing there on the sidewalk, his rugged face regarding her curiously. Her stomach flipped over and then dove straight down to her knees. Mike Beacon in a suit had always been her undoing. His tie was loosened already, showing her a glimpse of the contrast between his olive skin at his throat and the crisp white dress shirt. A five o'clock shadow dusted the planes of his strong jaw, gathering in the sexy cleft of his chin.

She used to put her thumb right there beneath his full lower lip as she tugged his face closer for a kiss.

"You okay?" he asked.

"Fine, thanks!" she insisted, snapping out of it. She tore her gaze off of the only man she'd ever loved and looked up Flatbush for the Rav4 Uber had promised her. Every muscle in her body was tense as she waited for the goalie to just walk away.

Which he did not do.

She turned and pinned him with what the assistants in the Manhattan office termed the Lauren Glare. The laser like effect of her stare made interns put away their phones and get back to work. It seared incompetent messengers into delivering packages in a timely fashion. It was a "powerful and terrifying weapon," according to her coworkers.

Beacon just smiled.

What an asshole.

"Why are you still here?" she asked.

"Because you're standing on a dark sidewalk at midnight?"

Seriously? This from a man so obviously unconcerned with her wellbeing? If he gave a damn, he wouldn't have walked out on her two years ago without an explanation. He wouldn't have tossed her heart on the street, stomped on it, and then vanished from her life. Forty-eight hours before she realized he was gone, they'd been circling real-estate listings in the newspaper together, discussing whether they needed a three-bedroom apartment, or whether two would be plenty. While naked. In bed.

Lauren didn't need to remind him, though, because she'd said it all before. For weeks she'd sobbed into his voice mail because he didn't pick up the phone. She'd begged for an explanation, wondering what she'd done wrong.

There was really no point in going there again. "Just don't, okay?" she demanded instead.

"Don't what?" his husky voice asked.

Oh, for christ's sake. She turned to face him, her blood pressure doubling. "Don't be nice. Don't talk to me. Don't *look* at me. Just stay between the pipes and guard the damn net. And leave me the hell alone."

He swallowed, and she saw a flicker of a shadow cross his face, but it was gone before she could name the emotion. *Note to self—never square off against a fricking goalie.* They were the masters of playing it cool when they wanted to. Lauren found herself staring again, trying not to remember how easy it had been to get him to toss off the mask and really *live*. "Nobody gets me like you do," he'd whispered into her ear.

It had been a lie, though. Obviously.

A quick tap on a car horn broke the weird spell over her. She turned to see a Rav4 against the curb, a man peering up at her that matched the profile picture of the Uber driver she'd requested.

Thank you, baby Jesus.

Without another word Lauren got into the back seat and shut the door. She couldn't resist a parting glance up at Beacon, though.

He stood there, hands jammed in his pockets, watching her car pull away.

ACKNOWLEDGMENTS

Thank you Patricia Nelson for listening so well. It's going to be awesome. Thank you Julie Mianecki, Kerry Donovan, Ryanne Probst, and the whole Penguin team. Thanks to Melissa Mayer for your help with Ari's massage therapy techniques. And thank you to Melanie Sen for helping me spot some errors. I'm so blessed to have all of your help!

Connect with Berkley Publishing Online!

For sneak peeks into the newest releases, news on all your favorite authors, book giveaways, and a central place to connect with fellow fans—

"Like" and follow Berkley Publishing!

facebook.com/BerkleyPub
twitter.com/BerkleyPub
instagram.com/BerkleyPub